You, Again

Kate Goldbeck

PENGUIN BOOKS

TRANSWORLD PUBLISHERS
Penguin Random House, One Embassy Gardens,
8 Viaduct Gardens, London SW11 7BW
www.penguin.co.uk

Transworld is part of the Penguin Random House group of companies
whose addresses can be found at global.penguinrandomhouse.com

Originally published in the United States of America in 2023 by The Dial Press,
an imprint of Random House, a division of Penguin Random House LLC, New York.

First published in Great Britain in 2023 by Penguin Books
an imprint of Transworld Publishers

You, Again is a work of fiction. Names, characters, places and incidents are the products
of the author's imagination or are used fictitiously. Any resemblance to actual events,
locales or persons, living or dead, is entirely coincidental.

A CIP catalogue record for this book is available from the British Library.

ISBN 9781804992975

Book design by Debbie Glasserman.
Printed and bound in Great Britain by Clays Ltd, Elcograf S.p.A.

The authorized representative in the EEA is Penguin Random House Ireland,
Morrison Chambers, 32 Nassau Street, Dublin D02 YH68.

Penguin Random House is committed to a sustainable future
for our business, our readers and our planet. This book is made
from Forest Stewardship Council® certified paper.

You, Again

"Fresh, witty, and utterly romantic, this is the deliciously offbeat modern reimagining of *When Harry Met Sally* I never knew I needed. Kate Goldbeck is an absolute star!"

—ALI HAZELWOOD, *New York Times* bestselling author of *The Love Hypothesis*

"This is a romance sung in perfect pitch! A spectacular debut!"

—CHRISTINA LAUREN, *New York Times* bestselling author of *The Unhoneymooners*

"*You, Again* reads like a romcom classic in the making. I've never read anything like it. This book is raw and sexy and radically vulnerable, and I'm already desperately missing Ari and Josh."

—RACHEL LYNN SOLOMON, *New York Times* bestselling author of *Weather Girl* and *The Ex Talk*

"*You, Again* is a knockout. Ari and Josh are my favorite type of couple—funny, flawed, and complicated, with prickly exteriors hiding tender hearts. I'll be first in line for anything Kate Goldbeck writes from now on."

—AVA WILDER, author of *How to Fake It in Hollywood* and *Will They or Won't They*

"Equal parts a studied homage and decisively modern, Kate Goldbeck debuts with a master class in banter. This is a luxurious contemporary romance to savor. Every character is as sexy as they are gloriously messy."

—ROSIE DANAN, author of *The Roommate*

"*You, Again* is one of those special, singular books you wish you could read for the first time again and again. It's funny and sharp, crackling with wit and chemistry, a clever homage to all the best parts of romantic comedies while making them feel new."

—ALICIA THOMPSON, bestselling author of *Love in the Time of Serial Killers*

"Not your average romantic comedy. Ari and Josh's love story is raw, chaotic, unconventional, very funny, and very sexy. An edgy, modern, slow-burn love story, with nipple piercings."

—GEORGIA CLARK, author of *It Had to Be You*

"The humor is sharp, the dialogue is equal parts poignant and fun, and the romance will make you giddy."

—TARAH DeWITT, author of *Funny Feelings*

"Kate Goldbeck is a genius. I laughed. I cried. I fell in love with her characters and her descriptions of New York and the food . . . This story has nuts and a big fat beating heart and I will be reading it over and over."

—ERICKA WALLER, author of *Dog Days*

IN MEMORY OF LAURA MEYERS.

IT'S ALL A PROCESS.

You,
Again

2014

"EXCUSE ME, SIR?" ARI STANDS HER GROUND, FEET SHOULDER-WIDTH apart, on the sidewalk in front of the Brooklyn Museum. "I know that someone who waited ten minutes for a six-dollar cold brew has the time to stop and talk to me about protecting the second-largest bobcat habitat in New Jersey."

Always best to start with a provocation. None of that "do you have a moment?" crap. No pedestrian in this city has "a moment" for a canvasser.

The tall man in sunglasses, expensive jeans, and a dark sweater—slightly hunched from the weight of a large backpack—slows down, not quite to a full stop. He glances at her neon vest and binder, realizing his mistake a half-second too late.

"I'm on a fucking call!" he snaps, angling his body to route around her.

It's fine. Ari is used to people faking calls to avoid engaging with her. She takes a step to the right, blocking his path again.

She needs one more donation to make quota, so Tall Sweater Nightmare Man can give her twenty seconds to make the case for the bobcats.

"Can I have a sip?" She reaches toward his cold brew cup with a minimalist Blue Bottle logo. "I've had a super long day out here." This trick—passed down from Gabe, her coworker-with-benefits—works about twenty percent of the time, which is a phenomenal success rate in the business of pestering strangers for (no) fun and (little) profit.

"Un-*fucking*-believable!" He lifts the cup out of her reach and jaywalks across Eastern Parkway, turning his head to look back at her and scowl.

Or maybe to ensure she's not following him.

When Gabe told their improv class about the "lucrative opportunities" with ProActivate, he'd assured them that they'd become accustomed to constant brush-offs, the lack of eye contact, the utter rejection. "It's good practice for comedy," he'd said. "And it pays better."

Everything pays better than comedy.

But at least onstage you can flop in front of dozens of people at once. Ten efficient minutes of agony. On the street, it's like extending your hand every thirty seconds and getting one of those extra-painful envelope paper cuts in return.

Something, something . . . the definition of insanity.

Ostensibly, Ari moved to New York to pursue comedy. When she met Gabe, one of the charismatic leaders of the sketch comedy theater where Ari had planted her flag four months ago, he'd spun tales of casting agents frequenting open mics and late-night encounters with *Daily Show* writers. He'd become a hero and a crush.

What Gabe neglected to mention is that most of those encounters occurred while he worked the register at the noodle place down the block from the studio.

On the drizzly walk home, she keeps an eye out for one last chance to make her donation quota. The woman with the promotional umbrella, letting her Yorkie pee on a flower bed? The stocky man with a gingery beard and thick-frame glasses, waiting in the doorway of a bar on Washington Avenue? But neither feels likely. Resigned, Ari turns to head toward home.

When she responded to Natalie's posting on Craigslist, looking for someone to sublet the "cozy" second bedroom in her "Prospect Heights–adjacent" apartment, Ari quickly discovered it was actually a twenty-five-minute walk from Prospect Heights. "The room is technically considered a closet," Nat had explained when Ari came to look at it, "but there's already a lofted twin bed in there and a desk would totally fit."

The desk didn't fit. But living with Natalie was definitely preferable to Ari's last living situation, which was a futon in a friend's cousin's living room.

Especially tonight. Natalie spent the weekend in the Hamptons and she won't be back until late. The apartment will be luxuriously empty: the perfect opportunity for Ari to use her noisiest vibrator.

That was the plan, anyway.

"Guess who met quota standing outside Whole Paycheck?" Gabe is leaning against the front door to her building, under the awning, just out of the rain. He has the classic good looks of an Eddie Bauer catalog model or someone who poses for stock photos, with his wavy-but-coiffed hair and twinkling brown eyes. "Like shooting fish in a barrel. How'd you do?"

Gabe pushes off the brick wall, his neon ProActivate vest tucked into the back pocket of his jeans. He's always a big hit with the leashes-and-strollers crowd.

"One short," Ari replies, fishing her keys out of her pocket.

"Bummer." He holds up a Blu-ray of *Inception*. "Wanna finish it?"

It's a flimsy pretense. They've been "watching" *Inception* for the last three weeks, in fourteen-minute increments. Last time, they'd paused after a particularly horny round of "Fuck, Marry, Kill." (Ari: Hardy, Watanabe, Gordon-Levitt. Gabe: Cotillard, Murphy, DiCaprio.)

"Natalie's out," Ari says, forcing her key into the lock. "I was planning on—"

"Perfect." He holds the door open. "I have a date in Boerum Hill later."

When they get in the apartment, Gabe pulls off his shirt before Ari gets the disc in Natalie's Blu-ray player.

It's convenient, this thing with Gabe. He's easygoing, open to trying new stuff. Proficient at undoing her bra with one hand. They both want sex and to *not* be boyfriend-girlfriend in equal amounts. He's the first man Ari's been with who doesn't take it as a huge personal failing if she introduces a vibrator into the equation.

And after dealing with face-to-face rejection all day, it's nice to be *wanted*.

At 1:06:47 into the movie and two pairs of underwear on the floor, the intercom buzzes in three shrill bursts.

"Did you order takeout?" Gabe asks, breathing hard. He flops back onto the sofa. "A sandwich actually sounds amazing right now."

"How would I have done that?" Ari sits up. "With my third

hand?" Two more buzzes trill through the apartment, followed by one sustained buzz.

Ari rolls off the sagging couch and stumbles to the intercom. She punches the TALK button: "Yeah?"

The response is a garbled mix of static, a low voice, "food," and "Natalie."

"Buzzer's broken," she says. "I'll come down." Ari tugs her tank top over her head. "Natalie orders these macrobiotic meals," she tells Gabe, who's already back on his phone. "Must be the delivery guy." She picks his boxers up off the rug, scanning the floor. "Crap. Where did my underwear go?"

"Underwear is overrated." Gabe heaves himself off the couch. "I'm gonna jump in the shower."

Ari pulls on his boxers, shoves her feet into her sneakers, and jogs down the stairs to grab the meals from the delivery guy.

When she reaches the ground floor, she sees a hulking shadow through the window at the top of the heavy door at the entryway. But as she begins to open the door, the shadow takes on a familiar shape.

Tall Sweater Nightmare Man is standing under her awning, holding a reusable shopping bag of produce that looks like an eighteenth-century Dutch still life.

He's pale and lanky—mid-twenties?—with dark hair and a longish face that's oddly proportioned.

But not in a bad way.

His eyes move back and forth across the slice of her face that's visible between the frame and the door.

Ari clears her throat. "Can I help you?"

He looks confused, but doesn't answer.

"Are you here to tell me about your Lord and savior Jesus Christ?"

"I'm Jewish." He peeks over her shoulder. "Are you Natalie's roommate?"

He smells like expensive botanical aftershave.

"Maybe," she says, raising an eyebrow. "Are these her gluten-free paleo meals?"

"This is olive oil–poached cod with mussels, orange, and chorizo," he says, shifting his weight impatiently. "Did Natalie not mention I was coming?"

As if on cue, Ari's phone chirps multiple times.

> NAT 🔒 : need huuuuge favor.
>
> I got my days mixed up.
>
> Josh is supposed to make me dinner tonight
>
> NAT 🔒 : the chef.
>
> he's already on his way with all these groceries.
>
> I'm on the earlier Jitney but still running so late
>
> could you let him in? 😳 😳

Shit.

This is typical Natalie bullshit, and she gets away with it because she has luminous skin and this amazing laugh and Ari has a crush on her in a way that's completely different from her occasional horny Gabe feelings. Namely, an inability to say "no."

"Wait, who are you?" Ari holds the phone screen to her chest, shielding it from his view.

"I'm Josh. Natalie's boyfriend." He doesn't phrase it in the form of a question. It's just a statement. A fact.

Ari spits back a fact of her own: "Nat doesn't have a boyfriend."

"YES, SHE *DOES*," HE SAYS WITH THE CONFIDENCE OF SOMEONE WHO BE-
lieves it to be true. Basically. "Me."

It's nearly imperceptible, but the roommate's brow wrinkles
at the word *boyfriend*. Josh prides himself on noticing the details
other people miss.

According to his schedule, in eight minutes Natalie should
be sipping a glass of Sancerre, watching him supreme oranges
with his Shun Dual Core Kiritsuke knife.

Instead, he's staring at a pink-haired stranger in men's
underwear and a faded Obama HOPE T-shirt with the sleeves
cut off.

"Nat's not here. She's running late," she says, not opening
the door any farther. "I can put the food in the fridge. There's a
bar down the block where you could hang out till she gets
home."

Seconds of wasted time tick away in his brain, growing
louder. Standing in the hallway, holding one hundred and sev-
enty dollars' worth of high-end perishable groceries, he considers abandoning the plan. Calling an Uber. Rescheduling for
another evening when all the elements of the concept can come
together seamlessly.

But that would be failure.

"Absolutely not," he says. "This requires thirty minutes of
prep plus fifty minutes cooking time. I need to get started now.
And it's raining."

Tonight, after the mousse au citron, Josh Kestenberg and
Natalie Ferrer-Hodges will transition from the confusing messi-
ness of *casually dating—question mark* to *full-fledged relationship—
period*.

Exclamation point.

No, *period*. More tasteful.

"If I do you this favor and let you in—"

"'Favor'?"

"—then you're going to atone for your rudeness earlier today and help me make my quota." The corner of her mouth tugs into the tiniest possible grin but her eyes are not smiling. A little dimple forms on the left side of her cheek. "I'll need a forty-dollar donation. I take credit cards."

"What the hell are you talking about?" It's not often that Josh feels three steps behind.

"Glad you finally asked! With the support of wildlife lovers like you, the Nature Conservancy is establishing 'Bobcat Alley,' a protected greenbelt where native wild felines can roam and—"

"That was *you*?" Josh sets the grocery bag down on the stoop.

"Un-*fucking*-believable, right?" There's a full Cheshire cat grin on her face now. Nothing coy about it.

"You're extorting me?" He steps forward, towering over her. "Is this some kind of scam you pull?"

"Yes, I pretend to live in apartments all over Brooklyn in order to guilt my roommate's angry trust-fund dates into making recurring charitable donations." *Recurring?* Fantastic, he'll be on a mailing list for the rest of his life. "Do you want to hear the talking points about the bobcats?"

"No."

"Thank you for helping to build a future where bobcats thrive," she recites by rote. She opens the door wider, letting him follow her into the building's vestibule. "This is like the cold open of a *Law & Order* episode, letting a strange man into my apartment. You could tie me up with an extension cord and steal our laptops or something. But now you'll be the last name on my donor log, so if I go missing, you'll be the first suspect." She stops for a breath at the foot of the stairs. "I'm Ari."

"Josh Kestenberg." His hand twitches in an automatic handshake response but he curbs the instinct. "I have a lot of prep to do, so you'll have to tie yourself up with the extension cord."

"Arianna Sloane," she adds, like she gets extra credit for also having a surname. "And don't threaten me with a good time." She gestures at the stairs. "You first. I don't want you staring at my ass the entire way up to the third floor."

Josh rolls his eyes and starts to haul the bags up the first flight. As he passes her, he smells cheap weed that reminds him of his whiny vegan classmates in his anthropology seminars at Stanford. Josh takes the stairs two at a time, hoping to get far enough ahead of her to make further interaction impossible, but she's right behind him.

"If you're a cook," she says, "shouldn't you be at work right now?"

"I'm a *chef*. I spent the last two years in Europe. I develop recipes." He'd freelanced at *Bon Appétit* on two occasions, thank you very much. "I just got back to New York."

"I don't know if I've seen Nat consume anything other than paleo bowls and Huel shakes," Ari says.

"She hasn't tried my food yet."

"How long have you two been 'together'? I mean, you're a cook—"

"Chef."

"—and you've never made her a meal; don't you think that's a little weird?"

"No." He picks up the pace, like he's trying to out-climb the accusation. *Is it weird?* "We've been seeing each other for six weeks."

"Does six weeks of dating mean a relationship? I hooked up with this guy, Nico, for three semesters and he was *not* my boyfriend. His name is still in my phone with three eggplant emojis, though."

Josh doesn't reply. She seems to be feeding off his answers, so it's best to cut off her supply. He's also feeling slightly winded.

"How is she labeled in your contacts?" she continues. "As 'girlfriend'? Is there a heart emoji next to her name?"

"No." Good fucking grief, this woman probably makes conversation with cab drivers and cashiers. "I don't need cartoon symbols to jog my memory about our relationship."

Why is it nearly impossible to meet interesting single women but so easy to attract people who have the uncanny ability to point out the small details that he's been consciously burying in his own mind?

When they reach the third floor, Josh turns to face her.

"Natalie never mentioned me?" he asks. It slips out, needy. Embarrassing.

"Let me think." Ari fumbles with her keys. "Are you the guy with the really nice bathroom with the dual shower heads?"

"No?" *What guy with the—*

"Oh! Were you Mr. September in last year's Babes of Bushwick calendar?" She looks him up and down.

"I don't know what—"

Ari forces the apartment door open with her hip.

Josh shakes off her disorienting questions; she's clearly just trying to fuck with him. He takes a cautious step into the living room, avoiding a pile of shoes by the door. He's always hosted

Natalie at his apartment, where he doesn't have to account for unknown variables: surfaces that haven't been properly wiped or hostile-yet-chatty roommates.

Out of the corner of his eye, he sees a scrap of lacy trim peeking out from under the couch.

Ari seems to follow his gaze. "*There* they are."

Before she can retrieve them, an interior door swings open. A shirtless man bursts out, surrounded by a cloud of steam, belting a show tune. "Bring *him hooooome*! *Briiing* him home!" He pauses his overwrought serenade and nods at Josh, friendly and completely unbothered by his presence. "Hey, man."

Ari makes no attempt to introduce them.

"Do I get my boxers back?" the guy asks her. "Actually, never mind, I gotta run." Humming the tune with heavy vibrato, he pulls a T-shirt over his head. "Call me in an hour in case I need a rescue?"

"'Kay," she responds, barely looking up. She's riffling through her Nature Conservancy binder. "Enjoy."

Josh watches him leave without kissing Ari goodbye.

As soon as the door slams shut, Ari appears at Josh's left side, holding out her donation binder and a ballpoint pen.

After he sets down his bags and prints his credit card number in neat block letters, Ari gestures grandly and announces, "This is the kitchen. Don't burn the apartment down."

Josh tilts his head, looking past her. "A fucking electric stove?"

Ari glances at the aging unit that doesn't even have a vent hood. "What's wrong with it?"

"There's no heat control, no subtlety, no flame. It's either scalding or lukewarm."

"I'm sure you'll figure it out." She shrugs. "Pretend you're on one of those cooking competition shows where you have to start your own fire."

He narrows his eyes at her and begins digging in his backpack, removing his supplies. There's barely enough room on the granite-patterned vinyl counter to organize the ingredients and the equipment he's brought. When he looks up, he's surprised to see Natalie's roommate opening the magnet-covered refrigerator door. He'd assumed she would make herself scarce.

"I'm also making dinner," Ari explains, bending at the waist to grab a box of MorningStar Farms veggie corn dogs out of the freezer drawer below.

"You have a little bit of an accent when you're ranting about appliances," she says, setting two corn dogs on a plate. "Did you grow up here?"

"Upper West Side."

She looks thoughtful as she shuts the microwave door. "Maybe it's the transplant in me, but I've always been jealous of the weird accent. I like it."

He blinks, unsure how to take the—well, it's not technically a compliment is it?

He removes a crisply folded list of timings from his bag and centers his maple cutting board over a clean white dish towel. With the space back under his control, he can channel his energy into transforming organic carrots into identical batonnets.

For a few minutes, they manage to ignore each other despite the tight confines. Once the carrots look as if they've been processed at a tiny lumber mill, Josh places a small kabocha squash on his cutting board and retrieves his cleaver. Overkill, perhaps, but the kabocha has extremely firm skin and he hadn't wanted to risk struggling with it in front of Natalie. Plus, cleaving anything provides a nice amount of drama. He gives the squash a small *thwack* next to the vine, covers the spine of the cleaver with a towel, and forces it down through the flesh.

"You didn't mention you were wielding a cleaver when you asked to enter my apartment," Ari says, removing her dinner from the microwave and setting it on the counter. "Can I try it?"

He takes a breath, but not so deep as to inhale the aroma of corn dogs.

The automatic response is obviously *no*. He hadn't planned on audience participation. But if he did hand her the cleaver, what could happen?

She could drop it. Dull the blade. Waste the squash by incompetently hacking away at it. He might need to demonstrate using a rocking motion. She would have to get close to him.

It's a terrible idea.

To his own surprise Josh nods at the space in front of him. "Stand here. Grip the handle like—*no*, like this," he says, moving her fingers.

"Are you always this bossy?" she mutters, setting the cleaver through the skin and pushing the blade down, leaning all her weight on it. "I mean, I'm not *not* into that."

As a rule, Josh doesn't let other cooks—let alone amateurs—touch his knives. He doesn't want their grubby fingerprints on his equipment, selecting the tongs when a spoon is needed, sprinkling an unnecessary pinch of salt over his perfectly seasoned protein.

And yet . . . the way she's touching something that belongs to him creates this strange, buzzy sensation on the back of his neck.

"I never learned to cook," she says. She cuts the squash into an array of sizes and wedge shapes that Josh will have to trim in a few minutes. At least she manages not to chop off a fingertip. "I lived with my grandma, and her culinary skills began and ended with the microwave." Ari rocks forward each time she presses the blade down and Josh is eighty percent certain that she's not wearing a bra.

He clears his throat. "So you came to New York to work for a pyramid scheme that tricks college students into marketing scams disguised as do-gooder bullshit?"

"I came here to do comedy." Josh makes a mental note not to ask a follow-up and risk being invited to a terrible open mic. "But I actually *am* an excellent canvasser. I'm very good at finding common ground with strangers." She looks up from the cutting board. "Except for right now."

He finds himself analyzing the details of her features. Round, flushed cheeks and a sharp chin, with a lower lip that's significantly fuller than the upper. There's some expression spreading over her face—confusion, if he's being optimistic; kindling annoyance, if he's honest. But he's always been better at arguing than flirting.

Not that he wants to flirt with her.

After a beat, Ari sets down the cleaver and pushes the cutting board toward him. He feels himself exhale.

"Thanks for the lesson." She wipes her hands on a towel and fills a water glass directly from the faucet. Josh makes a mental note to buy Natalie a filter pitcher. "But I guess it's the least you could do after interrupting my evening."

"*I* interrupted *your* evening?"

"Yes." Ari tucks a bottle of yellow mustard under her arm and returns to the living room, plopping down on the couch. "I had big plans for my night alone."

"But you weren't really by yourself, were you?" He pauses. "If you want privacy you could . . . go to your room?"

"It's sweltering in there. The window in my room is too small for an air conditioner." She reaches for the remote. "Why should I have to go anywhere? This is *my* apartment."

"ISN'T IT NATALIE'S APARTMENT?" JOSH GRABS THE HANDLE OF THE saucepan and shakes it around. "Technically?"

"I pay half the rent," Ari says, seething at the TV, unpausing the movie from where she and Gabe left off, dipping a corn dog into a giant puddle of mustard.

A couple weeks ago, she had just started *The Grand Budapest Hotel* when Natalie got home from some underground supper club, wine-drunk but not quite sleepy. Ari pretended to pay attention to the art direction, while breathing in the subtle scent of the mysterious product that makes Natalie's hair shiny and soft. She touched Ari's thigh every time she laughed. If making someone laugh is the best feeling in the world, making someone laugh *while they're touching your thigh* is like . . . the best feeling in the world plus a tiny hit of ecstasy. The arm touch was almost better than the orgasm Nat gave her ten minutes later.

Almost.

There have been two-and-a-half repeat performances of "movie night," after which they each retreated to their separate rooms to sleep. Or, in Ari's case, lie in her rickety lofted twin bed with a goofy smile on her face, staring at the remnants of some previous tenant's glow-in-the-dark stars on the ceiling. Perhaps she'd stumbled on the perfect sexual relationship: reasonably satisfying and free of emotional turmoil.

But she hadn't met any of Natalie's dates until now. Why has Nat automatically granted this guy "boyfriend" status, while Ari is an uncredited cameo? What makes him lovable (seriously, *how*?) and Ari merely fuckable?

The sound of a sharp blade against the wooden cutting board resumes behind her, in steady, exacting strikes, like a constant audio reminder of his presence in her space. His assumptions. His opinions.

"So you've never even cooked Natalie breakfast?"

"We go out," he replies, over the chopping. "Why? Do you usually treat your dates to Red Bull and Pop-Tarts when they finally roll out of bed?"

She lets out something between a laugh and a snort. "I'm long gone by the time they wake up."

There's a slight hiccup to the rhythm of his knife strokes. "What do you mean? You just get up and leave?"

"I like to wake up in my own bed," she explains, polishing off the second corn dog. "It's simpler."

"Ah." He resumes his knife work with a dramatic eye roll. "A true romantic."

"You think it's romantic sharing a bed with a stranger?" Ari stands up and walks her plate to the sink. "Either you wake up in a weird place in the morning or you have to kick someone out of your apartment. Anyway, I don't participate in the romance industrial complex." She scrubs the dish with enough vigor to leave scratches. "It's a distraction that keeps women dependent on men for validation." Maybe that statement is troublingly heteronormative but Josh is probably troublingly heteronormative, too.

She watches Josh place a pat of butter in a large pot on the stove. Upon closer inspection, he has the type of face that photos get wrong: a prominent brow, weak chin, serious dark eyes, and a long nose. His profile could've been chiseled into marble twenty-five hundred years ago. Handsome from some angles, harsh from others. The sort of person you meet once in passing but remember five years later.

Ari doesn't have that *thing*—that distinctive quality. People glance at her and decide there's someone more interesting to her left. Even dying her hair an outrageous shade of pink didn't help her stand out in this city. After attending just one festival in McCarren Park, she concluded that at least one fifth of all women in Brooklyn also have pink hair.

"Did you form these opinions based on life experience?" He fiddles with the knob on the dreaded electric stove, lowering the heat. "Or a handful of readings from Intro to Women's Studies?"

"Are you always this condescending?"

"Are you always this naïve?" He's still crouched down, at eye level with the stove top.

She reaches across him for a dish towel, blocking his access to the stove. "It's 'naïve' to buy into the patriarchal myth of monogamy."

"The patriarchal *myth*?" He grabs the towel from the hook on the lower cabinet door and thrusts it in her direction. "Move so I don't scorch my Le Creuset on this fucking Maytag coil."

"You genuinely believe the soulmate narrative peddled by Hallmark and those tacky Kay Jewelers commercials? Where a man surprises a woman with a little black ring box and it's supposed to be some kind of huge life achievement?"

"Hallmark didn't invent soulmates," he says. "They just made it more marketable." Josh places a cover on the pot of simmering water and turns to face her. "If you want to assign blame, take it up with Plato."

Ari dries her hands on the towel, debating whether to take the bait. "Plato?"

"*The Symposium*? Aristophanes's speech?"

"You'll have to refresh my memory. I went to public school in Arizona."

Josh reaches toward the counter and turns his neatly printed list to the blank side. "Plato says that the original humans were round creatures with four arms, four legs, and a head with a face on each side." Ari watches his pen glide over the surface of the paper, producing a sketch resembling Violet Beauregarde turning into a blueberry in Willy Wonka's factory. But this drawing has two heads, eight limbs, and a couple little scribbles above the legs.

"What's that?" she asks, pointing at the scribble on the left.

He glances down at the paper. "Genitalia."

"Oh." She squints at the drawing. "Yikes."

"IT'S AN ABSTRACT REPRESENTATION," JOSH INSISTS, DARKENING A FEW of the lines with his pen. "They could have any combination of . . . parts."

"How progressive. This is not where I envisioned this story going."

"You really haven't heard this before? My dad always told me it was the inspiration for the black-and-white cookie."

"Those shrink-wrapped things they sell at bodegas?" She shrugs. "Never had one."

Josh jerks his head up. "But you live in New York. It's basic cultural literacy."

"I moved here four months ago!"

He takes a clearing breath. "One of my jobs at my dad's deli was to ice the black-and-white cookies. No one else would make sure the lines were straight. It relaxed me."

"Did you at least get to eat the imperfect ones?"

"God, no. They're too sweet. Like spooning sugar directly into your mouth." He grimaces, remembering the sickly sweet smell of fondant and royal icing.

"Your dad owns a deli?" Ari glances at his perfect mise en place. "Did he teach you to cook?"

"My dad taught me the fine art of assembling corned beef sandwiches and scooping cole slaw." The sum total of his father's culinary training had taken place at the deli, working his way from busboy, to prep cook, to grill man, to cutter. His father had never cooked in another restaurant. He'd barely cooked in his own apartment, aside from opening cans of soup. "He's not a chef. That's a title you earn in a real kitchen. Not Brodsky's."

There's a glint of recognition in her eye. "Wait, your dad owns Brodsky's?"

"*That* you've heard of?"

"I mean, it's famous, right? It has a blue neon sign?"

Josh's dad, Danny, inherited Brodsky's deli in 1977 from his uncle with the tacit understanding that Danny was to be a custodian of a forty-year tradition. The name "Brodsky's" doesn't get mentioned without modifiers like "an institution," "a classic," "seen in such films as . . ." There's not a single person in the East Village, downtown Manhattan, or possibly the tri-state area who wants a thing about Brodsky's to change.

Except Josh.

He and his dad had butted heads since Josh was tall enough to use the stove.

As a child, Josh would spend hours in Brodsky's, begging to do odd jobs, while his father grilled frankfurters or mixed up enormous batches of pickling solution. He soaked up every bit of his dad's arcane knowledge—"moisture is the enemy of a good latke"—and studied the correct ratio of yolks to whites in a good egg salad. Then, one day, Danny decided Josh was old enough for the most important kitchen tools: knives and heat.

The element of danger unlocked something. Josh began cooking for himself—experimenting with new techniques, mastering challenging recipes, asking for *Modernist Cuisine* for his sixteenth birthday. When his little sister, Briar, refused to eat chopped liver, Josh made vegetable spring rolls for her school lunches. (It was a great way to practice his knife work.)

He was bursting with ideas—specifically, ideas for "improving" classic Brodsky's dishes. Couldn't they add caramelized leeks to the potato kugel? Some paprika in the egg salad?

His father's response was the same every time: He'd point at the weathered, hand-painted sign that had served as Brodsky's slogan since the 1950s: *The Food You Remember.*

"Food you wish you could *forget*," teenage Josh had muttered.

And for several years, he tried to do just that. Instead of afternoons spent at the deli, Josh doubled down on academic extracurriculars. He became a star Mathlete, joined Model U.N. and the debate team. There was little reason for father and son to have more than a passing conversation on the rare occasions that they found each other in the same place at the same time.

But three years into his economics degree at Stanford, Josh splurged on a meal at the French Laundry. Some dormant passion reignited that evening when he dipped his spoon into an impossibly silky egg custard. The subtle elegance of the presentation in a precisely cut eggshell, with one pin-straight chive blade providing a burst of sharp flavor. It wasn't just food; it was a sensory experience, offering a completely different set of possibilities than his dad's salty corned beef hash.

When Josh announced his plan to drop out of Stanford to attend the Culinary Institute of America, Danny shook his head in that specific disappointed way that only fathers can. "You want to pay thousands of dollars so someone else can teach you how to dice an onion?" he'd muttered.

Josh's mother, Abby, agreed to foot the bill, with the tacit understanding that Josh would one day apply his knowledge by taking over the deli. But Josh had no desire to be the heir to a fading pastrami empire: He had much more ambitious plans. After completing the program, he left for Europe to work in some of the world's greatest kitchens.

Josh and his dad haven't spoken since his return to the city. Abby acts as their go-between.

"The two-sided humans were so physically powerful," he continues, "that they became a threat to the gods. So Zeus sliced them down the middle." He draws a violent slash through the center of the circular body. "Now they're all running around on two legs, confused and distraught, trying to reconnect with their other half."

Ari leans forward, dropping her elbow onto a few square inches of empty real estate on the counter. "The soulmate?"

"Exactly." He nods once, throwing the towel over his shoulder.

FOR ONE SECOND, IN THE EXCITEMENT ABOUT AGREEING ON SOMETHING, Ari sees a glimmer of why Natalie finds him attractive. His voice is so much more pleasant when he's telling a story instead of arguing. And there's something annoyingly hot about men with towels on their shoulders and rolled up sleeves.

"That's pretty dark," she says, staring at the ink slash. "No wonder Hallmark rebooted this concept as a Candace Cameron Bure rom-com."

Josh's expression darkens. He stands up straighter, making her feel shorter than five feet five. "Your soulmate gives you the greatest possible sense of belonging," he says with genuine conviction. "They heal your existential wound. It's the basis of modern love."

Her brief flicker of interest in him must have been ninety percent towel-on-shoulder related. "You honestly think there's *one* person somewhere on this planet who can fulfill every single need you'll ever have?"

"Yes. And eventually you'll get sick of searching for your underwear at two in the morning!" His accent is poking through again. "You'll start looking for the person who won't bore you. Who makes sacrifices for you even when you don't deserve it. Who you want to hold all night until your arm falls asleep. Who's required by law to bring you matzo ball soup when you get a cold. No one with an eggplant emoji next to their name is ever going to care about you that way." Ari stares at him, mouth open, slightly alarmed by the volume of his impromptu monologue. He focuses his gaze on a chip in the laminate countertop and clears his throat softly. "What?"

"You're completely delusional."

Josh's phone vibrates across the kitchen counter.

NATALIE: hey! So sorry.
Gonna be later than i thought

Just getting to manhattan
😊 😊

The voice in Josh's head unleashes a burst of creative expletives. The cod is already poaching. The orange *sauce vierge* will be gelatinous in thirty minutes. By the time Natalie arrives, he'll be a sweaty mess.

Sometimes in his therapy sessions, Josh's emotions overtake his ability to answer questions like "what are you experiencing right now?" He can't take a clearing breath or do a fucking leaves-on-the-stream exercise. At this point, his therapist will inevitably advise him to "anchor." The idea is to focus on your physical surroundings: things you can touch, hear, smell. Forcing himself to be still and concentrate on the minutiae around him doesn't exactly come easily.

Except in the kitchen.

In no other place are all the senses so tightly interwoven. There's nothing *but* the present in the overpowering scent of rosemary or the gentle gurgle of water coming to a slow boil. The knife sliding easily through the flesh of a perfectly ripe pear.

So it's lucky that he finds himself in front of a cutting board, holding a plump heirloom tomato for the *panzanella* when Natalie's text comes through.

What's the alternative? Packing up his two hundred dollars' worth of half-prepped produce, his cutting board, and Le Creuset and leaving the apartment in a huff?

He's fucking trapped in this sweltering apartment.

"Something wrong?" Ari asks.

"No." He rubs his forehead. *Anchor.* "She's running late."

Ari raises her eyebrows and nods slowly. "This is exactly the scenario I never have to deal with." She turns away from him and opens the freezer, grabbing an ice cube tray. "If you weren't so preoccupied with locking down a relationship you could just shrug it off and do something else with your evening instead of spiraling about it."

"I'm not spiraling," he insists, even as he feels his pulse quicken.

Ari grabs each end of the tray and violently twists until the cubes detach from their molds. "Sure, you're not."

Quit talking to her. Let it go. Don't let her bait you. Anchor.

"How would you understand anything about a real relationship when you're obviously incapable of forming a connection with someone other than the briefest possible sexual encounter?" he utters in one unbroken, comma-less string of words.

Ari narrows her eyes—almost pleased to have set him off.

"I'm not 'incapable' of anything," she says, dropping the ice in her water glass. "I'm *honest* with people about what I expect. They can't hurt me and I can't disappoint them. We both get what we want."

"If what you want is to fuck someone you don't care about, roll over, put your clothes on, and see yourself out, you're set for life."

"Usually, we pretend to watch a movie first, but what difference does it make if I put my clothes back on ten minutes later or eight hours later?" She tilts her head back and takes four enormous gulps of water, as if the effort of the argument requires rehydration. The glass lands on the counter with a *thunk*. "We could have the hottest, most inconsequential hypothetical sex of your life and then—"

"*We* could?"

"*Hypothetically.*" She huffs out an exhale. "I'd quietly collect my panties and steal away into the night without waking you up."

"Assuming you can locate them." He notices a spot of mustard on the side of her mouth. It gives him a zing of schaden-freude.

"I always send a *thank you* text the next day." She pauses. "Unless you went down on me for three minutes with zero enthusiasm but also expected a messy blow job thirty seconds later."

It's not often that Josh is rendered speechless. Which is to say that his train of thought shifts to the length of Ari's shorts. Their intense little sparring contest. Handing her his knife.

There's something there—a frisson of excitement. Somewhere in between extorting him for charity and her description of their hypothetical one-night stand, Josh must have decided—begrudgingly—that she's pretty. Even if she does have pink hair that's starting to wash out. She's obnoxious and wrong about everything, but this is the most invigorating encounter he's had with anyone in—well, his social life hasn't been very robust lately.

"You're missing out on the exciting part." He sets down his knife. "Don't you ever have those conversations with people, when you're lying in bed after the first time you . . ." He trails off, like it's risky to use certain words in front of her. "And you're both vulnerable and nervous and hopeful because this could be a night you'll reminisce about years later? They tell you things you couldn't have known about them? The walls come down, and you start to understand who they really are?"

Ari squints at him, as if she's trying to see a color that doesn't exist yet.

"Have you spent ten minutes on a dating app?" Her voice is distinctive—maybe a hint of a rasp from shouting at strangers all day. "I don't want to see who these people really are."

Josh exhales a breath that clears nothing. He angles the cutting board over a salad bowl, watching the chunks of heirloom tomato slide slowly into the bowl.

Ari leans forward over the corner of the counter in a way that's both confrontational and an unexpected turn-on. "You just happen to be the only man on Earth who's not interested in completely meaningless, consequence-free sex?"

He isn't totally sure whether that's an accusation or an invitation.

"There's no such thing," Josh says finally. "You're leaving before the other person has a chance to point out the consequences." Ari raises an eyebrow, turns, and walks back into the living room. "At the very least, you're missing out on morning sex," he says, following her. "And still-awake-at-three-A.M. sex. And learning what someone's brunch order is—"

"You mean the awkward get-to-know-you breakfast?"

"If you knew me before we slept together, breakfast wouldn't be awkward!"

"Please." She positions herself in front of the air conditioner and lets the cool air from the A/C blow up under the hem of her tank top. "It's nothing but obligation and weak mimosas."

"Congratulations. You've figured out how to avoid any shred of intimacy that you could possibly share with another human being." The shallots and fennel on the stove sizzle too loudly, just on the edge of burning, but he can't force himself to drop the argument. "I guarantee you that the best sexual experience of your life won't be with a stranger."

"You're right!" she says, taking a step toward him. "It'll probably be hate sex with someone I despise."

It's Josh's turn to say something—hurl an insult or a self-righteous declaration. But instead, his mind replays that last sentence, the exchange hanging dangerously in the air between them.

"Or maybe not." Ari shrugs. "You know who *is* pretty high up on that list?"

"Who?" He tries to sound nonchalant, but fears it comes off pathetically earnest.

Ari doesn't blink. "Your girlfriend."

The high decibel scream of the fire alarm on the ceiling drowns out Josh's response.

HE LOOKS LIKE HE'S TRYING TO KEEP HIS BALANCE DURING AN EARTH-quake.

Ari grabs the broom from against the wall, stands on a rickety folding chair, and pokes at the screaming alarm until it stops assaulting their ears.

"*Natalie?*" Josh looks simultaneously appalled and confused. "What about your—your boyfriend?"

"My what?"

"You're wearing his underwear." He glances down at Gabe's boxers before averting his eyes again.

"Gabe?" Ari drops the broom against the wall. "He's just a friend."

Josh dismisses her statement with a judgmental *pfft*. His device buzzes.

"Natalie's in a cab," he reads. "She'll be here in twenty minutes."

Maybe it's the mention of a ticking clock that triggers the panic. The search for the exit. For the first time all evening, it occurs to Ari what might happen if she's still in the apartment when Natalie returns.

She would have to watch them greet each other with a kiss—the start of a romantic (albeit slightly burnt) dinner. Josh would smugly observe Natalie asking Ari if she could leave the apartment.

Better to get out of here while it's still a *choice* and not a humiliation.

Ari rushes into her room and pulls on a pair of jeans she'd left on the floor. She gathers her earbuds, phone charger, and water bottle and drops them in her tote bag.

"You're leaving?" Josh asks when she brushes past him, heading for the door.

"Yeah." She pauses in front of the door. "Why? Were you hoping for a threesome?"

He looks bewildered for a moment and then his eyes sweep over her face, giving Ari that weird tingly sensation down her scalp—like he's invading her personal space with his gaze. "Were *you*? Because two minutes ago, you were describing our hypothetical sex life."

"And forty minutes ago, you were staring at my ass."

"I wasn't," he insists, more indignantly than Ari would like. He tilts his head down, making his height advantage more obvious. "I know why you're like this."

It's like he can see through things: Intro to Women's Studies talking points, her anxious adjustments of Gabe's boxer shorts on her hips, the false bravado of someone feeling the sting of yet another potential rejection after a day full of them.

"You don't know anything about me," she insists, feeling behind her back for the door handle.

"You're so afraid of rejection, you have to latch on to some cultural studies bullshit to support your behavior." His accent is poking through. "It doesn't make you some brave badass. If you had any confidence in your . . . *connection* with Natalie, you'd wait for her to show up and let her decide who's more important to her."

"If Natalie wants to be your 'girlfriend,'" she says, letting the frustration and anger she's been pushing down all day rise up to the surface, "then why does she ask me to go down on her after she's been out to dinner with you?"

Josh stares at her, twisting his mouth. "If I had to guess?" Ari has enough experience with volcanic men to know that he's churning up a response designed to inflict damage. "She likes the convenience."

Ari wills herself not to show any trace of hurt. "I can hear everything she likes," she says slowly—really twisting the knife. "Even with her thighs covering my ears."

Josh's face is red. There's a blood vessel bulging from his temple.

Ari pulls at the door handle, hoping for a quick exit before he can muster a response. She has no idea where she's going, just the unstoppable desire to flee. Better to be the one who walks away than the person who gets left behind.

As she throws the door open, he adds, "You forgot your panties."

"Sorry, I can't hear you." Ari holds her phone up to her ear. "I'm on a *fucking call.*"

Three Years Later

ARI STANDS OUTSIDE THE RESTAURANT, JUGGLING HER PHONE, A VAPE pen, and an enormous street-meat skewer with two hands. Not surprising that her roommate, Radhya, isn't picking up, since dinner service at Scodella is still going. Radhya is somewhere in the kitchen, perfectly roasting and grilling expensive cuts of "carefully sourced" pork or things like squab, which is really just fancy chicken. Rad can press the pad of her index finger to a steak and tell exactly how done it is.

> Wed, Sep 13, 10:12 P.M.
> ARI: HUGE NEWS 🔪 👑 🐖
> gonna stop by, can you take a break?

Without them tacitly acknowledging best friendship, Ari and Radhya had become each other's emergency contacts over the summer, when Radhya kicked her husband out of her apartment and began the search for a roommate who wouldn't mind sleeping in the middle room of a railroad apartment. Enter Ari, who knew it wouldn't be a problem because she would never bring anyone home to spend the night.

They'd spent most of July and August smoking weed on the couch and bingeing various *Real Housewives* franchises, while Radhya revealed all of the worst things about her ex (cheating with a hostess, putting ketchup on hot dogs, cheating with a different hostess). Listening to the world's most depressing listicle every night only increased Ari's confidence in her own approach to sex and dating. (More of the former, as little of the latter as possible, thank you.)

Radhya makes delicious grilled cheese sandwiches at two A.M. Ari provides the deliciously strong pot brownies that induce the grilled cheese cravings. Radhya appreciates friends who don't judge her career choice, the men she hooks up with (often messily tangled with the career choice), or the amount of money she spends on cosmetics. Ari always asks before borrowing the cosmetics.

As friends, Radhya and Ari are a better couple than Radhya and her husband ever were.

ARI: loading dock? Or meet you at Milano's?

Ari tucks her phone into her bra to better focus on consuming the lamb skewer. She's ravenous. It's the buzzed feeling under her skin: this strange, unstoppable effervescence, like a soda that never goes flat. Making people laugh—causing them to lose themselves for a few seconds and surrender—is the greatest feeling in the world. Yes, better than sex. Stand-up is a different kind of high than improv or, like, actual drugs. It feels better when it works and ten times worse when it doesn't.

But tonight? *Worked.* Even though it was only one of Gabe's open mics. Even though most of the crowd was wannabe comedy men who never laugh at anyone else's material and run the gamut between shitting-themselves nervous and why-am-*I*-still-doing-open-mics cocky.

That didn't matter tonight. Because five hours ago, she heard the fateful little *ding* from her phone. The email. Subject line: *OFFER*.

Real money in exchange for a script. She's been reading the text of the message all evening, one little sentence fragment at a time, like she's slowly savoring wine from a chalice.

> KWPS (pronounced "quips") will be the Netflix of comedy,
> but *curated*.
> Only the coolest shit. No vowels necessary.

It's a game-changing career development. A tangible *thing* to add to her anemic list of professional accomplishments. She's a professional nanny for a family on Sixty-eighth and Park. A professional cashier at a panini place at Rockefeller Center. A professional assistant at the LaughRiot theater on Fifty-third Street, where she answers phones, cleans up after classes, and pours weak, overpriced drinks at their makeshift bar before the shows.

Maybe after tonight, she *could* call herself a comedian and not feel a giant shameful wave of imposter syndrome engulf her internal organs.

Ari's always felt slightly out of step with the intensity of the comedy "community" in New York. Most people love to talk about their "journey." They won childhood talent shows or edited *The Harvard Lampoon* or personally encountered the ghost of Del Close. Ari fell into comedy after a hookup with the leader of her college's improv team. The encounter was brief but the improv lasted four years. It was like rushing a tiny, nerdy frat.

The sense of absolute trust and camaraderie hooked her. The performances were an even bigger rush: Though she never got much attention growing up in her grandma's home, here were a hundred of her peers, hanging on her every word.

As a gainfully employed adult, Radhya is the closest thing Ari has to a proud parent. In fairness, Grandma Pauline never asked to be responsible for another child at age forty-eight when Ari's mom realized she "just couldn't do this anymore" and took off with a Phish Head. Over the years, her mom would reappear occasionally, sticking around just long enough to get Ari's hopes up, before disappearing in the middle of the night without waking her up to say goodbye.

Radhya, on the other hand, has never let her down.

> RADHYA: Come inside.
>
> Hot bartender working tonight. He'll hook you up
>
> ARI: the aussie?
>
> RADHYA: kiwi—he sounds exactly like the hotter Conchord

"RADHYA!" JOSH SHOUTS. "PUT YOUR FUCKING PHONE AWAY. HOW LONG on the steak?"

"One minute."

"One minute, *Chef,*" he corrects. "Watch the timing on that duck. Table Five is a contributor at Eater. I don't want duck juices running all over her plate while it's being carved tableside." Even though it's just past ten, the ticket printer is still whirring to life occasionally, spitting out the last of the night's dessert orders.

Josh tweezes a single curry leaf over a piece of poached halibut: The cut of fish is perfectly diamond-shaped, covered with glistening half-moon slices of zucchini "scales," floating on a shallow pool of turmeric fumet. He'd sketched the dish in his notebook last week and here it is: soigné, immaculate, willed into existence. The kind of thing his father would shake his head at— "What do you need to show off for?" Well, if they were on speaking terms, that's what he'd say. While Briar and Abby had been to the restaurant to eat several times, Danny refused to step foot anywhere near Josh's kitchen ("But I'm sure he would *love* it!" Abby would try to insist). Josh didn't care; it was better this way.

"The oven's been uneven," Radhya says, sliding a lavender-honey-glazed bird into the oven. "I'm leaving the duck in for ten minutes before I turn it."

"*Eight* minutes. It's *my* recipe. I don't want the risotto congealing into a disgusting, gummy mess on the pass because you're overcooking the duck." He pauses. "And it's 'eight minutes, *Chef.*'"

She shakes her head. Radhya can sear the fuck out of a scallop or expertly reproduce dishes he vaguely recognizes from Le Bernardin or Red Rooster. She's maddeningly correct about everything, like the amount of time it'll take to turn twenty artichokes (thirty-five minutes) or the exact number of salt grains to sprinkle on each heirloom tomato slice (seven). But lately, she's been sloppy. Forgetful. Distracted. Which are the worst qualities in a line cook. Even Danny was at least *consistent.*

Josh even thought he'd heard her sniffling in the walk-in last week, but when she reappeared at her station, her makeup was immaculate as usual.

A back waiter comes to collect the halibut and steak, balancing the plates expertly along his forearm. "There's a girl at the bar asking for Radhya," he says. "Says her name is 'Twattie'?"

There's a brief round of tittering from the other line cooks, who have a long-running joke about Radhya being gay, for no reason other than that she's a woman chef, seems to be a soccer fan, and has nicknames for everyone. Josh is pretty sure she mentioned a husband at one point.

"Radhya's busy babysitting this duck for the next eight minutes," he snaps.

"Ten."

"'Ten,' *Chef.*" When he started on the line at Scodella, Radhya outranked him. But as he endeared himself to their boss and was quickly promoted to sous chef, he'd heard the vague, displeased mutterings from the back-of-house staff about the circumstances of his swift rise in the kitchen hierarchy. The line cooks didn't seem to care about Josh's experiences *staging* in Denmark and Barcelona, but they certainly recognized the name *Kestenberg*. He still hasn't quite managed to check Radhya's occasional, subtle insubordination. It's probably resentment. Spite. Jealousy.

"I'm checking on the dining room," Josh says, untying his apron. It's a convenient excuse to escape the sweat and heat of the kitchen. And to spy on Table Five's first course.

Josh stops in his boss's empty office first to clean up a bit. He examines his reflection, appraising. He's never been able to let go of this habit of quickly cataloging the flaws in his appearance. The long nose that dominates his entire fucking face? *Check.* Bags under his eyes from thirty years of insomnia? *Check.* Nothing in his teeth from tasting dozens of spoonfuls of underseasoned red quinoa? *Check*—not that he's planning to showcase a slightly crooked open-mouth smile in the dining room. He's pretty sure less than half a dozen people on Earth have ever seen it.

He pulls out his phone. No text from Sophie. Again.

Things had felt precarious since last Sunday. As Sophie left his apartment, he'd spontaneously dropped an "I love you" into their standard goodbye as she walked to the elevator. She paused and turned her head. In that moment, Josh managed to convince himself that she would jog back to his door and embrace him with tears in her eyes. Naturally, sex in his small foyer would follow (against the wall, perhaps?), along with a full confession of feelings, and possibly the planning of a weekend trip to Rhinebeck.

What she'd actually said, with a smile that could best be described as *pleasant,* was, "That's so nice."

Then she'd stepped on the elevator.

He's been analyzing that specific intonation of "so nice" for four days. He's always struggled with that sort of ambiguity. "Nice" is positive; it's also not "I love you, too," which, as far as Josh is concerned, is the only response you want to that question. There's an art to navigating the space between *dating* and *relationship* and he'd fucked it up by rushing the climactic declaration. Now this incident is part of his brain's repertoire before surrendering to the REM cycle.

He drops the phone in his pocket. *Anchor.*

The dining room offers a different sort of sonic chaos than the kitchen. The laughter of a few loud blowhards booming over the self-consciously-cool-but-unobtrusive jazz playlist that the owner favors. The tinkling of dessert spoons scraping against plates. Chairs being pushed back by guests who are starting to feel the effects of the second bottle of cab sav as they stand up to leave.

If ninety-eight percent of a service is spent sweating, yelling, calculating, cajoling, tweezing behind the swinging door of the kitchen, then touching tables is his victory lap. Of course, a glowing review from a food publication is an even better form of validation.

Stopping at Table Five, Josh convincingly pretends that he has no idea who the woman is, even though he's careful to introduce himself with his full name. He politely inquires about their first course dishes. The *baccalà fritto* was "not too forward," she says. The *torchio* was "interesting."

It must be the least revealing conversation he's had this week. Well, aside from that exchange with Sophie.

Josh excuses himself, but something stops him from returning to the kitchen—a loud shriek of laughter from the marble-top bar.

There's only one patron there: Radhya's friend. Jace—which can't possibly be the bartender's real name—is chatting her up, showing her something on his phone. Only her back is visible. Brown hair and a black shirt—nothing remarkable, but there's something familiar about this woman prickling in his brain.

She tilts her head back and lets out another unrestrained peal of laughter—the kind you can't fake out of politeness. As far as he can remember—and he remembers all his successes and failures in vivid, high-definition detail—the only occasion on which he's elicited that kind of enthusiasm from a woman was during sex.

It's her speaking voice that gives her away—the specific, slightly throaty timbre that lodged in his head three years ago. There's no reason for it other than the simple truth that we remember horribly awkward incidents more clearly than pleasant encounters.

Josh approaches the bar, not to confirm that the woman is,

indeed, his ex-girlfriend's ex-roommate. He merely needs to know if there's another food order coming in from the bar. That's all.

Jace lifts his head to greet him. "How ya going, mate?" Josh has always suspected his accent is fake.

"*Chef*," Josh corrects, careful not to make eye contact with her. Yet.

Jace turns to his only patron. "Is that not the best thing you've ever put in your mouth?"

Ari Sloane places the tumbler down on the bar top. Without a coaster.

"That's a pretty high standard." She leans forward, forearms resting on the bar. "What else do you have up your sleeve?"

"A lot more tattoos, for starters." Jace watches Ari trace her index finger up his forearm. "Have you got any?"

She nods. "None that I can show you right now. Ask me again later?"

Josh clears his throat. "Unless you're planning to order food, we'll shut down the kitchen after that last table."

"Have you met Radhya's roommate?" Jace tilts his head. "Sorry, what was your name, again?"

"Twattie," she says with a nod. Ari is wearing a cropped black T-shirt. Glasses. An army green jacket with a scratched Bernie Sanders button fastened to the pocket is slung over the back of the barstool. And she has bangs now, so she's basically unrecognizable. Except for the dimple to the right of her mouth.

He knows she's wearing a bra this time because he can see the outline of her phone poking out of the cup.

"Charming nickname," Josh mutters.

"Well, Radhya is 'Cum Slut,' so that one was taken." She eyes his chef's coat. "Do you work for her?"

"No," he says, the neutrality slipping from his voice. "I'm in charge of the kitchen. She roasts meat."

Ari betrays no hint of recognition. Not the slightest furrow in her brow, no narrowing of the eyes. In the history of facial expressions, there has never been such a neutral countenance on another human being. Even Sophie's "that's so nice" was more scrutable.

"We've met," Josh says, unable to hold it in any longer. Her mouth is turned up ever so slightly at the corner.

"Oh?" she asks, curious rather than hostile. Taking in his face. Maybe trying to place the distinctive nose without being rude about it. "At Radhya's birthday?"

Josh shakes his head.

"On Tinder?"

"*No.*"

She furrows her brow. "OkCupid?" So she's scraping the bottom of the barrel now.

"Ari."

"Oh! I delivered medical marijuana to your apartment!" she announces triumphantly.

Jace perks up. "Are you still doing that?"

"We call it 'cannabis concierge service,'" she replies. "We can charge New School students twenty percent more that way."

"How entrepreneurial," Josh says tightly.

Jace rests both elbows on the bar, eyes ping-ponging between them. "Did you two ever . . . ?"

Josh winces. "We absolutely did not—"

"—I was fucking his girlfriend," Ari declares. "He botched a once-in-a-lifetime threesome opportunity."

"THAT'S NOT WHAT HAPPENED," TALL SWEATER NIGHTMARE MAN IN-sists.

Ari looks into the bartender's—Chase's? Jake's?—giant brown eyes. "I guess not every man can handle that kind of thing."

Josh scoffs, standing up to full height. He looks a little older, a bit more intimidating, bigger in the shoulders. There's a slight coldness in his eyes now, different from the needy, searching quality of two (three?) years ago. He's changed his look, pulling his hair back into one of those ridiculous half-ponytails with a bandana tied around his forehead, like he's some food warrior, trying to intimidate onions and potatoes with his headgear. It's baffling at first, seeing him in this new context, when he's only ever existed in her old apartment—like seeing your middle school algebra teacher at the convenience store purchasing a bag of Flamin' Hot Cheetos.

Josh turns to the hot bartender. "She was my girlfriend's roommate. We spent one nightmare of an evening together." He shifts his eyes to Ari. "I still get junk mail from the Nature Con-servancy."

"Sounds like the bobcats still need your help," she replies, sipping her drink.

"So you *do* remember?" Josh asks, annoyance seeping into his tone. Ari concedes nothing. "Have you talked to Natalie since she moved to California for her postdoc?"

"Who?"

Chase/Jake slides over another whiskey sour that she defi-nitely doesn't need. The alcohol is starting to muddle the dopa-mine hit of the windfall email and successful open mic.

"Your *roommate*." Josh shoots her the sort of withering stare he probably reserves for back waiters.

"Oh, *that* Natalie. Yeah, we Snap sometimes." She sips her drink, hoping her nonchalance gives off nail-polish-emoji energy. "She's on my nudes distribution list."

Chase whips his head up, God bless him.

Josh coughs. "And are you still harassing pedestrians—"

"You mean raising money for worthy charitable causes?"

"—or did you find a new line of work?" The hostility is still right under the surface, even after three years. His voice overcompensates for something. Probably a disappointing penis.

"I've been—" Ari hesitates for a few seconds, before remembering that she officially has the right to say it. Yeah, it's a fact now. No qualifiers. No *trying to "do comedy."* "I'm a professional comedian." Chase or Jake is no longer paying attention, occupying himself with closing tasks. A server stifles a yawn as she runs her last table's credit card, her nails clicking against the screen protector on the point-of-sale system. "I came here to celebrate with Rad. I sold a script."

"For television?" Josh asks. There's a slight dubious note in his voice.

"Yes." She clears her throat. "Well, a streaming platform. It's going to be the Netflix of comedy." She's surprised at the way she wants to keep chattering about this with Tall Sweater Nightmare Man. There's an enthusiasm in her voice—an almost coked-up vibe, but clear, too. "And I did a really great set tonight. It really flowed. So I thought Rad and I could celebrate by getting blackout drunk and trying not to barf in the cab home."

Enough. Jesus. Ari takes another sip of the whiskey sour to stop the giddy rambling.

"Your definition of 'roommate' hasn't changed, either," Josh says, shaking his head.

"Radhya and I are strictly platonic. Haven't you noticed she's hopelessly straight?"

He looks surprised by that. "We don't exactly keep up with each other's love lives during the dinner rush."

"So she hasn't heard your soulmate cookie theory? How's that working out for you, by the way? Did you find your other half and make her breakfast?"

"I HAVE A GIRLFRIEND." JOSH PAUSES, CONSIDERING HOW MUCH TO RE-veal. This conversation is a convenient excuse to be in the din-ing room for the tableside presentation of the duck at Table Five. "Sophie. She's in brand management consulting. Speaks four languages. She's the most intelligent woman I've ever met."

"Wow." Ari rests her chin in the palm of her hand. "Sounds like you really admire her."

"Yes," Josh agrees. "But it's mutual."

Out of the corner of his eye, he watches the server slice into the bird. It's a choreographed dance—the strokes of the carving knife revealing perfectly roasted duck.

"How many eggplants?" Ari asks.

"Three—no, four," he says quickly, feeling ridiculous for leaning into her eggplant scale, but oddly defensive.

"Lies!"

"I'm lying about my own girlfriend?" A girlfriend of two and a half months who likes responding to *I love you* with "that's so nice."

Maybe Ari and Jace will fuck each other later tonight. If he had to make a prediction, Jace will earn two emojis, max.

"See, I use the volcano emoji when—"

But she's interrupted by the sound of clattering cutlery over Josh's shoulder. Josh turns around, anticipating the delighted exclamation of a satisfied food critic at Table Five. Instead, he watches as the server looks over at him with a panicked expression.

"THAT DUCK WAS FUCKING UNDERCOOKED!" JOSH BELLOWS, SLAMMING the swinging door to the kitchen against the wall.

Radhya flinches, looking up from the counter she's scrubbing. "Jesus!"

"Turn the grill back on!" He heads straight for the walk-in, grabbing two Wagyu skirt steaks—the fastest entrée he can prepare. There's no time to roast another duck.

Radhya bursts into the walk-in behind him. "I was following *your* instructions."

"'Your instructions,' *Chef*. It's the most straightforward dish on the menu." Josh blows past her, heading for the meat station. "I need the fiddlehead ferns and the cipollini in seven minutes!" he yells to the line cooks.

Radhya reaches for the steaks. "I'll fire them—"

"Get the fuck off the line," he says, wrenching them away. "You're done tonight."

"This is *my* station."

The server rushes in from the dining room. "Table Five asked for the check, Chef."

"Tell them there's another fucking entrée coming!" Josh yells. He turns back to Radhya. "I told you to get off your phone and babysit that duck."

"And I told *you* it needed ten minutes," she retorts. "And it doesn't matter how it's cooked. Lavender and fennel is a disgusting combination."

Josh wipes down the surface in front of him in angry, slashing movements. "If you ever learn how to properly roast a duck as well as a first-year culinary school student, I'll ask for your opinion on my flavor profiles."

The kitchen falls into an awkward silence.

"I've been cooking just as long as you have—"

"I'm not going to warn you again, Radhya."

"Fucking off to Europe for a couple months doesn't make you Jacques Pépin." She pauses, like she hasn't quite decided whether to put a button on it. "It doesn't make you different than any other man in this city who got a job because of his dad."

A specific kind of rage boils up under Josh's skin. His knuckles turn white around the kitchen towel he's still clutching.

The rest of the kitchen staff breaks into an assortment of under-the-breath curses in English and Spanish and general tittering. They've all fully paused their tasks, devoting their full attention to the spectacle of an impromptu face-off.

Josh recognizes how precarious this is. There's probably a significant portion of the staff who believes Radhya should rightfully be in charge. Any sign of backing down and allowing dissent to flourish would be disastrous—a total loss of confidence.

And he has one trump card left. Or maybe it's the nuclear option.

Either way, the words fly out before he has a chance to think twice. "You're fired."

ARI DOESN'T NOTICE WHEN THE SERVERS BEGIN RESETTING THE DINING room. She's distracted by Jace and his accent. He's saying things that would be unremarkable in standard middle-American English, but sound like Neruda poems with the lilt of his accent combined with the whiskey sours he's been pouring her.

It's the muffled yelling from the kitchen that catches her slightly inebriated attention, followed by Radhya's heavy footsteps marching through the dining room, her backpack slung over her shoulder.

"We're leaving," Radhya announces, veering toward the bar. "Actually, tequila. Now."

Jace hurriedly grabs for a liquor bottle and a shot glass.

"W-wait." Ari gathers her bag and jacket, sliding off the stool, only stumbling half a step. "What's wrong?"

"*He's* wrong." Radhya slams down the shot and turns to face her, eyes watery. Even during the worst of the divorce aftermath, Ari can't remember seeing Rad cry. "I cooked that duck exactly the way he told me to. I was right, he was wrong, and he fired me."

"Who fired you?" Ari pushes Radhya's empty shot glass back toward Jace for a refill. Radhya is constantly outnumbered by aggressive mansplainers in her job so it's hard for Ari to keep track of every single one she complains about.

When Josh bursts into the dining room a second later, his face red, the pieces start to snap together.

"*You* fired her?" Ari asks.

"I can't work with someone who doesn't respect my authority in the kitchen."

"Your authority?" Radhya backs away toward the front exit. "You have an enormous fucking chip on your shoulder." She turns to Ari and Jace. "He only got this job because the owner's a regular at his dad's deli." She pushes through the door.

"That's a lie!" Josh says, even though Radhya's already outside.

Ari slowly turns back to him.

"What is wrong with you?" she asks.

"Me?" He takes a step toward her, gesturing at the door. "I'm not the person who just made a scene."

"Do you have any idea how hard she's worked to get here? How many born-on-third-base assholes like you she's had to deal with?" He opens his mouth, but Ari continues. "You can't fire someone over *one* dish."

"One dish served to a food writer can close a restaurant. There's no room here for someone who can't follow the most basic fucking technique. She's been sloppy and unfocused for weeks. I didn't spend seven months in Provence mastering *sauces mères* to look over Radhya's shoulder while she fucks up a simple duck recipe."

"You'd also be a little distracted if you were going through a divorce."

He appears momentarily caught off guard . . . possibly even slightly shamed? It doesn't last. "There are hundreds of Radhyas in this city who could churn out competent food." Josh wipes his hand on a towel. He stares down at Ari, that know-it-all look in his eye. "I'm not going to argue with someone whose great culinary achievement is microwaving a corn dog."

There's a moment where nothing happens. She doesn't blink or flinch or even breathe. Ari recognizes the look on his face. He thinks he's won.

So it's not a surprise that he doesn't see what's coming next, when in one swift motion, she grabs the remains of her whiskey sour from the bar and splashes it on his chefs whites and the lower half of his face.

Josh wipes his chin with his rolled-up sleeve.

Ari sets the empty glass on the bar with a hard *thunk,* blows her bangs off her forehead, and marches out.

She's definitely had better things in her mouth, anyway.

Two Years Later

THIS ISN'T HOW JOSH HAD PLANNED TO SPEND NEW YEAR'S EVE. IF HE had to rank the various options, attending a party thrown by his sister's college T.A. wouldn't have made the list.

Plan A: a quiet dinner with Sophie, not anywhere too obvious. One of the places on her *To Try* spreadsheet. Returning home just before midnight, they would have watched New Year's fireworks from the balcony of his apartment, flutes of 2006 Clos Lanson Blanc de Blancs Brut in hand.

But Sophie decided to stay in Vancouver, leaving Josh with a serviceable plan B: a recipe for cassoulet that takes eight hours to cook and a Gil Evans album spinning on his turntable. He could use the break after spending every waking hour of the last three months meticulously planning a "reimagining" of Brodsky's and fending off well-meaning people wanting to reminisce at him about Danny.

Josh's father passed away unexpectedly in the fall, leaving the deli in the hands of his family.

At first, Josh had wanted nothing to do with it. But his mother, Abby, an intimidatingly high-powered real estate broker, was dead set against selling the building. In her opinion, it was the perfect time for her son to make good on the vague promise he made when he'd entered the Culinary Institute. And while Josh never had any intention of griddling blintzes on a flattop, it wasn't as if his twenty-one-year-old sister, Briar, could be entrusted to manage Brodsky's.

So Josh reconsidered. The space itself had potential. It could be the perfect canvas for his culinary vision . . . with some cosmetic changes. He hired an interior designer to transform Danny's cluttered deli into a minimalist white box, banishing the yellowed wall décor and aged kitchen equipment to the cellar. According to Abby, it's "an unsubtle nod to his unexplored grief over his father's death."

But it's also a good strategic decision. For at least twenty years, Brodsky's business model revolved around indulging visitors from Omaha or Cleveland or Munich with a false sense of old New York nostalgia. Josh had watched seemingly permanent neighborhood establishments like Odessa Restaurant, Gem Spa, and Angelica Kitchen struggle for survival in the face of rising rents and shrinking profit margins. The Brod is the perfect pivot to take a barely profitable tourist trap into the echelons of fine dining.

His vision for "The Brod" includes a tasting menu designed to complement a list of natural wines. The dishes feature lacto-fermented vegetables—a tip of the hat to the kosher dill pickles for which Brodsky's was famed.

Over the past few months, Josh had been so preoccupied with the Brod, he'd missed his sister's birthday dinner (to be fair, it was a big ask to schlep all the way out to Fort Greene) and her apartment-warming party (he'd ordered her a very tasteful wood and marble cheeseboard from a listicle in *Architectural Digest*). Briar, therefore, would not accept "at home alone with a classic French stew and the *Twilight Zone* marathon" as a reason to turn down an invitation on a national holiday.

For most people, a party thrown by their former teaching assistant would mean a dozen bitter, insufferable grad students sitting on the floor of a dingy walk-up apartment, serving themselves from half-empty bottles of cheap wine. In Briar's world, it means an outrageously expensive Uber trip to a warehouse in Long Island City that someone had converted to a six-bedroom live/work space "after a successful crowdfunding campaign."

"Taran has a huge network," Briar explains as they climb out of the Uber. "Plus a lot of them are influencers. Exactly who you want taking selfies at The Brod. Now, when we get in there, if I do this"—she squeezes the bridge of her nose—"it means, pretend you don't know me. And I will not be sharing a car back to Manhattan with you. I heard Nicholas Braun might be at this party."

Josh doesn't bother asking who that is.

Behind a pair of heavy doors, the open space of the warehouse is flooded with a rainbow of colored light. A mumblecore film plays in a blurry projection against a cement block wall. Briar takes both of their coats up a set of metal stairs leading to a mezzanine. Maybe there's a hidden corner up there where he can escape to check in with Sophie; lately it seems they're rarely in the same place at the same time. She'd sent him a listicle titled "9 Creative Ideas for Long-Distance Power Exchange." Two days ago, he'd gotten to number eight: sending gifts with explicit instructions. According to the package tracking, Sophie should have received it at 4:13 P.M. today.

When Briar returns, a young woman hands them glow sticks branded with the BetterHelp logo.

"They got sponsors for this?" Josh says, noticing a bar in the left corner stocked solely with a tower of Truly hard seltzer cans.

"Oh! Cass is here!" Briar exclaims, greeting a woman wearing a Sleater-Kinney tank top under an artfully mismatched blazer. Mid-forties, if he had to guess. And imposingly tall. Briar pulls Josh into the circle. "You remember my advisor, right? Her class was a total life-changer."

Ah, yes. She of Briar's many fawning anecdotes.

Josh can understand why Briar changed her major from English to media studies after taking Cass Nichols's "Neoteric Queer Cinema" course last year. This woman is an expert at making herself the focus of everyone's attention.

Cass holds a champagne flute in one hand and a Moleskine notebook in the other, suggesting that she's perpetually on the verge of some brilliant insight that couldn't possibly be captured on a phone. She has the familiar look of someone who's been a recurring character on a well-regarded cable drama Josh should eventually get around to watching.

"'Advisor' sounds like hegemonic management consulting bullshit. It's really an academic partnership," Cass says to him, still clutching the notebook like a prop. "That bond is very important to me." She makes huge gestures, nearly hitting Josh's ear with her chunky statement ring. "I learn just as much from them as they learn from me."

Maybe that's why she socializes with her former students on major holidays.

She's surrounded by three or four of these other "academic partners." Grad students, probably, hanging on her every word. Josh is used to holding his own with people who think they're the smartest person in the room; usually, he takes pleasure in the challenge of it. For most of his life, there's been no one he couldn't talk over. His professors, world-renowned chefs . . . last month, he'd gleefully debated Stanley Tucci on the finer points of the Negroni.

He's about to serve up a counterpoint—something about how well strict hierarchy works in a restaurant kitchen—when he feels a hand press into his shoulder, gently nudging him to the left.

It's so unexpected that it jolts his body. The owner of the hand moves past him before he can turn around and see her face. She bisects the circle, cutting straight through the conversation about the various disappointments of the Toronto International Film Festival, and heads for Cass like a heat-seeking missile.

No greeting. No "I was looking everywhere for you." She just places herself directly in front of Cass, demanding her full attention. It wouldn't be hard: She's wearing black trousers and a bra, as if she'd had on a full tuxedo and simply removed most of the top half. Wobbling slightly on heels, she's still four inches shorter than Cass.

Josh still can't see her face from this angle, just the vague outline of her profile. It's mostly hidden by her hair, a platinum blond bob.

Taking Cass's jaw in the palm of her hand, she pulls her head forward greedily into a kiss. The woman is loose-limbed, keeping her hand on Cass's face and somehow kissing her with her entire body. Not a shred of regard for anyone else.

An indignant twinge of envy prickles in his chest—a "this is shameless and inappropriate and why can't I have it, too?" sentiment. When was the last time Sophie kissed him like that? Or vice versa?

At some point (the kiss either lasts a full minute or Josh's brain converts it into slow motion), the woman leans back and pulls away, her back arching. The colored light illuminates the side of her face.

His skin goes cold. There are nine million people in this city. Logic dictates that it must be someone else. But New York doesn't operate on statistical likelihoods. The city has its own agenda, and this—*this*—is exactly how Josh's life works. Every slight, every error in judgment, every regret—they all come back to haunt him eventually.

But usually not twice.

Cass tugs at the edge of Ari's bra, recomposing herself a bit. "My wife certainly knows how to make an entrance."

"WIFE! YOU GOT REMARRIED?" ONE OF THE YOUNG WOMEN SCREECHES an inch from Ari's eardrum. A former student, maybe. Cass is friends with so many of them. It's kind of remarkable. "Congratulations! That's amazing!"

Cass's acolytes immediately make those singsongy *awwww* noises, like a group of preteens looking at a litter of kittens. Suddenly, they're all too close, gathered in a tight circle, caging Ari in.

"You okay, Ar?" Cass asks in her sexy, husky voice. She sounds like an old-school country singer who's had too much whiskey and too many cigarettes.

"Just rolling," Ari mumbles, refocusing her attention on her wife.

The woman next to them laughs and then murmurs, "I want some of whatever she's on."

Ari leans back into Cass, trying to goad her into nuzzling her neck, getting her lips to graze against the nervy spot behind her ear. Every inch of her skin feels more sensitive right now.

My wife. *Wife.* Every time she hears the phrase out loud, her brain repeats it like an affirmation. A mantra from one of Cass's self-help books. Because it still feels slippery to the touch. It's technically legal but still this intangible fever dream. From *serial non-monogamist* to *spouse*? Maybe it *is* amazing.

Or maybe it's the Molly, which is magnifying everything, making the music pulse in Ari's limbs. Cass lightly scratches her nails up and down Ari's spine in a hypnotic rhythm. It has to be the most pleasurable thing she's ever experienced.

Ari was supposed to spend tonight in Hell's Kitchen, in the same place she's spent the last five New Year's Eves. Gabe *always* hosts a karaoke fundraiser for LaughRiot and Ari *always* dresses up in something hideous and sparkly. Together, they torture everyone with their rendition of "The Boy Is Mine" after fighting over who sings the Monica part.

There aren't that many holiday traditions in Ari's life. She's never gone back to Phoenix for Thanksgiving or Christmas, even when she was only a couple hours away at U of A. Making time-and-a-half holiday pay has always been a higher priority than enduring her mother's new boyfriends and Grandma Pauline's political opinions.

The only constant has been New Year's Eve with Gabe.

But three weeks ago, Cass and Ari became wife and wife on the deck of the *Jewel of the Seas,* just off the port of Nassau, and Cass didn't think it was too much to ask for her wife to be her date to a New Year's Eve party she had told Ari about an hour earlier.

Ari had spent most of December 31 staring at a text, feeling sorry for herself, willing the letters to rearrange themselves and form new words.

> so they liked your sample
>
> but it's a no on the staff writing gig.
>
> Your voice isn't the right fit for the project
>
> you open to an assistant job?

Cass had scoffed at that. "It's insulting. You are not an assistant."

The rejection stung doubly hard after a year-long slump: KWPS had folded less than a year after paying Ari a modest sum for her script, and there was no streaming series to show for it. None of her acting auditions had garnered more than one role as a sexual harassment victim in a corporate training film. She'd done a few four-month stints on a cruise ship with Gabe and their improv team, sailing between Florida and the Bahamas. But Cass didn't like Ari being away for long stretches.

Turned out that success was harder to come by on land.

"That's how it works," Cass had pointed out. "Your personal life is amazing right now." She gave Ari one of those affectionate caresses down her forearm. "Your career trajectory is . . . stagnant. It'll even out."

Of course, sometimes you even it out by ingesting small amounts of chemicals into your body, tricking your brain into a prolonged state of delight, where everything feels *good*.

Sometimes you watch the patterns of light projected on a concrete wall and allow yourself to disassociate while your wife monologues about her Substack and viable revenue streams for creatives.

"Ar watched Terry Malick's latest with me," Cass tells her

hangers-on. She slides an arm around Ari's waist, warm and re-assuring. "The entire thing."

She gazes at Ari like she's a living goddess. No one has ever looked at her like that. Not even close. Actual heart eyes.

Cass doesn't just teach at the New School. She's also a film critic. She calls celebrities by their first names, pitches think pieces to magazines, appears on podcasts, and has a two-bedroom (*Two! Bedroom!*) condo in Queens. She uses the tiny second bed-room as an office, like a real adult. It's half Ari's now.

Okay, yes, the office is basically still Cass's. But Ari has more than half the dresser drawers. And in this city, offering storage space is the ultimate expression of love.

Among the many pleasant discoveries when Ari moved in: Two of the three drawers in Cass's bedside table are filled with sex toys—a bounty of purple vibrating silicone that Ari could only have concocted in a dream. Maybe she would have been more open to the idea of committed relationships earlier if she'd known that married life is like a never-ending sleepover, with a lot more sex.

CASS TUGS AT ARI'S WRIST. "AR, THIS IS BRIAR AND HER DATE, JOSH, UH, Something."

"Ew, *no*," Briar says, backing away, pinching the bridge of her nose.

"Ar" takes a step forward. Josh braces himself for her to splash a drink over the front of his suit, but she doesn't erupt in anger. Her glassy eyes move around the room, unfocused, aim-ing at nothing—over his shoulder, to his left, up at the ceiling—before finding their way to his face.

"I *know* you." She squints through the dim lighting, pushing her index finger into his chest with each syllable. "Tall Nightmare Sweater Man!"

Briar watches this unfold in a hard-seltzer-tinged state of astonishment.

"W-what?" Josh angles his head back an inch as she lurches toward him again, squinting at his face. He blinks, trying to process this new version of Ari Sloane run through a high-contrast filter: the blond hair, dark lipstick, dramatic eye makeup.

"Ar, come on. Stop harassing him." Cass laughs. She tucks a shiny lock of hair behind Ari's ear, letting a finger graze her neck. "Ar" bites her lower lip and rolls her shoulder in apparent pleasure.

Sophie says his Love Language is "words of affirmation," rather than "physical touch." It sounds accurate. Reasonable. Convenient for two people who primarily communicate through their phones. But watching other people express affection, he feels the lack of it.

He and Sophie aren't the kind of people who need to be joined at the hip at social events. They don't have those unsubtle "help me" signals. They'd never developed a goofy shared dialect of nonsense inside jokes and nicknames.

In these moments—the occasional pang of envy over something subtly tender—he reminds himself that long-distance relationships foster a different kind of connection. All the mundane trappings of daily life get stripped away. You're left with the most important things, not the arguments over who ate the last of the almond butter.

"Will you keep touching my hair?" Ari asks. "It feels amazing."

But something draws Cass's attention across the cavernous space.

"Dasha!" Cass calls, looking over Josh's shoulder. She waves and turns back to Ari. "Be right back." With a quick glance over her shoulder, she pushes through the circle and marches across the warehouse floor toward a gaggle of podcasters and someone who probably played a corpse on two different iterations of *Law & Order*.

Briar's sitting on the floor in a circle of rich kids dressed like dirtbags, held rapt by one particularly loud dirtbag.

What a fucking mistake it was to come here. He makes two slow circles around the room. Josh climbs the stairs to the upper level and examines the spines on a dangerously leaning bookcase while nursing a subpar merlot from a clear plastic cup, clutching his phone like a security blanket. He taps on it every so often, as if to say, "I'm so in-demand and important that I need to answer my correspondence at eleven forty-two on New Year's Eve."

For a while, Ari is at the center of an impromptu dance floor, sometimes rubbing up against strangers, some of whom are very receptive. He wouldn't describe it as *good* dancing, but there's a fluidity to the way she moves. Not self-conscious at all.

After the second serving of wine, which somehow tastes worse than the first, he loses track of her.

He checks his phone again.

> JOSH: I'm ready to leave.
> BRIAR: who is this

No message from Sophie yet. The Uber app is stuck on an endless loading screen.

Josh wanders into an empty bedroom where a dozen coats have been deposited on an unmade bed, shuts the door, and calls Sophie. Being alone provides an immediate sense of relief, putting distance between his ears and the subwoofers. Straight to voicemail. He sighs, tapping the red X on his iPhone.

Maybe she's at a similarly bleak party. Maybe she's pacing around some stranger's bedroom, seeking refuge from the thumping music on the other side of the thin drywall.

Maybe if they were at the same party, in the same stranger's room together, drunk on mediocre wine, things would get more . . . interesting. It's not really Sophie's style. Or his. They're both the kind of people who don't touch the remotes in hotel rooms, so he can't imagine commandeering this stranger's bed for a tryst. But that doesn't matter in a fantasy.

When you can only see each other every other month, imagination becomes a key component in facilitating a sexual relationship.

He calls her again, listening to her voice on the outgoing message, her businesslike tone making what he's about to say feel a bit more transgressive.

Josh clears his throat as the tone sounds.

"You should have received the package this afternoon. If you read the note, it specifically instructed you to put on the items—all of them—and send me a picture tonight. It's eleven fifty-three and I haven't received a picture. Does that mean you're not going to be a good girl for me this year? How many times do I have to tell you? Only good girls get my cock." He lowers his voice. "Or do you want me to fuck you like you're a bad girl?"

There's a noise, like a cough or a hiccup that sounds like it comes from inside the room, nearly causing him to drop his mostly empty plastic cup of merlot. Josh hangs up and rushes around the bed, checking the opposite wall, peering around.

The room itself is empty but there's another sound just outside the window. He hadn't noticed that it was open.

There's a dark silhouette of someone seated on the fire escape.

"I have to know—what was in the package?" Ari barely gets the words out before breaking into giggles and then actual hiccups. "Please let it be a clown costume."

Josh takes a few cautious steps toward the window. "Are you stalking me?"

"I was here first." She's wearing an enormous parka, probably pillaged from the bed, holding a mostly full bottle of some sickly pink wine. "I was sweating in there. Needed some fresh air."

"Right. The crisp, clean scent of air pollution from the Con Edison plant." He leans his head out the window, not feeling confident enough in the structural integrity of the fire escape to share it. "So I'm 'Tall Nightmare Sweater Man'? Is that one of Radhya's charming nicknames?"

"No," she says, taking a swig directly from the wine bottle. "You earned that title long before you fired my best friend over a piece of duck."

"It wasn't just a piece of duck. It's about respect." He takes a deep breath. "I heard Radhya's working at Frenchette, so I'd say she's just fine."

Ari rolls her eyes. "She probably could've been an executive chef by now if she also had a famous dad—"

"Famous?" He lets out a bitter little snort. "The only thing he was famous for was kicking out anyone who asked for ketchup with their latkes." It's still strange to say it in past tense. Ari raises her eyebrows, as if clocking the change, but he's grateful she doesn't ask any questions or try to offer condolences. "I'm about to launch my own fine dining restaurant in the Brodsky's space. A tasting room. My menu. My vision. And no latkes." He doesn't know why he feels the need to tell her this, where this desire for validation comes from. "It has *nothing* to do with my dad."

Ari nods slowly. "You inherited a restaurant, and it has nothing to do with your dad, who *definitely wasn't* a New York icon. Right. Totally level playing field." She takes another drink. "Sorry, but I'll probably miss that opening. I only patronize establishments that offer fried potatoes."

"I wouldn't invite someone who likes to harass chefs in their kitchens."

She shrugs. "I did yell at Mario Batali on Sixth Avenue and he almost fell off his moped."

Josh laughs despite himself.

"Wine?" She thrusts the bottle in his direction. "I found it on the counter."

He examines the label. "Who shows up to a party with Trader Joe's white zinfandel?"

"Don't talk that way about the wine retailer of the proletariat," Ari mutters.

He should duck his head back inside and leave. Wait for an Uber outside. There's no reason to continue exchanging barbs with her. But something inside him—force of will, sheer stubbornness, pride—won't let her have the last word.

Josh clears his throat. "I suppose I owe you congratulations on your complete ideological U-turn toward monogamy."

"Of course you'd assume we're monogamous," she replies, staring at a brightly lit roof party in the distance.

Josh lightly chokes on the last of his terrible merlot and the corner of Ari's mouth curves up, creating a dimple, and why the *fuck* does he have to notice all these details about someone who loathes him while Sophie is a thousand miles away?

Finally, the loading icon on the Uber app stops spinning.

"Fuck," he mutters. "I can't even *leave* this party for another twenty minutes."

She settles against the brick wall. "It's not even midnight. Why the rush to leave?"

"If it's such a great party, why are you sitting by yourself on the fire escape?"

"When the MDMA wore off, so did my tolerance for conversations about Lars von Trier." She exhales, her breath forming a cloud in the cold air. "Your dramatic performance over the phone was an unexpected bonus."

"MY GIRLFRIEND AND I ARE DOING LONG-DISTANCE. WE'RE . . . TRYING TO keep it interesting," Josh says. "It's not . . . whatever you're thinking."

Ari isn't exactly sure *what* she's thinking.

The blissful little high of a couple hours ago is slowing to a crawl, heading for the inevitable comedown. She hates this part. There's not a shimmering coat of glitter over the world anymore. It's just Queens, with its slushy streets and row houses still decorated for Christmas. Just a few miles away from Cass's apartment—no, *Cass and Ari's* apartment. Ari looks out at the roof party again, where a clump of people are gathered into a loose circle. It must be close to midnight.

"Do you moan into the receiver while she folds her laundry?" Ari asks.

His phone buzzes. He takes it out and glances at the status

notification from Uber. "I'm positive that when we talk, Sophie isn't multitasking."

"I'd be crawling up the walls," she says. "I don't know how anyone manages a long-distance thing."

Josh rubs his forehead. "We've been together for three years. At some point, she'll move back here and we'll live together. And then I suppose we'll get married." Josh fidgets with his phone. "But we're both focusing on other things right now. The relationship will be here when we can prioritize it."

She glances back at him—the suit, the carefully disheveled hair. He looks almost camera-ready. Styled. There's a slick phoniness to this version of him. Or maybe this is the final state of his gradual evolution. Any fleeting attraction she might have experienced years ago can definitively be chalked up to the competence porn of watching a man with muscular forearms cook.

Before Cass, she'd never called anyone a boyfriend or girlfriend. Never heard *I love you*. Definitely never said it. In her twenty-six years, Ari had never woken up with someone without feeling a twinge of regret while trying to slip out of bed undetected.

She never believed they wanted her to stay.

Now she has someone who wants to share everything. Who wouldn't jump at that? Who wouldn't want to get off the cruise ship after twelve weeks of cruises to Nassau and never look back? Who wouldn't want to stop working as an after-school nanny for those obnoxious brats, Agnés and Raphael? Or those gigs as a bar mitzvah "party starter" on Long Island, dancing to Maroon 5 with middle schoolers while specifically *not* being creepy?

Cass encourages Ari to aim higher because she *knows* there's more out there for her than cruise ships and teaching Improv 101 at LaughRiot. She tells her to submit packets to late-night shows. To try pilot season again. That kind of encouragement is as valid a form of love as the way Cass always wants to go down on her.

And if she has to watch the occasional interminable Danish film or listen to Cass pontificate about the "monstrous-feminine," then that's a fair trade-off.

"Interesting," she says finally, more to herself than to Josh.

"What?" He looks up, a defensive edge in his voice.

Ari turns her head to face him. "I thought you were all about intimacy and morning sex and soulmate cookies. You just talk very differently about . . . uh . . . Good Girl."

"I'm certain of where we stand," he insists.

HE SAYS IT MORE TO HIMSELF THAN TO ARI.

The truth is, when Sophie leaves for the airport, he runs this mental checklist of relationship metrics. Was this visit better or worse than the last time? Did they get bored? Were there interesting things to talk about? How many photos of the visit did she post to her stories?

"Right," Ari says. "You're a hundred percent certain she's standing a thousand miles away."

"Two thousand four hundred, actually," he replies.

"What about your arm falling asleep?"

"She's always been a very light sleeper."

"The chicken noodle soup?"

"Sophie never gets sick." It's true. Josh has never seen her in anything less than peak physical condition. "And it's matzo ball. Chicken noodle is bullshit."

"I'll give you this: Sophie is a very moanable name," she continues. *"Sohhh-feee."* She draws out the two-vowel sounds into at least four. "If you want to work that into your next phone call. 'Cass'? Not a name you can moan. It's the short 'A' sound. Very nasal." Ari looks up at the hazy, dark sky and smiles a little bit, like she's recalling a private memory. "I guess the word 'ass' is in there, though."

"How did you meet?" he asks, surprised by his own curiosity.

"I was delivering her weed. I thought it was a rebound hookup for her," she says, "because she was going through this insane nightmare divorce." Ari runs her index finger around the mouth of the empty wine bottle. "It became this really great fling that I knew would peter out at some point. But one night, I was trying to work up the energy to get up and put my jeans back on and go back to Brooklyn. And she kinda rolled onto her side and faced me and said, 'I don't want you to leave.' And I realized . . . I didn't want to, either."

"The person who recoiled in horror at the thought of spending the night in another person's bed?"

Ari snorts—a cute snort. "I did have to smoke most of a bowl the first time I slept over." She presses her lips together like she can't summon the right words. "I dunno. It's *good*. She really wants me. Like, all the time."

"You"—he tilts his head, considering how to phrase it—"you've definitely evolved."

"Don't humans become a different version of themselves every four years? Like a total refresh with brand-new cells?"

"Seven years," he says. "But that's a myth. It's not even a rough average of every cell's life span."

"Right." She attempts to take another sip from the empty bottle.

From behind them, through the thin walls, the partygoers start chanting the countdown.

Ten . . . nine . . . eight . . .

"Aren't you going to call your girlfriend again?" Ari asks. "Wish her happy New Year?"

"She's three hours behind with the time difference." He glances over his shoulder. "Don't you want to ring in the new year with your wife?"

Five . . . four . . .

"We have our whole lives to ring in New Year's together." She stares into space, seemingly distracted, even disturbed, by the idea. "Like, sixty more New Year's Eves," she mumbles. "Shit, that's a long time. And I don't think I can get up right now."

Ari and Josh watch the celebration at the roof party a few buildings over: the jubilant hugs and a few kisses shared between partners.

They turn to look at each other and the timing is both perfect and awkward. *Should we? Just a peck on the cheek. A friendly thing.* Not that they're even friends.

But maybe . . .

Josh's phone nearly buzzes out of his hand and through the fire escape grate. "My car's here."

Ari nods. "Right."

Josh ducks his head through the window and back into the bedroom, fishing his coat out of the gigantic pile on the bed, praying that a dozen tiny bed bugs haven't crawled into the seams.

"Well, happy New Year." He adds, "See you," even though he can't imagine *another* circumstance under which they'd see each other again.

"Right!" Ari calls out. "Maybe next time, we can share that bottle of white zinfandel."

Josh shoves his arms into the sleeves. "No, thank you."

There's a beat of silence. "Okay, then we'll just share your girlfriend!"

Every muscle in his body contracts. *"What?"*

"Kidding," she shouts. Then, faintly, almost out of earshot, "Unless . . ."

Three Years Later

WHEN JOSH INITIALLY TOOK SOPHIE TO SEE THE LOFT, SHE'D BEEN thrilled to find that it was just one building over from The Smile. The proximity to one of her favorite brunch places loomed large over the rest of the tour, casting some of the more questionable elements—the long and narrow footprint, the grubbiness of the building's stairwells and elevator, the gut renovation that would be required—in a more positive light.

Sophie agreed that it had "a lot of character."

With The Brod on the verge of a splashy opening, pulling the trigger on this auspiciously located property felt like the right way to say, "I love you, please relocate to New York and move in with me."

Josh pictured waking up on Sunday mornings with Sophie. They'd complete *The New York Times* crossword together. He'd do most of it (in pen) with his neat block lettering, and she'd pull the occasional stubborn pun from thin air. Afterward, Josh would go down on her and—scratch that, she would insist on showering first and *then* he'd go down on her—and Sophie would return the favor but not in a sixty-nine configuration because it's "distracting." After that, he'd turn on NPR and make breakfast—baked eggs or avocado toast or lemon ricotta pancakes. Whatever she wanted.

He put in his best offer, using most of his inheritance, and they went downstairs to share what would be their first and only meal at The Smile.

SIX MONTHS LATER, THE SUNDAY CROSSWORD PUZZLE IS BLANK AND buried under a mound of folded newsprint. No sex in any configuration. No lemon ricotta pancakes or renovated kitchen. No Sophie. And yet, there's fucking Sunday brunch hipster bullshit right outside his front window, like a targeted assault. Even five stories up he can hear them: otherwise sane people spending hours of their weekend huddled in the cold, waiting for their names to be shouted by a hostess. All for the privilege of waiting forty minutes for a hungover line cook to spoon under-seasoned hollandaise over a couple of badly poached eggs.

If there's one thing Josh can't stand, it's an improperly poached egg.

If he's allowed a second thing, it would be women who take new jobs in Dubai when their boyfriends are in the middle of career implosions.

The wail of the buzzer reverberates around the cavernous brick walls, shaking him out of his half-hearted Sophie reminiscence.

Finally. His fucking Ess-a-Bagel order. He punches the DOOR button on the intercom and listens for the groan of the elevator, hauling the delivery guy up to the fifth floor.

When it lurches to a stop, Briar steps through the doors and hands him the Ess-a-Bagel bag without looking up from her giant phone. *Great.* Now he's being ambushed in his fortress of solitude.

"New job?" he asks as she brushes past him. "The digital marketing agency didn't work out for you?" He eyes her blue faux-fur coat. "Interesting uniform."

"I stalked the building and intercepted the delivery guy. He got an excellent tip and didn't even have to risk his life in your death-trap elevator."

Josh hears a familiar click of heels against the wood floors he has yet to refinish. "Bring everything right through here!" his mother, Abby, calls out, as three men in moving company T-shirts wheel an assortment of restaurant equipment off the elevator and into what is supposed to be Josh's living room. "Why aren't you answering our texts?" Abby asks, before taking a last sip from a La Colombe coffee cup. His mother looks around the loft in a way that a stranger would find innocuous, but Josh recognizes the undercurrent of well-meaning judgment. "There's another offer for Brodsky's. The accountant wants to meet again. You need to be involved, Joshua."

"What is all this?" he asks, as two of the movers haul the once-iconic (and constantly malfunctioning) neon Brodsky's sign into the apartment. Josh is convinced his career troubles began the moment he removed it from the façade.

"We cleaned out the cellar." Abby removes a measuring tape from her Goyard tote and extends it across the width of what was intended to be Sophie's office. "The building will show better without the clutter your father accumulated down there for forty years." In addition to storing Brodsky's deliveries, the cellar had become a glorified closet for all the junk Danny knew better than to bring back to the family's overstuffed Upper West Side apartment.

"Absolutely not," Josh protests.

Abby places a hand on her hip. "I'm not paying Manhattan Mini Storage a dime while three hundred square feet of space is sitting here unused. I thought you were renovating."

"I've been busy." For most of the summer, he'd successfully dodged his mother's texts by claiming to be in the Hamptons.

Briar looks up from her phone. "With what?"

It's a fair question. Since the failure of The Brod, Josh has been whittling down what was left of his savings. Ordering food, avoiding social obligations. Definitely not working.

He walks over to the kitchen counter—a very *un*renovated hideous orange Formica—and removes the contents of the Ess-a-Bagel bag, sulking.

The maddening part is the *idea* was sound. And at the beginning, everything had gone according to plan.

The Brod had been at the top of the city's "most anticipated" lists. Reservations for the early weeks were impossible to find. But critics, food bloggers, and the diners themselves expected The Brod to be a whimsical, modern upgrade to the original Brodsky's. What they didn't want was braised sunflower with sunchoke fumet for $37.

East Village locals wrote angry screeds on neighborhood blogs. The Yelp reviews called The Brod a betrayal and insisted that Danny Kestenberg must be rolling in his grave. When a review in *The New York Times* went viral ("The Brod is a culinary Oedipus complex"), reservations dried up. Josh had to lay off the staff just a few months after opening.

Briar pops up on his right side, her ridiculous coat giving her the look of a stubborn Muppet, brushing her bangs out of her eyes. "What if we didn't sell? We could reopen as a deli again—"

"No." The iconic neon sign, now sitting on his Restoration Hardware runner, is a nagging reminder of his giant fucking failure. He has zero desire to return to the kitchen where his dad would plant himself in front of the prep table to make the exact same bland egg salad every Wednesday afternoon.

At night, when he's trying and failing to fall asleep in his drafty bedroom, Josh hears Danny's voice, echoing around his brain, louder than ever. *Why do you gotta make everything so damn convoluted? My food wasn't good enough for you?*

This time, he can't shout back. Can't apologize. He'll just have to live the rest of his life with the knowledge that Danny was right.

Briar removes her coat and takes a seat at the dining table where Josh has never hosted a dinner party. Sophie picked it out.

"You can't just sit up here in a creepy apartment, licking your wounds for another six months," she says. "It's a high-risk industry. You misfired. Now you have to deal with it."

Bold words from a twenty-four-year-old who'd never so much as lifted a dishrag at the deli.

Josh unwraps his bagel, inspecting it and placing it on a small white plate. Untoasted sesame seed bagel loaded with cream cheese and a sliced tomato.

"Every fucking time. I said a thin—*thin*—schmear of *plain*. This is fucking scallion." He slides the plate to Briar. "Did you eat? You can have this one." He retrieves a second sesame seed bagel and a separate container of cream cheese from the bag. He always orders a backup because they load up the bagels like they're troweling concrete. "Salt the tomato first. They forgot the capers."

"For the record, I *warned* you not to respond to that review." His sister swipes a finger through the mountain of cream cheese and tastes it before reaching for the saltshaker. "I'm a marketing professional and you never listen to me. This isn't toasted?"

"You're an influencer—"

"Content creator *and* consultant."

"—and it wasn't a review." Josh saws into the backup bagel with a steak knife. He can't remember the last time he opened his knife roll. "It was a hit piece. And we don't toast bagels in this household. It's blasphemy."

"God," his mother says, from where she's directing the movers around the front of the loft, "sometimes you sound exactly like Danny." Josh nearly saws into his hand.

Briar continues on her new favorite topic. "Okay, so maybe the whole thing garnered a little more scrutiny than the typical negative review. But attention of any kind is good."

"I got an email from Guy *fucking* Fieri, telling me to 'keep my head up.'"

Briar pulls a bottle of green juice from her bag, along with a metal straw. "Okay, but the upside of a massive failure—"

"I thought 'it's a high-risk industry.'"

"—is that you have the opportunity for a redemption arc." She leans forward. "Give people a reason to root for you. This is your *Reputation* phase: messy as fuck, but more interesting than just being successful."

She takes an enormous bite of the bagel sandwich.

"No, I'd rather be successful." He tosses her a much-needed napkin. "And after we sell the building, I can get my life back."

He could move to Big Sur or Miami or Lisbon and start over without all the baggage.

When the timer on his pour-over beeps, Josh pours the

contents of the Chemex into his mug, letting his brain drift back to a time when he had everything to look forward to.

"Have you heard from Sophie?" his mother asks.

Right. The second reason for this ambush: a Sophie pile-on.

"She seems fine," he says, voice clipped.

Abby frowns. "Will she still come to the event at the Historical Society? They're honoring your father. I can't have an empty chair at our table."

"She unfollowed him last month," Briar says as if announcing time of death on a patient in the hospital. She grabs her phone and turns *EX?* into *EX* ☺ next to Sophie's contact information.

Josh spreads the correct amount of plain cream cheese over the top half of the bagel and tries to anchor.

"It wasn't about me," he says, leaning back in the chair, trying to look at ease. "She got a promotion."

Briar tilts her head. "It *is* a bit sus that she accepted a job halfway across the world a couple weeks after agreeing to move in with you, though."

"It wasn't 'sus.' It was a career opportunity."

His sister squints at him, as if trying to glean any sign of anguish behind his eyes.

He gives her nothing. He's fine. He's left the apartment *several* times in the last two weeks. Devastated people don't go to the gym and run the interval sequence on the treadmill for an hour at a seven-percent incline—a new personal best. They don't even get out of bed.

"God, Sophie's grid was a dream," Briar whispers as she swipes through his ex's carefully curated and filtered photographs, which stopped including Josh sometime last year. *Anchor.*

"Good," Abby says, continuing to take measurements. "Then you're ready to move on."

Before Josh can protest, Briar jumps in. "Here." She holds out her phone, open to a dating app he's never seen before. "I set up a profile for you last month. I've been chatting with this one for a few days."

There's a photo of "Maddie, 31," with long, dark brown hair, preternaturally white teeth, and a slight case of duck lips.

"This woman has been chatting with *you*?"

"Technically it's catfishing, but I think the two of you have totally amazing chemistry. Look, I think she took this pic *at* The Brod."

"She's an Elite Yelper," his mother adds, looking over Briar's shoulder.

"Great." Josh turns away from the screen. "I won't have to explain why I'm unemployed."

Briar ignores the bait. "I've tried to . . . reframe your aloof asshole quality."

"'Asshole quality'?"

"Women don't want to date a man who looks like he's in mourning." Briar glances at his black sweater and black pants— *which have a button closure, NOT sad sweatpants, thank you very much.* "Which you do. Just, like, normally."

It's bullshit. Everyone in New York looks like they're on their way to a funeral at this time of year.

"On the other hand," she continues, "you're basically the Darkling of the New York restaurant world. We can use that! And you two are definitely at the IRL meeting stage. We can set something up right now. I'm thinking bubble tea and Citi Bikes—"

"Absolutely not."

listening, half-wondering about the emotional intensity of her wife's "other relationships."

To be fair, Cass always hated hierarchy.

"Love is abundant," Cass reassured her. "It's overflowing."

But a month later, she had apparently run out of love for Ari.

She'd never *left* before. Not like this.

The past few weeks have been like living underwater—everything's blurry and distorted. Ari doesn't even remember putting on her least-flattering pair of jeans and an old hoodie this morning. She has no memory of getting on the train or meeting Rad at her restaurant's loading dock after the brunch shift.

Ari had intended to finish one of her freelance writing projects last night. Instead, she woke up at five A.M. on a mostly deflated air mattress, with a string of drool on the pillowcase, disoriented by the blank walls, just one nonsensical incomplete sentence in her open Google doc.

She's been picking at it all day, tapping out mediocre punch lines on her phone and deleting them.

The writing was Gabe's idea—one of his many side hustles. It's a platform for "creative entrepreneurs" called NeverTired where strangers pay professional comedians to craft wedding toasts, bat mitzvah speeches, even sermons.

Jokes written for her own stand-up material: none. Work-in-progress scripts opened: zero. One-off writing gigs that take way too much time and pay just enough to create the illusion that it's worth the effort? Seventeen in the past two weeks.

Plus, she doesn't have to leave the apartment.

It's the little things that are getting tougher to brush aside.

The stuff you barely notice while you're in the relationship suddenly require phone calls and paperwork to undo. Which utility bills are in Cass's name? Are they going to stay on the same Verizon family plan? Will they continue to share Cass's mother's Comcast log-in?

Instead of one giant knot, it's a tangled mess of yarn.

"Are you *still* texting Cass?" Radhya asks, holding up a harness across her hips. "I told you to block her." She puts down the harness and tilts her head. "Please tell me you did *not* send her another nude—"

"I'm trying to finish this maid-of-honor speech," Ari snaps, which is completely true and not technically a denial about sending Cass a very flattering image captured in the bathroom mirror last night.

Rad winces. "I don't know how you stomach writing about everlasting love when you're in the middle of a divorce."

Ari examines something that looks like a crescent wrench with a tongue at the end. "Why are they all purple? When did purple become the official color of sex toys?"

"So *are* you still texting Cass," Radhya asks, "or is it just the lawyers communicating now?"

"Can we not discuss that in front of the tongue?"

"You need to do a clean break. Cleave her." Radhya flattens her hand and makes a violent chopping gesture. "Throw your energy into something positive instead of hanging around an empty apartment feeling sorry for yourself." That's Radhya-speak for *let's move on to the next item on the breakup to-do list*. Radhya is the sort of person who would be able to sort out the internet-service-provider situation during a brusque two-minute phone call to customer service. And it's hard to argue with someone who's been in this exact position.

Ari doesn't like this stage, either. But wallowing feels heavy and comfortable. Like a gravity blanket.

Radhya shakes her head and makes the chopping motion again. "*Cleave.* Remember all those long weekends you had to spend with her awful friends?"

Without actually leaving evidence of their distaste, Cass's friends made Ari feel as though she radiated don't-quite-belong vibes. No-talent vibes. Just-a-phase vibes.

To be fair, the enmity goes both ways. Radhya wasn't exactly a fan of the way Cass had tracked Ari down while she was on one of her cruise-ship comedy gigs and publicly proposed to her next to the wave pool. Or the way Cass encouraged Ari to quit that actually-pretty-good job and "pursue more prestigious opportunities."

Radhya reaches in her bag for her phone. "Dammit. My grill guy called out. I need to get back to the restaurant." She's a sous chef at a "new American" place in the West Village while trying to turn the occasional catering gig into a series of pop-ups, with the help of Ari's connections in the cater-waiter world. "Crash on my couch? You don't have to be alone. We could make some headway with the pop-up concept. Test recipes, pick out the decorations, watch several seasons of *Below Deck Mediterranean*—"

Ari shakes her head. "I'm fine. I have the air mattress. And I'm gonna talk to the beer garden manager this week."

Rad puts her hands on Ari's shoulders. "I want you to know that I'm completely fine with you sleeping with him again in exchange for letting us use the location."

"I appreciate that support."

"Since you have the apartment to yourself, you should pick something loud." Radhya hands her an S-shaped coil of maroon silicone. "What about this?"

"That's a couple's toy," Ari says quietly, trying not to ascribe any poignancy to the moment. "We had one like it. I'm pretty sure Cass took that, too."

AFTER ABBY AND THE MOVERS LEAVE JOSH WITH AN APARTMENT FULL OF musty old crap, he agrees to walk Briar back to her Tribeca apartment just to avoid looking at the stuff for another hour. Josh shoulders past the hordes of SoHo tourists, listening to Briar's boring anecdotes about dating "a certain actor from the Marvel Cinematic Universe." Josh has nothing better to do on a Sunday afternoon, anyway. No dinner service to prep for. No one to expect him to be anywhere or do anything.

"If Maddie's too basic," Briar says, "I've been messaging with this girl Norah, who's—"

"I told you to stop with that."

"—almost finished with her orthodontics residency."

Josh rubs his temples as he bumps into someone taking a selfie on one of the city's remaining cobblestone streets.

"She lives in Jersey City—"

"No."

"It's just across the river. . . ."

"It's another *state*."

Briar comes to a sudden halt in front of a nondescript storefront with a brick-and-stainless-steel façade and one small, inconveniently placed window.

"Oh! I've been wanting to check this place out! Can we go in for a minute?"

The store has the pseudo-medical look of the high-end skincare retailers Sophie liked visiting on their trip to Seoul.

There's nothing on display. No claims of rejuvenation. Just one small, subtle sign engraved with *CreamPot*.

"I'll wait for you out here," he says. A year ago, Josh might have invested in a hydrating serum, but what fucking difference does the size of his pores make now?

"You have to come in. I want a photo of me in there for my feed. Potential spon-con! Plus, they only let cis men in here if they're accompanied by a woman or nonbinary person," she adds. "It's your lucky day."

On the other side of the heavy glass door, the space is stark white—like an Apple Store without all the greasy fingerprints. A concrete plinth displays a small sculpture in bold fuchsia that almost looks like a toy Sophie kept in her nightstand.

He stops walking. "I thought this was a skincare boutique."

"Chloë Sevigny swears by this place." Briar starts snapping photos of the layout from various high angles.

Josh shoves his hands in his pockets. It's best not to pick anything up and risk dropping it or touching some invisible ON button. "I'm not standing in here with you like we're shopping together."

Briar's attention abruptly shifts.

He follows her sight line to a woman in a plaid peacoat standing under a display labeled *Realistic Dildos* in a tasteful typeface.

Images flash through his mind, like someone flipping through a stack of half-developed Polaroids. Huge chunks of the past eight years are completely wiped from his brain, but every tiny interaction he's had with this woman is burned into his memory. He's never been able to overwrite them.

Ari is holding something phallic, turning it over in her

hands, while casting the occasional glance in Josh's direction. Her hair is longer than last time, brown again, falling softly around her shoulders under a slouchy winter hat. She's coziness personified, despite the sterile surroundings.

"Do you know her?" Briar whispers, elbowing him in the chest.

"She *married* your professor."

"*Wow*. Is that her?" she exclaims with dawning recognition. "Oh my God. She's coming over." Briar ducks behind a row of stark white shelves.

"Where are you going?" He finds himself instinctively looking for a hiding spot of his own, when—

"Josh?"

He turns around. Ari is two feet away. "Uh—"

She points at her chest with a coral-colored glass tentacle dildo. "Ari."

"No, I know." Josh watches Briar silently flee the store. "I was just—"

"Shopping for vibrators?" she asks, eyebrows raised.

"—leaving. What are you doing here?"

She shrugs and holds up the dildo again. "You just missed Radhya, actually."

That's a relief. It's within the realm of possibility that Radhya would try to knock him unconscious with something phallic.

"How are you?" he asks, after a few beats of awkward silence and weight-shifting.

"Great," Ari says quickly. "Yeah, really good." She nods and looks over his shoulder. "Fine."

"How's . . . your wife?"

A strange expression passes over her face. She shifts the tentacle from one hand to the other. "She's spending the semester upstate as a visiting scholar. She's . . . fine." Her mouth turns into a tight line before curving into an approximation of a smile. "According to Instagram, she's fine."

Josh is genuinely stunned for a moment. Not because of the apparent breakup—that doesn't surprise him at all. It's the uncharacteristic shakiness of her voice.

"I'm sorry," he says, actually meaning it. "What happened?"

"Two weeks ago, Cass showed up at the apartment with a 'totally brilliant young adjunct professor' she met at Bard. Katya. At first I didn't think anything of it, because we've been practicing relationship anarchy."

"'Relationship anarchy'?"

"Yeah, we unchained ourselves from society's expectations of a long-term relationship." Ari's nodding as she says it but she swallows hard enough that Josh can see her throat bob. "Then I saw the movers covering the furniture in bubble wrap and I realized that she didn't bring the woman with a PhD and huge breasts back to our place for a threesome."

Oh fuck. She's on the verge of tears because of his awkward attempts at polite conversation and how the hell do you navigate around divorce talk?

"I—"

"I guess she's doing the relationship anarchy thing with Katya now." Ari rocks back and forth on her boots with jittery energy. "I mean, this woman is twenty-six and raises goats on a hobby farm and Cass always liked blondes"—she spits the words out quickly—"so why wouldn't she reinvent herself yet again with an even younger woman?"

"That's—"

"Ironic? No. Maybe it's Alanis-ironic. The goats are cute.

Cass posts a lot of photos on Instagram." Ari takes a huge breath in, shrugging her shoulders tight against the side of her head. He just barely stops himself from reaching out to touch her shoulder. Is that a thing that people do to comfort each other? Too intrusive? Too intimate? "Anyway. That's my sob story. How are you?"

Josh blinks, still trying to process the last two minutes. It's been so long since he's had a conversation with someone who's not trying to set him up with a catfishing victim.

"Fine," he lies.

"Really?" Her eyes move back and forth across his face. It's the kind of close scrutiny he's been avoiding for months.

"Do I not seem fine?"

"You've literally never seemed 'fine.'" She lets out a little burst of laughter. Her right hand—the one that's not holding the tentacle dildo—jerks up, as if she's about to touch him on the arm. Josh braces himself in anticipation but she moves it at the last second, grabbing something that looks like a giant purple tongue. "Do *you* want to talk about it? We could finally share that bottle of white zinfandel?" It's something between a question and a suggestion punctuated with an ellipsis.

"No." He pauses for a half-second—just long enough for Ari's expression to shift into disappointment, ensuring that the invitation was genuine. "How about an actual drink instead?"

"THE *TIMES* RAN A HIT PIECE INSTEAD OF A REVIEW. SUDDENLY IT WAS open season on me just because my dad owned a deli."

Ari sits next to Josh at a bar in a boutique hotel around the corner from CreamPot, with a tumbler of Jim Beam and a glass of malbec, respectively. Josh looks less polished these days: There's a slump in his shoulders, like he doesn't want to take up so much space in the world. A patchy beard covers the lower half of his face, muting the way his feelings are written on the surface.

"The phrase 'just because my dad owned . . . ' doesn't exactly make you *more* sympathetic," Ari observes. The place is quiet in the lull between late brunch and early dinner. It's a relief to sit elbow to elbow, rather than across a table, where Josh would be able to see her every microexpression.

"That fucking piece made me radioactive. I was trying to breathe new life into the business. Suddenly, all these people who probably hadn't eaten at Brodsky's in years were accusing me of dishonoring my father's memory." He sets his glass down on the coaster with a bit too much force. "I'm not the heir to some great culinary legacy. My father believed that any dish with more seasoning than schmaltz, salt, and pepper had no place on the menu. I'm allowed to want more than that. I was supposed to create something important. I was supposed to have a Michelin star by now."

"Maybe to some people," Ari says, "a pastrami sandwich with just the right amount of mustard is more impactful than an award from a tire company." Josh stares at his wineglass, unconvinced. She clears her throat and grasps for a subject change. "Well, at least you have . . . Sarah?"

"Sophie."

"Right." She leans in. "Your 'good girl.'"

He rolls his eyes. "You don't remember her name, but you remember that?"

"Seared into my brain," she says, tapping her temple. "Did she end up being the missing half of your black-and-white cookie with the arms and legs and the weird little penis?"

The bartender looks up.

"That drawing was not a self-portrait." He swallows another gulp of malbec and shakes his head. "Sophie had only seen me at my most successful. That's the part she signed up for. Not . . . this." He gestures vaguely at himself. "You know what bothers me? I spent my best years on that relationship. Two years ago, I appeared on *Chopped*. I had a spread in *Food & Wine*. I got invited to festivals and food events. I'd get messages from women. One of them always referred to me as 'the biggest boy' and kept asking me to step on her neck."

Ari nearly spits out eight dollars' worth of whiskey. It might be her first unforced laugh all week.

"And now when a woman googles me, the first thing they'll see is . . ." He trails off, like he's unsure of the right terminology.

"A dumpster fire?" Ari suggests.

"A feature on Eater where I'm portrayed as a petulant child, ruining his father's legacy by adding orange zest to a blintz recipe." He exhales and his whole torso seems to crumple.

"Okay, but she'll be dating a man who can make blintzes. And you can still cook," Ari points out, because for some reason, other people's problems always seem obviously fixable. She hasn't had a reason to absorb someone else's pain since Cass left. It doesn't feel *good,* but it's an odd sort of relief from wallowing in her own misery.

Josh stares into the dregs of his wine, his shoulders rising and falling with heavy breaths. "I have no interest in stepping foot in another kitchen, not that anyone wants to hire me." His voice is softer than she's ever heard it. Resigned. Like the furious, know-it-all energy that used to surround him burned away and left a shell of a person. "Every morning I wake up and remember I have no plans and nothing to look forward to."

"Well, that's not true." Ari swallows, searching her brain for a way to cut the grim direction of the conversation, even though she had the exact same realization when she lay awake at four A.M. on the inflatable mattress. "You just spent eighty-six dollars at CreamPot."

"I did *not* need to buy a hands-free lube dispenser," he points out.

"It's convenient *and* hygienic." She laughs, the last sip of whiskey still burning a streak down her throat. "You'll thank me the next time you bring a girl back to your place and you're not fumbling around in your nightstand."

He finishes his wine. "Don't be nice to me. It makes me uncomfortable. And I don't deserve it."

The Jim Beam makes her want to reach over and squeeze his arm or something. But that much human contact would probably shatter him at this point.

"I think I prefer this version of you. You're morose as shit, but for once, you're not acting like an entitled prick."

The look on Josh's face is hard to parse, like he's both offended and pleased. When their eyes meet, it's as if he sees behind the tight smile she's been plastering on her face.

Ari slides down from her stool, grabbing her shopping bag—filled with high-end vibrators that she cannot afford—from the hook beneath the counter.

"And men rebound quickly," she says. "You'll be knee-deep in some soulmate-level romance in a month or two and you'll forget we ever had this conversation."

Ari glances out the window, watching pedestrians move down Greene Street, meeting friends outside restaurants or hurrying home to their loved ones.

There's no one waiting for her anywhere.

She nods at the street. "Do you . . . want to take a walk?"

"AT LEAST YOU DON'T HAVE TO GET DIVORCED," ARI SAYS.

Josh watches her wrap a crocheted rainbow scarf around her neck as they walk north, auto-piloting vaguely toward Washington Square Park.

"Sophie thought weddings were tacky." He pauses. "She used the word 'gauche.' I always pictured a city hall ceremony. Something simple."

A trio of tourists brush past him, their Zara shopping bags trailing behind them.

"We got married while I was working on a cruise ship. I wore a striped two-piece." Ari takes out her phone and scrolls through approximately ten thousand pictures—many of them distractingly . . . flesh-toned—before selecting a photo and holding it up for him.

He tries to focus on Ari's bright smile in the photograph and not the bikini. Her nose is a little scrunched up, like she's about to burst into a laugh next to Cass. There's nothing artificial or posed about it.

"You keep this picture on your phone?"

"I know, I know." She tosses her phone back into her tote bag, shaking her head. "Radhya tells me to delete all that stuff but sometimes I find it comforting? The tangible artifacts of happiness. Every time I get a text, it's like . . . . my heart leaps because I think it might be some huge apology." Ari buries her chin a little farther into the rainbow scarf. "I can't believe I just told you that humiliating tidbit."

I'd give anything for Sophie to text me, he thinks, unclenching his cold, stiff hands.

"You still have the apartment, though?"

"Yes, but I'm living the involuntary minimalist lifestyle," she continues. "Eating on the floor. Re-inflating my mattress every night."

"She took the furniture?"

"Well, I guess almost all of it was hers." A little wrinkle appears above the bridge of her nose. "When I moved to New York, I had one set of utensils and my water bottle. After a couple days, I bought myself a single bowl at Pearl River Mart.

It was white, with a blue border around the rim and a dragon at the bottom. I thought it was beautiful. It felt like a New York 'thing.'"

He nods. "It's a classic pattern."

"I never kept more stuff than I could haul around in a duffel bag but everything in the bag was *mine*. If nothing else, no matter what shitty apartment I had to live in, I always knew I had the equipment to make myself cereal." Her voice grows a little more agitated. "Cass used the bowl all the time and I thought that was kind of cute. She already had tons of kitchen stuff, but this was my symbolic contribution to the apartment. After the movers left, I went into the kitchen and threw open all the cabinet doors, looking for it."

"And it wasn't there?"

"I assumed she'd make sure they left that *one* thing." Her voice rises in pitch. He's afraid she's on the edge of tears again until she recomposes her face into something nonchalant. "At least she didn't take my bong." Ari laughs, but there's a razor-sharp edge to it, giving Josh the sense that the bowl represents the outer bound of some bigger hurt, pulsing under the surface.

They take one of the looping walkways around the park, leaves crunching beneath their boots, following the paths without either one of them leading the way. The orange-pink light of sunset filters through the Washington Square Arch onto the surface of the fountain water, creating an ideal backdrop for a handful of couples taking selfies.

Ari stares at a man and a woman, his arms slung around her shoulders, her right hand outstretched to hold her phone.

"How do you think those two will break up?" she asks.

"Break up?" Josh tilts his head at the couple. "They seem

happy enough." They're each wearing L.L.Bean fleece pullovers in muted earth tones.

Ari gives him an "oh, please" look. "It's easy to be happy at that stage. But in a couple months he'll start to suspect that she's cheating on him with her work husband. He'll notice her smiling at some after-hours text and check her phone when she's in the shower. He'll tell himself he's doing it to prove himself wrong. That she's totally innocent. And instead, he'll discover that his intuition was spot-on. She's been boning her co-worker for months."

"Is this a new hobby of yours?" Josh asks, searching for whatever invisible signs of future infidelity she's picking up on.

"More of a lifelong aptitude." Ari starts walking again, hugging her coat closed. "Weird how I didn't foresee the demise of my own relationship. I guess we always think we're the exception."

Something about her dejected expression triggers his empathy, revealing a sliver of common ground between them. Josh clears his throat. "When we first met, I was—"

"A total shithead?" Ari keeps her eyes straight ahead as they pass beneath a stretch of scaffolding.

He exhales, recalibrating. Apologies have never been his strong suit. "A bit arrogant."

"But you're a softboi now?" She gives him a gentle little jab in the ribs. It gives him a jolt in a way he's certain she didn't intend. There's a pause—an opening—but they let it pass.

"I honestly don't know if that's a positive or a negative." He makes a mental note to check the meaning of *softboi* on Urban Dictionary later.

"You also said you were completely certain that the best sexual experience of my life wouldn't be with a stranger."

Interesting that she memorized the exact wording of his pronouncement. Of course, this exchange burrowed deep in his hippocampus, too.

"So . . . was it? With a stranger . . . or . . . ?"

"I'd like to believe the best is yet to come." A smile spreads across her face. "Pun intended."

She stops in front of him once they reach the red light at the corner. They're standing close enough that she has to tilt her head up and . . . *Fuck,* he misses having another person focus all their attention on him. They look at each other for a beat too long. The WALK sign flashes. People with dog leashes and over-stuffed backpacks and knockoff Louis Vuitton handbags brush past them. Everyone has somewhere to be.

They don't.

They've been talking for almost three hours. To keep going might be pushing his luck.

Ari takes a big breath. "Well, I should—"

"My apartment's down the block," Josh blurts out to his own surprise. "Do you want to come up?"

She squints like she's trying to read the bottom line on an eye chart. "Come up?"

"We could watch a movie?" His voice is slightly breathless, like he's desperate to avoid being alone again.

"Really?" Ari raises an eyebrow.

"Why not?" The question comes out immediately, even though it's humiliating.

"I don't think I've ever actually sat on someone's couch, just the two of us, and watched a movie past the fourteen-minute mark without . . ."

A beat passes while Josh attempts to process that statement. It's been years since he's had to decode these kinds of semantic nuances. "No, I didn't mean—" He swallows and starts over. "I meant it in a strictly . . . platonic way."

She raises her eyebrows. "Netflix-and-chill, but actually watch the movie? Like, silently?"

"You're one of those people who talks through movies, aren't you?"

"Are you a watch-the-credits-through-to-the-very-end-out-of-respect-for-the-craft guy?" In his defense, something feels *wrong* about leaving a movie as soon as the credits roll. "The thing is," she continues, "I feel like . . . one fingertip and I'd probably disintegrate." Josh might, too, but probably for a different set of reasons. "I'm hoping the vibrators help," she adds, holding up her shopping bag.

She hugs her torso again, fighting off the chill, and he can't part ways at the corner like this. He's tempted to offer her his coat, but it's probably too intimate a gesture. At this moment, he employs the only useful piece of wisdom Danny Kestenberg ever imparted to his son: Anytime you're standing on a street corner with another person and at a loss for what to do next, there is *one* valid suggestion.

"Want to grab a slice?"

Ari's face brightens immediately at the prospect of pizza. "I'm actually kind of starving." Josh nods in a southerly direction down Lafayette and they start walking again. "I think that's the title of my memoir: *Hoping the Vibrators Help, But Actually Kind of Starving: The Arianna Sloane Story.*"

Josh chuckles.

Ari glances back at his building. "Hey," she says, her tone a bit softer, almost hesitant. "Just so you know, at any other time in my life—if I wasn't feeling like human garbage—I'd probably ask you to take me up to your place right now."

The left side of her mouth curves into a tiny smile, forming a dimple. He hadn't noticed before that she has the kind of hazel eyes that seem to change color depending on the time of day. Josh finds himself taking new mental snapshots to augment the ones that have stubbornly refused to fade.

"For the record," he says, "you wouldn't have to invite yourself up to my place. At any other time."

"God," she says, releasing a huge exhale. "I'm too sad to fuck someone. I didn't know that was possible."

"That's mine: *Too Sad to Fuck Someone: A Portrait of Josh Kestenberg as a Young Man.*"

It earns him a full-throated, head-tilted-back laugh. It feels a little thrilling. A minor victory. He's never been so confused by a woman in his life. They wait for a red light to change at the corner.

"We can be . . . friends in misery?" he asks.

"Okay," she replies. "Friends. But I should warn you: Historically, I haven't had the best track record keeping things—"

"Platonic?"

"Sex-free. I mean, it's way harder to make a new friend than to find someone to fuck around with. This is, like, a really great growth opportunity for me."

"I can't even remember the last time I made a friend."

"I'm also a really great wingwoman." Ari grabs his hand and pushes his index finger into her shoulder. "If you want someone to help drag you out of your hermit state."

"I'll keep that in mind," he says. "What about you? What do you need?"

"Furniture. Maybe an actual bed . . . in which we will not have sex." She takes a deep breath. "Now, do friends fight over the pizza place?"

6

MOPPING THE FLOOR OF THE GENDER-NEUTRAL BATHROOM AT THE
LaughRiot theater was not the comedy career Ari envisioned
for herself when she got off the plane at LaGuardia eight years
ago. At least, she didn't think she would *still* be cleaning the
theater bathroom after taking classes, performing, and teaching
here for her entire adult life.

But LaughRiot is a collective—a fancy way of saying that
everyone's a ticket-taker, a bartender, a custodian, and a master
of side hustles. Maybe there's no such thing as a comedy career
that doesn't include wiping a fine mist of pee molecules from
the tile floor of a public restroom.

At this point, Ari would rather clean toilets than get back
onstage and try to make people laugh.

From one of the two cramped stalls, Gabe belts out the last line
of "Giants in the Sky," his aggressive vibrato bouncing off the tile.

The stall door swings open. "God, I love the acoustics in
here."

"The climactic toilet flush at the end really sells it," Ari says, scouring soapy residue from the ancient porcelain sink.

He hums the melody again, grabbing Ari by the arms and whirling her around against her will. Gabe is perpetually over-caffeinated, a loud talker, and always has a questionably relevant story at the ready in both English and Spanish. His smile is insane—his actual *teeth* are large. He played Gaston in Tokyo Disneyland for the better part of 2012. Radhya still calls him that and he believes it to be a compliment.

Gabe leans close to the mirror, examining a tiny blemish on his forehead. "Did I ever tell you that I played Rapunzel's prince in a production of *Into the Woods* at that dinner theater outside Minneapolis?" He did, multiple times. "Fell in love with a waiter. Got cheated on by the waiter. Started doing stand-up to get some control over my feelings about the waiter." He looks at her through the reflection in the mirror. "Comedy about break-ups is relatable as fuck."

So, this isn't just janitorial work—it's a learning moment. "I didn't get cheated on," Ari says, returning her attention to the sink.

He turns from the mirror and Ari feels a monologue coming on. "We perform because we are desperate for praise and approval and we're deeply troubled people and I'm *challenging* you to take all of that grief and mine your pain for material that's both emotionally raw and hilarious."

"Challenge not accepted." He's right, though. When a personal disaster happens, you turn it into a bit. Use it as inspiration for a sketch or a relatable one-liner that you hope will go viral on Twitter. But Ari can't bring herself to do that.

"You haven't showed up to practice with our Harold team in weeks," he points out.

Okay, so maybe she'd missed some rehearsals with the improv group she's been a part of for six years. "There's no 'grief,'" she insists, scrubbing at the porcelain. "I'm fine. I'm just busy with my five jobs and NeverTired gigs."

"It throws off the chemistry when you're not there." A wrinkle appears above his brow. "We're splintering. Half the team is talking about relocating to Chicago to do corporate improv-training for Second City. That's how they make money, you know. Sellouts."

"You're being dramatic."

Unfortunately, when you say that to an actor, the insult doesn't land.

"Okay, then how about getting up at Therapy tonight? Seven minutes?"

This "Therapy" is *not* a garden-level office where a pleasant woman tilts her head while she asks you to "say more about that." Ari is certain she will never, *ever* want to say more about that. In Gabe's world, Therapy is the bar around the corner where he hosts a comedy show on Thursdays and flirts with aspiring Broadway performers Friday through Wednesday.

Performing has always been Ari's escape from her problems— she usually feels more at home onstage with her friends than anywhere else. But she had a few disastrous improv shows the week after Cass left. It felt like her neurons failed to fire. She froze up. Two nights later, she'd bombed—like, *bombed*—a stand-up set. More evidence of her personal failure. The last thing she needs is a stage. She'd rather be anonymous or ignored right now. Why give an audience of strangers the opportunity to validate all the toxic thoughts brewing in her mind? Better to throw herself into catering and freelancing and jobs where people don't punish her with stony silence because she's just a *little preoccupied with the way her wife left her with an empty apartment because she's decided she's "beholden only to herself."*

Ari exhales. She'd scoured off the top layer of white enamel on the sink.

She shoves a stack of fresh paper towels into the dispenser and slams it shut. "I've told you. I'm not capable of being funny right now. I'm busy writing customized eulogies for fifteen dollars each."

He narrows his eyes. "All this moping over a woman who used to tell people she conjured you out of Manic Panic, nipple piercings, and secondhand bong vapor?"

"That's basically a compliment." Ari aggressively sprays glass cleaner over the mirror, blotting out her own reflection. "And I'm not moping."

"There's a cute new bartender at Therapy." Gabe leans closer to the mirror and examines his chin, tapping beneath it as if to check for signs of sagging. "Amazing ass. Never wears a bra." He pauses. "Glasses."

Ari tries to muster some enthusiasm. She pictures leading a braless, near-sighted bartender into the alley behind the bar. Feeling a new pair of hands in her hair. The damp brick wall against her back. Dragging her mouth across a shoulder, a collarbone, a nipple covered by the thin fabric of a stretchy tank top. Clouds of breath in the cold two A.M. air. Being pushed to her knees. Quiet little whimpering noises barely audible above the muffled, thumping bass from inside. Just picturing that kind of encounter would normally send flickers of live-wire energy through her body.

But the swooping sensation in the pit of her stomach won't materialize.

"I can't tonight." After what is sure to be a few mind-numbing hours of pouring cheap merlot at an opening at the

Whitney, she has huge plans to go home and try not to look at her soon-to-be-ex-wife's Instagram. It features pictures of Cass and Katya cuddling on a hammock in the Catskills, captioned "New beginnings," followed by some quote from Brené Brown.

"You're isolating yourself." Gabe turns to face her. "You should get over her by getting under a bartender. Or two. At the same time."

"I'm not getting under anyone." She gives the mirror one last swipe with the rag, catching her disaffected facial expression in the reflection. "Plus, you know I like to be on top."

Thurs, Oct 13, 6:26 P.M.

ABBY: Financial advisor will be at the restaurant in 7 mins.

It's on 55th.

I have a booth in the back.

Bring your laptop.

7:10 P.M.

Are you coming?

7:28 P.M.

We ordered you the salmon.

You like ponzu, right?

8:00 P.M.

You need to be part of this decision, Joshua.

We have to present a united front.

Emailing you a recap of the offers.

If we move forward, I'm inclined to wait until after the Historical Society event.

Optics.

Josh braces himself against the chilly October wind whipping down Great Jones Street. He's started adding evening runs to his gym schedule. Spending a full quarter of his waking hours at the Crunch on Bowery is a perfectly acceptable way to pass the time. Better than meetings with the humorless bald man fielding offers for Brodsky's—property developers who want to turn the space into "athleisure concept labs" or "bitcoin bodegas."

Inside his building, the old elevator shudders to a halt, opening directly into his fifth-floor apartment.

The fluorescent lights take a full two seconds to buzz to life, revealing the chaos, courtesy of his mother. In what's supposed to be his living room, there's half of a booth that his dad never got around to reupholstering, an industrial mixer, assorted hotel pans and racks, his dad's old records and paperbacks, and questionably functional home gym equipment. A physical testament to Danny Kestenberg's stubborn refusal to let go of things. His home now functions as a twelve-hundred-square-foot junk drawer.

At some point, Josh will pry the hideous avocado tile off the bathroom floor, rip out the chipped kitchen cabinets, and finish demolishing every non-load-bearing wall. But he's not going to bother with the renovations he and Sophie had planned. Someone else can come in with their Miele appliances and Herman Miller chairs and create the most generic version of a Manhattan "dream home," complete with a wife and a French bulldog.

He's been telling himself that for the last six months. The only progress he's made is a smattering of half-hearted sledgehammer holes, created after an especially brutal bout of self-loathing. Instead of dropping an anchor, he'd swung it through drywall.

He does some light social media stalking: monitoring restaurant openings and closings on Eater, sifting through the social accounts of every chef he ever worked with. All the James Beard winners, the *Top Chef* contestants. This form of masochism is supposed to propel him into action, but it only brings the bitter feelings back up to the surface.

Peeling off his shirt, he walks back to the bathroom to start the multistep process of running the hot water in the ancient claw-foot tub. Everything in this apartment is half-broken. Josh misses the walk-in steam shower from his previous apartment. He misses Sophie in his walk-in steam shower. Or maybe he misses *the idea* of Sophie in his walk-in steam shower because they'd only had sex in there once. (She'd said it was awkward and possibly dangerous.)

Sometimes it boils over into a mix of hostility and anger: a longing for her to call while fantasizing about rejecting her offer of reconciliation. He wonders when he'll have another sexual experience aided by more than his own hand and his porn stash.

So, when his phone abruptly buzzes to life in that very hand, it's reasonable to conclude that he'd conjured a text from Sophie with the power of regret and self-pity. He gives himself a half-second to imagine her sheepish, apologetic message before glancing at the screen.

But it's not Sophie's name.

ARI CURLS UP ON HER AIR MATTRESS—AS MUCH AS ONE CAN CURL UP ON a large plastic balloon—her fingers hovering over the keyboard, on the verge of the last line for another maid-of-honor speech on NeverTired.

Ari's been describing the apartment as "empty," but that's

not exactly true. It's full of piles: piles of clothes, piles of books, piles of random shit she never bothered to put away that used to be on the nightstand. Which is also gone.

Several times, Ari has felt the automatic impulse to clean up the piles, in case Cass comes home late and stumbles over them in the dark.

But no one's coming home anymore.

No one's sending a wildly inaccurate ETA text with the kiss emoji.

No one's getting up in the middle of the night to make kimchi grilled cheese sandwiches when Ari has the munchies.

No one's purchasing the ingredients, either. There's just a steady diet of microwave popcorn, takeout, and bowls of cereal. Cooking had been Cass's thing. Ari had moved in and joined Cass's life, already in progress.

Maybe it's the emptiness of the room that emboldens her. Ari pulls her T-shirt over her head and snaps a couple selfies. *Very tasteful,* she decides after reviewing them. *Definitely not trying too hard.* She goes into the messages app to unblock Cass, sends the selfie, and blocks her again.

There. Some little gremlin inside her feels sated.

Ari likes to imagine that Cass tries to respond with words like *Yes, please* and *More.* Or maybe just the tongue emoji. But as long as Ari has her blocked, these responses live in a liminal zone. They are Schrödinger's text messages.

Ari opens Netflix—Cass still hasn't changed the password—and lets the cursor hover over the looping trailer for one of those Hallmark-esque holiday romances. The thought of watching this alone, while eating an entire sleeve of saltines and drinking wine from the bottle, feels unbearably sad, even though that's probably how this film is consumed most of the time.

These things are only fun if there's someone else to appreciate her snarky commentary.

> Thur, Oct 13, 10:03 P.M.
>
> ARI: u up?
>
> Wanna do shrooms and watch the 4th Christmas prince movie???
>
> 10:11 P.M.
>
> RADHYA: bitch I'm roasting swordfish for another hour 🍴
>
> any update on the beer garden?
>
> ARI: yes!
>
> your pop-up is ON for January 15 🎉
>
> (and I didn't even have to exchange sexual favors)
>
> we can go over there next week and talk beer pairings
>
> he said to go heavy on the salt
>
> RADHYA: thx Twattie 😚
>
> ARI: anytime, Cum Slut 😎

Ari falls back on her pillow, making the plastic mattress squeak and echo around the naked walls.

She sighs. The sound seems to bounce.

Her right thumb scrolls through her contact list and circles THE BIGGEST BOY twice before pressing down. Why the hell not?

> Thur, Oct 13, 10:13 P.M.
>
> ARI: Wanna hatewatch a mediocre movie with me?
>
> JOSH: I thought movies were off-limits due to your inability to keep your pants on the moment you see the Netflix logo.
>
> ARI: yes, for the sake of my virtue, we will not be in the same room
>
> We turn on a movie at the same time and watch it together while we text

Her device lights up with an incoming call.

"Dude," she says, "what is your obsession with talking on the phone? Who even makes actual calls anymore?"

"I'm not going to spend an entire movie texting on an even tinier screen. Or are you going to talk incessantly so that I can't hear the dialogue?"

"Oh, you won't want to hear the dialogue." Ari sits up on the air mattress. "Because we'll be watching *The Expendables*—"

"Absolutely not."

"It's the perfect choice for our overwhelming isolation and fear of dying alone. Even the title speaks to me." She lies back on her pillow and the air mattress squeaks in protest. "And I won't lose the plot while I fold my laundry."

"Do you even own a dresser for the clean clothes?" he asks.

"No, but I'll be able to find one for free at the end of the semester. NYU kids always put perfectly good stuff on the curb."

"You can't put your underwear in a piece of furniture that's been on the street and then put it on your body. I'll help you pick out a new dresser. We can go to CB2."

"On whose budget?" she counters. She'd promised Radhya a trip to Ikea this month. "What do you want to watch?"

She hears the quiet bleeping sound effect of Josh scrolling through the interface on his TV.

"*Tree of Life. Birdman. Blue Valentine. Requiem for a Dream*—"

"I'm gonna stop you right there. I spent three years living with a Gen X film critic. Let's watch something that won't make me want to slit my wrists."

It's not that Cass would express her disapproval outright. It was the barely raised eyebrow working in concert with the rest of her face to create a slight suggestion of disappointment. The noncommittal *hmmm* sound followed by footsteps and the swift shutting of her office door.

Josh sighs. "Fine. *The Princess Bride*. A safe crowd-pleaser. A film everyone likes but is nobody's favorite. The Foo Fighters of movies."

"I've never seen it."

"How is that possible?" he exclaims, his voice distorting over the connection. "It's basic cultural literacy."

"I'm a *youth*," she insists. "And I'm not in a state of mind where I can watch something with 'bride' in the title."

"There's enough self-awareness that it won't bother you. And I overheard two college students at the gym misquoting it and referring to it as 'that old movie' and I'm still upset about it."

"No," she says firmly. "No love stories. I don't care how ironically detached they are. I don't want to feel anything."

Ari looks up at the light fixture. It has a dark bronze finial that reminds her of a nipple. Or maybe she's just missing Cass.

"But you're okay with subjecting me to *The Expendables*?"

"If I watch it with someone else, it's social. Otherwise, I'm just a sad, lonely person, waiting to get divorced, sitting on a hand-me-down air mattress, watching an ensemble action thriller by myself."

"You're right," he says. "That's definitely not what's going on here."

"Oh, and if I go quiet for a few minutes it's because someone hired me to write a eulogy."

7

Sat, Oct 22, 1:32 P.M.

ARI: i can't find the mattresses

JOSH: Where are you?

ARI: I turned a corner at patio furniture and now i'm lost and also I want to buy this sofa table?

JOSH: I'm waiting near the bed frames.

ARI: i've heard THAT before
ok I'm in the middle of a sea of desks
Shout PENIS and I'll follow your voice

"Everything in here is slightly sticky," Josh says, shuddering.

"It's either the soft serve or the meatball gravy." Ari sits up from the showroom mattress she's been lounging on. "If I don't leave here with a box of unassembled particleboard, cartoon instructions, and a jar of lingonberry jam, we'll have failed the mission."

"I refuse to consume meatballs from a discount furniture chain." Josh examines the store map. "What about a nightstand?"

"I have a cardboard box next to the bed."

"Okay. Well, we came here for a dresser."

She crosses her arms. "I have a stack of clean clothes and a pile of dirty laundry. It works fine."

"Okay. Get up." Josh is standing over her with his hands on his hips like an annoyed-but-hot poli sci professor. "You can't treat your apartment like a campsite. Why did you let her take everything from you?" His voice has a trace of the self-righteous teen he must have been—a kid who grew up knowing he could claim everything he wanted.

She hauls herself to her feet. "It's not technically 'my' apartment. And what was I supposed to do? Throw my body across an eight-year-old West Elm side table?" There's a twitchy edge to Ari's voice that somehow makes her feel more defensive. "Do you know how pathetic I felt, watching the movers struggle to maneuver the bed through the front door? I hid in the bathroom, okay?"

She braces herself for the look of pity that people offer her when she brings up these embarrassing details about that day and loses control of her emotions.

Josh moves his jaw like he can't quite decide on the right response. They're stopped in front of a $329 six-door dresser. "Red, Red Wine" plays over the sound system.

"Did you ask me to help you shop because you wanted someone to smile and nod and keep their mouth shut while you refuse to help yourself?" he asks. "Because I'm not going to do that."

"No, obviously I wanted you to experience the meatballs." They stare at each other for a few beats while a couple holds up the paper measuring tape across the width of the dresser. Josh raises an eyebrow, expecting something more. Ari swallows. "You go to the gym a lot, so I know you can carry heavy boxes. And you're tall so you can reach things on high-up shelves in the warehouse area."

His expression remains stern. Concerned. Unwilling to accept her one-liners as actual answers. "Ari."

"What?"

He folds his arms across his chest. "Why did you ask me to come here with you?"

Grimacing at his persistence, she walks over to an untreated pine dresser and pretends to examine it. "I thought you could help me pick out some pans?"

"You're absolutely *not* using cookware from Ikea. You'd get the same result with a folded-up piece of aluminum foil. We'll go to Sur La Table. Try again."

She opens the top compartment and looks down. Inside the drawer is a crude drawing of a penis. It's a fun surprise. Like finding a quarter on the ground. "I guess . . . I like being with you more than I like being by myself." She takes a deep breath and glances up. Josh has this way of focusing on her face. There's a potency to it. "Why did you come?"

"The meatballs." A stranger would say his face appears blank, but Ari can tell he's pleased. "Obviously."

Fri, Oct 28, 5:27 P.M.

BRIAR: Have you looked at any of the proposals from developers?

JOSH: Mom sent you after me now?

I don't care about the proposals. It's prime real estate on Avenue A.

Sell it to the highest bidder.

Sell it for parts.

BRIAR: You need to come to my deep stretch yoga class.

There's a new instructor that's VERY pretty

JOSH: I already have a gym routine.

BRIAR: She has NYE date potential!

You can't show up at a gala by yourself when your family is

being honored!

That's just sad.

JOSH: Mom said you aren't even coming.

BRIAR: Excuse me, I've had a luxury yurt booked for over a year! I will

be glamping under the stars at Joshua Tree.

"I'M DEFINITELY COMING DOWN WITH SOMETHING." ARI IS STARTLINGLY loud as she blows through the swinging doors of the Duane Reade on Broadway and Fourth Street. "It's either a cold or diphtheria."

"You came down with several shots of tequila and rang my buzzer at two in the morning," Josh says, following her past the bored security guard, the cough suppressants, and an aisle of greeting cards. She hadn't wanted to come upstairs, though.

Actually, Ari has never been to his apartment, even though they've watched six and a half terrible movies over the phone, ordered four coffees, shared two pizzas at Arturo's, and this is their second—no *third*—joint shopping excursion.

Not that he's counting.

"Where did you say you found her underwear?" she asks, slurring slightly.

"In my laundry. It was just sitting there," he continues, steering her toward the cold drinks. "Mingling with my whites and light colors."

"You have clothes that aren't black?" She stops in front of the fridge and reaches for a six-pack of Coors Light. "Throw them out immediately. If you let your ex's stuff linger in your home, it will slowly poison you, like the One Ring."

Josh wordlessly takes the beer out of her hands, replacing it with a bottle of water. She barely seems to notice as she continues walking.

"Did I tell you that Cass took the time to go through every single one of the books and take the ones that belong to her? Except for one little pile. And I'm positive she left them on purpose." Ari pauses in front of another fridge and exchanges the water for a Red Bull. "*Get Out of Your Mind and Into Your Life*? *Daring Greatly*? It's all the shit the yoga teacher reads during shavasana when you just want to fall asleep. Clearly I have to get rid of them. Burn them or something."

"You can't burn books," he says. "We'll take them to the Strand and sell them."

Ari nods seriously. "Less violent but more profitable."

"Try to be sober for five seconds and focus." Josh grabs the Red Bull can as she attempts to open it. "Am I supposed to send the underwear back to her? I spent two hundred dollars on a tiny triangle of mesh and now it's mocking me."

"*You* bought them?" Ari abruptly turns down a different aisle. "Did I tell you that Cass has this *thing* about plain cotton briefs?" She raises her eyebrows like he's supposed to read something into that. "She never wanted me to wear anything else." She grabs a ten-pack of generic women's underwear off the rack, holding it out to him. "I have a drawer full of these from Costco!" She drops the package of briefs and Josh retrieves them from the floor. "Okay. Your turn. You need to tell me one really aggravating thing about Sophie."

He places the briefs back on the rack. "Why?"

"This woman left you high and dry at a time when you needed support and you *never* talk shit about her. Like . . . would she leave one square of toilet paper on the roll without replacing it? Did she quietly fart as soon as you left the room when she thought you wouldn't hear? Does she own NFTs? Does she have any weird rashes or unconscionable hot takes on Zack Snyder?"

Josh scans the Sophie Archives for an anecdote that's interesting but not painful. A fondness for rioja, the fact that her Kindle was never charged, her fondness for having sex while blindfolded with her sleep mask . . .

"Sophie has to be listening to this very specific podcast in order to . . ." Josh performs a noncommittal hand gesture. "You know . . ."

"Have an orgasm?" Ari shouts.

He shushes her, glancing around the store.

"What was it?" She leans in like she's going to whisper but speaks in the same loud drunk voice. "Like . . . an ASMR thing? Erotic short stories?"

"That's the worst part." He waits for another shopper to move past them. "It was *This Week in Tech*."

Ari nods slowly. "You know what you should do?" She grabs the lapel of his coat and he inhales the scent of Jose Cuervo and citrusy perfume. Her mouth curves into an evil grin. "You should get another woman to put the panties on and take a picture of *her* and send *that* photo to Sophie."

Josh stares at her, impressed and a little intimidated. "Fuck, I'm glad I'll never have to break up with you."

She drops her grip on his coat and continues down the aisle, already on to the next topic. "Why don't you have NyQuil in your apartment? How do you *live*?" Her voice sounds like truck tires over gravel.

"Klonopin." He picks up the dark blue NyQuil package. "You shouldn't be taking cold medication when you're drunk."

"Nonsense! That's the best time to—" Ari stops in her tracks, nearly tripping him. "Oh my God."

"What? What is it?"

She bounces over to a cardboard display at the end of the next aisle and grabs a box.

"Josh." She clutches the package to her chest. "Will you be my Dust Daddy?"

He flushes for a second before she flips the box around to show him the logo. It's some kind of phallic as-seen-on-TV vacuum-cleaner attachment and she's definitely about to make a scene.

"I'm begging you not to turn that into a nickname."

"It's for cleaning. Your favorite. Ooh, it gets into the tiniest cracks and crevices." She holds out the box at arm's length so they can both read it. "Flexible tubes with 'powerful suction.' How can a girl compete with that?" She bites her lip. "Should we get it? Is this my new boyfriend?" She drops the Dust Daddy back onto the display. "Oh! I have the best idea!"

Josh makes frenetic shushing motions, which only seem to amuse her. "Does it involve a giant bottle of Gatorade and some aspirin?"

"Pervertables."

"What?" He feels the flush creeping back, not that she'd notice subtle details like that right now. The entire store must look like an expressionist painting to her.

"You pick out items that are normal on their own but could be sexual in the right context. When you buy them together, it

looks like you're preparing for a low-budget kink scene. Like"—
she squeezes her eyes shut for a moment—"clothespins and a
jump rope."

"No."

"*Yes,*" she insists. "I challenge you to a pervertables duel.
Hamilton versus Burr."

"Is this some awful improv game you force your students to
do at the first class?"

"No! That would probably constitute sexual harassment."
Ari grabs a stick of deodorant off a display rack, opens the cap,
and inhales the aggressively strong fragrance. "Usually this is
something I do with people I'm trying to go home with."

It's exactly the kind of maddeningly ambiguous statement
that sends his brain in five directions at once.

On the other hand, she probably won't remember this conversation tomorrow.

Josh sighs. "We're not leaving until this happens, are we?" If
his coping mechanism is logging hours at Crunch, apparently
this is Ari's.

"Three things, Dust Daddy." She walks backward—
stumbling slightly—toward the tower of plastic shopping baskets
at the entrance. "One minute. Set your timer?"

"Okay," he agrees, converting one Drunk Ari minute into
five Regular Person ones. "If you also buy an enormous bottle
of water."

"I hope you have a plan." She hands him a basket. "I'm
really good at this."

"I always have a plan."

"Aaaaand . . . go!" she yells, tearing down the aisle toward
the kitchen supplies with no warning, no three-two-one countdown. "Let your dirty little imagination soar!"

Three minutes, twenty seconds, and two incoherent shouted verses of "My Shot" later, Ari sprints to the register, where Josh has been waiting patiently with his basket.

"I can't believe I did that before the timer went off!" He stifles a laugh as she reaches for her selections. "Okay, I got"— she gasps for air—"spatula"—she hits him on the chest with a satisfying *thwack*—"that's an impact implement. Toothbrush case, with ridges, obviously. And plastic wrap, extra clingy." She peeks into his basket, still out of breath. "Your turn."

"Hairbrush. Latex gloves. Baby oil."

Ari gets quiet, stares at him, looks down at the items in the basket again, and then back up.

"*Josh*. Josh, I feel God in this Duane Reade tonight. You *total*"—she's yelling now—"*Fucking. Perv.*" Without warning, she launches herself at him, wrapping him in a giant bear hug. Or a petite-medium bear hug, considering her size. A rush of warmth courses through his body. She hasn't ever touched him this much. It feels like months since anyone so much as shook his hand. He tentatively raises his arms to reciprocate—for once, the motion seeming automatic, rather than forced—when she suddenly breaks the hug and sets his basket on top of the counter at the register. He tries to mask his disappointment. And his hard-on.

"Congratulations, we are purchasing all of your items to commemorate this moment," she declares. "God, a *paddle-style* hairbrush?" She cackles. "You should add this skill to your dating profiles."

"No," he says firmly.

Her expression changes to something like panic. "Oh shit, we forgot the Dust Daddy!"

Josh avoids eye contact with the bored-looking cashier, who

sighs as he scans each item. When he gets to the baby oil and then the NyQuil, something seems to snap into place.

The cashier looks up. "Not throwing away your shot, huh?"

"ANOTHER ONE?" ARI ASKS, WHEN THE CREDITS START TO ROLL ON *Grown Ups 2,* the ninth terrible movie they've watched over the phone in the last two weeks. It's becoming a routine: *How to be pathetically alone, together.*

Josh turns off his TV, letting his eyes adjust to the dark. "I really thought we exhausted the Adam Sandler oeuvre last week."

"Nope. That man is a renewable resource. There is *always* another Adam Sandler film. But if you're tapping out, I'll just hang up and get some work done."

"What kind of work?" he asks, sitting up.

He double-checks that his alarm is set for five forty-five A.M., which should give him enough time to shower and do his complete morning grooming routine before the deep stretch yoga class Briar forced him into. Well, not so much "forced" as sent him unsolicited screenshots from the instructor's Instagram account, which demonstrate her passion for fitness, her flexibility, and her great taste in athleisurewear.

"You refuse to laugh at any of my Rob Schneider hot takes, but I bring up something boring and now you're interested? All right. Would you rather help me write a funny-yet-touching father-of-the-bride toast or an essay about why it's critical to provide free access to menstrual hygiene products?" She takes a breath. "That one is for a best man speech, obviously."

"What about your own material?" he asks, broaching the subject cautiously. He may have very casually stalked @ari.snacks69 and watched some of her old stand-up sets and improv videos.

There's a one-second pause, just long enough to throw off her rat-a-tat rhythm. "Excuse me, this *is* my material. I definitely do *not* regularly visit a blog post titled 'Ninety Hilarious Maid-of-Honor Speech Examples' and punch up the jokes."

Josh hesitates, cognizant of the nerve he might be touching. "I watched some of your clips."

She takes a breath in. "You did?" He's not sure how to continue the conversation. There's so little to go on without seeing her face.

"It was—" He racks his brain for the right adjective.

"Don't say 'interesting.'"

"—impressive."

"Really?" There's something so pleased in her inflection. He's forgotten that it feels good to pay compliments.

And he means it. Under normal circumstances, being in the audience of an improv show would hold the same appeal as watching a college a capella group perform an eighties medley. But the videos had provided a glimpse of an alternate version of Ari—someone with their defense shields up at sixty percent, rather than ninety.

"Really."

"I used to love it," she says. "I pretty much used to get off on the high. But last time I went onstage, my stomach was in knots and I was sweating and my heart was racing. It wasn't typical nerves. I mean, total paralysis. I left the stage, which is a cardinal sin in improv. You don't just walk away from a scene. You don't leave your team hanging."

Josh hesitates. His entire life feels like it's hanging. "But you want to get back to it at some point." It's half question–half suggestion.

"I'm not sure." She pauses. "When I got married, I didn't have to pass hors d'oeuvres or walk dogs. Cass supported me so I could submit my comedy writing packets and perform and go on auditions. I threw *everything* into it and I'm still exactly where I started. So what's the point? At least these NeverTired projects allow me to fail in private," she continues. "Imagine hiring someone who failed at marriage and grew up without a dad to write a toast for your daughter's wedding. He probably really hates the groom."

"In that case, maybe you could have him warn them not to go through with it."

"Rachel," Ari says in an imitation of an older man's voice. *"If you'll indulge this fifty-five-year-old, twice-divorced man for just a few minutes, I want to offer some advice. When you fall in love with someone, you're all optimism. You have no sense of the hardships you'll face in a few years. You're thinking 'This is it!' because Caleb makes you happy. But I need to tell you the truth—"*

"Happiness is bullshit," Josh offers, deepening his voice to match her impression.

"Jesus. This is going to be one entertaining reception. Poor Caleb."

"No one should marry the person who makes them happy," Josh continues. *"Marry the person you want by your side at your absolute lowest point."*

"Seriously, *Rachel,"* Ari interjects in the gruff old man voice. *"Imagine Caleb eating Cheez-Its for dinner, watching* Grown Ups 2, *while writing wedding toasts for total strangers during the off-hours when he's not a cater waiter.* Now *do you want to marry him?"* She laughs at herself and then grows quiet. "Kind of a self-own, I guess."

Josh clears his throat, feeling the urge to spin the sentiment into something optimistic. *"If you genuinely want to spend years watching Caleb fuck up while he grows into the person you know he can be, that's when you get married."*

Ari says nothing. The dead air gives Josh a brief sensation of panic. This is the problem with the immediacy of the phone: every nonresponse can be a subtle hint that the other person is about to hit the eject button on the conversation. Sophie would always say things like "well, I should let you go" or "wow, it's so late on the East Coast" at the first moment of silence.

"Shit," Ari says finally, "it's almost one. Time to put on a grisly true crime podcast that definitely won't give me nightmares." Her polite sign-offs are at least disguised as frothy remarks.

"Maybe you should expand your horizons and learn something aside from how to commit murder and get caught."

"What do you suggest?" she asks. "*This Week in Tech*?"

"Not if you want to fall asleep. Apparently." There's a luxurious fifteen seconds of quiet that Josh feels no pressure to fill. Just Ari breathing and the occasional sound of tires bumping along the cobblestone street five stories below.

"You know, every night," she says, "I lie here by myself and think, 'Tomorrow is the day I'll wake up and feel okay about this.' There has to be a tipping point, right? Do you ever feel like you're living a depressing ending, but you never get to the last page? There's no pithy final line? It just keeps going."

Fragments of thoughts and observations and painful experiences offer themselves up in his head but nothing comes out of his mouth. She probably needs comfort—not exactly part of his repertoire.

"God, I should hang up." She laughs in a way that sounds forced and then, "Sorry for the cringe . . . I'm just—yeah . . ."

If landlines were still a thing, there would be a dial tone, but there's no sense of finality when she ends the call before he can respond.

"WHO ARE YOU TEXTING?" GABE ASKS, CRANING HIS NECK TO GLANCE AT Ari's chiming phone as they reach the fourth-floor landing of Radhya's apartment.

"Get off." She swats at his chest as they walk down the hall.

Tues, Nov 22, 9:23 P.M.
JOSH: I actually slept last night.
Midnight to 6 A.M. according to my tracker.

Ari hesitates for a half-second before rapping on the door. "Are you decent?" she calls. "It's not a dealbreaker if you aren't."

Ari's had a key for five years, but the courtesy knock has been a habit since they'd shared the railroad apartment.

ARI: ooh nice of you to let me win at insomnia 🏆

Rad's door flies open with a loud groan. A tall man with floppy, sandy hair and a beakish nose ducks past Ari and Gabe with a tiny acknowledging nod. He's clutching his coat and a light blue button-down shirt that's unmistakably part of a server's uniform at Radhya's current restaurant.

Gabe's gaze follows him down the hallway. "Radhya's celebrating early."

NoFucksgiving is a sloppy gathering of wannabe entertainers and people with master's degrees who realized they could double their arts nonprofit salaries by waiting tables and bartending during "the most magical time of the year." For the next month and a half, they'll be working overtime while tourists descend on the city and office workers put on their finest cocktail attire for a slew of awkward annual holiday parties.

Ari hangs up her plaid peacoat. It's been weeks since she's trekked out to Brooklyn. Not because she doesn't want to see Radhya. But maybe there'd been a bit of an overdose of advice and tough love in the immediate aftermath of Cass moving out. In the past month, Ari hadn't quite figured out how to integrate her best friend back into her life once the shock had worn off. And Rad can't stop asking questions like, "Did you call my divorce lawyer?"

JOSH: Have your recent . . . purchases helped at all?

Ah yes, her radical acts of self-care are currently plugged into her spiderweb-like network of charging cables—each one unique, for some reason—on the floor where her nightstand used to be.

ARI: I've been trying a new thing where I use them in the morning. supposedly it improves your math skills.

JOSH: At least you have a reason to wake up.

"Who was that?" Ari calls out.

"Back waiter," Radhya answers from the bedroom. "Cute, right? Hey, can you call my phone? I can't find it."

Ari taps on her contact name. A robotic British accent declares *"Calling Rah-dee-yah Am-bah-nee Woman Cook Medium Skin Tone"* through Radhya's Bluetooth speakers.

She nudges Gabe. "Do you know how to stop my phone from announcing every single call like there's a tiny aristocratic butler in there? I changed the settings *one* time to play DJ during a party and now it automatically connects every time I'm in this apartment. What if some accidental porn popped up on my phone?"

"Since when is porn 'accidental' to you?"

Radhya walks out of the bedroom, heeled boots under her arm. "I don't want to know the context of this conversation." She lifts the couch cushions, searching for the device. A muffled buzz sounds from the floor beside her armchair. Radhya lifts up a pair of jeans, the back pocket glowing. "A*ha*!"

Radhya ends the call and gives Ari a hug. "I'm glad we're doing this. I haven't seen you in forever."

Ari straightens a cushion and plops down on the couch, making the springs creak. "I had to clear my busy schedule of quietly moping."

> ARI: you were in a long-distance thing.
>
> You slept alone for most of your relationship

"So, that's where you've been." Rad glances at Ari's phone suspiciously. It does feel slightly illicit to sit in Radhya's apartment, texting with Josh. "Are we still on for Ikea next weekend?"

"Oh." *Shit.* "I already went," Ari says carefully. Slightly guiltily.

Radhya frowns. "You went by yourself?"

"Now I can enjoy a tiny bit of lumbar support with my despair," Ari says, sidestepping the actual question. "I'm the proud owner of a shoddily constructed, hastily assembled, untreated-pine bed frame."

"I need a new duvet cover." Radhya lets her boots drop onto the rug with a thud. "Why didn't you tell me you were going?"

"Now you don't have to help me complete a construction project with those tiny hex wrenches." Ari hasn't been hiding her shopping partner, it just . . . hasn't come up organically.

A loud *ding* sounds through the Bluetooth speaker. Ari plops down onto the now-orderly couch and glances at the message.

> 9:26 P.M.
> JOSH: Yes, but she was there in theory.

Radhya's expression shifts from confusion to detective mode. Avoidance doesn't slip past her. Distraction it is.

"You look amazingly hot in that dress," Ari says, nudging the conversation in a new direction. Radhya's wearing one of those loose-but-sexy sweater dresses that always look like shapeless tents when Ari tries them on. She glances down at her own jeans and old T-shirt. "And I look like the babysitter you hired to watch your fashionable toddler."

"Wanna borrow something?" Radhya asks as she puts on chunky gold earrings.

"Anything Ari borrows is guaranteed to come back with a whiskey sour stain on it," Gabe warns.

> ARI: having a bed to yourself is the best

> I would think you of all ppl would appreciate never having to find a loose hair in your sheets
>
> JOSH: Or crumbs.

Ari lets out an inadvertent cackle. Gabe and Radhya glance at each other.

"Okay, out with it," Rad says. "Why are you smiling at your phone? Who's the rebound?"

Ari forces her face to slacken into something neutral. "It's not a rebound. Jesus."

"The bartender?" Gabe asks.

Radhya continues to press. "Was Ikea a date?"

"No!" Ari insists with more vehemence than the question demands. "I have *friends*."

Rad takes the seat next to her. "No one makes new friends after a breakup. It's hard enough to be likable when you're actually happy."

"This is a person I can be miserable with."

"So, there *is* a person," Gabe says.

Ari stands up. "Why are you interrogating me?"

"The goofy smile? Hiding your phone." Radhya steps into one of her torturous-looking boots with a grimace.

"Well, let me reapply my resting bitch face," Ari says, waving her hand in front of her nose.

Ding!

> JOSH: Can I call you?
>
> I need your take on this interaction I had with this yoga instructor.
>
> I'm not sure I can accurately capture the tone over text.

Radhya zips up her other boot. "If you're texting Cass again, I'm staging an interven—"

The aristocratic butler cuts in: "*Incoming call from*"—Ari curses as she fumbles to silence the phone—"*Josh Kes-ten-butt poodle emoji.*"

At first, nothing happens. Radhya and Ari simply stare at each other.

Maybe the name was indecipherable with the British accent. Maybe she hadn't heard it. Maybe—

"Is this a joke?" It's like Radhya's face hasn't yet figured out how to accurately express this particular form of betrayal. "An ironic code name you use for someone who's *not* a toxic asshole?"

"Wait." Gabe appears to be solving a math problem in midair. "'Poodle' who?"

"Don't freak out," Ari says, voice laced with panic. "I ran into him a few weeks ago—"

"Weeks?" Radhya turns to Gabe, as if to verify.

"—we commiserated over our depressing lives and—I don't know . . . we just hang out sometimes."

"You 'hang out sometimes'?" Radhya stands up from the couch, wobbling a little in her boots. "With fucking *Kestenberg*??" She looks at Gabe again. "*That's* who she's talking to?"

His eyes ping-pong between them. "Wait, who?"

"He's moving on from his asshole phase," Ari says. "I think that if—"

"It wasn't a 'phase,' Ari." Radhya shakes her head. "I realize that all chefs who happen to be angry white men receive second and third chances, but I didn't think he'd get the opportunity to redeem himself with my best friend."

"To be fair," Gabe says, holding up his hands. "Ari does have a thing for bossy people who think they know everything."

"Stay out of it, Gaston." Radhya shoots him an intimidating glare.

He backs out of the living room and steps into the kitchen to observe the argument from a safer distance.

"No." Ari can't come up with the right words fast enough. It's easy to put his past offense with Radhya aside when he's just a weirdly engaging voice on the other end of the line. "It's not like that."

"Then what is it like?" Radhya cocks her head to the right. "What kind of 'hanging out' have you been doing? Because I'm pretty sure I'm the only friend without benefits you have."

"There aren't any benefits!" At least this is one answer where the truth isn't the worst-case scenario. "None. Rad—"

"Is this why I haven't seen you? Do you get how insulting this is? *I'm* your friend, Ari. Not him."

"Then listen to me!"

For the first time ever, Ari briefly wishes she and Josh *had* just hooked up that evening instead of splitting a pizza. She could have snuck off an hour later, Radhya would never need to know, and they each could've gotten their first post-breakup sex out of the way with minimal fuss.

"If you wanted me to listen," Radhya says, "why did you keep this a secret for weeks?"

"Probably because I knew this exact argument would happen!" Ari stands up from the couch.

"You always do this," Radhya continues. "You deflect and avoid until things blow up and then you walk away."

Ding!

JOSH: Hello?
She mentioned she does personal training.
Is that flirting or a sales pitch?

Radhya stares at the phone in Ari's hand. "Are you coming to NoFucksgiving or not?"

Ari heads for the door and shrugs her coat back on. "I'm going back to Queens."

"Why? So you can text him in private?"

"So I can *wallow* alone." Ari lets the door slam.

A bitter, muffled "Happy Thanksgiving!" echoes down the hallway.

On the street, the wind bites at Ari's face. Fighting with Rad always permeates every aspect of Ari's emotional state. She could get the silent treatment from Cass or flub an audition—those disappointments stay in their clearly marked lanes in her brain. When Radhya's upset with her, it's a jackknifing semi. Heavy. Messy. Uncontrolled.

Ari exhales a cloud of warm breath and marches across the street to the bodega on the corner. If she's not going to get sloppy drunk on cheap cocktails with friends, at least she can buy a can of wine and drink it alone, on the Q, through a straw.

A chonky bodega cat guards the entrance on the other side of the glass door, peering deep into Ari's mind with a disapproving, soul-piercing gaze, and shaming her out of purchasing train rosé.

She grabs her phone out of her pocket, Radhya's totally reasonable words circling the background of her mind like a carousel.

> ARI: plans fell through tonight

> JOSH: Movie?

> ARI: It'll take me an hour to get home from brooklyn

> JOSH: This is why I don't date women outside Manhattan.

Preferably, they live below Madison Square Park.

ARI: this is exactly why you're not getting laid
I guess I could come to your place

JOSH: And watch a movie in person?

ARI: no, just dinner and yoga instructor advice
I could stop at that taco place

JOSH: Which one?

ARI: the one where you got the thing with the stuff on it?

JOSH: The place with the chambray onions or the carnitas huaraches?

ARI: the one with the hot guy at the counter and a clean bathroom

"OKAY, I THOUGHT ABOUT IT ON THE WAY OVER AND HERE'S WHAT YOU'RE gonna do." Ari steps gingerly off the scary elevator and into Josh's loft, handing him a grease-soaked paper bag. "After class, take an extra minute to wipe down your mat and ask her about stretches that work your adductors. Trust me, works every time. Yoga classes are a great place to meet women." He's dressed in black jeans and a dark sweater that probably cost more than Ari's entire outfit, including her shoes and coat. "You wear pants at home? With a button fly? Are you a psychopath?"

"They're comfortable."

She shakes her head, brushing past him, fully taking in the space. "Holy shit. This could be a sitcom apartment."

"It would look more impressive without all the junk." Josh retreats to the kitchen to set the table. "I'm in the middle of a renovation."

To Ari's eye, the front of the apartment looks less like a "renovation" and more like someone deposited the contents of a basement all over the floor, started trying to put it in order, and gave up halfway through. As a veteran dumpster diver, she can't help strolling around the piles of treasures: a Thighmaster resting on a cracked boom box, heavy ceramic lamp bases with giant beige shades, the remnants of Brodsky's giant neon sign. The smell of old paperbacks and dusty vinyl.

Her gaze catches on a familiar silhouette.

"You can't get rid of the Bowflex, it's one of the best pieces of sex furniture known to man." Ari rushes over to the angled bench. She pulls at the lat tower assembly, testing the stability. "Do you have any carabiners?"

Josh's expression is both stern and laced with panic. It's so easy to make him uncomfortable, it's almost unfair.

She perches cross-legged on the bench. "Just so we're clear, there's no universe where any form of pants is more comfortable than no pants. I take mine off as soon as I walk in the door."

"So every time we watch a movie, you're not wearing pants?"

"Actually, I'm totally naked." She heaves herself off the Bowflex and walks toward the table, where he abruptly stops setting out the to-go containers. "Sorry, I'm fucking with you again. I can't watch movies naked. It's embarrassing. I'm an old T-shirt and underwear kind of girl."

He doesn't look up. "Like the shirt you're wearing? Which isn't even yours?"

"It's mine," she says, voice tinged with indignation.

"Really? Bikini Kill is a little before your time." He raises an eyebrow, waiting. "More of a . . . Gen X media studies professor thing."

"Legally, this shirt is half mine," she declares. "Am I supposed to throw it away?"

"*You* told me to toss out everything that belonged to Sophie. It's hypocritical."

She lets out a little huff. "It's a comfortable shirt! That's different from keeping someone's lingerie and you know it."

"Is it?"

"Everything else is gone. I can't have this *one* stupid shirt?" She's surprised at the way her voice almost cracks. Josh falls silent. It's just as well—Ari doesn't have the energy to pick a fight so soon after the Radhya debacle. "Can we eat now?"

He gestures at the table, which is set as if he's hosting a formal dinner. Ari can't help but observe that it's large enough to accommodate sex: a true New York luxury.

"Eating on dishes instead of takeout containers helps you stay in touch with your humanity," he says. "According to my therapist."

"I guess that makes me an animal." She takes a seat. His kitchen is in disarray—old cabinets and countertops with fancy new appliances, some still wrapped in plastic. "I thought cooking was your passion," she says.

Josh carefully arranges the tacos on a platter. "I refuse to fill my free time with something that reminds me of failure."

As she dumps a mountain of tortilla chips onto her plate, a dating app notification splashes across Ari's lock screen.

> Any one of these matches could be The One!
>
> Tap here to find out who.

"Ugh," she says, wrinkling her nose at the message. "How do I tell this app I don't want 'The One'? I'm not even ready to have totally forgettable rebound sex yet." Ari clears her throat, reading from the profile. "'Adam, thirty-eight. Big white one. Uncut. Huge loads. Can't an Uncut guy just get some head.'"

She drops the phone on the tabletop, disgusted. "This is what you put up with when you date men."

He reaches for her device and stares at the moonfaced man featured in a driver's seat selfie. Josh has one of those faces that never seems to relax into a casual expression. It's like his eyes are always scanning, seeking more information. "There's no question mark. And why is 'uncut' capitalized?"

"*That's* your critique?" She wipes her greasy hand with a flimsy taco place napkin. "Clearly you have the luxury of thousands of profiles of nice, normal women at your disposal."

He looks up, narrowing his eyes. "Then why aren't I spending time with nice, normal women right now?"

"You're probably disqualifying them for completely petty reasons." Everything she's deduced about his ex and the other nameless previous relationships he's vaguely referenced seems to indicate that *yes,* he absolutely does have a history of dating lovely women with real jobs, who actually read *The New Yorker* and don't let all the issues pile up for several months before going through them and skimming only the movie reviews and the cartoons. "What's the worst that could happen?"

"I could be trapped for hours at some mediocre restaurant with someone who doesn't respect the rules of grammar."

"Whenever I got stuck on a really bad date, my friend Gabe would show up at the restaurant and pretend to accuse me of cheating on him. It brings the date to a screeching halt, while eliminating any chance of future contact."

"I'll keep that in mind if I ever decide to date again."

"You need someone more objective to do the swiping." She places her open palm in front of him and gestures for him to hand over his phone. "I'll show you my terrible future dates if you show me yours?"

He opens an app and begrudgingly hands his device across the table. Ari stares at the Raya profile of "Lauren," who has a passion for travel but also loves relaxing at home. She swipes again on a "Hannah," who does part-time fitness modeling. "Your entire feed is beautiful overachievers?"

Josh swipes left every few seconds with one hand and rubs at his fledgling beard with the other. "Are you actually going to meet any of these people?"

"I'll risk it if you will," she says, examining a photo of a different Lauren, who's always up for an adventure. "So have you actually *talked* to the yoga instructor?"

"Two after-class conversations this week."

"You went *twice*?" Ari asks, a little embarrassed by the odd tone of her voice.

He scowls at her phone and makes another swipe. "'No fatties'? Really? This asshole is holding a fish."

Ari sits up taller, craning her neck to see what Josh is doing on her device. "Did you make sure it's set to all genders?"

"I assure you, I'm combing through every available human in the entire tri-state area. It's quality control. Unless you want to end up with someone who uses a bathroom selfie in their profile?" He's giving her that focused gaze again—the one that makes her feel exposed.

Ari returns her attention to Josh's phone, now very cognizant of the way the conversation tapered off into a real-life animated ellipsis, and swipes right on "Ashlyn," who works in program management and uses proper punctuation on dating apps.

11

UNDER NORMAL CIRCUMSTANCES, ARI WOULD TEXT RADHYA, MEET HER at the loading dock behind whichever restaurant she happened to be working at, and they'd grab a drink or five at the closest dive bar. She'd be buzzed from a set at one of the lesser-known comedy venues on MacDougal Street, either because it went really great or it really didn't.

There aren't any normal circumstances anymore. Their text thread has been silent for over a week. There haven't been any stand-up sets for months.

Nevertheless, Ari cuts through a narrow alley, the air thick with that familiar ripe smell of kitchen trash from several restaurants—the Korean place, the Irish pub, and the "new American" from Radhya's current sous-chef gig. Rad is a creature of habit, so she is exactly where Ari expects to find her: sitting on a milk crate against a brick wall. Phone in her right hand, cigarette in the other.

"Hi, Cum Slut."

Usually, Rad would respond with a tired but cheerful "Twattie!" But after a poorly masked look of surprise, she barely moves her eyes from the glow of her screen.

"I just want to know why." Radhya says it the way people sigh at their fuckup nephews who ask to borrow rent money.

Why what? Isn't necessary.

"I like talking to him," Ari says, choosing her words carefully.

"No one likes talking to him. Try again."

"He doesn't judge me or try to fix me."

Radhya hauls herself up from the crate. "And *I'm* the one judging *you*?"

"I didn't say that."

"You needed me in the immediate aftermath. You needed me when you didn't want to be alone in your apartment. You needed me every time you wanted to vent about Cass's moods. You were that person for me when my life blew up." All true. But it felt so much easier to be Radhya's support system; it's exhausting being the dud in a friendship. "Now you're fooling around with—"

"We *aren't.*"

"—my nemesis?"

Ari narrows her eyes. "I thought your nemesis was the chef de cuisine at Marea."

A sweaty-faced guy in a stained apron swings open the kitchen door, observes Rad's body language, and quickly retreats.

"I'd almost rather it was just some meaningless sex thing," Radhya says, sitting back down on the crate. "*I'm* supposed to be the person you confide in."

"Given your previous experience with Josh, it didn't seem

as simple as calling you up and saying, 'Hey, I want to tell you about this guy I know.'"

"But it was easier to sneak around behind my back?" Radhya takes another drag of the cigarette.

Ari opens her mouth to dispute this interpretation of events, but instead, what comes out is a trite analogy. "It's like . . . I got pushed into the water. But it's not a nice, heated pool. There's no shallow end. I got shoved over the railing of the *Titanic*."

"Say what happened. Cass pushed you. Stop using the passive voice."

"I've been treading water and I'm so exhausted that I can't bring myself to"—Ari inhales a back-alley-scented breath—"like, wave my hands and shout for help."

"I'm right here, offering you help, and you're waiting for Kestenberg to rescue you?"

"No," Ari says, her voice full of conviction. "He's in the water, too. We're both clinging to the same shitty piece of debris."

"According to that metaphor you're drowning in open water with someone who shoved my head underwater and never looked back." Radhya exhales a cloud of smoke. "Don't be the Leo in this situation. Don't let him hog that fucking door."

"I'm not the Leo." Ari's never actually seen *Titanic* but she knows the reference from the memes. "He's mostly just . . . going through a self-loathing thing." It feels like a slight relief to swivel the spotlight away from her and onto Josh and Radhya. "He doesn't even cook anymore. I think he'd like to apologize to you." Even as she says it, she can't quite remember him actually stating that.

Radhya stubs out the cigarette. "I'm not interested in being the next stop on his journey of 'listening and learning.'" She groans like someone twenty years older than she is as she stands up from the milk crate. "I should get back inside." She pulls the kitchen door halfway open and hesitates. "Did you at least talk to my lawyer?"

There's an odd swell of nerves in the pit of Ari's stomach. "How bad is it to send your ex a topless selfie from the bathroom of a divorce lawyer's office? Asking for a friend."

Radhya turns around to look at her. "Tell your friend dubcon nudes are . . . not great."

"I'm self-medicating."

"Meet me at Johnny's in an hour?" Ari nods, her giant exhalation creating a cloud in the cold air. "You're buying the drinks, Twattie."

"HOW HAVE YOU LIVED IN THE CITY FOR EIGHT YEARS AND NEVER BEEN TO the Frick?" Josh asks in a tone that's both exasperated and reverently hushed. "It's basic cultural lit—"

"Literacy. I know, I'm a heathen."

Late afternoon light streams through the glass windows of the Fragonard Room, illuminating gilded sculptures, porcelain vases, and a series of large paintings that the label describes as "exuberant depictions of romance." Josh and Ari have been wandering through the museum for almost two hours. Well, *wandering* is generous. It's more accurate to say that Josh has been coaxing and sometimes literally dragging her between the wings.

"Let's see," Ari says, glancing at the panels depicting subjects who definitely lost their heads to the guillotine. "I'm not interested in robber barons, colonialism, or celebrating thousands of years of sexism."

"Is there anything that's not problematic for you?"

"Are you suggesting that I shouldn't have unzipped my hoodie to reveal my KILLMONGER WAS RIGHT T-shirt in front of the docent?"

Josh stops in front of a giant mirrored mantelpiece and meets her eye in the reflection. "This is one of my favorite places in the city," he says. "It hasn't changed in . . . I don't know, a hundred years? I'm not going to apologize because a wealthy industrialist once bought a Persian rug."

"'Bought'?" She lets out a little *cough*—"white male privilege"—*cough cough,* but Josh isn't listening.

He's stopped in front of an enormous painting of a torturously corseted lady swooning at a foppish man in a wig. A small crowd is gathered around a heavyset man in a Nike baseball cap. He gets down on one knee and holds out a small box to a young woman in jeans and a Florida State sweatshirt.

It's not that Ari begrudges anyone else the whole fantasy of "that moment." But the trappings of weddings conjure up memories of terse phone calls with lawyers and an empty, silent apartment rather than flower girls and passages from Corinthians.

Endings like that have a way of overshadowing beginnings.

The woman tearfully nods and embraces Nike Hat. Josh continues watching, as people in the small crowd clap and take pictures of the newly engaged strangers. He turns and gives Ari a cryptic look, and she forces a sort-of smile, because that seems like the appropriate response to witnessing an engagement. But ten seconds later, she feels an urgent need to escape the imposing confines of the gallery, the fawning well-wishers, the smell of tourists sweating into their winter coats. Josh follows her out of the entrance hall, close enough that she catches the subtle botanical scent of his cologne.

"No commentary?" he asks as they exit into the cold early evening air of Seventieth Street.

"Well, for eighteen dollars I'm sure I could have written him a more memorable proposal." Ari buttons her coat, thinking. "They'll get married, have two kids, and Florida State will drag herself out of bed one morning, stare at the motivational word art on her desk, and realize that maybe she *doesn't* want to be trapped in a domestic jail cell with Nike Hat for the next fifty years."

"So, they're yet another couple destined to meet an untimely demise," he says, a shade of weariness in his voice.

"I mean, what's really the point of being married?" They cross Fifth Avenue, taking a winding path into Central Park. It feels easier to keep walking, as if she can sidestep the entire conversation as long as they're in transit. "It doesn't have to be *that* or nothing."

"So, you don't want . . . *that* again."

Her boots crunch on the fallen leaves. "Is this a trick question?"

"No." He slows down in front of a large arch made of brick and stone. "It's pretty straightforward." Ari gazes at the bare tree branches that form impossibly complicated webs in front of the orange and pink watercolor sky. She'd rather not face him while he's standing in front of something so photogenic, talking about marriage. "Technically, it was a statement."

"*Technically,* that's not what I said," she clarifies. "Shoveling thousands of dollars into the wedding industrial complex has nothing to do with making a long-term relationship work."

"Getting up in front of family and friends and saying, 'I love this woman and I want her to be my wife' doesn't have to involve an 'industrial complex.'"

I want her to be my wife loops in her brain, only with Cass saying it. Then it morphs into something indecipherable.

Ari shakes it off and turns around, walking backward in front of him, passing under the arch. The cool, musty air fills her lungs. It feels like a different world for the nine seconds it takes to pass beneath it. "Since when do you want to attend *any* event with your 'friends and family'?"

"Good point," he concedes.

When they emerge on the other side, Ari nods toward a bench at the edge of the footpath. They sit on the weathered wood, leaving a healthy distance between them, like they're each enclosed in their own protective force fields.

"With Cass, it was like . . ." She trails off, trying to remember why being married seemed necessary. "Getting that piece of paper would somehow validate that she chose *me*. Because without that, I was just part of someone's midlife crisis." She picks at the loose button on her coat. "Turns out, even with a government document, midlife crises end eventually."

"You should light some candles before you say something so romantic." She looks up at him. The sunset creates some distractingly beautiful golden hour lighting across his face. He crosses his arms tight across his chest. "I have a ring—a family heirloom from my dad's side. When Sophie was in town, I'd carry it everywhere, just in case I felt this shining moment of certainty. I didn't want to propose unless I was absolutely sure the answer would be 'yes.' But it never happened."

Ari folds her legs underneath her on the bench. "Do you still want to be married someday?" she asks, even though it's uncomfortable to bring the question to the surface.

Josh finds some point in the middle distance to stare at. "In theory," he finally says.

It's completely expected and a little disappointing. Now she's forced to imagine meeting Josh and his hypothetical . . . *wife* for dinner. A Lauren, probably. Smiling at their inside jokes—their own little language that Ari wouldn't know. The two of them would have stupid, petty fights, followed by amazing make-up sex. Josh would make his wife whatever healthy dish she wanted for breakfast. They'd go grocery shopping at Fairway and buy organic produce while pushing a state-of-the-art Bluetooth-enabled baby stroller.

He would completely move on with his life, the way people do when they're in relationships—when friends become people you squeeze into your schedule because your world revolves around your significant other. The idea of it makes her heart constrict—thinking of Josh as another person who'll inevitably leave her behind.

"But I don't think I'd propose in public, in front of a Fragonard. It's a bit on the nose," he adds, rising up from the bench, oblivious to her spiraling thoughts.

Ari breathes out and it's like opening a relief valve from the conversation. She shakes her numb hands and winds a scarf around her neck, bristling against the cold, following Josh as he starts to walk south.

She catches up to him, nudging slightly. "Let's stop at the halal cart for dinner."

He stops in his tracks. There's this funny, sheepish expression on his face that Ari hasn't seen before. "Oh, I . . . have plans."

"'Plans'?"

He looks up at the trees, avoiding eye contact. "The yoga instructor."

"Oh." Something in her chest burns but she manages to utter, "Yoga instructor pussy? I think I'm jealous." Yeah, it's definitely jealousy, but she can't tell if it's directed at Josh or his date.

"It's just dinner."

Is he grimacing or suppressing a smile? Her fist clenches around her phone.

"Wow. Straight to dinner. Not even vibe-check drinks first?" Ari takes a couple steps away from him. "This could be the first night of the rest of your life and I can barely handle the emotional intimacy of sexting."

It comes out a touch more bitter than intended.

"I thought you were going to get back out there, too."

"Totally." She puts a little distance between them. "I definitely am." *What if his date goes well?* "I'm— I should let you get home." Ari gestures at nothing in particular, backing away. "I assume you'll be changing into a different black outfit."

What if he gets laid? Her stomach twists, considering that possibility. The fact that she even *has* nervous feelings about it at all intensifies the stomachache.

"I'll call you after?" She's far enough down the path that he has to shout it.

"Sounds great!" Ari yells back. *Totally! Can't wait to find out whether the yoga instructor spends the night!*

She speed-walks toward Fifth Avenue, heading east when she'd meant to continue south. Ari glances behind her and he's rubbing at the back of his neck. She's never felt the need to escape a conversation with Josh before. Hadn't she told him she was a "really great wingwoman"?

What if Josh and the yoga instructor have brunch the next morning and the date lasts into Monday, when they'll both walk over to Crunch together for class at six A.M., where she'll demonstrate (again) how flexible she is while easing her body into a series of Instagrammable #yogagoals poses?

Once she's a safe distance away, with shin splints hobbling her right leg, Ari retrieves her phone from her bag. She'd been saving this move for a truly critical sex-life circumstance. A break-glass-in-case-of-emergency situation.

Apparently, this is that moment.

Ari updates each of her active dating profiles to *single, seeking couples.*

"Fuck it," she murmurs, editing her username to include unicorn emojis for good measure.

If Josh can date someone, Ari can date two someones.

12

Sat, Dec 10, 8:47 P.M.

JOSH: You said yoga classes were a great place to meet women.

ARI: they are.

All that flexibility and stamina and sweat . . .

Date not going well?

JOSH: She's not just a yoga instructor, she's also trying to sell me microbiome superpowder.

ARI: so you're saying she's more employed than you are.

You should see my date

Dates

JOSH: What?

ARI: Last minute thing with a couple I matched with

JOSH: A couple?

ARI: He's got a beard, she has a nose ring

They live in Red Hook

Stop me if you think you've heard this one before

JOSH: Dating one person is too much intimacy for you but two people is no problem?

ARI: they're looking for a unicorn

they have each other for the intimacy stuff

I bet they'll cuddle with each other afterward and won't want me to spend the night

Jackpot!

I can't believe this didn't occur to me earlier

8:59 P.M.

JOSH: Oh great. Her suggestion for a second date is a halotherapy salt room.

She says I need to cleanse my respiratory tract.

ARI: Is she into women? 👀

Where are you btw

JOSH: An oyster bar "partially owned by Zach Braff."

She brought her own food.

Where are you?

ARI: Burp Castle

b/c apparently men need to prove that they enjoy obscure beer or it's not a real date

JOSH: I like that place. It's quiet. You can bring a book.

ARI: you WOULD like a bar where the employees dress like monks and shush the customers

Cute bartender tho. He has the aura of a quieter
Jason Mantzoukas 😵‍💫
God. now there's a great voice

9:07 P.M.
JOSH: Her practice is rooted in a "mind-body-soul perspective."
I need to leave.

ARI: Use your Plato material!
She'll love it

JOSH: You're really going to sleep with a couple?
What if this affects their marriage?

ARI: they messaged ME!
Clearly you haven't experienced an extra set of hands 👐 👐 👐 👐

9:16 P.M.
ARI: Oh no
Oh god
the guy's real passion iS hOstINg TrivIA niGHtS

JOSH: Fuck.

ARI: it just so happens he's hosting trivia tonight
At the pub 3 blocks away 🫠
I'm being nonconned into attending trivia

9:37 P.M.
ARI: oh goddddd he thinks he's funny. He's doing bits 🆘 🆘
Why do people think this is a back door into stand-up? WHY
how does his wife put up with this???

JOSH: Maybe he's one of those men who go down on a woman for
more than three minutes with the right amount of enthusiasm.

ARI: doubtful

9:41 P.M.
ARI: Did you know Rembrandt's first name was Rembrandt??

JOSH: Everybody knows that.

ARI: Rembrandt Rembrandt?? 😭 😭
I went outside for a cigarette.

JOSH: You don't smoke.
Van Rijn. Rembrandt van Rijn.

ARI: I assumed he was like cher 🙄
ok i'm making a run for it
I've taken enough shit from men in actual comedy. I draw the line here

9:52 P.M.
JOSH: Well, mine's over.
Maybe seeing her in something other than Lululemon was off-putting.

10:02 P.M.
JOSH: Want to meet up? Debrief?

10:12 P.M.
JOSH: Hello?

Sun, Dec 11, 1:25 A.M.
ARI: sorry, phone died just coming back from Brooklyn

JOSH: You went back to their apartment?

ARI: Nope. Went back to Burp Castle
Wound up at the bartender's place with him and his wife 🍷
and uh . . . he does NOT whisper at home

1:29 A.M.

JOSH: I thought you could "barely handle the emotional intimacy of sexting."

ARI: We didn't exactly bare our souls

Sun, Dec 12, 1:31 A.M.

JOSH: I'll meet one of your catfishing victims.

BRIAR: Excellent!
I'll reopen communication with Maddie on Raya tomorrow morning.
It'll seem less desperate.
She has New Year's Eve potential!

JOSH STARES DOWN AT HIS WINEGLASS, WHICH HAS A FINGERPRINT smudge on the base of the stem that he desperately wants to wipe off. It's a respite from making prolonged eye contact with Maddie, a self-professed "food influencer, but not obnoxious about it" who's monologuing about the YouTube chefs she finds "most fuckable."

His mind wanders, cataloguing the Smith's décor clichés— Edison bulbs, wood paneled ceilings, subway tile walls. It's a copy of a copy of a New York bistro. Of course this fucking chain thrives, while his thoughtful, unique venture went down in flames.

Thur, Dec 15, 8:23 P.M.

ARI: sup
i'm playing beer bong w/ gabe in hell's kitchen and I'm bored
where are you

JOSH: I'm on a date.

The Smith on 63rd.

ARI: ooh nearby . . .

JOSH: 27,000 restaurants in this city and a "foodie" chooses the Smith?

ARI: glad youre not being judgmental this time 👏 👏 👏

"It's so ironic," Maddie says—and Josh is sure whatever she says next is guaranteed *not* to be ironic, "because I think I had a little crush on you, but I actually only gave The Brod two stars?"

JOSH: Actually, call me and pretend it's an emergency.

ARI: Why??

Wait

actually I'll do you one better

He reaches for his knife and fork, half-listening to Maddie's monologue about her ex-boyfriend, who never supported her food blogging and who she's "totally over." Luckily the acoustics are so bad that his date's voice fades into the general cacophony of the restaurant. The couple at the next table appear to be having a lovely dinner, with no need to feign interest in the other's early-stage dating anecdotes.

Had it felt that effortless with Sophie? Or was he a nervous-fucking-wreck the entire time?

Josh surreptitiously checks his watch under the table as their entrées arrive: his steak and Maddie's salad with five substitutions. She photographs the unremarkable dish. Fifteen minutes have passed and no emergency call. Had Ari gotten distracted? Forgot? Gone home with her beer pong opponents?

Maddie glances up at something over his shoulder: a sharp, insistent tapping sound coming from the window behind him.

Josh turns around, expecting to see some bizarre only–in–New York event unfolding in front of a crowd along Broadway. But there's only one person standing there, an inch from the window, her face contorted in outrage.

"*What the fuck, Joshua?*" Ari yells into the insulated glass, creating a cloud of condensation on the window. Josh freezes, racking his brain for an explanation.

"Do you know her?" Maddie asks, sitting up straighter.

Before he can say anything, a blur of plaid peacoat appears at the periphery of his vision.

"I knew it!" Ari bursts through the door and past the host stand. "Liar!"

It takes her only a few seconds to march past five other tables and plant herself in front of their crowded two-top. He slouches automatically but there's nowhere to hide.

"'Working late'?" Her eyes are glassy from beer pong. "It's *bullshit*! You're cheating on me!"

"I—" His mouth won't close. He blinks and lets the dual feelings of shock and confusion fight for dominance.

Ari slams her open hand down on the shiny wood tabletop. The couple at the next table pretend not to stare. "And at our favorite restaurant!"

"Our *fav*—" He clenches his jaw, tamping down whatever emotion is fighting to make itself known. He's either on the verge of laughter or genuinely scared of her.

"Wait," Maddie says. "You have a girlfriend?"

He's about to offer . . . well, *something* in the realm of a denial when Ari leans down so that her face is only a few inches from his.

"I'm his *wife*."

His date jerks her head back, like she's been hit by a particularly vicious dodgeball headshot.

Josh isn't often rendered speechless but something short-circuits between his brain and his throat when Ari looks down at him, her expression fiery anger, cut with a dash of mischief that almost no one else would notice.

"M-Maddie, it's not—" He exhales. "This isn't real."

"Not real?" Ari shakes her head slowly. "Not *real*?" Josh reaches for his water and takes a gulp. "It felt pretty real when I got my nipples pierced because you said it was 'more intimate than a wedding ring.' They took an entire month to heal!"

Maddie's mouth falls open. Josh coughs up some of the water.

Dropping her tote bag on the floor, Ari takes a seat on the banquette, trapping him. The side of his body is pushed up against the cold poly wool blend of her unbuttoned coat, which absorbed the aroma of cheap beer.

"You're *married*?" Maddie asks, leaning forward.

Ari looks at him, eyebrows raised to cartoonish heights, daring him to join the act.

Josh does some quick calculus. He's never been good at improvising, but Ari hasn't given him much choice.

"I guess we've been"—he breathes in, scanning Ari's face—"avoiding the truth for a long time. Going through the motions."

Maddie lets out a little gasp. She should be reaching for her coat any moment.

The tiny divot at the corner of Ari's mouth turns up ever so slightly. "So all that phone sex was just your way of 'going through the motions'?" His neck gets hot. She glances at Maddie. "He makes crazy noises, you know." She leans across the table. "One time, he wanted me to wear a clown suit."

"Jesus, this is so toxic," Maddie mutters, pushing the bread basket toward Ari.

Ari's slightly inebriated affect really helps to sell the idea that she'd downed three glasses of pinot noir back in "their" apartment before marching over to Sixty-third and Broadway to confront her lying husband.

"When we met," Ari says, grabbing two slices of focaccia, "it was like he couldn't get enough of me. He gave me a drawer after our second night together."

"Such a red flag." Maddie nods, making absolutely no move to leave. "But also romantic?"

Ari faces him. "You told me you loved me and you didn't care that it was too soon. And it scared me because I never said that to anyone before." She places her palm against his cheek and he's certain she can feel his racing pulse through his skin. "But I did. I said it because I felt . . ." There's a tiny wobble in her voice. "I thought we belonged to each other. I let you in. I let my guard down. I used the drawer and you just got . . . tired of me."

Josh swallows. If this monologue is pure invention, she really does have great improv skills.

"What a fucking asshole," Maddie says, heartbroken by proxy. "I'm so sorry."

The two women stare accusingly at Josh and he feels momentarily guilty for fake-perpetuating an entirely fictional crime of the heart.

Ari slides her right hand in front of him and reaches for his plate, quietly slicing into his steak. After she ingests half his meal, finishes his wine, and signals the server for another, Ari turns to the bewildered woman across the table. "I'm sorry, what was your name?"

"It's Maddie," she says, apparently surprised to become a direct participant in the drama. "Hi. But I'm not—" She pauses. "This was our first date."

Ari whips her head back to him. "How many women did you neglect to tell me about, Joshua?"

"Aren't you even going to say you're sorry?" Maddie asks him, shaking her head in disbelief.

Great. So, he's capable of disappointing people in made-up scenarios in addition to the real world.

Ari slices off one more bite of his steak. "This is really good," she mumbles, somehow acting convincingly distraught while thoroughly enjoying his food.

Josh and Ari stare at each other for a beat. The blaring noise of the restaurant—the laughter at the bar, the clinking of silverware, Le Tigre pumping through the speakers—recedes into the background.

"I'm sorry," he says in a sober tone. He doesn't issue apologies often; even this fake one feels oddly potent. "I haven't been completely honest with you." He takes a breath. "Because I don't think you want to hear the truth." She stops chewing. Her eyebrow does the slightest little quirk. "And it would force a conversation that could blow up our . . . *marriage*." When she looks at him, it's like she's eighty percent certain of something. That extra twenty percent will keep him up at night. "So I've been keeping things from you"—he glances at Maddie and back to Ari—"my *wife*."

Maybe the little moment could've lasted longer if not for the server manifesting table-side to cheerfully inquire if Ari is "still working on that steak."

She is, obviously. But he doesn't miss the hint of a smile on her face before she grabs his napkin off his lap and pretend-dabs at her eyes.

"God." Maddie looks down at her highly customized salad like she's reading tea leaves. "Now I'm rethinking my breakup with Kevin. We were together since college and I thought I was missing out on all these wild sexual adventures in my twenties, but—"

"Oh?" Ari perks up, dropping the napkin.

"—being single is just so bleak," Maddie says, taking a gulp of her chardonnay. "I mean, no offense, but like, looking at you two, I'm not sure if it's worse to be out here dating or to end up in a nightmare relationship like yours."

Josh wrinkles his nose at the criticism.

Ari reaches for another piece of focaccia.

"So . . . tell me about these wild sexual adventures," his "wife" says to Maddie, not quite innocently enough, sliding the bread through the bowl of olive oil without breaking eye contact.

13

"REMIND ME WHY WE DECIDED TO SCHLEP TO THE STRAND ON THE COLD-est day of the year so far?" Ari whines as she steps off the elevator, hunched over with the weight of a backpack sagging on her shoulders.

"It might help if you invested in a real jacket," Josh replies. "Your coat is an embarrassment to outerwear."

"At this point, I'm just hoping I make enough cash back on these books to buy myself pierogis at Veselka afterward." She drops the bag on his dining table. She pulls *Daring Greatly* out of the bag and holds it up, examining the back cover. "Why is everyone always trying to get me to read this book? Maybe I don't want to 'dare greatly.' Maybe I just want to dare the regular amount and wallow." She walks over to his fridge and peeks inside, pulling out a bottle of Pellegrino, taking a second to study the stack of identical reusable containers, all labeled and dated in his neat block lettering. Chef habit. "Is it possible to wallow greatly? Somebody write *that* book."

Josh reaches into the backpack. "Did she leave you the entire Brené Brown collection?"

"Wait, don't look in there. I have a surprise." Ari rushes back over to the table, sloshing some water over the rim of the bottle. "Now, before you say anything"—she slaps his hand away from the bag—"I know you don't celebrate Christmas. This is a nondenominational winter holiday present." She pulls out a large box wrapped in one of the free daily newspapers they hand you at subway stops. Maybe Cass took their supply of wrapping paper, too. "Congratulations. I hope you're ready to be a father."

After tearing into the newsprint, the first thing he sees is the as-seen-on-TV logo. She'd taped over the little cartoon Dust Daddy character on the box with some old photo from a profile that ran in *Saveur* two years ago.

"It's not a gag gift," she assures him. "I know how you feel about crumbs. This is basically like when Aragon got that giant sword from those dwarves."

"This doesn't give you permission to eat crackers on my furniture," he says, turning it over. "And the *elves* re-forged that sword. Not the dwarves."

"I know." She grins and shrugs off her plaid peacoat. "But when I fuck with you, you get this look on your face like this . . ." She furrows her brow, creating a little wrinkle over her nose.

The gift is so perfectly casual yet evocative of a specific time and place that's only meaningful to them that he briefly second-guesses himself as he retrieves the present he'd purchased for Ari two weeks ago. He'd wrapped it the way they do on sitcoms, where the lid just lifts off.

He might have watched several tutorials.

"Is it the tiny sleeping golden retriever puppy I asked for?" She shakes the box near her ear before lifting the lid.

Ari's smile fades. She looks down into the box, eyebrows knitted together.

"They still sell them at Pearl River Mart," he says quickly. "I know it's not *the* bowl but it's the same pattern with the blue rim and the dragon design. I wanted you to"—she looks up at him with the corners of her mouth turned down, like she's trying to contain something—"be able to eat cereal again."

After a few seconds she manages to shift it into a lopsided smile. She picks up the bowl. It was $3.50—less than he'd spent on the wrapping paper. Probably the least expensive gift he's ever purchased.

"Damn," she says quietly. "You really go for the jugular, Kestenbutt."

"Well, it's . . ." he starts, having no idea how to finish the sentence. "Make sure you wash it first."

"Thanks." She traces her index finger around the rim.

"I had a slight ulterior motive." He takes a breath in like he's preparing to inflate a balloon. "What are you doing on New Year's Eve?"

"Gabe hosts a karaoke fundraiser every year. We sing obnoxious songs and raise money for LaughRiot while wearing ridiculous-but-sexy outfits." He glances up at that. "Cass never wanted to go. Do you want to? Maybe sing a terrible rendition of 'Piano Man'?"

"There are good renditions of 'Piano Man'?" Josh retorts automatically.

"I'm more of a 'We Didn't Start the Fire' girl." She tilts her head. "Why, what do you have planned for New Year's? You've already done Zach Braff's seafood place. Are you challenging an aspiring actress to a match at Susan Sarandon's ping pong bar? Bringing a fitness influencer to Jeremy Renner's Cajun bistro?"

"Really?"

"You're right." She nods. "That's more of a Bastille Day spot."

Josh hesitates. Every word he's about to utter sounds embarrassing in his head. "On New Year's Eve, my father is being honored at a black-tie event at the New-York Historical Society."

"Seriously?"

"They're opening a new exhibition on Jewish foodways," he explains with a dismissive gesture. "My dad sat for some interviews a couple years ago. Begrudgingly, I assume. My mom donated some Brodsky's memorabilia and they're expecting the family to show up at the gala."

"You can't get out of it?"

Josh shakes his head. "Briar has our mother convinced that it will be a good way to move on from the whole son-who-killed-his-father's-beloved-Jewish-deli narrative."

Ari nods. "Tough rep. I get it."

"Meanwhile, Briar will be off in the desert on some sponsored influencer trip while my mother spends the whole evening accusing me of being rude to all her real estate developer friends. They'll serve steam-table brisket and some Broadway ingénue will perform a couple Stephen Schwartz songs. And if I run into someone I know I'll have to explain why Sophie's not there. . . ." Josh lets the sentence trail off, raising his eyebrows at Ari in a way that communicates his request without him having to complete the ask.

"Ahh," she says, narrowing her eyes and nodding slowly. Ari collapses onto a kitchen chair. "The thing is, I'm bad arm candy at parties for one-percenters. Cass made me go to a few with her. No one finds me funny and I can't dance."

"And you act like a brat at museums," he adds.

"You're really selling this. Keep going."

He takes a seat on the other chair, so they're back at the same eye level. "If you show up and let my mother fawn over you for two hours, you can complain all you want."

"Will she think I'm your date?"

"I'll make it clear we're just friends."

Ari narrows her eyes. He can't tell if this is a good sign or not. "Fine. But if I agree to this, you'd owe me a favor, right?"

"Fine," he agrees. "Do you need me to reach something on a high shelf?"

"Radhya's holding a pop-up at Bohemian Garden next month. She's making Gujarati bar snacks." She pauses. "You could finally apologize to her."

"Apologize?" He stands up from the chair, crossing his arms over his chest. "No."

"That's like, one tenth the effort of a *gala* with your mother on the biggest date night of the year!"

"Radhya wouldn't want me there." He knows he's right. *Ari* knows he's right.

She sighs, clearly disappointed, and stands up with a full body stretch. "Do you have books to sell? I think they close at eight."

"YOU REALLY DON'T WANT TO KEEP ANY OF YOUR COOKBOOKS?" ARI watches Josh pack up a stack of pristine hardcovers as a gust of wind rattles the large window at the front of the loft.

"The whole point is to rid ourselves of these reminders of

the past." Josh has that "please wade no further into this subject" look on his face, so Ari drops it, looking out the window. A light snow has started to fall, visible in front of the glow of a streetlamp. "Ugh, it looks windy."

"Here." He walks over to the front closet and pulls out a bulky black parka. "You can borrow this."

When she puts it on and checks the mirror, it appears that her entire body is being swallowed by several yards of heavily insulated Gore-Tex.

Josh stifles a laugh. "You look . . ."

"Like three kids in a trench coat?"

"Cute." He seems surprised to hear himself say it. "Cute and probably warm."

"Sweating, actually." The goose down filling probably isn't the cause of her flushed cheeks. Josh isn't exactly doling out *cute*s with great frequency; it feels surprisingly nice to receive one. No, two.

Outside, heavy wet clumps of snow melt into slush on the sidewalk. The streets are quiet as they walk up Lafayette, shoulder to shoulder, along the narrow stripe of sidewalk next to the clumps of snow on the curb. He points out Chase and Citibank locations that started out as something with character—sheet music retailers or restaurant supply warehouses. She tells him a story about getting trapped in the restroom at the Kmart that used to be across the street from Cooper Union.

When they pass a bodega, Ari insists on purchasing a black-and-white cookie "for the sake of basic cultural literacy." She breaks it in half so that each of them has both vanilla and chocolate.

"Still too sweet," Josh says after the first bite. "I always told my dad they need a secondary flavor. Some spice or a citrusy note." Watching him eat his half of the cookie—which, in Ari's opinion, is the perfect amount of sugary—it occurs to her that their friendship exists in a perfect, fragile bubble of *right now*. If Josh was five percent less picky, he'd have a rebound girlfriend. If the fog of breakup failure wore off tomorrow . . . well, Ari probably wouldn't be "dating" in the same way, but she'd be a functional human who wouldn't need someone else to talk her to sleep over the phone several nights a week.

She imagines Josh walking into Pearl River Mart—like, the mundane process of pushing through the doors, walking down the stairs, searching through the massive selection of dishes. Looking through all the variations on blue-and-white bowls to find that one.

It stirs this inkling—maybe it's an ounce too affectionate? Accepting that kind of small but meaningful gesture almost feels like a cheat. A crutch. Why hadn't she thought to do that for herself? What's so hard about replacing a bowl or buying furniture or an insulated winter coat? Now she'll get used to Josh being a person who would do those things, right up until the moment where he'll get out of his own way just enough to invite a nice woman on a second date.

Then he'll disappear into the warm embrace of a healthy relationship, never to be heard from again.

Ari kicks at a fresh snow drift—releasing a tiny bit of her frustration—and a rat the size of a calzone bolts out from underneath.

She shrieks and takes off running for half a block, stumbling inside the confines of the too-long coat.

"How long have you lived here?" Josh shouts from behind her as she slows to a stop. "This is why you should never jump in a leaf pile in Central Park. Anything could be under there."

"I'll never get used to the rats."

"Rats are the real New Yorkers," he says, catching up to her.

"I'll give the rats credit for being badasses on the subway tracks, but that creature can pry this half-cookie out of my cold dead hands." Ari defiantly raises her right hand to reveal the remaining black-and-white chunk.

JOSH NOTICES IT AS THEY WALK UP BROADWAY TOWARD UNION SQUARE. Maybe it's the sugar rush from the fondant on the cookie. Maybe solving his New Year's Eve date problem tweaked one of the default settings in his brain. But he's suddenly aware that anyone passing Ari and him on the sidewalk would assume that they're on a date. It's probably because they're subtly comfortable with each other in a way that's impossible to achieve on a first or second date—which is the limit of his recent experiences. He's not wearing his gloves; her mittens are peeking out of her tote bag. With every other step, the backs of their hands just barely brush against each other. Obviously, if they were, in fact, two random people in a burgeoning love affair, they'd take advantage of the fleeting contact and suddenly intertwine their fingers. It could be a casual gesture or something full of significance.

Since they're not random people, nor in the early stages of a romance, neither of them grabs the other's hand.

But they also don't move farther apart until they approach the entrance to the Strand.

The store is packed with tourists on the ground floor: people milling around the tables of ubiquitous paperback bestsellers, picking out pencil bags and tote books and bookmarks screen-printed with the Strand logo.

"This is the perfect first-date location," Ari says, as they weave through the crowded aisles. "Because it's very easy to lose someone on the lower level."

Josh has never brought a date here. But among the tall shelves and less congested corners, the store feels so steeped in romantic possibility, it's almost as if he and Ari parachuted into a scene from another couple's love story. The whole evening has this new, vibrant undercurrent, like their comfortable vibe is stretching into a different shape.

"*Whoa.*" Ari stares at her phone, as they wait in front of the bookselling desk.

"Is everything okay?"

"I think it's an elbow?" she squints at the screen. "Or a knee?"

Josh leans over her shoulder, curiosity getting the better of him. "Someone's sending you unsolicited photos?"

"No, they're solicited." She unlocks her device to enlarge the image. "I should have dropped that unicorn into my profile years ago. This is a real game changer. It's literally impossible for me to get rejected by these couples. So validating."

He rolls his eyes. "Should I leave you three alone?"

"Is it suspicious that the man is a lot chattier than his wife? I think he copy-pasted one of those listicles with sexting tips. Look." She hands him her device. "'What panties are you wearing?'"

"Costco?" He scans the brightly colored text bubbles. "You responded 'none.'"

She's labeled her conversational partner 👀 *salt & pepper man + blond hotwife* 🐊.

He continues reading. "'You look so beautiful, but you'd look even better with my tongue inside you.'" He places the phone back in her palm without looking her in the eye. "These are people you want to spend time with?"

"I know, right? They didn't even specify whose tongue!"

The clerk offers Ari a grand total of $1.35 in store credit, even though Cass's copy of *Daring Greatly* had been inscribed ("To Cass, without whom I would never have dared at all. —B").

His cookbooks fare better, but he doesn't care about the $7.78. It's the principle of the thing. He doesn't need David Chang and Grant Achatz taunting him from the covers of their memoirs.

Ari grabs a shopping basket and pulls a half-dozen books off the shelves on the main level. Josh peels off and spends a few minutes in the Linguistics section, eventually meandering, accidentally or not, to Cooking.

The glossy covers—grinning chefs holding artfully composed dishes—remind him of the life that seems like a false memory now. The food itself looks appealing, even though it's all lighting and shellac. He can barely remember what part of it appealed to him.

Josh descends the stairs to the lowest floor, where Ari is leaning against the railing on the landing.

"See, I could've ghosted you ten minutes ago." She's standing one step above him, making them almost the same height. "But here I am."

Maybe it's seeing her face from a shallower angle, or the way her mood lifted after getting rid of the last remnants of Cass. Or the slight case of raccoon eyes from wearing non-waterproof mascara in the falling snow.

"You probably realized that you need my seven dollars of book-selling profit to pay for your pierogis."

"Actually, I need your muscular forearms. Here," she says, handing him her full basket of books and nearly overextending his elbow with the weight of it. "Put the gym time to good use."

"You're expecting me to carry these all the way back to my place?"

The elevator dings.

"Yes, because I just agreed to spend a national holiday making small talk with your mother." Ari makes a sweeping gesture in front of the bright red elevator door. "Reason number two why the Strand is the perfect date location: good make-out spots."

"You bring dates into the elevator to make out?" he asks, stepping inside. "It's only four floors. I hope you didn't have anything gymnastic in mind."

"I meant the Rare Book Room. But I like the way you think." They stand shoulder to shoulder, watching the doors close. The elevator lurches to the next stop. "You're the one taking all those yoga classes." Ari turns her head and looks up at him. Her parka—*his,* actually—grazes his cashmere coat.

"Are you asking for a demonstration?" His eyes move back and forth across her face, taking in the small details that are only visible close-up: the little scar on her forehead, the flicker of a smile, the dimple. She's leaning against the back wall of the elevator so casually. *Too* casually? He can't quite decode whether she's merely playing along or there's some glimmer of potential behind it. Had they met *here* eight years ago—or five years ago, or three years ago—as total strangers, maybe everything would've been different.

"That depends," she says. The doors open onto the Rare Book Room but neither of them move, even though there's someone—a tall figure in glasses and a blazer—waiting just outside the elevator, reading a brochure. "Are you one of those men who goes down on a woman for three minutes with minimal enthusiasm, but also expects a messy blow job thirty seconds later?"

Before he can summon a response to . . . *that,* the figure looks up.

"Ar?"

14

NEITHER JOSH NOR "AR" LOOKS OVER RIGHT AWAY, LIKE THEY'D RATHER not break whatever spell they'd been under by acknowledging the metaphorical elephant standing three feet away.

"Oh my God." Cass takes a step forward. "How are you?"

Ari reaches out with her left hand and Josh feels his muscles tense at the possibility of being trapped in a steel box while watching them embrace. But Ari's index finger swerves to the CLOSE DOOR button, which she mashes repeatedly, her face blank.

This act seems to confuse the elevator. It makes a loud buzzing noise, as if to shoo them out. Cass throws her arm against the door, keeping it from sliding closed. There's nothing to do but step forward into the Rare Book Room.

"Fine," Ari says, keeping her arms stiffly at her sides as her ex-wife forces her into an awkward embrace. Her voice is hollow. "I'm fine."

Cass looks refreshed. Glowing. Josh tells himself it's Botox.

She's wearing a dark blazer (likely a more expensive one

than last time) over a gently distressed Hole T-shirt. Clear frame glasses, Blundstone boots. Every aspect of her feels precisely curated. She places her hands on Ari's shoulders, taking her in: smudged eye makeup, messy bun, a giant men's parka. Objectively speaking, it's not the way anyone would care to run into their ex.

And yet . . . he can't help but wonder if Cass thinks he and Ari are *together*. Is it wrong for him to take some pleasure in the slight amount of annoyance that might cause?

Cass looks at Ari, letting her gaze run up and down her face. "Did you set up a time to meet with my broker about the move-out dates?"

"Um, working on it." Ari remains stock-still. No fidgeting, no shifting weight. "I'll figure it out."

She'd never mentioned anything to Josh about a broker and move-out dates.

Cass loosens her grip on Ari's shoulders. "Good," she says, with no trace of conviction. She glances around the space like she's looking for someone. "It's so weird to see you here. I was just meeting with the events director."

"Are you . . . giving a talk?" Ari asks, still wearing a vacant expression that Josh has never quite seen from her. It's like she's looking through a portal into another reality.

"No, actually—"

"Did you see the dressing rooms, babe?" The new voice belongs to a young woman in an oversized, unbuttoned cherry-red coat who appears in Josh's peripheral vision. Cass grabs the woman's hand, pulling her forward. Ari visibly flinches before managing to regain her composure. "Oh. Hi, Ari." The woman gives her a limp, awkward nod. "Katya Kulesza," the other woman says to Josh, while nestling closer to Cass.

There's silence all around as both women shift their attention to Josh. He waits for Ari to say anything—introduce him, provide some conversational lubrication to move them all over this hump.

She doesn't move. Doesn't breathe.

He nudges Ari gently.

Still nothing. She barely seems to register his presence.

"Josh," he says finally, extending his hand to Cass, even though it's the last thing he wants to do. "We've met before."

"Have we?" Cass regards him with a steely, even gaze, tilting her head slightly, the faintest hint of a smile forming at the corner of her mouth. She steps forward as if to demonstrate that they're approximately the same height, gripping his hand firmly. Her chunky ring presses uncomfortably into his palm.

"My sister was one of your students," he adds. "Briar Kestenberg."

"Oh, *Briar*. Of course!" Cass nods, clearly having zero recollection. "This is new for you, Ar." She gives Josh a once-over, conveying both skepticism and pity with a subtle raise of her eyebrows.

Ari seems to wake up from a trance. "Oh, we're not tog—"

"Babe," says Katya, "we need to ask about swapping out the folding chairs." She turns to Josh and Ari. "We're scoping out venues." Under the coat, she's wearing a blazer and a vintage T-shirt, like a shorter, curvier, younger version of Cass. "Engagement party."

Ari's face flushes red. She's frozen, mouth open just a centimeter or two, staring at the two women in front of her, knees locked, muscles tight with pure tension.

Something catches Katya's attention across the room. "Excuse me!" she shouts to the ponytailed woman who must be the events coordinator, before excusing herself by telling Ari "you look great." There's no real malice in her tone, which somehow makes it more cutting.

Maybe Josh should also occupy himself elsewhere with some fake book-shopping task, but he can't bring himself to cede any ground, physical or otherwise, to Ari's ex. Instead, he grabs the basket off the floor and plants his feet.

Cass, unfazed, touches Ari's shoulder—*again*—initiating a private conversation between the two of them.

"Ar, I know this is awkward." She's speaking just above a whisper, but Josh can hear the tender inflection of her tone. "But we're really hoping you'll sign the documents this week. It's so much easier for all of us to do this uncontested. And you'll return the broker's calls?"

"Okay," Ari says, barely audible.

He grips the handle of the basket almost hard enough to break the plastic, waiting for the bomb to explode. She can have until the count of three to tell her ex to *fuck off*.

Cass's fingers stay pressed into Ari's shoulder, as if she still has some claim. Some right to be there. "I hope you're okay. If you need anything . . ."

Three . . .

Two . . .

"She's fine," Josh snaps.

They both turn their heads accusingly, as if he'd interrupted *their* moment.

What happens when Ari needs something? Who does she call? Who's been picking up the fucking pieces? *Fuck this presumptuous—*

"In that case," Cass says, turning back to Ari, "you should stop texting me. No more . . . pictures, okay?"

The way she says *pictures* sends Josh's mind spinning in twelve directions.

Ari nods, defeated. Her eyes don't seem to be focusing on anything.

Cass gives Ari's shoulder a final squeeze as she takes a step past her. Josh is about to let himself exhale when she pauses and turns around, her face now just an irksome inch above his. Must be the heels of her boots.

"Oh, and, Josh? I'll give you a tip. Eating pussy should be the main event, not a three-minute warm-up."

Six semi-formed comebacks fail to fully materialize in his brain. He blinks dumbly, watching Cass walk away.

Ari reaches past him, pressing the elevator button. It groans to life from the floor below.

There'd been no outburst. No argument. She'd passively absorbed everything that came out of that woman's mouth: the false comfort, the performance of kindness, even the judgment.

"Let's go," she says, her voice carefully modulated in that indifferent tone that drives him fucking insane.

The shock of the whole encounter wears off into something sinister. She'd seemed almost . . . embarrassed to be seen with him.

"What about the books you picked out?"

"What do I need books for?" she snaps. Her cheeks are crimson. "I don't have shelves. I have a move-out date."

"I can keep them—"

"No!" Ari doesn't look at him. She's staring straight ahead, face red. "I don't want your help. I don't want the books. I want to go home." Eventually, the elevator door creaks open. "Except 'home' just reminds me of . . . *that*."

He sets the basket down, abandoning it to the Rare Book Room, and follows her into the elevator.

"Then let's go to Veselka. You wanted pierogis."

She lets out an aggravated sigh, which Josh takes as a "yes." If he sticks to the script, a normal activity—something they do all the time—he could stabilize the situation.

They stand in the same positions as before but now everything's changed around them, like the elevator is some kind of emotional teleportation torture device. Maybe he'll encounter Sophie chatting with the ghost of his father on the first floor.

When the door opens again, it's a random couple waiting to get on, holding hands and laughing about something that's only funny to them. They're locked in their own little bubble, oblivious to the disaster that occurred three flights up.

JOSH CAN HEAR ARI'S FOOT TAPPING ON THE FLOOR IN NO DISCERNIBLE pattern, even though Veselka is noisy tonight. She turns the laminated menu back and forth.

"You're not getting the pierogis?" he asks. It's the first time he's spoken since they left the Strand. This time, there hadn't been any cookie-splitting or not-quite-hand-brushing. Just awkward silence and the sound of boots scraping against wet pavement.

She shrugs, tossing the menu down on the table and pointedly not making eye contact. They're surrounded by couples, but Ari makes no predictions about the nature of their forthcoming breakups.

When the waiter returns, she orders a fucking salad, which is somehow the most insulting thing she's done all evening.

With the distraction of the menus gone, they sit in continued silence: Josh looking at Ari and Ari looking anywhere but at Josh, her refusal to engage keeping his anger at a low boil.

There's something almost disrespectful about her brittle demeanor inside the homey, unpretentious atmosphere, drenched in the familiar smell of carb-heavy comfort food. It's a warm Ukrainian blanket of a diner.

"Should we talk about what just happened?" he asks, after giving her a reasonable two minutes to speak first.

"If you want," she says. If *you* want. Like this is for his benefit.

"Are you okay?" He keeps his tone steady and devoid of feeling. They could be two chatbots exchanging pleasantries.

"Oh yeah, perfect," she replies, letting a drop of sarcasm through whatever filter she's using to sift out emotion. "I've been holding my breath for months, waiting for it to happen." She continues to tap her foot. "I ran into my wife—"

"Your ex."

"—looking like a drowned rat ragamuffin. And that's fine. I'm fine."

"You certainly seem 'fine.'"

"Yep." Her foot taps harder against the tile. There are no distractions: no food on the table, no menus.

After a beat, he tries a new strategy. "It's okay to be upset."

"Oh, I have your permission now?" She picks at the corner of the table and finally looks up. "Great. I'm upset with *you*."

"Me?" Josh sits up straighter.

"Why were you acting like that in front of her?"

"I could ask you the same question." He unrolls the paper napkin and wipes off the water spots from each piece of silverware. "You acted like you didn't even know me. You should have just shoved me down the elevator shaft in front of her, it would have been subtler."

Ari raises her eyebrows to cartoonish heights. "That's why you're mad? Because I panicked and didn't perform a round of gracious introductions? Sorry if I was distracted for two minutes by the person who shattered my *fucking heart*."

The waiter chooses this moment to serve Josh's matzo ball soup and Ari's salad, dropping the dishes down on the table with a clatter.

"I was trying to help," he says, as much to himself as to her.

"I never *asked* you for help, so you can stop trying to live out this fantasy where I'm your girlfriend."

The word lingers in the air like gun smoke.

"Excuse me?" he shoots back, driving toward some heretofore unacknowledged line. The border of the demilitarized zone of the friendship. "You were practically begging me to kiss you three seconds before your ex showed up."

Her mouth falls open. "We were joking around! And *you* started it. You pushed this on me."

"What did I push on you?" He feels over-caffeinated, like he's barely in control of whatever might spill out of his mouth next.

"Really?" She cocks her head to the right. "Why are you eating soup in a diner instead of taking a Lauren to some under-the-radar Argentinian wine bar? Why don't you dress up the yoga instructor in your giant coat and humiliate her in front of her wife?"

"*Ex*-wife. I made you wear the coat because I don't want you freezing your ass off because I *fucking care* about you."

She stares at him, saying nothing.

The middle-aged couple at the next table pause their own

conversation and give each other painfully obvious "look at these two" glances.

The adrenaline that was coursing through his body a few seconds ago dissipates into dread, tepid and stagnant.

Ari looks down at the plate and pokes at the lettuce with her fork. Her shoulders start to shake. When she finally looks up, her eyes are spilling over with tears. "Is there more to me than bong vapor and nipple piercings?"

"Ari." He modulates his voice into something soft. "That's a ridiculous question."

"I was supposed to be her muse," she says, her voice drained of all levity.

"That sounds very convenient for her but you're not her love interest. You're not the character without a personality who only exists to make someone else seem desirable." Josh picks up his soup spoon. "That's not you."

"You're right. I'm supposed to be the person who's happier being alone."

"If that were true, you wouldn't be here right now," he points out.

Her chest heaves and she can't swallow down a sob. "How are they engaged?" Two more whimpers and tears start to fall. "When you love someone y-you don't just erase them—"

Her face crumples; in a second, she's full-on bawling into the salad.

He's seen Ari wavering on the precipice of tears, but she'd always managed to hold them back.

"I-I'm not even sure I wanted to get married. I did it for her. She wanted that official commitment. Somebody *loved* me and I was finally on the inside of this circle." Her breathing stutters and the sentences come out in a torrent. "I tried to be what she w-wanted because it felt so good when she was happy with me. All that bullshit about anarchy and demolishing hierarchy had nothing to do with it. She just didn't want *me* anymore." She chokes on a sob. "I hate myself for it. I'm s-so lonely and I don't want to cry about it because if I let myself cry, I won't stop. I know i-it wasn't working, so why am I—" She gasps like she needs to refill her lungs. "I don't cry. I d-don't—"

There's a series of desperate, gasping inhales with no release.

Ari pushes the salad to the side and lays her head down over her arms and continues to cry.

In another timeline, Josh instinctively reaches out his hand to touch her hand. He jumps out of his chair and rushes to the other side of the table. He embraces her hunched shoulders and whispers soothing platitudes into her ear.

But in this reality, he's still unsure whether he has an actual role to play here. He settles for moving his foot so that it pushes gently against her boot. She's not tapping against the floor anymore.

Slowly, he slides his bowl of matzo ball soup across the table in front of her.

When Ari lifts her head, she's red in the face, cheeks damp, what's left of her eyeliner streaking across her temples. Her brow furrows, like she's confused about why he's still there. But she sucks in a breath, picks up the spoon, and bisects the matzo ball.

"Thank you," she mutters, wiping her eyes with the back of her hand.

He passes her a stack of napkins.

"Don't be nice to me." She blows her nose. "It's making me feel worse."

"You're the only person I'm nice to. If you weren't around, I'd have no redeeming qualities."

Ari dabs at the outer corners of her eyes with a napkin.

"You don't want to witness this. I'm going to cry until I'm dehydrated, smoke a bowl, and fall asleep with my hand inside a bag of Takis. It's my process, I've been refining it over many years." She slices the other matzo ball.

Josh watches her swallow another spoonful of soup. How is it possible to be so goddamn frustrated with someone, while also wanting her to close her eyes and rest her head on your shoulder?

"Jewish penicillin," he says. "It cures anything."

"Grief?" She slurps on the broth. "Self-loathing?"

"No." He collects a thick stack of napkins. "You have to order the borscht for that."

15

Sat, Dec 31, 9:13 P.M.
JOSH: ETA?
It's on 77th. The New-York Historical Society.

ARI: oh no

JOSH: What?

ARI: bad news: i'm waiting at the entrance to the Staten Island
Historical Society.
Good news: there's an amazing wu-tang exhibit
I'm down the block—I had to stop at Gray's Papaya

JOSH: We're about to attend a dinner.

ARI: ok but have you had the papaya drink?

JOSH: No.
No one orders the papaya drink.
Can you hurry?

The sooner I show up to this event celebrating a family business I ruined, the sooner I can leave.

ARI: So glad you invited me to this!

Ten minutes later, Josh spots a long, gray puffy coat bobbing down Seventy-seventh Street. Ari is walking a bit unsteadily through the slush in high heels. Her hair is down in loose waves, longer than he remembers. Maybe. He can't recall the last time he saw her without a messy bun or a ponytail. Or wearing lipstick. It's not a huge transformation—except that the last time they were together, she had a serious case of raccoon eyes after running into her ex-wife. But she clearly put effort into this and there's something . . . affecting about it. Even if she's clutching an enormous Gray's Papaya cup.

"Hey, Dust Daddy!" She moves a bit closer, into his personal space. Are they supposed to hug? Air-kiss? "I updated your contact name."

"To 'Dust Daddy'?"

"Hey, what's my contact name in your phone? First and last?" Ari reaches for his device, which he quickly holds up out of her reach. They end up colliding and she blinks and steps back. "Oh my God. You shaved." Ari takes her hand, still warm from the pocket of her coat, and presses it against his face, rubbing her thumb along his cold cheek.

"What do you think?" It's been so long since someone touched him with any degree of tenderness, he's tempted to tilt his head and lean into it.

"I'm still processing," she says, withdrawing her hand. "I like seeing your face."

He pulls himself together, swallows, and checks his phone. "You're late. It's almost nine-thirty—"

"There was no chance I was going to be on time, walking in heels this high." She takes a step back. "And see? I ordered a coat. It's like a sleeping bag with sleeves and it was on sale for the equivalent of five best-man toasts on NeverTired." Ari spins around. "Are you happy now?"

Josh considers it for a second, trying to tease apart "happy" from a confused swirl of other emotions that have been bubbling up since that evening at the Strand and Veselka and the not-date that felt suspiciously more . . . *something* than any of the actual dates he's been on in the last month. More like the best and worst parts of a brand-new relationship, after you've both broken the surface of polite conversation.

Ari looks at him with raised eyebrows, still waiting.

"Oh," he replies. "Yeah. Good."

It forces him to consider what she's wearing underneath.

Why hadn't they discussed their outfits? Did Ari even own a dress for a black-tie event?

"Let's strategize. If you give me this signal"—she mimes a blow job with her fist and her tongue pressing against the inside of her cheek—"from across the table, we'll make a run for it?"

He nods toward the museum entrance. "Come on."

"Want the rest of this?" she asks, thrusting the papaya drink at him. There's lipstick on the straw.

He wordlessly grabs it and throws it in the trash can on the corner.

In the lobby, a dour young woman holding an iPad—who is *not* amused when Ari gives their names as "Dust Daddy and Plus One"—directs them to the coat check.

Ari slips off the puffy coat, revealing a fluid silk dress with a slit that comes way up her thigh. She glances at him for a nanosecond, but his eyes lock on to her back first, because, well, it's *bare,* except for two dangerously thin straps that cross once. He's never actually seen this part of her: graceful curves and muscles that reveal themselves when she hands the coat across the counter. He's still staring—had the coat-check person said something?—when she turns around and asks if her dress is okay.

"I stuffed a cardigan into my coat pocket if it's too—"

"No!" Josh says too quickly. "It's"—*the straps are so precarious. One unplanned twist of the shoulder and*—"nice."

"I thought we could go all in on the goth-wedding-guest aesthetic," she says. "I took a wild leap of faith that you'd also be wearing black."

He allows himself to look again. The neckline plunges into a low V. This, too, provides new visual information. Her breasts are covered by two small triangles of fabric held up by those tiny straps—the kind of thing where it's very apparent that there couldn't be a bra underneath. "I like it."

"I've had it for a while," she explains, fiddling with her gold earring. He hands over his coat and takes the claim ticket, feeling slightly deflated that this was a Cass-era dress. "Can we hit the bar first?"

Josh points in the direction of the elevator, happy to delay this interaction with his mother.

"You look really nice, too," she adds.

His right hand keeps trying to place itself on the small of her back as they walk. He clenches it in a fist.

The bar is set up in a gallery that resembles a dark jewel box, lined with antique Tiffany lamps, all dramatically lit.

"Why are these parties so upscale and expensive if the point is to raise money?" she asks, stopping in front of the translucent staircase in the middle of the gallery and turning around to face him. Her face is illuminated by the softly glowing colored glass.

"I suppose I did agree that you could complain the whole time."

She pauses to read a text panel next to a glass display case. "Huh. Turns out that Louis Comfort Tiffany didn't even design most of these. As usual, it was a woman, toiling in obscurity."

Josh scans the paragraph.

"It says she and her staff were 'well-compensated,'" he points out.

"Yeah, well it doesn't say 'Clara Driscoll Gallery' on the door. Clara Driscoll's ancestors aren't benefitting from generations of inherited wealth."

"Seriously, no more museums for you."

"Am I getting the hairbrush again, Dust Daddy?" she says loudly as a gray-haired couple passes by.

Josh feels a buzzy sensation, but this time it really is his phone. Mostly.

9:47 P.M.

ABBY: Where are you?

JOSH: Getting a drink.

ABBY: Dinner starts in 10.

JOSH: Ari wants to look at the lamps.

ABBY: Oh! Your date? Tell her to enjoy and take as much time as she wants!

After taking more time than necessary to down two more drinks, they meander upstairs to the dinner.

His mother isn't hard to spot; she's holding court in a semi-circle of well-dressed benefactors in the center of the room.

Abby hones in on Ari like a heat-seeking missile before Josh can weave through the crowd and set expectations. He'd planned to introduce her as a friend. Instead, he watches his mother hold Ari's shoulders at arm's length as if she's examining a sweater at Bergdorf Goodman.

"IF ONE MORE WOMAN IN NICOLE MILLER PRETENDS TO COMPLIMENT MY Louboutins so she can ask me if it's a good time to list a two-bedroom, I'm going to lose it. Thank God you're here."

What Ari had presumed would be a polite handshake with Josh's mom turns into a "hello hug," which becomes a full-on, lingering, motherly *embrace*. Ari stiffens at the unexpected tenderness. Sometimes it's not until she encounters genuine parental affection that she recognizes the utter lack of it in her life. It hurts more to fill the cavity than to leave it empty.

"It's nice to meet you, Mrs. Kestenberg," Ari says while they're still mid-squeeze. She doesn't mention that Cass *is* listing their two-bedroom, but from what she's gathered from Josh, Queens isn't exactly his mom's market.

"Call me Abby. And it's Cohen, not Kestenberg, by the way. I kept my own name before it was a thing. Women weren't doing that in the eighties. Are you planning to keep your name?"

"Oh, um," Ari says, unprepared for this line of questioning. Josh is somewhere behind them, caught in a conversation with someone. "I actually never thought about it." Which is true. She and Cass never discussed it.

Ari finds herself distracted by the charmingly imperfect application of Abby's eye shadow as she tilts her head down, conspiratorially. "Josh never liked introducing us to his girlfriends, so when he told me he was bringing someone—"

"Oh, I'm not, like, a *someone*," Ari protests. Ten feet away,

Josh maneuvers around partygoers with a panicked expression. "We're just—"

"Joshua!" Abby drops her arm and gives her son a careful peck on the cheek without actually touching his face. "Before we sit down, let's take a picture in front of the step-and-repeat. I think we have time before the amuse-bouche."

Josh rolls his eyes. "This isn't prom. I don't want to draw more attention to myself with photos."

"We should definitely take a prom picture," Ari suggests, letting her nervous-babbling coping mechanism take the reins. She subtly readjusts her dress, making sure her right boob is safely hidden behind a piece of black silk that feels way too flimsy. Clearly, it was a mistake to choose something unabashedly sexy knowing she'd be meeting Josh's mother. "The classic pose on a staircase, so you're three feet taller than me. I never got to do that." Abby's eyes light up. Even though it's probably because she's envisioning future grandchildren, it feels like validation. "Did you go to prom?"

"No, he didn't," Abby answers. "Anyway, half the people in this room have been canceled or Me Too'ed. You're hardly the only person here trying to control the narrative."

"I wasn't canceled," he mutters, but Abby's already hustling them to the photographer, where she insists on multiple poses with Ari and a begrudging Josh.

"Let's do one with just the two of us," Abby says, putting her arm around Ari, like they've known each other forever. As if this woman—a high-powered real estate broker? Venerated restaurateur? Friend of Countess Luann?—has any reason to pose in front of a New York City Department of Cultural Affairs logo with her son's inappropriately dressed friend who ghostwrites raunchy maid-of-honor speeches. "Now, Ari, what do you do?"

"She's a comedian," Josh volunteers.

"Really!" Abby exclaims with genuine excitement. "Now, is it 'comedian' or 'comedienne'?"

"Usually it's 'waitress'!" Ari quips, making Josh's mother laugh a lot harder than the joke deserves. Ari's brain begins scanning for new potential ways to achieve the dopamine hit of making Abby crack up again. "Comedy doesn't really need more ways to make gender more obvious."

"You're absolutely right," Abby says with a serious nod. She leans in and whispers, "Josh could still be the David Chang of pastrami sandwiches, you know."

A voice over the sound system announces the start of the dinner. Ari tries not to think about which catering company booked this gig and whether she could have been getting extra holiday pay tonight by refilling glasses of champagne instead of drinking them.

"I feel like I'm at church," Ari observes, looking up at the stained-glass windows and fifty-foot ceilings that ring the space.

"They do absolutely beautiful weddings in here," Abby says. She's unstoppable. "Only twenty thousand for a Saturday night reception."

A woman with blown-out hair and questionable lip fillers touches Josh's mother on the shoulder to congratulate her on a closing. Abby holds up a finger to pause the greeting.

"Ari, sit next to me? I want to hear all about your comedy and how you two met. Joshua is always so secretive. Taking an interest in your son's life isn't 'meddling.'" She doesn't wait for a response, taking a step away from the table to graciously listen to the woman's complaints about her co-op board.

Ari turns to Josh, who pulls out the chair in front of her. "Do you want to describe the tentacle dildo, or should I?"

"My mother thinks she can speak things into existence through sheer force of will," he whispers over the cacophony, his mouth very close—almost ASMR-close—to her ear. "I'll straighten it out."

They both sit as a waiter offers them a champagne refill. A curator on the left side of the table blathers on about how his team selected the featured photographs for the exhibition, all the while focusing his eyes approximately ten inches below Ari's face. He introduces himself as "Dr. Davison." No first name mentioned, probably to force everyone to use the title "Dr." She longs for her cardigan.

Abby returns to her seat next to Ari and picks up where they left off.

"So have you performed with anyone I'd know? I love Amy Schumer."

Ari disguises a snort and shakes her head. "I don't think so. Though I might have opened for a guy that wiped down tables at the Comedy Cellar before one of Amy Schumer's sets."

"I find it absolutely fascinating." Abby places all her focus on Ari and it feels like something in between a beam of sunshine and an interrogation lamp. "The kind of self-confidence you need to get up in front of strangers and try to make them laugh."

"My friend Gabe always says that performing is equal parts masochism and praise kink." Ari feels her cheeks heat. She should've paraphrased that, but Abby lets out a laugh. "Improv gives you something totally unique as a performer." She pauses in case Josh's mom is just making polite small talk. But Abby's still listening intently, with her chin in her palm. "You're part of a team and there's so much trust there. With the right group of people and a good audience, you can feel it under your skin, just this . . . giddiness. You're in control, but only to a certain extent, and you have to be vulnerable enough to accept the surprises. It's this series of moments that are never going to happen quite that way ever again. You can't hold on to it. You can't repeat it. You can make the most perfect joke in the universe and you know it'll only happen once. It's magic."

Abby nods. "That's exactly how I feel when a property goes into escrow."

Ari continues, barely pausing to breathe. "And if I can get another comedian to laugh at my joke or to get my team member to break onstage? I'll wake up the next morning thinking about it. Replaying it. I could live off that feeling for days. What other profession gives you that high after seven minutes onstage, making up ridiculous shit?"

"Politics?" the leering curator offers. She hadn't noticed the entire table listening.

Ari smiles and digs into her limp salad, suddenly self-conscious about the whole monologue.

"I like her, Joshua." Abby takes a big gulp of her drink. "I *like* her."

EVEN THOUGH THE EVENT OSTENSIBLY CELEBRATES PURVEYORS OF "iconic New York cuisine," Josh finds the "late dinner" predictably bland, even by his dad's standards. Maybe Danny Kestenberg didn't have an adventurous palate, but he'd never serve people soggy latkes. Josh looks down at the black square plate in front of him, wishing it was one of his dad's thick white dishes with perfectly juicy slices of brisket and a sauce that was always a touch too sweet.

Following the meal, there's an endless presentation about the museum's "groundbreaking" upcoming exhibition on New

York's deadliest maritime disasters and, finally, a brief musical performance. This is supposed to be the impressive part but it's the third fundraiser he's attended in five years with John Legend as the featured entertainer.

He watches a smattering of couples give each other "should we?" looks and decide to get up out of their seats after John Legend invites everyone to the dance floor during a slow cover of "Open Your Eyes." In a move that Ari surely could not miss, Abby shifts forward to give Josh a hard stare. He doesn't turn his head, just works his jaw, willfully ignoring her. If his mother could somehow manage to kick him under the table with Ari sitting between them, she would.

Before Abby can utter any embarrassing verbal prompts, the insufferable curator materializes behind them. Josh braces himself for some additional anecdote about funding for the exhibition.

"Shall we?" the man asks, extending his hand to Ari.

Josh blinks, immobilized. Twin flames of outrage and jealousy spark in his chest, witnessing the guy's sudden chutzpah.

"I'm way too sober to dance," she replies.

"It's three minutes of your life, tops."

"You're definitely not the first man to tell me that."

The guy cackles. *Cackles.*

With what Josh interprets as extreme reluctance, she places her palm in the curator's hand.

"I *knew* there'd be dancing," Ari whispers in Josh's ear as she rises from her seat.

Josh watches her follow him to the dance floor. She's asking him why they couldn't have spent the John Legend money on historic preservation.

"Why didn't you ask her?" his mother scolds when they're barely out of earshot. "This is his last song. It's almost midnight."

"I don't want to dance," he says. His mouth tenses into a flat, tight line. Possibly a scowl.

"You're a terrible liar," Abby notes, examining her buzzing phone. "And stubborn. Just like your father." She can push his buttons at the worst moments. "You have to put your pride aside occasionally. If either one of you had . . ."

Josh tunes out his mother's unsolicited diagnosis. He watches the curator spin Ari around. She's not exactly graceful, but she's good at finding enjoyment in stupid shit like this in a way that Josh just can't. He works his jaw again, wondering how many dresses Ari tried on before choosing that one. Wondering if this is one of those situations where *she'd* want to be rescued.

After another vigorous spin, they slow down. Ari catches his eye and silently mouths "help." Or, at least, Josh convinces himself that she does.

"Why are you still sitting here, Joshua?"

He isn't sure if Abby says it or his champagne-soaked subconscious imagines her saying it.

Either way, Josh finds himself pushing back from the table.

It doesn't occur to him until he gets within a few feet of Ari and her partner: He has no fucking clue how to cut in on someone in real life without looking like an awkward, lumbering creep.

Luckily, looking like an awkward, lumbering creep forces insufferable curators to step back and drop the hands of other people's New Year's Eve pity dates. Who knew?

He remains still as everyone else on the dance floor moves around him, like he's a minor nuisance. A giant orange cone in the middle of a sidewalk. Ari's a foot away. Facing him. Alone. In that dress.

It takes a beat for Josh to remember why he's standing there.

"I was just getting a lecture about the pneumatic-tube waste system on Roosevelt Island." Ari takes a tiny step closer. "Good timing."

"That would be a first for us."

And then they get confused about where to put their hands.

Somehow Ari's left arm ends up around Josh's waist, while his right hand is on her left shoulder, as if they're junior high school students forced to partner up in gym class.

"I'm used to dancing with a woman," she points out. "What's your excuse?"

John Legend croons about sitting alone. Regretting an old love. Finding the right one.

Back at the table, Abby positions her phone to take a candid photo.

He'd mind *more* if he wasn't enjoying the fringe benefit of dancing, which is that the correct position of his right hand is against Ari's lower back.

Neither of them says anything as they shuffle back and forth. He can't quite find the beat but he can feel her breathing. She's looking over his shoulder, watching couples—who are more comfortable holding each other—do a box step.

"Despite your assurances, your mom seems to be under the impression that we're . . ." She looks around the room like the right word will appear in one of the gobo lights projecting color onto the walls. "An actual couple."

He's close enough to catch the scent of her shampoo—grapefruit? Something subtle that he wants to keep breathing in. "It's wishful thinking."

She finally looks into his eyes. Her cheeks are red. "'Wishful thinking'?"

Did it have to be a song about seeing the light? At this specific moment?

Dozens of other couples sway around them: older people, second or third marriages, if he had to guess. They all had that moment when they weighed the risk of another failure against the possibility of forever.

"Josh . . ." She swipes the back of her hand against her forehead. He can't tell if her tone is in the realm of "letting you down gently" or "confused about my feelings, too."

It's selfish to want more from this. But he's always been selfish.

He spins up a few possible responses, most notably: *It just occurred to me that you're the perfect height for me right now and if I just tilt my head down slightly—*

"Can we—can we leave before the countdown?" She gulps a breath, like there's not enough oxygen in the ballroom. "And the kissing?"

She looks over his shoulder with a pained expression and Josh pushes aside the uncomfortable truth that dancing with him apparently flipped her mood.

"We don't have to kiss."

"It's just that . . ." He notices a sheen of sweat on her forehead. Despite their lethargic dancing, her breathing is rapid and shallow. "I need air."

"Oh." *Fuck.* "Of course. We can get out of here," he says, hoping to fend off the possibility of a romance-induced panic attack. *Fuckfuckfuck.* "Do you want to go home?"

"I can't. I rented out my apartment on Airbnb. I'm staying at Gabe's."

"Right." His mind skims a quick geographical survey of their current location. "I think I know where we can go."

"CONGRATULATIONS," ARI CALLS OUT. JOSH IS A FEW STEPS AHEAD OF her on the paved path, moving faster than she can manage in heels. "You're the first and last man I will follow into a poorly lit park at eleven-fifty P.M."

If there's a trace of lingering awkwardness from when they abruptly left the gala, Ari is determined to push past it. Being outside in the freezing air helps, cooling her face and neck. It felt tropical in the library or the ballroom or whatever it was. She'd been breathing in too much Chanel No 5.

"There's a good spot up here, just around this curve," Josh says. They make their way down a path that meanders and loops through Central Park. They'd passed a surprising number of bundled-up pedestrians streaming in through the Seventy-second Street entrance to the south.

"I've never seen this many people here at night," Ari says, stumbling on her heels as she ducks under a temporary barrier blocking off West Drive. "Are they here for the fireworks?"

"The New York Road Runners have a race every New Year's." He leads her across Oak Bridge, toward something that looks like a stone wall with a narrow arch, nestled between two giant rock outcrops. "They fire the starting pistol right at midnight and a thousand people run four miles around the park."

"That's an admirable commitment to physical fitness, considering the wind chill." Ari takes careful steps, balancing on her toes. "Seems like a thing *you* would do—skip a party in order to exercise."

"I don't run outside," he says. "Controlled conditions produce the best results. The treadmill helps me maintain focus and proper pacing."

". . . in bed," Ari adds, a step behind him. "Do you do that with fortune cookies? Add 'in bed' to the end of the fortunes and they somehow make more sense?"

He shakes his head. "Those cookies are always stale and flavorless."

His cookie standards must be as impossible to meet as his dating standards.

Though the trees are bare, they create an effective barrier from the cacophony that reminds her of New Year's Eves past.

Ari feels a jolt of panic as her stiletto slips down the pavement, now slick with a thin coat of frost.

"Josh!" she shouts, barely catching her balance. "I can't get down the hill in these shoes."

He turns around, sizing up her predicament. "The 'hill'? You mean this gentle slope that's graded for wheelchair access?"

"Spoken like someone who's never worn heels. Just give me your hand or something."

Josh lets out a deep sigh, as if this is the biggest possible chore.

Ari grabs his hand, takes a tiny test step, and slips again. "Shit." She looks up. "I'll have to live here."

With a shake of his head, Josh bends down, places his shoulder at her hip, and lifts her off the ground in one fluid motion.

"The hell?" she yelps, smacking him on the back, trapped in some kind of humiliating fireman carry.

"First, I don't trust you not to take me down with you," he says, heading down the slope. "Second, there's finally a point to all the lumberjack presses and triceps dips I've been doing at the gym: lifting shopping baskets and women in non-functional shoes."

"Hey!" she mutters. "Be careful where you put your hand, I can feel everything through this coat."

"Watch your head." He ducks down, passing through the arch to the other side. She can faintly catch the scent of his hair product.

"It's not my head I'm worried about."

"I'll let you carry me on the way back." He takes his damn time setting her back on her feet, with a grunt of effort. She tries to readjust her dress beneath her coat. There's a good chance her breasts escaped their insubstantial constraints. "This spot is off the race route," he says. "There's a boarded-up cave somewhere around here."

Ordinarily, Ari would be scrambling down the rocks to check out the cave, but at the moment, she has a more pressing need.

"Mind if I smoke this?" She retrieves a joint from her little clutch. It seemed classier than a vape pen.

He shakes his head and brushes some microscopic dirt off a large boulder before taking a seat.

"I kind of felt a"—she makes a jittery hand gesture—"*thing* coming on at the party."

"I noticed."

Ari flicks her lighter and slowly creates a cherry, rolling the joint between her fingers over the flame, pausing to take a small drag. She probably should do some deep breathing that doesn't involve smoke inhalation, but when has that ever worked in a crisis?

She takes a long hit before offering it to him.

His gears turn for a few seconds, but she's pleasantly surprised when he reaches for the joint. Ari leans against the cold rock wall of the arch, watching him draw the smoke in.

"It's bad for your palate," he says, "but who fucking cares now? It's not like I'm at risk of oversalting someone's duck confit."

There's a retort on the tip of her tongue, but who is she to lecture anyone about giving up?

"Your mom was pretty much running a visual analysis on the childbearing capabilities of my hips."

"It's hardwired in her amygdala." He carefully passes the joint back to her and their cold fingers brush for a second. There's a quick flash in her mind's eye: Josh's hand pressing against her lower back twenty minutes ago. Then tangled in her hair, holding it back. Pulling. That part's not a memory fragment. It's . . . something else. Too many cocktails, maybe. "My mother can't help trying to fix my life."

"It's nice. I mean, I can see how that would be comforting—to have someone want that for you." The contrast between the icy December air and the hot smoke shocks her lungs.

"When my dad and I weren't speaking, she was the go-between. I think she still believes she can stitch that relationship back together even though he's gone." He takes a second hit and passes it back, leaning against the outcrop. "Fuck, this stuff always makes my heart race."

Ari looks up at the night sky. The canopy of tree branches obstructs any view of the stars.

"I hate that I'm still wondering what Cass is doing tonight," she says, letting the words spill out. "I hate that I can't brush my teeth or pee without remembering how I hid in the bathroom while she cleared everything out of our apartment. I hate that I'm a creep who still sends her these photos just to provoke a reaction and prove to myself that she wanted me at one point." Josh opens his eyes. "I'm one hundred percent sure that I'll never give another person this . . . power ever again. I just want someone who makes me feel good for an hour and who won't trick me into thinking it's anything more than that."

She waits for him to either argue or reassure her.

It feels like a full minute before he responds. "Just an hour, huh?" He blinks up at her.

"Too optimistic? Fine. Thirty minutes."

Ari takes one more hit and gently stubs out the joint, taking a seat next to him. She lets the THC and the cocktails dilute the noise from other people's celebrations. For right now, it doesn't feel like a park shared with millions of other people.

"You had one bad experience," he says.

She shakes her head. "That's the thing. There were really good parts. If it was all bad it wouldn't hurt so much and I could just let it go."

It's quiet except for the occasional crunch of leaves or errant police siren in the distance.

A long lull.

"Music?" she suggests, not wanting to risk Josh gently drifting off to sleep in Central Park in December.

He reaches in his pocket for his phone, sitting up a little bit.

"'Auld Lang Syne'?"

Ari shakes her head. "Play something that feels poignant but not overly celebratory."

He furrows his brow, sighs, and then types something into Spotify. A few seconds later, the reverb-heavy opening strums of "Don't Dream It's Over" ring out through his iPhone.

"This is a perfect fucking song," he says as the bass guitar kicks in. "Just as Neil Finn intended it to be heard: from a speaker the size of a pebble."

"Neil who? I thought Miley Cyrus wrote this." Ari smiles

innocently, taking too much pleasure in his exasperated expression. She stands up, immediately feeling stiletto torture pain. "Hey, if we stand under the arch, the sound will bounce."

"Technically, it'll reflect."

She takes a step forward and holds out her hand. "Want to?"

"Dance?" He raises his eyes to hers, like he's not completely sure if she's being sincere.

"I mean, we clearly both need the practice and I spent most of that song making sure that curator couldn't see my nipples." She makes a more exaggerated gesture. "If you're waiting for me to lift you over my shoulder you can forget it."

He grabs her hand, and she pulls him up to stand. They step inside the narrow passageway.

The curved walls amplify the sound, enveloping them in a ghostly echo, with a sliver of the harsh light from a streetlamp streaking across the ground. They forego the hand/shoulder/waist combination they got wrong before. Ari puts her arms around his neck, and he puts his around her waist, with the phone in his hand gently poking into her back through the down coat. They sway from side to side, not really to the beat.

"I'm never sure if this song is melancholy or hopeful," Josh says, looking down—or is this gazing?—at her in that specific intense way, where it feels like he can see inside her. It's not banter. It's not amusement or anger or frustration or any other emotion they've volleyed back and forth for two months.

"Can't it be both?" Ari rests her head against his shoulder, maybe to escape the intimacy of unbroken eye contact, maybe because the music and the rocking back and forth feel like a lullaby.

Or maybe it's all the cocktails and weed.

It's probably that.

With her ear pressed to his chest she feels his pulse pounding, fast and erratic. He'd said that was a side effect of smoking, hadn't he?

Somewhere beyond this cluster of trees the occasional celebratory *Whoop!* goes up, followed by cheers and noisemakers.

"Almost midnight," Ari points out.

A strong gust of wind cuts through the archway and the layers of synthetic down she'd just purchased yesterday. Despite her best efforts to channel a warm boozy feeling from the champagne, she visibly shivers.

Which is why she nestles into him.

Josh pulls her in closer and tries to wrap his coat around both of them. It doesn't quite work—they're making a shadow on the pavement in the light from the streetlamp that resembles Frankenstein's monster—but the gesture is nice. Ari waits for him to take a half-step back, but he doesn't.

Neither does she.

"This year was terrible." She looks up at him, waiting for him to agree. He's still giving her that look. "But I'm glad I met you again. Becoming friends was the best thing to happen to me in a long time." She hears herself sounding sloppier, the pot and the alcohol teaming up and wresting control of the wheel.

He works his jaw like he's fighting the urge to say something. She's both desperate to hear it and terrified.

"Ari, I—"

"Because you're so important to me. You have no idea. You're kind of the best thing to happen to me in a long time."

"You said that already." His eyes move across her face.

"I did?"

The arch seems to be rocking back and forth like a seesaw. She puts her head back down on his chest and closes her eyes.

That helps. Neil Finn sings about counting the steps to the door of your heart.

The fuzzy sounds of revelers on Central Park West become louder. A noisy group stops on the bridge directly above them, over the arch.

"I think it's almost midnight," she says, lifting her head. The cheering in the distance grows louder.

"You said that already, too." Friends don't look at each other like that, eyes darting down to her lips every so often. "You're so—"

"Are we going to—you know . . ." Ari trails off, feeling him breathing through his tuxedo jacket, heavy and even. "Um . . . after the countdown?"

"Yes."

The song seems to grow bigger, the bass line of the chorus echoing off the stone over their heads.

There's chanting from the buildings across the park. *"Ten! . . . Nine! . . ."*

She swallows. "Like, a peck on the cheek or—"

"No."

"Eight! . . . Seven! . . ."

"So, quickly, but on the lips?"

"No."

"Six!"

"I just want to know—"

"Five!"

"—so we don't do something awkward, because—"

"Four!"

"—it's kind of a one-shot deal."

"Three!"

"It is."

Ari feels his right hand move up her spine all the way to the back of her head, and God, she really *can* feel everything through this coat. They stop the half-hearted swaying, even though the song isn't over. His fingers twist slightly in her hair.

"*Two!*"

The prickly sensation running along the back of her neck is probably from the wind kicking up. It's not because he tugs her head back a little bit and looks at her in that way that makes her feel completely exposed, even though she's wrapped in a thick layer of polyfill and down. She closes her eyes.

There must be a "*One!*" but neither of them hear it.

Her head tilts to the right and she feels Josh's lower lip graze hers. That tiny amount of contact ignites something in her chest. Ari grabs at his lapels, pulling him closer, parting, opening, inviting. He obliges with a trace of caution, pressing in again.

His lips are soft and tentative against hers, the friction warming them against the winter air. He pulls back for a moment, just far enough to search her face. His expression is resolute but he's waiting for something. Ari lets out a shaky exhale and nods.

He doesn't move yet.

"Josh . . ." She's about to tug at his coat again, when he suddenly lowers his head, moving just past her left cheek.

Her breath hitches as Josh's nose brushes behind her ear, followed by his lips. He pulls her hair again, this time to the right for better access to her neck. Her whole body shivers as his mouth passes over a thousand tiny nerve endings, all of them firing at once. Her stomach tightens. How is he doing this? Why does he have this innate sense of where and how she wants to be touched?

Some first kisses are hurried—an awkward tangle of hands and noses.

But Josh takes his time, spurred on by little whimpers that she can't hold in, moving lazily down her neck and kissing along her jawline until they come face-to-face again.

This is the first point at which they could—*should*—stop.

But they don't.

The celebratory roar of a million strangers recedes into the background. Ari murmurs his name just before she pulls his head down, so their lips meet again. Some element of his restraint snaps as he slides his tongue into her mouth with an urgency that leaves her breathless. Josh's fingers move across her collarbone, thumbs meeting at the base of her throat.

That's the second point at which they don't stop.

The third is when his hands find their way under her puffy coat, meandering down the bare skin of her back, and then slipping beneath the silky fabric of the dress. He palms her ass and she can't help moaning into his mouth and he could take one step and back her up against that wall.

There's a part of Ari's mind that's throwing caution tape all over the encounter. The acceptable boundaries of "just friendship" are getting pulled and stretched to the point of imminent tearing.

But they don't stop here, either.

Because something is incredibly *right* about it. There's a pleasant ache in her belly and a tangled web of surging emotions and *who the fuck cares about friendship when you can feel like this instead of being numb?*

She's reaching up to run her fingers through his hair—something she's always thought about doing, if she's honest—when a loud *CRACK* rips through the freezing air, snapping both of them out of their shared feverish haze.

They both recoil. Ari knocks against the back wall and Josh

pulls his hands away like an old-timey schoolmaster smacked them with a ruler.

A sustained cheer erupts from somewhere to the south.

The thing that finally stops them from committing a misdemeanor is the starting pistol of the New York Road Runners Midnight Run.

They stare at each other for what seems like a full minute, both of them waiting for the other to do something. It would be easy enough to just step forward again. She could bite her lip. He might shrug and glance at the ground. They'd get back into it with a certain shyness this time. With more intention.

But as two, five, ten seconds pass, the strange, electric energy that enveloped them dissipates like a breath in the cold air.

Maybe it hadn't been the pistol. It could have been a lightning bolt thrown down by the goddess of *For Fuck's Sake, Don't Run This Friendship Off a Cliff*.

Her throat is burning with the urge to explain why the kiss shouldn't be the start of some epic romance. That they can just stay right where they are. Or, wherever they were yesterday. If one more precious thing in her life falls away, it'll be unbearable.

But the world is still spinning a bit, like she's just stepped off a carousel.

"That was . . ." She trails off, unsure what she'd intended to say.

Right now, "just friends" is a comfortable certainty. A gravity blanket. A subtle vanilla-scented candle.

And the alternative is a giant blinking cursor and a blank document. Sometimes it feels like Josh has already been poking around that page. Writing passages and deleting them before she's ready to open it.

Something in his expression turns cloudy.

"It was just a New Year's kiss," he says after an eternity of honking horns and off-key renditions of "Auld Lang Syne." "And the pot."

"Right," is all she manages, all her rhetorical skill apparently buried under the combination of mind-altering substances, adrenaline, and unfulfilled need.

"It doesn't have to be . . . anything." His voice is firm; his face tells another story. He must be transmitting some kind of clue, but Ari can't decipher it.

A sharp gust of wind billows around her unzipped coat. He turns toward the incline that leads back to Central Park West. "We should move before they close off the path for the race."

He heads through the arch, not waiting for her, not hesitating when she doesn't immediately follow.

Ari stays put for a few more seconds, wondering if he might stop and turn around, giving her time to catch up. But he keeps walking away, not even slowing his pace.

Pushing off the wall, she hurries after him.

Maybe this will be fine. Maybe this is how normal people deal with mistakes. They just keep moving forward. She reminds herself to take some deep breaths, but the freezing air hurts her lungs.

As soon as she gets to the spot where the hill starts to rise, her beautiful, impractical stiletto slips on the frost-covered pavement again, sending a jolt of panic through her body as she catches herself.

"Josh!" She turns to the side and takes tiny, shuffling steps, feeling ridiculous. "I can't get up the hill."

"I guess you'll just have to live there," Josh calls over his shoulder. He takes his time coming back for her.

16

Wed Jan 4, 11:24 P.M.

JOSH: I already selected tonight's film.

Does Donnie Darko hold up?

Disaffected teen Josh Kestenberg thought it was the height of cinema.

11:34 P.M.

ARI: sorry can't tonight

really busy

JOSH: At 11:34 pm?

ARI: didn't you say I should get back out there?

Catch up later?

Mon, Jan 9, 9:57 P.M.

JOSH: Hello?

Still busy?

10:26 P.M.

ARI: hi

I served all the canapés in the tri-state area

JOSH: Are you serving canapés on Sunday?

There's a Buster Keaton series at Film Forum.

ARI: can't

Helping with Radhya's popup

JOSH: Right.

Sun, Jan 15, 10:23 A.M.

UNKNOWN NUMBER: Ari! Abby Cohen here.

Had a lightning bolt idea. Would love to discuss.

Can you meet for a quick coffee tomorrow morning around 9?

THE INTERIOR OF BOHEMIAN GARDEN HAS A CERTAIN UNPRETENTIOUS charm. The smell of spilled beer and grilled sausage has been seeping into the dark wood paneling for fifty years. For today only, Radhya has masked it with turmeric, cardamom, coriander, and tamarind. She and Ari covered the beer promos with decorative pieces borrowed from Radhya's cousin's wedding: thick garlands of artificial marigolds in yellow and red, parasols hung from the ceiling, long strands of tassels and pompoms.

"Let's review the evidence." Gabe expertly spreads a block print tablecloth over a four-top. "You hang out. You text all day."

"We really don't," Ari says, placing stainless steel spice boxes at each booth. It's not a lie because they've hardly exchanged more than a handful of *hey*s in the last week.

Conveniently, the gig economy provides evergreen excuses such as: "Can't tonight, I'm pouring wine/serving shrimp puffs/

walking five dogs/signing terrifying relationship-severing legal paperwork/writing a bar mitzvah speech."

And it's not avoidance if you actually answer the text.

Besides, Ari's been going out more than ever—she's never experienced this level of popularity on dating apps—but navigating the dynamics of dating and sex and boundaries and comfort levels with *two* strangers instead of just one has been exhausting. Witnessing "new to poly" couples steer themselves through the volatile waters of opening up their relationships for the first time, Ari feels a profound sense of relief that she can walk away from any of them, at any moment.

And there's a Josh-shaped indent underneath all the new conversations.

"You spend hours on the phone at night, talking about God knows what—"

"Movies." Ari busies herself by pouring Radhya's spiced nuts and poppadoms into small bowls.

"I happen to know that Ari Sloane doesn't actually *watch* movies."

"I've been watching them," she insists.

"You should've banged immediately and gotten it out of your system." Gabe is loving this drama, practically dancing to the next table. "You let it fester—"

"Can you not use the term 'fester'?"

"—then you bypassed the meaningless sex part and went straight for making out on a national holiday. Now he thinks you're dating."

"He doesn't." She's pretty sure he doesn't. "He's a friend. We've been very clear about that." *Have we?*

"Okay, but I bet he fucks." Something clatters from the

kitchen, as if to underline Gabe's assertion. "From what I've seen, he has that ugly-hot thing happening."

"Will you stop saying that?" Ari sets down a trio of decorative candles on the long, communal table. "It's rude."

Great, now all she can think about is whether she personally agrees that Josh is "ugly-hot" or just "regular-hot" and whether the distinction even matters.

"It's a compliment!" He unfolds more brightly colored linens. "Don't pretend you're *not* into it."

She's spent the last couple weeks in only two alternating modes: wiping away the memory of the Ramble Incident and carefully preserving the visceral details in a mental scrapbook, decorated with bespoke lettering and Washi tape. No matter how many times she closes the book with a hard *thwack* and shoves it in a drawer, twenty minutes later she'll find herself running the pad of her thumb over her lower lip. Thinking. Remembering.

Shit. *Shit.*

"Are you set up out there?" Radhya yells from the kitchen. "Service was supposed to start three minutes ago."

Ari walks to the front entrance, peeking through the small window, hoping to see a mass of people outside the entrance, queued up for Radhya's Gujarati delicacies. There isn't a line, but there is someone in a black parka waiting just to the left of the door, looking up every so often, as if waiting for a first date to show up.

Gabe continues setting the tables. "This is the worst time of year to accidentally get involved with—"

"Oh God." Ari takes a second peek.

"—someone. You need to deal with this *today*—"

Josh is dressed in various shades of black, standing outside

Bohemian Garden with his arms crossed. He's not radiating nervous energy. Not occupying himself with his phone while monitoring the passersby. More like telegraphing annoyance. Tall, imposing. In absolutely no danger of cracking a smile.

She presses her back against the front wall, even though it's impossible that Josh could see her from this angle.

"—or you're locked into this through Valentine's Day. Who are you hiding from?"

"He's outside."

Gabe raises his eyebrows and unabashedly takes a look. "Hello, there."

No reason for nerves. They'd both agreed it was just a case of getting carried away by a national holiday. No big deal. Fine.

And then they hadn't spoken about it for fourteen days.

"I'll help you out," Gabe offers. "Grease the wheels."

"*No.* Things are . . . delicate right now."

He clears his throat. "Rebounds aren't supposed to be delicate. Or complicated."

"This isn't a rebound. There aren't any rebounds in this situation. Only Bumble snacks, Tinder treats, and the occasional slutty couple on Feeld."

The best thing to do is step back and reestablish some boundaries. If the last week proved anything it's how much she doesn't want to mess this up. How critical it is to get back to normal.

Gabe throws the door open and Ari feels like she's boarding the *Hindenburg.*

IT'S BEEN A LONG TIME SINCE JOSH HAD TO WAIT IN THE COLD OUTSIDE A building, giving passersby the impression that he's being stood up for a blind date.

Actually, no. The last time he lingered at an entryway, it was two weeks ago, and he was anticipating the arrival of the same latecomer.

He checks their last text exchange, in which she'd clearly stated she'd be at Bohemian Garden at three P.M. And while she hadn't explicitly invited him to Radhya's pop-up a second time, it had occurred to him that showing up to the event might present him in a magnanimous light.

Better than continuing to send her texts and receiving half-hearted, noncommittal responses.

It stands to reason that after you kiss like two people who have really, *really* been wanting to kiss each other for several long months, you are obliged to have at least one substantive conversation about what it meant.

New Year's Eve had cleaved their friendship into a clear *before* and *after*—he's only beginning to understand what the *after* looks like.

In the *after*, he and Ari haven't talked since he walked her over to Gabe's apartment from the Ramble. He'd spent the first day of a new year ruminating, caught in between the heady excitement of replaying the kiss and the disappointing way it fizzled.

And wondering if Ari and Gabe still "watch movies" together.

It's the little things he can't quite get out of his head: touching her hair for the first time, the way her cheeks were freezing and flushed and *soft,* her voice murmuring his name. New versions of things that are already so familiar to him.

But over the last two weeks, the confusing aftermath has painted over the memory of New Year's with a dark, muddy wash.

He checks his watch: 3:05 P.M.

She's never fucking on time. Is she like this at her various jobs? Does she show up late for meetings? Appointments? Dates? Does she get away with it because she always arrives with some kind of diversion? Shouting a nickname or slurping from a giant cup?

When the front door swings open, Ari is standing in the entryway, elbowing a familiar-looking man in the ribs. Why had he assumed she'd be alone? They probably have inside jokes and nicknames, too.

On second glance, they're clearly too comfortable with each other to have just met. The sight of her being so cozy with someone else makes his throat tight.

What makes it worse is that she's clearly *un*comfortable when she finally greets Josh . . . with "What are you doing here?"

"Briar wanted to come," he lies. He'd had to beg Briar to meet him here.

Josh stares at Ari for a moment, evaluating her expression. Waiting for her to betray a hint of any reaction to his surprise appearance. Relief? Satisfaction? A hint of excitement?

He sees nothing but poorly masked panic. After a beat, she leans forward and gives him a little half-hearted hug.

A hug. Since when do they hug? They've hugged *once*, at Duane Reade, when she was drunk and he was holding baby oil. Josh is certain of this.

And of course, he'll probably remember this second awkward hug as the time she felt like she had to perform a normal act of friendship in front of her *actual* friend, who she probably hugs all the fucking time.

Fuck.

He presses his boots into the sidewalk, anchoring as much as one can when already standing.

"Gabe Mendoza," the guy says, thrusting his hand out. *Right.* The "friend." Josh feels a wave of relief before he remembers it was Gabe whom Ari chose to spend the rest of New Year's with, after she kissed Josh.

"I think we met." Josh examines Gabe's face; his eyes actually appear to be twinkling. He has a smile that has either been subject to a lot of orthodontia or he's been blessed with a specific magnetism Josh certainly never received.

"Most people recognize me from the Geico commercial," Gabe says. "Or T-Mobile? The Off-Off Broadway production of *Godspell*?"

"I believe it was leaving Ari's apartment without your boxers seven years ago."

"Eight," Ari mumbles, wrenching open the heavy door as a handful of customers move past them. She's wearing a short dress—black with pink flowers—and Josh tortures himself with the thought that she's dressing up for someone else. A date?

Ever since he got back to his apartment, alone, on New Year's, his mind has been churning. Playing out scenarios. Identifying the missteps.

What if he had suggested that Ari could crash at his place instead of Gabe's? Would reality have set in under the harsh lighting and weird smells of the B train? Would they have watched a movie? Would she have slept on the sofa? Asked to borrow one of his shirts?

What if she were to peek inside the bedroom and ask to stay in his bed? Would she softly knock? Enter quietly? Maybe it wouldn't happen that way at all. He could carry her inside, with her legs wrapped around his waist and his hands firmly gripping her ass, and push her up against the wall he was supposed to paint elephant gray weeks ago?

The possibilities stretch out like tree branches, prompting endless *what-ifs*.

There's a distinct sense of unease about her today: avoiding eye contact, positioning Gabe in between them, fussing over the décor in the vestibule. She's so fucking frustrating in the way she forces him to be exactly what she needs while disregarding what he wants, or how he feels about any of it.

Mostly to separate himself from Ari, he finds himself following her friend to the bar for a drink (actually, Gabe calls it an *aperitif,* which Josh finds only slightly grating). Gabe is too glib, but at least he's not this new version of Ari who won't look at him.

While they wait for their grapefruit Boulevardiers, Gabe manages to orchestrate a conversation with a pretty redhead nursing a gin and tonic at the end of the bar.

"TWATTIE!" RADHYA JOGS OUT FROM THE KITCHEN. "PRETEND TO BE A customer? It's more obvious when spaces are empty in the daytime."

"It's filling up, though," Ari says, pulling a little bowl of chili-covered poppadoms within snacking distance, even though she'd already consumed a lunch's worth of calories in crispy flatbreads while setting up. "It's a great menu for selling drinks. Everyone will be thirsty. Maybe I can get the manager to commit to another weekend next month."

"Let's hope." Radhya adjusts her chef's coat. There's a confidence to her posture that says, "I'm in the right place, I'm taking the right steps." She's like a Mario, jumping bravely over the chasm to the next platform.

Sometimes Ari feels like a Luigi wandering back to the start of the level in search of hallucinogenic mushrooms.

Radhya shifts her focus to the bar, where Gabe is busy talking at Josh and a woman perched on a rickety barstool. It's unclear which of the two Gabe is flirting with. Probably both.

Ari sees the exact moment when Radhya's eyes double back to the taller figure. She freezes and then shakes her head slowly. "Are you fucking kidding me?" Radhya pronounces every syllable. "You brought Kestenberg? *Today?*"

Ari pulls her shoulders back. "He didn't tell me he was coming. Maybe he just wants to support you."

"I bet he does." Radhya reaches up to tighten the knot on her bandana headband. Her brown eyes ping-pong between Ari and Josh, taking stock of the way they are quite obviously communicating something by performatively *not* communicating. "You slept with him."

"I didn't!" Ari recoils like she's been shot with a paintball. "I don't even get the courtesy of you phrasing it in the form of a question?"

"Okay, well, now you're acting like you committed a crime, so that's not weird at all."

"Hel-*lo*, Ari!" A set of brightly manicured nails tap on Ari's left shoulder. She turns to see a grinning face, framed by long, glossy hair. Ari isn't sure she's ever officially *met* Briar, but she kind of wants to be her when she grows up. "Those photos of you and Josh on New Year's Eve? My fucking *heart*?"

Radhya smiles smugly. "I didn't see any New Year's pics." She hits the consonants hard on the word *pics*.

"My mom sent me these adorable candids," Briar continues. She pulls out her phone and scrolls to a photo of Ari and Josh dancing, with charmingly incorrect hand positions. Looking at it only underscores how uncomfortable everything feels right now.

Radhya arches an eyebrow. "You're his sister?"

Briar nods eagerly, offering Radhya a European-style double-cheek kiss. "I'm at 'A-Briar-Commitment' on all socials. Do you mind if I shoot some stories about the pop-up? Is there a hashtag? I know tons of food influencers. I'll post something right now. Ooh, can we film some behind-the-scenes material?" Briar asks, heading for the kitchen.

"Just sit here and try to make the table look full," Rad calls over her shoulder, leaving Ari by herself in front of a large round table. "Manspread or something."

Ari collapses onto a wooden chair and shoves a handful of spiced nut mix into her mouth. Minutes later, Briar AirDrops her eight photos documenting the final hours of last year. Ari scans them, zeroing in on Josh's hand against her bare shoulder, the ghost of a sensation making her skin tingle.

She allows her gaze to pan over to the bar. There's no reason Josh shouldn't be meeting people.

Casually dating.

Casually dating women with tight sweaters and thick, shiny auburn hair.

Ari opens her text messages, dismissing the low battery warning. The couple she'd gone home with last week are game to grab a drink ("or something") later that evening.

🐷 SALT & PEPPER MAN + BLOND HOTWIFE 🐽 : my wife is really looking forward to seeing you again

She puts her phone back in her bag, feeling temporarily buoyed, even though there's something unsettling about how the texts never come from "my wife," herself. At least he doesn't use the thumbs up emoji like most middle-aged men.

A minute later Gabe sets down four glasses and a full pitcher of pale ale on the table.

"Your *buddy* already got a number," he says in an obnoxiously chipper tone of voice.

What's the Chill Girl response to this? *Interesting! I didn't realize we're both attracted to women with breasts the size of oranges!*

Josh places napkins beneath each glass. His cheeks have more color than Ari's noticed before, but his expression is tight, like he's straining not to betray any emotion.

Ari silently helps herself to another handful of nuts while Gabe pours, filling the glasses all the way up to the brim.

He holds the pitcher over the fourth cup. "Expecting someone?"

She allows herself a half second of eye contact with Josh. "Briar's here. But she went back to the kitch—"

"Holy shit." An ounce of beer splashes onto the back of Ari's hand. Gabe lets the pitcher slam down on the table as he stares at someone behind her. "I've been following her for years!" Ari turns to see Briar returning to the table, phone in hand, coat slung over her arm. "She's 'A-Briar-Commitment' on Instagram." Gabe glares at Ari. "Why didn't you tell me that?"

"Wait. *Wait.* I know you," Briar says, pointing and trying to place him. "What's your handle?"

"I'm at 'Bye-Bye-Bi-Boy.'" He holds his arms out, almost smacking Josh in the face.

There's an earsplitting squeal and Briar scurries to the other side of the long communal table to embrace her kindred social media spirit.

"Oh my God! I had the biggest crush on you." Briar holds her hand over her mouth. "Is that okay to say?"

"Fuck, yes." They squeeze each other like long-lost friends, swaying back and forth. "Except for the 'had' part."

Ari finds her gaze dipping down to the other person at the table not involved in this hug. She can't help it. He has a face that's begging to be scrutinized. He's looking at her, too, but not in a way that makes her feel at ease.

"You know each other?" Josh asks.

"He's 'Bye-Bye-Bi-Boy'!" Briar says, like this is a common point of reference. "We've been mutuals for years. Here, Josh, sit next to Ari, so we're even."

Does Josh look reluctant as he pushes his chair back? Annoyed? Ari takes three enormous gulps of beer as Josh takes the seat next to her, like they're third and fourth wheels on an impromptu date.

THREE HOURS MUST GO BY WHILE BRIAR AND GABE GLEEFULLY DEBATE the finer points of Taylor Swift's *Folklore* and gossip about actors Josh has never heard of. Beyond a vague sense of unease, he's no closer to understanding Ari's state of mind. He pretends not to notice Radhya poking her head out of the kitchen every so often, looking increasingly frazzled as Briar's followers pack themselves into the dining area.

But when Radhya suddenly appears at their table a rush of pure anxiety shoots up his chest. Her expression is strained, like she's about to unleash a long-awaited tirade on him.

"I'm out of rotis," she hisses, squatting next to Ari. "I need you to help me griddle them. Please. It's just like making grilled cheese."

Ari is halfway out of her chair when Briar calls out, "Wait, Josh can do it!"

Radhya recoils. "God, *no*—"

"Absolutely not," Josh declares at the same instant.

"He's a professional!" Briar beams. "No offense, Ari." Josh shoots her an unsubtle warning look that she pretends not to notice. The last place he wants to be is in a kitchen—and especially not with someone who's been nursing a grudge for years.

Radhya looks like she'd rather sink into the beer-stained floor than accept Josh's assistance, but she grits her teeth (literally, she makes an actual *grimace*) and gestures toward the kitchen.

Josh pushes his chair back, letting the legs scrape against the floorboards. He follows Radhya past the other tables, into the kitchen, steeling himself and feeling conspicuous as fuck, even though he doesn't recognize any of the other diners.

It's clearly a beer hall kitchen, with multiple deep fryers and other pieces of equipment in which Josh isn't exactly well-versed. Every surface feels like it's coated with a fine mist of grease.

"Two hundred twenty-six grams of whole wheat flour in this plate," she barks, pushing a wide metal dish toward him. "Then lukewarm water—gradually."

Josh blinks at the plate for a few seconds, relieved to default into kitchen jargon instead of unwieldy apologies. He scrubs his hands in the sink. "How mu—"

"One-twenty mil, but you need to bring it together bit by bit. Watch me do the first batch before you fuck it up." Radhya drizzles the water over her own plate of flour, mixing it together with her left hand until it turns into a soft dough. She dips her hand in water and starts to knead it, keeping her hand a little more open than Josh remembers from culinary school. "Do you have any idea how aggravating it was to look at your stupid, smug face in *Bon Appétit* last year?" She says it without turning around, focusing on her roti-related tasks at the prep table.

Straight into it, then. Fine. "I want to clear the air about—"

"No. There's no 'air' to clear. This isn't one of the twelve steps. I don't care about your personal growth." Radhya finally turns her head to the left to glance at him, her hand still working the dough. "I'm happy to go on resenting you. It motivates me."

"It was a heated moment," he says, spooning the flour onto the scale. "We both went too far."

"For months, I tortured myself, going over it again and again in my head. And every time I interviewed for another job, I'd have that fucking little inkling. The imposter syndrome. This inferiority complex because I didn't get to go to culinary school and work abroad."

"I never said your technique was bad."

"Yes, you fucking did. You undermined me in front of the entire kitchen over that bullshit duck preparation at the lowest period of my life."

"Believe me," Josh says, "I'm familiar with the human cost of being humiliated."

"No." She leans in. "We're not the same. I've spent ten years taking shit from white guys like you in the kitchen," Radhya says, pushing the dough away from her, like she needs to focus on the argument without multitasking. "Watching them get promoted. Laughing off everything from microaggressions to outright sexual harassment. I've had to be twice as good and I don't get the luxury of multiple chances."

There's a good response to this but it isn't in his arsenal. "I'm glad we're finally talking about it," is all he manages.

"Wow! After five years?" Radhya takes a huge gulp from her water bottle. "What a sense of urgency you have."

"The situation was mishandled," he concedes.

"That's a passive-voice non-apology."

"I'm sorry?"

She points her index finger at Josh's chest. "Now you're getting the hang of it. Try it once more, with feeling."

"Okay." He takes a deep, fryer-oil-coated breath in. "I'm sorry." Exhale. "On some level I probably felt . . . insecure about being in charge. I was trying to maintain control and I felt . . . defensive. And I didn't realize you were going through a divorce." He pauses, trying to decipher her expression; it's both dubious and exasperated. "The truth is, I'm glad you're doing these pop-ups. You're a talented chef and the food was . . . excellent."

She doesn't reply, but nods at him to take over the kneading and he tries to mimic her actions. The dough is smooth and strangely pleasing to knead. He pushes his thumbs into it, turning it over and over.

"Where are you working these days?" she asks.

"I haven't taken out my knives in almost a year."

They work in silence for a few minutes. Josh doesn't mind. There's a soothing aspect to it, similar to his perfect knife work. Maybe a bit less violent.

She watches him add a bit more water to the flour. "I've known Ari for a long time—"

"So have I."

"No, you *haven't*," she snaps before he can add any additional evidence. "You've known her for—what?—a few months?

And for most of that time she's been miserable." Radhya grabs a thin rolling pin and starts rolling flour-dusted discs into flat, perfect circles. "Maybe you've noticed."

"Maybe I've *noticed*?" He would be gesturing wildly if his hands weren't covered in dough. "Who do you think she's been confiding in? Who spends hours on the phone with her? Who put together her Ikea furniture with those tiny hex wrenches?"

"*You* went to Ikea?"

"Who watched her melt down in front of her fucking ex? I don't remember seeing you there."

Radhya stops rolling. There's a trace of hurt in her eyes. "Right. You're treading water together."

"What?"

Radhya shakes her head and continues pushing the rolling pin in controlled, even strokes.

"I need you to understand something." There's a pointed quality to the way Radhya pauses there and meets his gaze. An unfair implication. "Ari is extremely guarded, okay? She never had a real relationship before Cass. There was a very lopsided power dynamic."

He'd clocked that almost immediately upon meeting the woman—a living, breathing lopsided power dynamic. He turns it over in his mind, the other pieces of the Ari puzzle somehow joining together with a satisfying click.

"She doesn't have many people she relies on." Radhya pats a roti with flour. "It takes time to bounce back from feeling blindsided and abandoned." Josh feels his fist clenching and unclenching. "Time and *space*."

"Why are you telling me this?" he asks, knowing full well where this is going.

"When you have a crush on a friend, there's always going to be—"

"That's not what's happening." His voice is low. He feels the dough becoming too dry in his hands. "We're both dating other people."

It's the truth. No one can say it's not.

"—an imbalance. It can upend things."

"She kissed me!" He accidentally sends a bit of dough flying. "I mean, it was mutual." He lowers his voice, straightening his body to full height. "Totally reciprocated. There's no 'imbalance' here." Radhya has no fucking clue how perfectly balanced it was. Basically the fucking Justice statue with the blindfold and the scale. "Didn't she tell you about it?"

There's that glint of hurt in her eyes again.

"No." She sighs like this is her last task on a ten-page to-do list and heats a cast-iron skillet over one of the burners. "Ari holds things in until they explode."

"Not with me." Josh says it with a little shrug that probably comes off as a touch too self-righteous. Cocky. He can't help it—it's been too long since he's felt that twinge of earned satisfaction.

Josh passes Radhya his batch of dough.

"Don't. Push." She pokes her index finger in it three times and adds a splash of water. "She thinks you're her life raft or some shit. If you're going to be her friend, be her *friend*. But it's not a shortcut into something more."

"I'm not pushing."

Okay, *yes*, that phrase sounds like a telltale sign that the speaker *is*, in fact, pushing. But that's not the case! She kissed him. It happened. And Radhya can't manipulate him into thinking otherwise.

"Ari needs time." She shapes a knob of dough into an almost perfect circle. "I happen to know something about this."

Timing has already fucked them over twice.

"I TRULY THINK ARMS ARE THE NEW THIGHS," BRIAR PROCLAIMS, RUN-ning her hand over Gabe's biceps. "I mean, traps? Scaps? Fore-arms? We're gonna see more rowing gyms and, like, rooms full of pull-up machines." She's managed to tuck her legs beneath her on a small wooden chair and look perfectly comfortable.

"Yes!" Gabe cries, slapping his open palm on the wobbly table, making the beer slosh out of Ari's glass. "I *just* tweeted about how I think monkey bars are the next big thing in gym equipment and the runner-up from *The Bachelorette* retweeted me. He's starting a weekly running club in Central Park."

"Ryan?" Briar exclaims. "The fitness influencer? I can't be-lieve he's not the next Bachelor."

They stopped including Ari in the conversation thirty min-utes ago, except to ask her to take photos on each of their phones. She looks back toward the kitchen occasionally, waiting for yelling or for someone to storm out.

But when Josh finally emerges from the back there's a con-templative look on his face, like he's trying to crack Gödel's in-completeness theorems. He takes his seat without saying anything.

"Your boyfriend's back," Gabe announces in a singsong voice.

"He's not my—"

"—I'm not her boyfriend," Josh insists. Loudly.

Really loudly.

They glance at each other for a moment before looking

away. Ari begins stacking the empty dishes in a desperate bid to occupy her hands. She feels Josh's knee bouncing next to her.

"Methinks the lady doth protest too much," Gabe tells Briar. Ari shoots him a vicious warning glance, causing him to put up his hands in surrender and declare, "Okay, I'll stop."

Ari has sat across from drunk Gabe at enough tables to know he probably won't.

"How'd it go in the kitchen?" Briar asks, sitting up a bit straighter from the intimate little huddle she'd had with Gabe.

"It was . . ." Josh twists his mouth, like he's choosing his words carefully. "Interesting."

"You and Radhya should do a collab!"

"And I think that you and Ari should just"—Gabe makes some gesture with his index fingers that could be interpreted in several ways—"get it out of your systems. You already kissed. It's not going to get *less* awkward now."

So much for Gabe's promise to stop.

"Oh my God." Briar's jaw drops. "You *kissed*? Is that why you keep blowing off my Raya picks?" Briar reaches across the wood table, knocking over an empty glass, and grabs Josh's and Ari's wrists. "Guys, I ship it." She looks pointedly at Josh. "When did this happen? Why didn't you tell me? How *was* it?"

Gabe dings his beer glass with a fork like he's egging on a newly married couple at a wedding reception.

Ari feels like she's been buckled into the passenger seat of a car that's careening out of control. She wrenches her hand out of Briar's grip. Why are people so eager to bury a genuine friendship under the weight of a romantic relationship?

"It was nothing!" It comes out as a shout. A group sitting at the next table pauses their conversation to stare. "People kiss on New Year's!" Ari glances at Josh for confirmation, to show a united front, but he's staring at her like she just shivved him between the ribs. "It's a tradition." *Shut up.* "That's all it was. No big deal." *Stop. STOP.* "So just drop it."

No one at the table says anything. In fact, everyone in the vicinity seems to take a momentary break from speaking. Ari's heart thuds against her chest.

A little voice pings in her mind: *Something's wrong, something's wrong, something's wrong.* Josh looks at her with a wild mix of confusion and . . . something else. Shit. *Shit.*

Gabe clears his throat. Briar says something that Ari can't quite hear. Josh's phone buzzes and he spends a long time looking at what seems to be a short message.

She blinks against the sting of tears, watching Briar and Gabe resume their drunken half-cuddle like it's the simplest thing in the world.

Why can't it be that easy anymore?

Josh doesn't say anything when his phone buzzes again. He deposits his deeply creased napkin onto the empty plate in front of him, pushes his chair back, and stands up, towering over everyone at the table.

"I have somewhere to be," he announces.

17

JOSH HAS NOWHERE TO BE.

He hasn't had anywhere to be in approximately eight months.

He just can't sit at that table with Ari.

The moment Josh shrugs his arms into his parka—the one he'd lent her a few weeks ago—Ari jumps up from the table, too.

"Wait," she says. "I have . . . a thing. I'll walk out with you."

She trails him to the exit, ruining his attempt to leave the building in a cloud of quiet, stoic anger. Josh ignores her, letting the heavy front door slam behind him. Without the barrier of his patchy beard, the wind bites at his face.

The hinges on the door squeak and Josh picks up his pace, hurrying across the intersection, forcing himself not to look over his shoulder.

Ten seconds later, he hears a pair of footsteps, jogging behind him in double time.

"Hey!" Ari shouts. "Wait up. Where are you headed?" He doesn't slow down, but she manages to catch up, breathing hard. She looks at him expectantly, like there's no reason they shouldn't walk to some new destination together. "Train?"

Josh racks his brain for an alternative before coming up empty—because where the hell else would he be going in Astoria?—and giving her a curt nod.

"Me, too," she says, putting on the mittens that she claims are warmer than gloves. An adult wearing mittens. This is who he's losing his goddamn mind over? "I'm meeting up with that couple in Chelsea. Salt-and-Pepper-Man with the hot wife." Of course she is. *Of course* that little dress was meant for someone else. She's not even wearing her new coat today, despite the frigid temperature. Like she doesn't want to risk reminding him of anything. She'd rather shiver in her unlined, sale-rack-at-T.J.Maxx peacoat.

"This weekend went so fast," she continues. Since when do they exchange banal pleasantries like this? He should ask Ari what she did yesterday to make the weekend pass so quickly, but he doesn't actually want to know. Probably went home with one or more near-strangers and left their apartment fifty minutes later.

He's too fucking agitated to anchor. The emotional storm clearly blew his shitty boat out to sea.

Maintaining a steely silence, Josh takes even longer strides as they round the corner onto Thirty-first Street, as if perhaps he can outwalk the possibility of a conversation.

Instead, she keeps going. "So that girl at the bar was hot, right?"

"Yes," he says through gritted teeth. It should feel like twisting a knife, but it's a hollow victory. Mutually assured destruction.

"Gabe said you got her number."

Josh turns around in front of the wide staircase leading up to the subway platform. "Yes."

He examines her face for signs of hurt, but her tells are frustratingly subtle. Her lips pinch together into a tight line but there's nothing he could snapshot and file away under *visual confirmation of Ari's true feelings*.

"Cool." Every monosyllabic word she utters jabs him in the sternum. She takes a few steps up the staircase, transforming her expression back into a placid mask of indifference.

And that? That is *exactly* why he owes it to himself to try this. To take this nice girl from Connecticut—or was it Philly?—with big brown eyes and full lips on the most standard date possible. Just dinner or a drink. A slightly awkward kiss at her doorstep. It would be perfectly fine and nothing more. There wouldn't be any stomach-tightening, slow-churning agony.

Which is much better. Healthy. *It's what I deserve*.

He takes the stairs two at a time, brushing past Ari.

ARI FUMBLES FOR HER METROCARD AS JOSH MOVES SWIFTLY THROUGH the turnstile.

She's tried bland conversation. Following him at close range. No tactic she can muster seems to mend whatever is broken.

As she swipes her MetroCard, her hips slam against the turnstile bar. *Insufficient fare*. Dammit.

Josh is probably praying for the train to whisk him away before she can refill the card. He'll return to the safe confines of Manhattan and go on with his life, satisfied in the certainty that he's dodged a bullet.

Ari makes a show of retreating to the ticket machine, half-hoping he'll turn around and offer to swipe her through. Not so much because of the $2.75, even though that's the equivalent of about thirty minutes of NeverTired labor.

She just needs something—one gesture—to build on. To prove this crack won't deepen.

Tapping her index finger on the fingerprint-smeared glass to select the $5.50 minimum, she watches Josh walk a few steps in the other direction, past clumps of bundled-up people waiting for the next Manhattan-bound N.

By the time she swipes the refilled MetroCard and pushes through the turnstile, Josh is pressing a pair of AirPods into his ears.

It stings.

No. It doesn't just sting, it *hurts*. It's the kind of petty silent-treatment bullshit Cass would pull anytime Ari wouldn't capitulate and apologize for some crime against their relationship. Like a little warning of things to come.

Which means she can't let it go and walk away; she has to hurt him back a little bit.

She taps him on the shoulder. "Are you experimenting with passive aggression instead of original formula aggression?"

"What?" He removes the AirPods, pouting with all the subtlety of a silent film star.

"Ghosting out of an actual friendship with someone who just got abandoned is a real asshole move."

For once, he looks expressionless. "I don't understand what you want from me, Ari."

"Stop avoiding me!" She hasn't picked a fight with him before, at least not since they've been friends. Not a real fight. There's no sign of any train yet . . . so they're doing this.

"*I'm* avoiding *you*? Are you fucking serious?" He takes a half step closer, like it's the absolute maximum proximity he can stand. "You've been pretending like nothing happened for two fucking weeks."

Something small and bright and sharp pulses under her ribs. "I'm not pretending," she protests. "We just don't need to give it more oxygen." She pulls off her scarf, which feels way too tight around her neck. "*You're* the one who said it was nothing. 'Just a New Year's kiss'? 'It was the pot'? That's exactly what you said."

"That's what I said because you didn't—" He looks down at the platform. Josh always shows hurt on his face like he never figured out how to hide it. "You seemed so fucking relieved when I"—he pauses to breathe—"walked it back."

"We got carried away," she says. "I had a lot to drink, I was feeling lonely." She's recited this narrative to herself plenty of times over the last two weeks, but in her head, it hadn't landed with such a resounding thud.

"Great description for our 'friendship.'" He starts to pace again. "I happened to be standing nearby while you were feeling sorry for yourself."

"That's not what I meant."

"No." He shakes his head. "You've made your feelings completely clear. You keep me around because you're depressed and you don't want to be alone and I seem to be the one person in this city who you specifically *don't* want to fuck."

"You want to be my fuck buddy now?" It feels good to accuse him of something. "That's what you wanted this entire time? I don't even *like* half the people I go home with."

"You'd rather fuck people you hate than someone you love."

"Who said *anything* about love?"

"Definitely not *you*," he spits. "That would require you to drop this act where you pretend like nothing matters to you.

You broke down sobbing in front of me. *That's* the reality of your life." Her flight impulse kicks in and she turns on the heel of her off-brand Ugg boot to escape, but Josh catches up. "I don't want to hear about the couples or your awful ex or the roommates you used to fuck. You want to entertain someone? Get back up onstage and don't call me."

He turns away again, apparently trying to get the last word, but she can't let him have it.

"Let's talk about the reality of *your* life for a minute, then," she says, walking after him. "*You're* choosing to sit at home. You hold every random woman you date to a ridiculous standard of perfection, but your most intimate relationship is with the floor of the shower at Crunch."

Finally, Ari can see the headlights of the N heading south from the Ditmars stop.

"I literally met someone an hour ago." His voice is low and hoarse. The train is close enough to the station to create a rumbling sound.

"But you're not gonna sleep with her, are you? You're going to take her out for an expensive meal, find one stupid imperfection, and text *me* about it."

At least a dozen people are now staring at them.

"You know exactly what that kiss was." He's almost yelling over the crescendo of noise. "You've known the truth for two weeks and you're pretending you can't see it but it's *there*. I can't look at you, waiting for some acknowledgment of this enormous fucking *thing* that happened. I can't do that."

He rakes his hand through his hair and blows out a breath. It seems impossible to look at him, too.

"I just—" The words feel trapped in her throat. "I don't . . ." The platform shakes under her feet.

"The next time I fuck someone," he shouts, nearly drowned out by the roar of the train blowing past them, "it's not going to be because I'm desperate to eradicate the memory of my ex." Ari holds her breath. If she doesn't exhale, time will stop right here. "I haven't slept with anyone else because the only person—"

"Josh, please—"

The train screeches to a rough stop, obliterating their voices.

The doors open with a calm mechanical hiss—like everything is still totally normal and Ari's stomach didn't just plummet down to the sidewalk along Thirty-first Street. A generically cheerful pre-recorded voice announces, *"This is . . . Astoria Boulevard. This is a Manhattan bound . . . N train. The next stop is Thirtieth . . . Avenue."*

Josh steps backward onto the train. This is it. This is the last image of Josh she'll keep locked in her brain.

"I want *you*," he says. An indecipherable sound escapes Ari's throat, but it's not a word. She's certain she'll hear that phrase—that specific serious intonation of it—in her head forever. Like the best part of a song. The bit of "Hey, Jude" that builds into the *na-na-na-nanana-nahh*s. The part that gives you goosebumps.

"I just . . ." she hears herself say. "I don't want this to change." She gestures in the space between them. "I can't lose this."

"We aren't losing anything." He holds out his hand, his eyes shifting from hopeful to resigned, as people brush past them and she stands there, paralyzed.

The gap between the car and the platform might as well be a giant chasm. Ari could walk it back. She's good at shoving down inconvenient feelings. Josh's always bubble right up to the surface.

"Stand clear of the closing doors please."

The doors jerk and start to slide again and the only thought banging like a drum in her head is that she can't stand here on the platform and watch this train pull away. She can't let Josh be one more person who leaves her behind.

Ari reaches for his hand and he pulls her inside just in time.

18

THE TRAIN SHUDDERS AND HEAVES FORWARD, SLAMMING ARI AGAINST him. It's an unsexy collision, despite the new, uh, *context* established two seconds ago. Her unwound rainbow scarf snags on one of the closures on his coat.

They should probably be sharing a passionate kiss, or at least, like, making eye contact. But Ari rearranges herself so that they're both standing side by side, with their backs against the doors. Facing him feels impossible. Like being pushed out onstage without knowing her lines.

Kind of an ironic fear for an improviser. But this is different.

At least he doesn't turn his head, either. That's a small relief.

The train bumps along and she counts the remaining stops in her head. *Broadway . . . Thirty-sixth . . . Thirty-ninth . . . Queensboro Plaza . . .*

There's a look on his face that's reminiscent of his expression during the New Year's Eve countdown, but it's different under the fluorescent overhead lights. Clearer. More obvious. Underlined in bright red pen. No lingering questions.

Except their relationship has been nothing but questions up until this point, so what the hell happens when there's an answer? Right there? An *I want you* staring her in the face? Literally.

He doesn't say anything, but Ari feels Josh shift his hand so that their fingers are interlocking. He strokes the pulse point of her wrist with his thumb and *aren't we going to talk about this?* The car empties and fills up again, multiple times. Ari takes this trip every day but this time it seems both endless and like it's playing in fast-forward.

"*This is . . . Times Square. Transfer here for the . . .*" She feels Josh squeezing her hand tighter, like he's afraid she might jump out.

A family clutching giant M&M's store shopping bags crowds into the car, forcing Ari several inches closer to him.

It's stuffy in here. No air circulation at all. Just heat.

Okay. Think. When there's too much pressure, you let off steam. It's very logical. Mechanical. Maybe even what the friendship needs. They'll do it and get it out of their systems. Maybe even go back to being friends.

Sure. Yes. She's still friends with Gabe, after all.

"It's *showtime*!"

"Fuck," Josh mutters, stepping back as a dance troupe filters into the car. Booming music kicks in and the tourists eagerly join in on the kind of arrhythmic clapping only a family from northern Minnesota can produce; the New Yorkers instinctively wince and push themselves against the walls as the aerial gymnastics start.

Ari sympathizes. "Showtime" dancers are basically the street canvassers of the NYC subway system, except with a slightly higher likelihood of kicking a bystander in the face while somersaulting off the ceiling of a moving train car.

When a sneaker comes within an inch of Ari's head, Josh pulls her behind him, tucking her into the corner near the door.

It's both a chivalrous gesture and a convenient way for Josh to maneuver them into a face-to-face position. Actually, more like her-face-to-his-chest.

If she's flushed, it's because she never feels comfortable when she's not facing an exit. Which he probably doesn't realize because she feels funny admitting that to people. Radhya picked up on it after a couple months of living together. Ari had chalked it up to feng shui; Rad called bullshit and rearranged the furniture without saying anything more about it.

But Josh doesn't know that and it's too weird to mention it now, so she looks straight ahead, right into his shirt, which is peeking out from his unzipped, heavily insulated parka. Her stomach is one giant, tightening knot.

"You're warm." Josh's voice is barely audible over the thunderous bass of the music. The back of his hand feels like ice against her cheek.

She nods and he lowers his hand down to her coat, slowly undoing the oversized buttons one by one, brushing his fingers against the front of her dress as he moves down, down, down. It doesn't help at all. Every passing fantasy she's had about Josh is playing out in her mind's eye and the way he's looking at her kind of indicates that he can see this montage, too.

A bead of sweat is dripping along her back, she's sure of it.

"Josh?" She's almost shouting. "Are we gonna talk about this?"

"What?" he yells. His hand is still hanging on to the open flap of her coat.

She reaches in her pocket for her phone and dismisses the increasingly dire battery life notification.

> Sun, Jan 15, 5:16 P.M.
> ARI: should we talk about this?

He pulls out his device and Ari stares over his shoulder at an ad for a mattress startup promising "the best snuggles of your life" with a photo of four entangled feet sticking out from underneath a soft, gray duvet.

She swallows as her phone lights up.

> JOSH: All we've done for months is talk.
> We've said every fucking thing to each other except what we really want.
>
> ARI: what do you want?

"Stand clear of the closing doors, please."
The "Showtime" crew exits the car as the applause peters out and the train rumbles down the track again.

The train empties a bit. They sit down and let their knees brush. She wouldn't have noticed it before, but now? The friction of her tights against his pants feels so . . . *apparent.*

> JOSH: We walk to my apartment.
> I take off every winter layer you have on.

She runs the knuckles of her right hand across her lips, reciting the stops in her head . . . *Twenty-third Street, Union Square, Eighth Street . . .*

Maybe this will be a sort of freebie. A blip.

JOSH: Probably in the elevator.

Even though another bead of sweat meanders down the curve of her lower back, Ari takes her crocheted rainbow scarf out of her bag and winds it around her neck, high enough to cover the lower half of her face.

JOSH: You get on my bed, or my kitchen table or any
surface you prefer.
And I make you come all afternoon.

Ari bites down on the inside of her lower lip almost hard enough to draw blood.

It would be smarter to pump the brakes right now. Give it some breathing room.

But her brain is only providing one piece of data: *I want you.* She plays it back, trying to decide whether he'd placed the emphasis on *want* or *you.* He's not looking at the person to her left. He's not evaluating. He's tugging on something—some loose thread that never quite got mended after Cass left.

She swallows hard. Her thumbs say *fuck breathing room* and press down on the gas.

ARI: The surface I prefer is your face.

"*This is . . . Twenty-third Street. This is a Brooklyn bound . . . N train.*"

She peeks at Josh, now wearing a smug little grin on his face. Just two more stops. They'll be getting off soon.

WHEN ARI PACKED HER POTENTIAL-SEX TOTE BAG THIS MORNING, SHE did not think she'd be potential-sex-ing with Josh.

Josh has a sudden burst of energy: barreling ahead, unaffected by the blasts of frigid wind down Great Jones Street, practically jogging five steps ahead of her to his door, already gripping his keys. Like he's shedding any doubts with each giant step, while she's letting them whip her in the face.

In the cold, fluorescent light of the elevator lobby, her final text feels like a slight misstep. It's not untrue—it's just the wrong format for communicating with nuance. Instead, she might've gone with: *Hey, I think I've always kind of wanted to ride your face, but I'm currently suffering from acute emotional distress and it's so much easier if I only sit on faces I don't have memorized.*

At least it's more specific.

They step into the elevator. Josh jabs at the 5 button and turns around to face her. The nervous tension in her stomach calls to mind their elevator ride in the Strand—but this is different. Less playful. Quieter.

Everything that moved at fast-forward on the walk over transitions to slow motion. The elevator lurches upward in a way that suggests it also has concerns about this scenario. The delay gives Ari more time to consider the various ways this could play out. Are they about to dismantle the friendship they carefully forged, knocking down one brick after another? Or pick up those bricks and form something new?

Will this eventually become fodder for a set of inside jokes? *Remember that one time we did it? When we couldn't figure out how to navigate the height difference and you got annoyed because I stretched out your Egyptian cotton boxer briefs? Crying-laughing emoji.*

But when he pulls the lapel of her coat and tilts his head down, it becomes clear that this is something very different from her usual frenzied hookups. That now, there's all the time in the world and he'll want to kiss her—slowly—and touch her and look at all the parts of her that he hasn't seen before and that hadn't really been part of the discussion on the train, had it?

Turning her head to dodge the kiss, Ari tugs on the sleeve of his coat. She's always been good at pivoting, downshifting, making situations more manageable for her brain. She places his hand under the skirt of the dress—*this, here, now*—guiding his fingers inside the waistband of her tights. He's more than willing to oblige. She might be death-gripping the sleeve of his coat with her other hand because *holy shit.* Her legs are tense, even though she's used to this part of the repertoire—a little show-and-tell so new partners can feel what she likes. But Josh's face isn't screwed up in the "I'm concentrating, gotta remember this" expression that she's used to. He's *looking* again, watching her. And, for once, she's not talking.

Which is not to say that she's quiet. She's surprised to hear herself whimper—a pathetic whine that confirms how easy it would be to lose control. Ari lowers her gaze into his parka-covered chest because if they stare at each other like that while this is happening, it's just . . . way too much.

When the elevator gears grind to an abrupt halt at the fifth floor, they stumble into the apartment. Ari takes the opportunity to reset expectations. Lingering too long at this part will make it impossible to explain it all away tomorrow.

"Take this off," she orders, tugging at his parka, regaining a bit of her composure. "Take everything off."

If he's a bit thrown by the shift in tone, it doesn't make him less cooperative. He lets his jacket drop to the ground without so much as a wince.

Ari steps out of her boots, hastily grabbing the fabric of his shirt in her fist and pulling up.

"I'm starting to understand why you don't even need an

hour with these dates." He sounds amused. "Do you have somewhere to be?"

She *was* on her way to a date, but she can't remember where
it was or with who. Every brain cell is currently focused on how
to steer this ship over the waterfall without smashing it to smith-
ereens at the bottom.

Ari takes a step back, letting the shirt fall to the ground. She
simply hasn't pictured him so specifically before. At least not this
part of him. Her hand skims over his chest; it's the perfect
amount of give.

"You're . . ." Her voice trails off. It's not that his muscles are
spectacularly well-defined. He just looks so *solid:* like a person
who could chop large quantities of firewood or help a woman
carry a giant stroller up a flight of subway stairs.

Josh gives a little self-conscious shrug. He moves to unbut-
ton her dress again, but she swats his hand away. Easier to keep
this focused on the physical if she remains in control of everything on her body. Her hand migrates downward, and in three
seconds, he's in his boxer briefs.

His abs contract as Ari reaches beneath the waistband
and . . . *um* . . .

"Wow," she says softly. "I've been casually sitting next to this
for months?"

He swallows with some effort. "Your loss."

And now she really is irreparably stretching the Italian-
cotton blend material, but for once, proper garment care doesn't
seem to be on his mind.

The boxers join the pile on the floor. If Josh feels embarrassed or awkward about being the naked one, he doesn't show
it. Under normal circumstances, she'd have no problem dispens-
ing with her dress, but this isn't exactly normal, is it?

She takes a step back, out of his reach. Without being too graceful or alluring, she rolls down her tights and underwear, leaving them in a heap on the floor.

The dress stays on.

"Bedroom?" he suggests. She can physically feel the word *bedroom* vibrating in her chest.

"No!" She's almost surprised by the vehemence of her own response. They can't do this in his bed, which is probably covered in crisp sheets with the subtle fragrance of expensive laundry detergent.

She looks around for the least romantic alternative. *Couch?* Too bed-adjacent. *Chair?* Too comfortable. *Table?* Her eyes land on something intriguing near the front windows.

Perfect.

It's impossible to catch feelings on a Bowflex.

"Here," she says, leading him over to the angled bench and pushing him down.

Josh glances at the five-way hand grips and lat straps. "Are you planning to torture me or something?"

"You should've bought the carabiners." She turns her back to him, letting her calves press against the ripped black vinyl upholstery. Maybe they don't need to look at each other at all. "Reverse cowgirl?" There's a whiff of desperation in her voice.

"Ari." Her name sounds different now when he says it—like things have already been altered on a molecular level. "Turn around? Let's just . . . keep it simple."

Turning around isn't *simple*. Looking at each other isn't *simple*. Nothing about this is *simple*. How does he not see that? They're supposed to be ripping into each other. Releasing three months' worth of pent-up sexual tension. Not gazing.

"It's my favorite position," she says, facing away from him.

"There's no way that's true."

"It is," she insists. "You're saying you *don't* want to look at my ass?"

"Later." Even without seeing his expression, the depth of his voice makes her anxiety flare. Why is he promising a *later*? This is only ever going to be a *now*. "You're skipping past some of the good parts."

Except one person's good parts can be someone else's minefield.

A bit of motion draws her attention to the window—a dusting of snow pelting the glass.

"Look," she says, standing up and walking in front of the north-facing window, possibly out of desperation to change the vibe. "It's snowing." She exhales and draws back the curtain and watches thick white clumps stream down from the sky in efficient diagonal lines. It's like an establishing shot for a holiday episode of *Friends*.

She doesn't mean for him to follow her but five seconds later his warm body brushes up behind her, but cautiously, like a zookeeper approaching a skittish animal.

They're reflected in the windowpane, juxtaposed against the snowy scene outside. They could be a picture of any kind of couple: a one-night stand, friends with benefits, newlyweds, exes about to backslide. A dozen emotionally devastating scenarios unfurl in her mind.

"Is this okay?" he asks, grazing her arm with his knuckles so lightly, it raises goosebumps on her skin. *Is it?* What purpose is it serving besides digging this confusing hole even deeper?

Elsewhere in Manhattan, thousands of people are lying in bed with their partners, switching off lights, reading, cuddling, ignoring each other, having sex. Their hearts aren't racing.

Their mouths aren't dry. They're taking comfort in sharing a bed, not stacking up layers of anxiety like people playing a game of Speed.

A little montage of their friendship plays out in her mind's eye, like an "In Memoriam" segment at an awards show. Is she really going to call him up on Wednesday night to watch a Kevin James movie after this? *No.* Half the city will be tainted with "walking around with Josh memories" when this goes awry.

"You don't have to do all that. We're just"—she glances down at her arm, swallowing hard—"getting it out of our systems."

Josh stills his hand. "Are we?" He stares at their reflection, finding a way to indirectly look in her eyes even though she's not facing him.

Ari can hear the thumping of her heartbeat over the muted ambient noise. Shoes scraping the pavement. Distant horns. The sound of breathing—either hers or Josh's, she can't really tell at this point.

Josh's mouth brushes against her neck. She feels his left hand beneath the hem of her dress, drifting up between her thighs. Gentle. Deliberate. Practiced.

Ari turns to face him—to make a joke or play it off. But there's no clever line at the ready. She has nothing to say. Because some random Hinge match will never look at her in this specific way that breaks her heart and melts it back together in the space of one breath.

He touches her face and she can see his eyes moving across everything—like he's taking it all in again from this closer angle. There's a little burst of tenderness, warming her chest, smoothing over sharp, painful edges. There aren't any more layers to strip away. Just the slightest push and she'll bruise.

The rattle of the furnace punctuates the quiet.

The kiss doesn't come the way she's expecting—just the soft, lingering press of his lips against her cheek.

She lets a tiny pleasurable prickle unfurl at the back of her neck. It feels like an admission. *More, please.*

Their lips touch once and part. And *no,* that's clearly not enough because they meet again. And again. A little deeper, a little bolder every time, until they don't separate at all and his hands tangle in her hair and they breathe each other in and—

Aside from the Ramble Incident, Ari hasn't Kissed in a while. She's lowercase *kissed,* the way you do when your date isn't terrible and you feel like it would be rude not to. Usually, making out is mostly a box to be checked en route to some other activity.

But this feels urgent—like they wasted the last hour by not kissing on the train, on the walk, waiting for the elevator. His mouth meets the hollow of her throat and Ari tips her head back, hungry and dizzy with his tongue in her mouth and his fingers sliding over the flowery fabric of her dress, bunching it up in his fists.

Her heavy exhales sound inordinately loud in the quiet room.

"Can I take your dress off?" he mutters into her neck.

Ari nods, letting out some feral noise of assent, needing the last scrap of a barrier to fall away. Right now.

Out of the corner of her eye she can still see them reflected in the windowpane. It's a nice picture. Now it doesn't look like two depressives bonding over shared loneliness and coping mechanisms. They could be any normal Sunday couple. They could take trips to Bed, Bath, and Beyond and walk around the city holding hands and share boozy brunches and spend all afternoon in bed, checking items off their fuck-it lists.

You never know.

This goes wrong one hundred percent of the time—until the one time it doesn't.

THE WALK TO THE BEDROOM ONLY TAKES ABOUT TEN SECONDS, BUT IT gives Josh a moment to turn over the Rubik's Cube of the whole encounter and look at it from a new angle. To push aside the vague, formless dread that she might get up, run out of the room, and send a text from the elevator: *Thanks for the sex*. 👀👀👀

It means something—crossing the mystical threshold into his space. Every step and gesture and piece of removed clothing and point of contact feels like moving deeper into the unknown.

Josh lowers her down onto his bed—it's not the most fluid transition, but at the moment, it's not like his body is capable of nuance.

Ari rolls over onto her stomach and he immediately misses seeing her face, getting that crucial bit of visual feedback. But it's better to follow her lead and the caution tempers his desire to go fucking nuts. He drags his fingers down her back, over the delicate curve of her spine, observing every tiny manifestation of her nervous energy, examining tattoos he'd never realized she had.

He tries to quiet his brain, which is racing two or three minutes ahead, visualizing all the possibilities laid out in front of them: flashes of the most tantalizing mental porn he's ever concocted.

Josh finds himself unable to shut up—he's never been so talkative in the bedroom.

"Why did we wait so long to do this?" he hears himself say, like the thought was so loud in his head that it had to come out.

He continues kissing down her shoulder, taking his time, feeling the way her body responds to him. This is an exploration. Something to build on.

There's this idea of her that exists in his mind: where she's some kind of enigma, where the passcodes are always off by one number, where she almost opens up, but not quite.

He gathers up Ari's hair, winding it around his hand. He slides his hand between her legs, mimicking the position of her fingers over his in the elevator. She makes a little incomprehensible sound. Josh is good at memorizing these things. Leaning down to her ear, he tugs lightly on her hair.

"This okay?" he murmurs.

"J-just keep . . ." She nods and closes her eyes. "Shit." He'd wanted to draw more words out of her but this is almost more satisfying. "Josh, please."

He lifts his head up. "'Please' what?" He stills his fingers. "Tell me what you want."

She fumbles for his hand. "Don't stop."

"Give me more feedback or we're just going to cuddle."

"Really?" Ari cranes her neck to the right to look at him. "You think you're cute?"

"No. That's why I got good at this part."

She squirms. "Keep going, exactly like you just were." After a few stubborn moments of silence, she adds, "But don't let me come on your hand."

He pauses. "Okay."

"Make me come while you're inside me? It doesn't usually happen that way for me but . . . I feel like it could."

A burst of pride hits his chest like a lightning bolt.

"You still need to use your fingers, though. You know that, right?"

Josh stops again. "Yes, Ari. I have done this before." He imagines that she's biting back a smile. Then he nudges her over onto her back. "Is this okay? I really want to look at you."

She hesitates for a moment and then nods.

It's like he has a mission now. For years, Josh's accomplishments relied on his belief that his hands could do anything. Even though the last year had put an enormous dent in that conviction, at this moment, he's never been more confident in his sense of touch.

Actually, he hasn't felt this good in months. Maybe he just needed to be given a task—specifically, the best task in the entire fucking world—which is making Ari whimper and arch her back off his mattress.

Unvetted words start tumbling out of his mouth again. "I feel like I've been waiting eight fucking years for this. I want this, Ari." With his other hand, he traces a finger behind her left ear and down her neck. She shivers. It's the tiniest involuntary response, but the serotonin shot from that one little movement could power his workouts for the next few weeks. *Fuck.* "I want this."

The condoms . . . *where*? His brain isn't working. His hand gropes across the bedside table, where he'd optimistically placed them a few days after moving in; they hadn't been touched since.

Ari grabs the foil packet before he can even fumble with it. Because she's fucking perfect.

The judgmental voice somewhere in his subconscious mocks Josh for these erection-driven thoughts but he can barely make it out over the sound of Ari's heavy breaths. He's going to turn them into moans in about ten seconds.

His first instinct is to fuck her into his mattress immediately, but she might not want to be caged in.

His brain rotates the Rubik's Cube again. He slides over to sit on the edge of the bed.

"Come here." He pats his thigh. "Like this."

He's dangerously hard—one slide of skin against skin with the right angle and friction could be his undoing. Ari climbing on top of him seems to render all his usual calming tactics completely ineffective.

She straddles him, sitting up on her knees, granting her a clear line of sight to the door and providing him with the best possible view of her nipple piercings, already pointing at him in the cold air. He runs his mouth along the gentle curves of the undersides of her breasts while she watches from her slightly elevated position, digging her nails into his back. She's claimed to be dissatisfied with their size; making her feel otherwise could be his new mission in life.

When she's had enough of the teasing, Ari tears into the foil package. He looks down at her hand stroking along the length of his cock a few times before unrolling the condom.

She stills for a moment, searching his face. "Point of no return?"

Her voice has an edge of uncertainty, but his doesn't: "Good."

Josh puts his hands on her waist, supporting her as she slowly eases herself down. It's not like she needs the assistance, but there's something about them doing this together—as partners—that excites him.

"Breathe," he says, not breathing. She exhales unsteadily until she sinks all the way down, pressing her fingers into his shoulders. "Good. So good, Ari."

His vocabulary has shrunk considerably over the last hour.

They stay like that for a few seconds, adjusting to a new center of gravity.

"Don't move yet," she murmurs.

Resisting every urge to do just that, he watches as she drags her knees forward, bringing their bodies closer, letting him nudge half an inch deeper. Running her hand up to the back of his head, she pulls on his hair to tilt his chin up.

Ari sucks along the side of his neck, up to his earlobe and whatever she's doing with her tongue is making it really fucking difficult to remain still. The pleasure centers in his brain that have been dormant for too long light up in neon.

She leans back, placing her palm against his cheek. It's like she sees everything—the self-loathing, the judgmental tendencies, the mistakes that haunt him at night. The face that's made him self-conscious his entire life. And she wants him.

He can feel how much she wants him.

Fuck.

He has to move. Now.

With a soft grunt, he holds her hips and thrusts up, making her gasp.

"You feel so good," she whispers. "God, you feel so good." Her vocabulary is also operating at a first-grade level.

He rolls his hips up into her again, watching her body respond. She lets her head hang back and he can't help reaching for her neck, running his hand down to her collarbone and between her breasts, which shake slightly as he moves again.

"Look at us." He moves his hand to her head, tilting it down. "Don't close your eyes. Look."

"Josh!" She tenses around him again. "Shiiit . . ." she breathes out.

That fucking does it. He has to be on top.

"Hold on to me," he says, pulling her back into his chest. She rests her chin on his shoulder, clinging tightly as he stands and, for a brief moment, contemplates using the wall, but *no*. It's not the right time for that. He turns them around, lowering her down until she's on her back. He rests his weight on his elbows. Thank fucking God he's been doing planks.

"Okay? Can I—"

"Yeah." She wraps one of her legs around his waist, pushing her heel against his back.

Finally, he moves the way he wants to. Not too fast, but deep. Really fucking deep in her. She meets each of his thrusts, the crown of her head just barely bumping up against the headboard each time. It's a little mesmerizing.

Her left hand grabs at the corner of the mattress, like she needs something to hold on to.

Josh grasps it with his right hand, intertwining their fingers. She can hold on to him.

They move together without speaking. Not that there's total silence. He's quite happy to have only their breathing and moaning reverberate around the room.

Actually, *fuck*, he's being pretty loud right now.

Maybe that's why Ari turns her head to the left, breaking the eye contact they've been holding. Is she trying to imagine she's somewhere else? With someone else? Someone with enough self-control to not lose his goddamn mind over missionary sex?

Then he follows her gaze and realizes what captured her attention. She's looking at their clasped hands. Her eyes are welling up.

The icy shard of anxiety stabbing at his brain melts into warm water.

She waited for this, just like you did.

Yeah, he's not going to last much longer.

"I want this, Ari." Words are tumbling out again. "All of it."

She turns her head back up to face him, letting out a sob.

"Josh . . ." she chokes out. "I-I'm . . ."

He moves faster, losing some control, unclasping their hands to focus his fingers on her clit. His, uh, technique lacks some of the nuance he'd demonstrated before, but he can already feel the pressure building in his own body.

"I know. I feel you. You're so close—"

She babbles nonsense syllables he wishes he could decipher. Not that he's making much sense, either.

What a fucking stupid and amazing idea this was. It doesn't matter that the rest of his life is in shambles, as long as he can have this. *We fit together—we literally fit together.*

"We're so good for each other," he says, opening the floodgates. "I know it. It's—"

"Josh . . ."

He leans down an inch closer, testing her flexibility. She's panting, legs shaking, just on the edge. He can feel himself about to explode.

"You're so fucking beautiful like this." He touches his forehead to hers.

Her face screws up, her eyes squeezing shut, and he feels her clench as she cries out, pulsing around him.

Fuckingshitgoddamngonnacumfuckfuck.

In a fraction of a second, everything tightens and releases. He feels simultaneously powerless and almighty as he lets go.

Josh takes three of the deepest breaths of his life. His mind feels blank, like there's a blinking cursor waiting for a line of code.

He lets himself roll onto his back and disposes of the condom, missing the trash can and not caring. He pulls Ari closer, resting her head on his shoulder. Her eyes are still closed. He can feel her pulse racing, her slightly erratic breathing slowly growing steadier until she drifts off.

She might wake up and feel differently about everything. Which, now that he's coming down from whatever the fuck possessed him thirty seconds ago, seems increasingly, terrifyingly plausible.

On the other hand, Ari is nestled into him, perfectly calm and trusting. That's fucking amazing, too.

He could let himself sleep.

But he won't.

He feels good so rarely—why waste it on his traitorous subconscious? Not when she's clinging—actually fucking *clinging*—to him. He strokes her hair with his left hand.

No. He'd stay awake for days for this.

19

ARI BLINKS HER EYES OPEN WITH A JOLT. TEN FEET OVER HER HEAD, there's a beige plaster ceiling with a long, disconcerting crack running from the light fixture to the molding. It's been forever since she's woken up in a strange bed.

Ari wipes some drool from the corner of her mouth. Her hand connects with a shoulder. Which she's apparently been using as a pillow.

Oh no.

Several key memories from the very recent past flood her brain. This isn't a strange bed. She's seen it several times before. Just not from this angle.

It doesn't seem to be fully light out. There's frost on the windowpane but it's about a million degrees under the covers. She's forgotten how men magically become radiators at night.

Ari carefully turns onto her side to better position herself for a silent escape, but his shoulder stirs and seems to follow her, definitely shutting the window in which she could have surreptitiously slipped out of bed and retrieved her dress from the living room. *Shit*. He closes the gap between her back and his chest and *hello, yes, we are both extremely naked*.

"Hey." The voice is low and soft. It's Josh, but some new, weird version of him that's already speaking to her in a different tone.

"Is it, uh, morning?" She grabs the duvet and holds it to her chest the way women do in PG-13 movies. "Did you fall asleep, too?"

"A little bit." His mouth twitches. "There was also some quiet snoring and I lost circulation in my left arm."

"Oh my God." Ari pushes back, scrambling closer to the edge of the bed. "Why did you let me do that? You should've just rolled me over." Untangling herself from the sheets—when did she even get *under* the sheets?—she touches her feet to the creaking floorboards and hesitates. "Do you have a shirt or something I could borrow?" It's not that she's usually shy about the journey to the bathroom. But right now, in the quiet and without the rush of adrenaline or hormones or pheromones or whatever the hell was coursing through their veins last night, she feels even more exposed. And cold.

Josh looks up at her with a bemused expression. "With your reputation for stealing shirts? No, I'm sorry. I can't risk it."

She waits for him to relent and point to a drawer full of black T-shirts, organized by cotton weight.

He doesn't. There's the hint of a grin on his face—some new boldness, as if the mischievous element of their dynamic flipped overnight.

"You're ridiculous." Ari doesn't see anything in the immediate vicinity, so she steels herself and rushes out of the room, hoping that motion blur is a thing in real life. She retrieves her tote bag from where she'd dropped it in the living area and locks herself in the bathroom: her preferred location for emotional meltdowns.

After peeing and washing her hands with the kind of fancy soap you'd expect to find next to Ina Garten's sink, she checks her face and hair in the mirror. Predictably, it's an eyeliner catastrophe. She gathers her hair back into a bun, thereby discouraging Josh from trying to run his fingers through it again. *Reset expectations.*

She finds a towel—of course he keeps a neat stack of luxury bath sheets in here—and sets it down over the freezing tile, just sitting for a few minutes in the merciful privacy.

It was supposed to be *just sex*. An inevitable resolution. It fits in a compartment that has a label and a lid and a compactor pushes it down and out of sight. That's how this usually works.

Sure, every so often when she's enraged or can't stop crying or when the weed isn't dialing down the feelings from an eleven to a manageable four or five, the compartment explodes and litters the other chambers in her brain with emotional shrapnel. She takes a day off, watches every filmed version of *Pride and Prejudice,* consumes a couple edibles, and starts the containment process over again.

She doesn't have any mind-numbing substances right now. Not even a Xanax. In fact, she's never felt more terrifyingly sober.

Sex was supposed to resolve the tension. So why is her stomach still a giant knot?

There's no way to rationalize it. Ari is almost certain she's never used a cringe term like "making love" before. Her stomach tightens just thinking it, silently.

She cried. Fucking *cried* while he declared things to her.

She's never done that—not with Cass or anyone. Ever. And she had several borderline-religious experiences with Cass.

Ari forces herself to take some deep breaths.

Find the exit. It's the smartest course of action. She has put her underwear back on in an elevator on several other occasions; she can do it again. Her brain serves up an array of excuses. "It would be terrible to ruin the friendship." "Let's not rush into anything." "Your dick is phenomenal and I need time to process that." Or, better yet, "I have an early appointment." A valid reason that also has the benefit of being true. It's just not the Reason.

She hasn't *slept* with anyone since Cass. Nothing like burying the lede in your own mind.

Maybe she should say these things with clothes on. *Yes, clothes first, then excuses, then exit.*

She's about to tiptoe into the living area to track down her dress, when a ringtone shatters the silence.

"Call from . . . Dust. Daddy."

Ari grabs her phone out of the bag and swipes away the notifications she's racked up. The battery is at two percent. She clears her throat.

"Twenty-four hour Erectile Dysfunction Hotline, how may I direct your call?"

There's a quiet moment in which Ari can hear the trace of a resigned sigh.

"I'd like to file a complaint about one of your service providers."

"Oh," she says, quickly transitioning into a singsongy customer service voice. "I'm sorry to hear that. What's the nature of the problem? Failure to deliver a blow job?"

"I'd describe it as a failure to communicate. Sometimes she even uses humor to fend off serious conversations."

Ari gasps. "I see. There must be some malfunction in our training program."

"Clearly." There's a long silence. "Are you planning to come back to the bedroom?"

"No," she admits.

"What's the worst thing that could happen if you come back?"

Ari searches her potential-sex bag for her toothbrush. "Spooning."

"You can be the big spoon," he offers. "It could just be sleeping."

"It really couldn't, though." The wood floor creaks beneath her feet as she pads back to the bathroom. "I don't do this—"

"This is different," he insists.

Except, it's not different at all. Every relationship starts this way. And most of them end in tears and half-empty bookshelves.

"You said some really intense things." She squeezes some of Josh's toothpaste (Colgate Total—she'd expected something more exotic) onto her toothbrush.

"*I* was 'intense'?" he replies. "You invented a new dialect. For all I know, you proposed marriage."

"Yeah, because I can't wait to jump back into one of those again." She brushes vigorously and spits. She's never been more passionate about dental care.

What the hell does she do with her toothbrush? Just set it in the little stand, mingling with Josh's Oral-B 7000?

Ari snoops around the artfully distressed metal basket attached to the side of the tub, which contains a lot of "product."

"You use Russian leather scented body wash?"

"Ari."

She pops open a bottle of Aesop "Calming Shampoo" and inhales a whiff, hoping for some immediate effect.

Nothing.

What the hell does someone with such ridiculous taste in grooming products know about the reality of relationships?

Ari stares at her reflection. She has a terrible case of raccoon eyes and a burgeoning hickey where her neck meets her shoulder. "I haven't had missionary sex with a man—like, vanilla, face-to-face, whatever—in a really long time."

"What? What about the couples?"

"They usually want to do that with each other. It's too—"

"Intimate?" Josh suggests.

"—awkward." She makes a face. "All that eye contact."

"You know," he says, "Zeus ordered Apollo to rearrange the entire human body so people could have sex face-to-face. When they found their missing half, it healed their existential wounds."

"So, that's why I'm such a disaster." She turns away from the mirror. "I've been bleeding from my existential wound this entire time."

"We should definitely spiral about it in separate rooms for twelve hours," he says, probably lowering his memory foam pillow over his air passages.

"Works for me."

Her phone goes dead.

Ari shuts off the bathroom light. Pushing against all her deepest impulses, she peeks into the bedroom, hiding her body behind the doorframe. "I'm scared, okay? We could really, really hurt each other."

"Do you think I don't know what it's like to be hurt?" Josh sits up on his elbow. "You're the only good thing in my life."

Ari stares at him, holding her breath. She could raise serious objections to that statement. There's a construction worker in a neon vest waving a SLOW DOWN sign in front of that statement.

"Let's just . . . watch a movie or something. Please."

She shifts her weight. "You know I don't watch movies naked."

"I know." He tosses a soft white ball at her. "Put these on then." She looks down at a neatly rolled up pair of socks.

Ari sits on the edge of the bed and pulls the enormous socks on; they're more luxurious than some of her shoes.

"I don't do this," she says again, gesturing at the bed. "I told you this the first time we met. I don't sleep over." *And I'm scared shitless of this entire thing, so I'll be going and probably not contacting you for three weeks.*

"So we won't go back to sleep." Josh peels back the covers so she can slide in next to him. These sheets must have a thread-count in the thousands. It's like staying in a very nice, austere hotel. There's an awkward silence hanging like a cloud over the room. Or perhaps that's a fancy Japanese diffuser.

This is the weird thing that happens after sex: Once you've unraveled all the tension, you're just two naked people sitting there like nervous idiots.

Josh rolls onto his side and his right arm snakes its way around her hip.

"This is dangerously close to spooning," Ari says.

"And yet, you haven't disintegrated." His skin smells like the sandalwood/camphor/Russian leather fragrance of his stupid organic body wash. Maybe part of her wants to smell like those nonsense words, too.

Shit shit shit.

"I—I have things to do tomorrow. I mean, this morning." Seems best not to mention the meeting is with his mother. "I need to get up soon."

"Hmm." His thumb grazes the soft, ticklish area where her thigh meets her hip, making her squirm. "Didn't you say orgasms jolt you awake?"

"At this point, my vibrator is my main reason for waking up, period, so . . ."

His breath tickles the nervy skin on the back of her neck.

"Show me."

20

"I DIDN'T BRING MY EQUIPMENT," SHE REPLIES, UNSURE IF SHE'S TRYING to escalate or defuse. But frankly, this is far more appealing than snuggling.

"You have hands." Josh shifts himself up toward the headboard, moving his left arm under her neck.

"But that's a lot more effort." It's been forever since she touched herself without the aid of buzzing purple silicone.

She's keenly aware of the way his erection presses insistently into her ass and she finds herself arching her back, pushing against it. Her legs part just enough to slot her right hand between them.

"I have hands, too," he says. There's a second or two of conspicuous silence before he shoves the duvet down the bed. "Roll over onto your stomach."

He pushes down on her right shoulder so that she's lying on her belly and there's a thrilling little sensation streaking up her spine. Maybe Gabe was right about her having a thing for bossy people who think they know everything.

She lets an approving *mmm* slip out when he moves his hand between her legs, brushing it over hers. One—no, two of his fingers slide all too easily inside her and she sucks in a breath. Thank God they're not staring at each other this time.

His fingers press down and—*shit, shitshit*SHIT. It's the difference between *let's see where this pleasurable feeling leads, shall we?* and *there is definitely, one hundred percent an orgasm in my near future.*

"Do you ever think about me when you touch yourself?" His mouth is right next to her ear.

She lets out some incomprehensible moaning sound in response and loops her left arm around the pillow, needing to hold on to something.

Part of her brain screams at her to say anything necessary to get *more, more, more right now.* That part is expanding like a helium balloon. The sensible part that knows all these statements could be used against her in the inevitable argument they'll have later today when they've both come to their senses? That part is shrinking down to the size of a pea.

"I think about lots of things." She bounces the question back to him. "Why? Do you think about me?"

"No. Never. Not even once."

"You're so fucking weird," she says.

"You're so fucking wet."

He slowly pulses against this certain spot in a maddeningly steady, controlled rhythm. Ari hates being edged. Hates it. So, so, so . . . much. "I know what you're doing."

"Hmm?" he replies, obviously reveling in making her ask for it.

"I do this to other women." She squirms to reposition herself, seeking a little more friction. He holds her firmly in place with his other hand. "It doesn't work on me."

That makes him laugh. *Enraging.* "Answer the question."

Ari huffs but she'd rather be satisfied than indignant. "Statistically, I've probably, uh . . ."

He lays a series of kisses down her back, his nose dragging along her lower back, inching lower . . . and lower until he lifts his head.

"Yes?"

Admitting it feels like the final nail in the coffin they've been assembling for the last twelve hours.

"I have a very dirty mind, okay? But I don't— *Ahhh.* Oh God."

"That's it." He rubs firmly against the same spot. "Do you want to come like this?"

"P-pretty much always. How are you doing that?" And why hasn't she been doing it to herself for the last ten years?

He eases his fingers out and she makes a disappointed little moan.

"Want me to keep going?"

"If you stop, I'll cut you."

That earns another chuckle. His weight on the bed shifts and she hears a rustling on the nightstand.

After eight seconds of packet-opening struggle, he pulls her hips up a bit, kneeling behind her. Her pulse is racing and she hasn't felt this combination of tension and excitement flood her brain without chemical assistance in years.

He places one hand on her left hip and the other between her shoulder and neck. Ari can't help but look back at him, like she needs to double-check an answer she knows is right.

"Okay?" he asks softly. He lets go of her hip to guide himself inside her. "Tell me if it's too much."

"I've taken a whole fist, you know."

"Not mine." He spanks the fleshy part of her ass. "Brat."

God.

Despite her fist-related bluster, a soft curse escapes her lips because this angle feels like . . . uh, more than she was anticipating.

He waits for them both to breathe in and out a few times before pressing her flush against the mattress, legs straight.

It's slow at first—which is good because she has no leverage; it's the kind of thing she never allows herself to do with random hookups. But not being in control at all is a minor revelation, and she's just never trusted a man like this before, maybe ever, and it's . . .

Well, she usually thinks of herself as fucking the other person.

His hands move over hers, fingers intertwining again, like a pervy inversion of yesterday's intimacy.

There aren't any tears this time.

He lowers himself onto his elbows, covering her back with the weight of his torso, thrusting deep and slow. Ari catches her breath just before he moves her hair aside and drags his mouth over the back of her neck.

"Just keep . . . doing . . . that," she mutters.

They breathe in the same rhythm, both groaning when he nudges that same spot, over and over.

Josh reaches underneath her, palm flat against her rib cage, and pulls her up and onto her knees in front of him, until her back is pressed against his chest. The angle is shallower and his movements are more careful, but now he can reach his hands everywhere—cupping around the underside of her breast, thumbing the nipple, making her whimper.

It's on the verge of too much.

"Are you always this . . ." She can't come up with the words. What are words? "This . . . this—" Her hands reach back for anything to hold on to: She scratches at his shoulder, his back, pulls at his hair. She really has been missing out on morning sex. Holy shit.

His mouth is just barely on her ear and if he says *anything*—a deep vibration of any kind—she'll fucking lose it.

"Arch your back more." *Gah!*

She complies without a second thought, pushing her shoulders back against his chest. Maybe sex *is* better than a killer stand-up set.

"I'm almost— Don't stop. I'm—I'm—" *Pleasepleaseplease.*

"You could be waking up like this every day." His other hand nudges open her legs a little wider, just enough to position his fingers almost exactly where they need to be. But not quite. "Better than a vibrator?"

"W-why not both?"

"Bring it next time."

Maybe she shifts her weight; maybe he changes the angle a tiny bit. Maybe it's the mention of "next time." Whatever does it, the smallest adjustment sends a lightning bolt down her spine, straight to her core, blotting out everything else.

"Right there, right there. Oh God. Josh. Oh God." He holds her tight against his chest. "God, I fucking love this. I love you. Fuuuuuuuuck."

She catches it just after the tidal wave rolls over her body. *Shit. SHIT.*

Her heart thuds against her chest—and not because of the orgasm.

What was that?

For a second, she's not sure if she'd actually said it. Like, maybe some insanely impulsive part of her brain was just super loud inside her head.

She lets herself go slack as Josh presses her down against the mattress again. He utters her name a few times and comes in several long bursts before collapsing on top of her like the world's heaviest weighted blanket.

But, like . . . she wasn't in her right mind. People say all sorts of insane things in the heat of the moment.

He knows that. He must know that.

The phrase rolls around her head like a marble in one of those handheld maze games.

Why? Why did it have to be *those* words?

She's sweating. Physically and metaphorically sweating. A flashing neon sign in her brain warns: *Get out of here. Leave. Get your shit and go.*

Funny. That's the exact same thing she tells herself immediately after some random hookup. It's like a mantra.

She reaches behind her to tap on whatever part of him is accessible. "You're, uh, kind of crushing me."

"Oh. Sorry, I just—" He rolls himself off her, running his hand through his hair, still breathing hard. "Fuck, that was . . ."
She slides cautiously off the mattress, finding her footing on the floor. "Where are you going?"

"I need to get up," she says, careful not to set off any alarm bells.

"You're leaving?" Josh sits up a bit on his elbow and stares at her with a faint hint of suspicion. "Now?"

"I need to pee," she adds, backing away from the bed. "And

I have the dog-walking tryout. And then I'm meeting"—*oh God*—"I have an appointment. I told you."

He can't argue with any of this.

"We could get breakfast. The Smile?"

"You hate that place."

"Yeah, but it's right downstairs. Or bagels? Russ & Daughters? Tompkins Square? David's? Wherever you want."

"It's six in the morning, Josh. They're not open yet."

"You could cancel. Say you're sick."

Ironically, she does feel quite ill.

"I don't get sick days." She searches the floor for any fallen belongings because she really doesn't want to have to re-enter the bedroom in search of a hair tie or something. "I'll text later?"

"You'll *text*?"

"I have to go. I'll be late."

"Fine." The tightness in his voice indicates that it's really not *fine* for her to leave like this.

But every fiber of her being is screaming to flee.

She's halfway through the door when she glances back at him. His expression makes her wince. *Confusion? Disappointment?* But she doesn't turn around.

In her entire life, she's never gotten dressed faster.

21

JOSH STARES UP AT THE PLASTER CRACK IN THE CEILING THAT HE'S failed to address for the last eight months. It feels like an apt metaphor for his current emotional state.

He'd worried she'd slip out in the middle of the night, so it was a pleasant surprise when he'd awoken twice and found her softly snoring next to him.

Maybe the encore this morning was a bridge too far. Instead of pressing his luck, he could've gotten up and made her breakfast. She's incapable of leaving a room where food is on the table. This would occur to him *now*, two minutes after she's out the door.

Or maybe it all unfolded exactly as it was supposed to.

Because she fucking said "I love you" clear as day and that has to *mean* something no matter what the context is and she didn't explain it which means she didn't take it back but she also didn't acknowledge it and holy fucking shit he's going to spin on this unless he gets his mind under control.

He's not letting himself celebrate it. Not yet.

Instead, he's running the events of yesterday over and over in his mind on a loop, where all the questionable shit gets warped and exaggerated and interrogated until it seems like the entire twelve hours was a long, tense argument with a few minutes of sex thrown in.

And now every single variable needs to be reexamined in order to create the right circumstance for the last twelve hours to happen again, but with a different ending.

What if he was supposed to run after her? If he's already fucked that up, then should he call? Or, if that's too much, what—does he text her? And when? There's a decision tree here, already branching out of control. If he had something better to do with his time, he could distract himself.

But he doesn't have anything else.

What he needs is an objective opinion. Someone who knows Ari and isn't related to him and doesn't hate his fucking guts.

He reaches for his phone. There is one someone who knows Ari, isn't related to him, and well . . . does hate him. But he'll have to settle for two out of three.

> Mon, Jan 16, 7:36 A.M.
>
> JOSH: I need you to decode something.
>
> RADHYA: Who is this?
>
> JOSH: Josh.
> JOSH: Kestenberg
>
> RADHYA: we do NOT have a texting relationship after one lukewarm apology
>
> Especially before 10 am

JOSH: Did she talk to you already?

RADHYA: who?

Who? Before he can answer, another notification comes in.

BRIAR: Morning, sunshine.
You left so fast yesterday.
What do you think of Gabe?? 👀
I thought we had a really great dynamic?

He flips back to his primary objective.

JOSH: We did it.

RADHYA: ?

JOSH: Yesterday. We did it.

RADHYA: are you trying to say you had sex?

JOSH: Yes.
Ari and me.
We had sex.

He considers wrapping up the conversation right here, so it could feel like a win. As soon as she offers her begrudging congratulations, he can convince himself that Ari is just about to text her friends and shyly confess her true feelings.

BRIAR: Would it be weird because he slept with ari?
I mean I know they're totally just friends now
But maybe still awk?

Josh drops the phone in disgust, only to pick it up again, impatient for Radhya's response.

JOSH: Ari didn't call you yet?

Hypothetical question:

An "I love you" during sex.

Does it count?

BRIAR: askdfjsalgkjawoegjoi

FUCK. Wrong fucking text fucking MOTHERFUCKER.

BRIAR: I'm—

I cannot.

☻ ☻ ☻

He tosses the phone across the bed. But then it buzzes again, and he has to pick it up because Radhya might suddenly have some crucial insight.

BRIAR: Alexa, play "Paper Rings"

JOSH: Delete my number.

BRIAR: Okay, let me think

Was there eye contact?

He should just put the phone down, but her excitement is strangely gratifying. He flops down dramatically on his unmade bed.

JOSH: Not possible at the time

BRIAR: Dirty!

What happened after you said it?

JOSH: Why do you assume I said it and not her?

BRIAR: Do you really want me to answer that?

JOSH: She said it. And then she panicked and left.

Hold on, Radhya's calling.

BRIAR: omg start a gc rn 👀

JOSH: Absolutely not.

7:46 A.M.

JOSH: How do I do that?

Mon, Jan 16, 7:49 A.M.

JOSH: I can explain.

BRIAR: Hi Radhya! 😵‍💫 😵‍💫

Did you see my stories?

Btw where did you find those linens for the two-tops?

JOSH: FOCUS.

BRIAR: Start from the beginning. Tell us everything.

RADHYA: I do NOT want to hear everything.

JOSH: We were arguing.

BRIAR: Ok but did you yell at each other with your faces really close
and then just KISS?

was it *Lover* era or *1989*?

RADHYA: Are you fucking kidding me?

Didn't I tell you to give her space?

Like, yesterday afternoon?

BRIAR: was it a little magical tho?

Did she touch your hair?

🫠 🫠

RADHYA: ffs

BRIAR: At least give me an emoji to describe it.

JOSH: I don't use emoji.

BRIAR: THEY'RE PICTURES! PICK ONE

JOSH: 🔥

BRIAR: I'm screaming

RADHYA: What time did she leave?

JOSH: 40 minutes ago.

BRIAR: Did you make her matzo brei for breakfast??

RADHYA: Wait, she spent the NIGHT?

JOSH: Your shock is very flattering, thank you.

RADHYA: Don't do anything.
Don't text, don't call.
Wait for her to initiate contact.

BRIAR: I dunno . . .
3:25ish is a GREAT time for a "sup?"
Very casual.

RADHYA: No.
GIVE HER SPACE.
She might call me in the meantime.

BRIAR: Good strategy. Triangulate!
Gtg team. Peloton is starting.
🚲 🦵

ARI HURRIES AROUND THE CORNER TO THE BLEECKER STREET STATION,
hugging her peacoat closed. It's hard to believe she was sweating
a few minutes ago. She sifts through her unanswered texts with
the charging cord still attached to her phone, slapping against
her inside-out tights as she runs down the stairs.

Fumbling in her bag for her MetroCard with one last fare,
Ari pushes through the turnstile with the slightest sense of relief
that there's at least one physical barrier between current Ari and
the Ari of ten minutes ago. It'll feel even better to get out of this
neighborhood. There's no arrival time on the LED displays—
just a random pattern of red pixels.

She checks her phone. There's an angry red dot with the
number 104 over the MESSAGES icon. She's sure that number was
in the 80s yesterday.

> Sun, Jan 15, 5:31 P.M.
> SALT & PEPPER MAN + BLOND HOTWIFE : Still on for 6:15?
> The place on 20th.
>
> 6:21 P.M.
> We're here.
>
> 6:42 P.M.
> We're in the dining area in back. Ordered some tapas.
>
> 7:05 P.M.
> What's your ETA?

7:23 P.M.

Look, we were willing to wait over an hour because Cara
liked that thing you did with your chin but this is extremely
rude.

7:31 P.M.

How challenging is it to send a text?? "Sorry, can't make it" would
fucking suffice.

Do you know how hard it was for my wife to get comfortable opening
things up?

7:47 P.M.

Your time is not more important than OUR TIME.

Women like you don't give a shit about anyone else.

You happy?

Ari blinks at the screen until the words turn into clumps of
letters. *Cool.* Not only is she blowing up her own life; she's de-
stroying other people's relationships, too. A rat with a long white
scar down its back casually meanders over the rumbling tracks.
The headlights of the 6 light up the tunnel. Ari watches the rat
wander, unconcerned, along the rail.

The train slows to a stop and she chooses a car with enough
people in it to indicate that it's free of horrific smells.

Ari's thumb hesitates over DUST DADDY.

ARI: hey

Delete.

She watches the letters disappear. Maybe if they just never
speak of it again, it'll be like it never happened.

It'll be fine.

It's fine.

The train surges forward and service cuts out in the tunnel. Putting her head in her hands, Ari becomes one of those women who softly cries on the train while the other passengers mercifully ignore her.

WHEN ARI ARRIVES AT THE ADDRESS JOSH'S MOTHER TEXTED HER, SHE recognizes the front windows, now papered over with a smattering of posters for a new HBO series and a bit of graffiti. Abby is already inside the old Brodsky's building, pacing back and forth across the mostly empty floor. She has two white AirPods pressed into her ears, facilitating a spirited conversation with an invisible person.

She waves Ari over, continuing her call while pulling a metal folding chair over to a table with a laptop and scattered papers. "It has a thirty-five-year tax abatement. Mixed-use. Yes." She crushes Ari into one of those maternal hugs that rock back and forth a few times. "A hundred eighty rental units at the base of the Williamsburg Bridge? Text me after you connect with him. Okay." Abby rolls her eyes. *"Okay."* She hangs up and drops the phone to the table. "I swear to God, men refuse to read emails. They need me to tell them the information three times before it takes. Sit, sit."

Ari's phone chimes.

> BRIAR: 🍔😊
> SO great seeing you yesterday.

At least it's not from Josh.

"Thanks so much for meeting me here," Abby says. She holds up two Starbucks cups. "I'm doing a walkthrough with a potential buyer this morning."

BRIAR: the first of MANY hangouts! ☺

If Ari had come here two weeks ago, she'd be scanning the place, looking for clues, trying to glean those tantalizing bits of information that Josh never wants to talk about. Did ten-year-old Josh sit at the counter and refill salt and pepper shakers after school?

Except she doesn't really want to imagine Josh doing anything right now. Not while she's wearing clothes that she picked up off his bedroom floor. Not after what happened this morning and *especially* not in front of his mother.

"Cute dress." *Is Abby a mentalist?* "I'll get right to the point," she says, taking a seat in a folding chair on the opposite side of the table. "I hope this isn't overstepping, but does the name 'WinProv' mean anything to you?"

"WinProv? Is it a startup?" Ari sips the coffee. "Or some kind of online platform?"

"Management consulting. They provide improv workshops for corporations. It's incredibly lucrative. I met the CEO last week—Brad's a lovely guy. Really sharp." Abby tilts her head forward. "He wants to talk to you about a job."

"Me?"

"Absolutely. He's hiring comedians. Give him a call sometime this week. He's expecting to hear from you." Abby slides her phone across the table to show her the WinProv website, featuring a man and a woman clad in matching blue buttondown shirts, mugging for an audience of insurance salespeople. "His business is booming. Look at that client list."

"Oh. Wow . . ." Ari scrolls down to the cloud of recognizable logos at the bottom of the website. Big pharma, Silicon Valley, predatory lending.

"He books these workshops all over the country. I think he's even opening a new office. There's a ton of opportunity right now."

Mon, Jan 16, 9:11 A.M.

GABE: You coming tonight?

I need you. The show's a bringer.

$23 at the door + 2 drink min

Ari may have evaded Josh's attempt at the awkward morning-after breakfast but somehow being doted on by his mother feels worse. It's probably just paranoia, but Abby's expression is a little smug. Knowing. Maybe even . . . delighted.

Ari's phone chimes again.

Mon, Jan 16, 9:13 A.M.

RADHYA: it's been 3 hrs

When were you planning on telling me about last night?

Ari's stomach drops. First Briar, now Radhya?

"Abby, this is so kind of you but you barely know me."

"Nonsense." Abby waves her hand. "I'm helping his cousin buy a co-op in Murray Hill. He owes me a favor."

Some rogue emotion makes Ari's throat constrict. A sudden pang of missing Cass. The mix of caring and concern. Aggravating and gratifying. Being mothered.

Abby opens an expensive-looking handbag, removing a tube of lipstick and a compact. "Ari, when someone offers you a boost, take it. I mentor the young women in my office." She applies a fresh coat of color to her lips. "Encourage them to seize every opportunity, the same way a man would." Abby snaps the compact shut and leans forward. "Where do you see yourself in the long run? What's your five-year plan?"

Ari buys time with a long sip of coffee. *I plan to be financially stable enough that I don't need to beg grooms to let me write their wedding vows* probably isn't the best answer. *I've been trying to 'do comedy' for my entire adult life and I have nothing to show for it because*

I never 'made it' and I spend the vast majority of my time as a waiter or a dog walker or a nanny isn't great, either.

> 9:15 A.M.
>
> RADHYA: call me
>
> And then call him
>
> I can't take any more of his spiraling texts

Ari silences her phone and turns it facedown on the tabletop. "I've been dealing with a . . . divorce." She says that word carefully. "I'm just trying to do a five-day plan here."

It's more than she'd normally share with a near-stranger, but her emotional reserves must be reaching capacity and starting to leak.

To her credit, Abby appears unfazed.

"Following your passion is so important. I learned that lesson far too late. When I sold my first property, I had a teenage son who resented me, a precocious kindergartner, and a husband who had been doing things the same way for twenty years. Everyone *needed* something from me. But I couldn't live a life where my only purpose was to make theirs more manageable. You can't just wait around, letting things happen *to* you." Abby clicks her nails against the tabletop. "A divorce is the perfect time to rebuild your career." She pauses. "And relationships."

Oh no. Abby looks at her with a shameless grin.

"I think you have the wrong idea about—"

Abby's hands shoot up in surrender. "You don't have to explain."

Then she winks. *Oh God.*

Ari reaches for her water and Abby surprises her by closing her warm palm over the back of her hand.

"Give Brad a call. It might be exactly what you need. It's improv, right? There's travel. And it pays well. If you're not moving forward, you're moving backward. I think they only pass around that memo to men." Abby gives her hand a little pat and settles back into her seat. "And I want you to know, I'm not offering just because you're sleeping with my son."

TWELVE HOURS, TWENTY-SEVEN UNANSWERED TEXTS, AND TWO HUNdred passed canapés later, Ari hears Gabe's laughter outside the comedy club, where he's standing in the center of a cluster of smokers, his laugh bellowing a decibel louder than anyone else's.

"Why do you smell like ham?" he asks when she forcibly inserts herself into the circle.

"Four hours of serving pancetta-wrapped peach slices." Ari musters up the simmering anger that she hadn't gotten the chance to unleash at Radhya's pop-up. "And what got into you yesterday?"

"Funny. I was about to ask you the same thing." He exhales a smoke ring. "Let's have a drink. I'm not up for another half hour."

Gabe claps her on the shoulder and leads/shoves her through the door to the bored host, scrolling her phone behind the podium. The woman barely looks up as she collects Ari's $23 cover, heaving a little sigh.

There's no one onstage yet inside the club's "Rising Star Room," which, frankly, resembles a community center basement where one might attend an AA meeting. Accordingly, Ari heads immediately to the bar for a Long Island Iced Tea.

"That kinda day, huh?" Gabe observes.

Ari answers by flaring her nostrils, determined to give him nothing. She sips from the plastic cup, scanning the room, squinting into the darkness at a tall woman with heavy bangs lying perfectly over her forehead.

"Is that . . . Briar?" Instinctively, Ari stumbles two steps back, moving out of her line of sight.

"It's a bringer. I blasted out invites to everyone I've ever hooked up with." He shrugs and does something weirdly seductive with his left eyebrow. "She likes me."

Ari leans forward. "Did you—"

"We made out in the bathroom of the beer garden." He pauses. There's a threat of mischief in his eye. "It's not like I said 'I love you' or anything."

If he follows that up with another punch line, Ari doesn't hear it over her internal screaming.

"Why does everyone know about this?"

"Probably because you sprinted out of his apartment this morning and he immediately started spiraling and you haven't talked to each other all day?"

"I've been . . . processing." Yes. *Processing*. Processing and avoiding.

"You sound a little hoarse. Is it from all the screaming?" Ari is certain cartoon daggers shoot out of her eyes, puncturing Gabe's perfect, waxed chest. "Okay, look. It was less of a frat-boy-bragging-about-banging-a-girl-on-Reddit recounting of the mechanics and more of an 'all my dreams came true last night so how do we avoid fucking this up' thing."

"I don't want to be anyone's dream." Josh couldn't even casually gloat, like a normal douchebag?

Gabe moves a little closer, creating the illusion of intimacy. "How was it?"

"It was . . ." Ari chews the inside of her cheek. "You know that old song lyric, 'we make love and then we fuck'?"

Gabe barely stifles an impressed sort of chuckle. "No, but it sounds like you each got what you wanted."

Ari downs the rest of the drink, tossing the cup in the trash can by the exit. "I need to leave. I can't do this right now."

Gabe grabs her biceps and walks her back to the bar. "You already paid the cover and I need you to laugh incredibly loud at my set and sit there stone-faced for everyone else." He flags down the bartender. "Seriously. I invited a casting assistant."

Ari orders a double as she looks at the back of Briar's head. "Were you and Briar sitting here, discussing it?"

"Of course not," he says, checking the time on his phone. "We discussed it over text first thing this morning."

"See, *you're* the ones making it into something more than it is."

Gabe puts his phone in his pocket and puts his hands on Ari's shoulders. "There's a window. You waited too long. The window for a no-strings hookup closed on the two of you months ago."

"That's not true. I always leave the window open a crack."

"Say whatever you want, but it's gonna be one hell of an awkward DTR conversation," he adds. "He has heart-eyes."

"I think we can just . . . walk it back." Even as the words leave her mouth it feels hopeless.

Gabe gives her a patronizing "sure you can" nod. "I have to ask . . . what the hell was he doing to you that made you say the phrase that shall not be named?"

Ari chokes on her comically large drink. She feels nauseous—not just because of the smell of sour alcohol and musty garden-level air. "Hey," she says after the coughing fit subsides, "have you ever heard of something called WinProv?"

"Great segue. You should teach classes on avoidance." He tosses back his drink. "Some corporate comedy training bullshit?"

"Bullshit with travel and an actual paycheck." Ari pulls out her phone and shows him the WinProv website.

Gabe scans the screen, narrowing his eyes.

"No," he says. Something passes over his face—worse than actual anger. Disappointment. "What about LaughRiot? Our Harold team? You're really going to walk out on us?"

"You guys have been performing without me for months. You don't need me."

"Please don't tell me you're actually considering doing *this*." He thrusts her phone back at her. "Not you."

"You played Gaston in Japan for six months!"

"That's *acting*," he insists. "This? Is disloyal. It's selling out. You're better than this."

"I'm just considering my options."

They stare at each other for a long beat before Gabe shakes his head and walks away. It's somehow more cutting than a huge blowup. There's something especially awful about his subdued disillusionment.

Ari takes a breath in, turns around, and heads for the exit, fumbling to swipe the WinProv website off the phone screen.

Something even more fraught replaces it.

> Mon, Jan 16, 9:57 P.M.
> JOSH: Sup.

It's almost worse than heart emojis.

She stumbles through the doorway and into the chilly night air, hitting CALL before she can decide not to.

JOSH PACES THE LENGTH OF HIS APARTMENT IN LARGE, STEADY STEPS.

"You were chatty today," Ari says. "Is there anyone in this city you didn't contact this morning?"

"That was an accident," he points out.

"I don't want to get a congratulatory message from your mom next . . . or your therapist, or your accountant." There's a long pause.

"Can we talk about this?"

"Can we?" The line goes silent for thirty seconds. His jaw is practically grinding into the phone until she adds, "It was—"

"—fucking amazing."

"—kind of insane?"

"But in a good way." He's careful not to add any hint of a question mark to that statement. He wanders aimlessly into the bedroom and flops down dramatically on his uncharacteristically unmade bed.

"Why is this hard all of a sudden?" she asks. "No pun intended."

"Because there was no way we could keep going like that forever."

There's another long pause. Too long.

Uncomfortably long.

Finally, she breaks the standoff. "Like *what* forever?"

"Like two people who desperately want to be more than friends but never act on it." There's another thirty seconds of silence. "We could just start with a normal conversation," he suggests. "You could tell me about your day."

"Okay, let's see." She clears her throat. "So interesting thing happened yesterday. I went home with this guy I've been hanging out with. And we just, like, boned. Out of nowhere."

"You *boned*?" he says. To be fair, this *is* the kind of thing she would tell him on a random Monday. "How intimate. Definitely the biggest dick you've ever encountered, right?"

She makes a kind of squeaking noise. "Honestly," she says in a solemn tone, "I was frightened of its massive girth."

Josh nods. "I can see why you're so into him."

"When did I say that?"

"That's true." He leans back into the headboard. "You never have."

"That's the thing," she says. "Who am I going to text about you?"

"You can text me about how adequate I am. It's probably the most positive feedback I've received in a year."

"I hate when you say things like that—"

"Do you want to have dinner? Just dinner." *Fuck it.* "Unless you also want to have sex. In which case it would be both."

She sighs. "I'm waiting for Gabe to go on. I promised to come to a bringer show. That's, like, a sacred pact." There's another interminable silence before she says, "Let's just . . . pause for a few days?" There's a careful quality to the way she says it that sets off alarm bells in his head. "Don't read too much into this, but"—*great,* now his brain is ready and waiting to assign subtext to words she hasn't even spoken—"I don't think we should get swept up in something without really considering it in the cold light of day."

"It sounds like you're considering it in the dark confines of a comedy club."

"Josh, every part of my life is in some stage of upheaval right now." He can hear the swirling panic in her voice. "I like you in, like, fourteen specific ways and we probably just blew up our entire relationship. Can we just . . . give ourselves some time to—"

"Okay. Okay you're right." He adopts the calming inflection of a hostage negotiator. "Let's talk in a few days."

"Cool." Hearing the obvious relief in the sigh she lets out makes his own throat feel tighter.

"You know," he says, adjusting his tone, "I noticed I didn't get a polite thank-you text today. I thought that was your standard operating procedure."

"Well, you didn't actually go down on me."

"Because you never put on the clown costume like I told you to."

He imagines her smiling at that—that little glint of sly charm that feels so fucking good to see. "I'm not much of a good girl. More of a brat, really."

And now *he's* fucking smiling, despite himself. Maybe it'll be okay. An intermission, of sorts. Give her time to adjust.

It's fine.

It'll be fine.

22

Thurs, Jan 26, 4:53 P.M.

BRAD HOENIG [SFW ⬤]: Ari! Thanks for jumping on another call at the last minute.

Being able to roll with the punches is mission critical at WinProv.

Just to confirm, you have a valid driver's license, correct?

"YOU WEREN'T EXAGGERATING ABOUT YOUR DISTASTE FOR PANTS." JOSH stands at Ari's door, holding a cardboard box and two grocery bags.

Ari is wearing a pair of boxers and a tank top because the thermostat in this apartment has always been something out of her control. But it creates an odd dynamic when someone shows up appropriately bundled for January and the other is dressed for a sweltering July.

Particularly when the someone is Josh, who she hasn't seen, spoken to, or texted in the past week. That he's extremely dressed only makes Ari feel extremely not-dressed.

"What's in the box?" She crosses her arms over the Lilith Fair logo on the front of the tank top, hiding the outline of the piercings that poke through her unlined bralette like, "hey, remember us?"

"I'm making you dinner. A real dinner."

"*You're* going to cook? Here?" She peers over the cardboard flap of the box and sees something shiny and metallic. "Really?"

"Really." He walks back into the kitchen, brushing past Ari, leaving her staring at the door.

When she turns around, he's swinging the strap of a duffel bag off his shoulder. It could be a gym bag, sure. Or his potential-sex bag. With outfit changes.

How had she failed to see this coming when she texted him and asked if he wanted to come over and talk?

They're wandering around a no-man's-land between buddies and lovers without a rulebook. Maybe the Tall Sweater Nightmare Man version of Josh was right: There really is no such thing as consequence-less sex.

She walks cautiously toward the kitchen, watching the explicit competency porn of Josh separating the produce into neat groups and lining up his knives next to his cutting board.

"You stole salt and pepper shakers from a diner?" He holds up the two mostly empty little glass bottles that had been sitting next to her stove. "I'm buying you some decent kosher salt. This is unacceptable."

"The food I eat doesn't usually need *more* sodium," she mutters, brushing some stray crumbs off the counter before he can comment on them. "Hey, so there's something I need to talk to you . . ."

She trails off because Josh pulls his sweater over his head and there's a slice of pale skin between his waistband and T-shirt. For a second, she has this ridiculous thought that he's just . . . casually undressing because that's how things are between them now. Like he's going to continue removing layers of dark clothing until—

"It's so fucking hot in here," he says, folding the sweater—of course he *folds* it—and placing it on top of his duffel.

He methodically opens each empty overhead cabinet. *Why are his shirts always straining slightly?* Of course Ari's dirty Josh thoughts leach up to the surface now, at a time when she needs to be rational. "Where are the mixing bowls we bought?"

"Uh . . . lower left." Ari watches him take over her kitchen, fussing over various stainless-steel gadgets. "What are you making?"

"*Lasagne in bianco,*" he replies, like this is a normal thing. "Is it possible that you own a baking dish?"

She crouches down to the lower right cabinet and holds up a rectangular Pyrex dish. "I use it for pot brownies."

He gives her a slightly titillating look of disapproval before taking it out of her hands. "Is that another one of Cass's shirts?"

Ari shrugs, looking for a conversational pivot. "You brought your pasta machine?" She turns the little handle.

"My dad's. This is elevated comfort food."

Ari leans her lower back against the countertop, trying to find a position that seems casual before she tells him why she will not need kosher salt or these mixing bowls in a few weeks. Instead, what comes out is: "You think I need comforting?"

She's way off her script now. He wasn't supposed to come over here and boil water, let alone make pasta from scratch.

Josh picks up his grater and walks toward her—only one step, because he's a big man in a New York kitchen.

"Do you?" He looms over her, leaving just a couple inches of space between them. There's a dish towel over his shoulder. He's not playing fair.

"Do I what?" The black cotton of his shirt just barely brushes against the thin barrier of the faded Lilith Fair logo.

"Need. Comforting." His eyes move up and down her face, like he's maybe going to lean in.

Ari holds her breath, tilting her chin up very slightly. He lifts his right arm and—

—reaches for half a pound of fontina cheese.

"Make yourself useful and shred this."

She exhales. "Sure, give me the dangerous job." He opens the package of flour and searches the drawers for measuring cups, as if she might actually own some.

"While this is in the oven, we'll go in the bedroom and clean out your ex-wife's T-shirt drawer."

They're perfectly good shirts, she wants to point out.

But something feels tight in her belly when he says *bedroom.* Her mind slips out of rational mode and begins generating images of sex they could be having.

No, no, no. She has to stay focused. There's no point in disturbing their fragile peace now, not while he's cooking for the first time in a year.

So they'll eat. And then they'll talk.

It'll be fine.

"You know," she says, looking for a subject change as she picks up the grater, "I do have a huge bag of bacon bits from Costco. They're delicious in mac and cheese if you just sprinkle them—"

"Absolutely not." He furrows his brow. "I brought prosciutto."

JOSH EXPECTS TO FIND MAYBE HALF A DOZEN OF CASS'S SHIRTS IN THE dresser he and Ari assembled two months ago. Instead, it's almost like this woman forgot to empty one drawer in her haste to vacate the apartment and it happened to house the contents of Cameron Crowe's laundry basket, circa 1995.

It doesn't matter now. He won.

Overall, he's really fucking proud of himself for the restraint he's shown throughout the evening. There hasn't been a hint of desperation. No pushing. It even felt *right* to cook again, to demonstrate certain steps, even show off his knife skills a little, just like the first time they met.

They hadn't kissed, which was also okay—almost like they didn't need to prove anything. On the contrary, their lack of physical contact up to this point has only added to the tension.

And yes, her bare-bones communication over the last few days was aggravating. But he understands Ari now: When there's something this big—*this* important—she clams up. If anything, it's confirmation of her feelings.

Which explains why she's nervous, standing at the foot of her bed, rocking back and forth on her feet, watching him rummage through the shirts. Everything about her is slightly heightened now—she somehow gained freckles, her lower lip is fuller, her topknot is more unruly.

He pictures himself on top of her, the lights still on, her legs wrapped around him. She might even say "I love you" again but looking into his eyes so there's no mistaking it. And he'd have the presence of mind to say it back this time.

He holds a trash bag open.

"They're just shirts." Ari bends at the waist and unceremoniously grabs at the contents of the drawer. "They're not, like, symbolic of anything."

"It's about moving on with your life."

"I *am* moving on. You're just depriving me of pajama tops." She sinks back down onto the bed, clutching two handfuls of shirts. "That's what I wanted to tell you."

"That you're moving on without pajama tops?"

"Actually, yes." She sets the clothing down in two little piles on either side of her. She picks at the material on one of the shirts. "We're putting the apartment on the market. I need to be out of here by the end of the month."

He lets the trash bag drop. Hearing her casually refer to Cass as part of a present tense *we* stings.

"So I had to figure out what to do." Ari folds her legs underneath her again, as if she needs to buy a little extra time to formulate the words. His mind floods with possibilities.

A sign?

He turns his back to her and stands in front of the dresser, staring down at the open drawer, giving himself some privacy from her gaze. "There's a solution for that."

"Actually—"

"Move in with me." He shuts the drawer with a satisfying smack.

"Wait, what?"

Josh turns around, leaning against the dresser. Ari's expression is more surprised than he would like. "Move into my apartment. Or we can look for a new place. Together."

"Like roommates?"

"No." He drops his head for second, taking a breath, reminding himself to be fucking patient. "Not like my roommate." Lifting his head back up, he looks her in the eye. "Like the person I'm in love with."

The room is silent except for the occasional clank and hiss from the radiator.

He'd thought maybe her eyes would well up, that the corners of her mouth would curve into a disbelieving smile and she'd slowly rise up from the bed and embrace him. They'd hold each other, finally feeling some sense of relief.

But instead she just sits there, stock-still, mouth open.

Easing himself down beside her on the bed, he slowly reaches for one of her hands.

"Josh." Her voice is low and quiet. She watches him run his thumb across her knuckles. *Soft.* "Saying that only makes this more complicated than it already is."

"I'm so fucking tired of *not* saying it. I thought we were being honest now. You already said it. I know this can work. I'm sure of it. You don't think you're ready. But you are." He pulls her hand up to his lips and presses a kiss into her palm. "You are."

"Don't tell me what—" She forces herself to slow down and breathe. "Josh, listen to me—"

"What do you think we've been doing this whole time? We've been fucking dating, Ari. It happened so gradually, we just didn't see it. We didn't use the word. We only needed that final piece and now we have it."

He moves her hand down his cheek and it feels almost like she's doing it of her own volition.

Josh tilts his head and leans down, placing his other hand on the back of her head and pulling her into the kind of kiss they should have had before she ran out of his apartment last week. Her mouth is warm and open and inviting and says everything she won't express in words.

They fall back onto the mattress. He props himself up, hovering over her.

"This isn't the right time," she says. "I'm—I'm depressed."

"I'm depressed, too. Over half the people in this fucking city are depressed."

"Josh—"

"Depressed people can be in relationships. We could be waiting forever for the 'right time.' You're perfect for me, exactly how you are at this moment."

He kisses the hollow of her throat, listening to her breath get heavier and a little ragged as he sucks on a particular spot on her neck in a way that's definitely going to leave a visible mark.

"Josh . . ." Her fingers dig into his shoulders.

He lifts the hem of the shirt (of *course* Cass went to Lilith Fair), exposing the skin between the waistband of her shorts and her bralette. "You needing a new apartment? This is a sign." He kisses along her rib cage. She's soft and warm and everything just makes *sense*. "It's a fucking sign that this is right."

"*Josh*." The volume of her voice makes him pause. "I'm not looking for another apartment."

"What?" He stops moving.

"I accepted a job. I'm leaving New York for a while."

"What?" He lifts his head, not quite processing those sentences. "Where are you going?"

"Washington, D.C., for now. Your mom put me in touch with the CEO of a consulting firm. He's hiring comedians to do improv training."

"My mom?" *When did this happen? Why hadn't Ari mentioned this?* "Consulting?"

"I'll be traveling around, teaching improv games to employees of different companies." She pulls her shirt back down to cover her belly. "It pays really well. Like, an actual salary."

"Hold on." Josh shakes his head. "Since when do you want to be a consultant?"

Ari scrambles into a seated position. "You have *no* idea what I want."

"What about getting back to performing? What happened to 'comedy is like magic'? You're just giving up?"

Ari's eyes flash with anger. "Says the person who hasn't stepped foot in a kitchen for . . . a year?"

"What about *me*? Where do I fit into this?" He doesn't bother to filter out the desperate edge to his voice. He waits for her to present some solution: long visits, weekends in Philly, phone sex. Could he go with her? It's not like he has a reason to be in New York. He doesn't have a reason to be anywhere.

She continues in the same suspiciously careful tone: "We can go back to the way things were. Over the phone. Before the . . ." Ari tilts her head and gives a little shrug.

"Before the *what*?" He waits for her to utter the word, knowing it's not coming. "Say it."

"You know exactly what I'm talking about, Josh. You can keep dating. I'll keep, you know, whatever—"

"We had *sex*." *God-fucking-dammit.* "And I don't want to go back, Ari. You'd rather be lonely together, over the fucking phone? Do you honestly think I want to hear about you doing 'whatever'? Listen to yourself." He feels his hands balling into fists and unfurling and balling again. "It unlocked something."

"I'm not good at this part," she insists. "It's not personal."

"'It's not pers—'" He looks up at the ceiling like he's begging for divine intervention. "We're not pretending this didn't happen. Not this time. We already crossed that line, Ari. You can't move it again." Josh's face turns from confused to mildly accusatory.

"You're not listening to me." It sounds like a warning, but she doesn't get just how much he already understands her. "I'm not ready to unlock anything right now. I'm still grieving."

"You're 'grieving'?" He grabs one of the shirts and throws it down onto the wood floor with a surprising amount of force. "She's a narcissist who cheated on you and left. You're letting this woman dictate your life and she doesn't give a fuck about you anymore. I know it hurt your pride when she walked out. Because *you're* the person who disappears in the middle of the night. *You're* the one who leaves. Which is exactly what you're trying to do right now."

The look on her face is surprisingly wounded. "You already got the fun part. I don't know what else you want from me."

Josh gestures at the space between them. "*This* is supposed to be the fun part."

"I'm having a *great* time, how about you?"

He leans closer to her, so that he can see her exact reaction to the words that are on the tip of his tongue. "I know what I want." He has a heady, dizzying feeling like this is *it*. The last shot. "I want everything and I'll give you everything." He reaches out and brushes his hand over her hair. "You don't just *find that* with someone and walk away."

"We're already fighting!" Her head moves back, away from his hand.

"I know there's something here. I *know* it, Ari. I know you feel it, too."

"Every bitterly divorced couple feels that way in the beginning. None of your problems matter because there's someone to be your everything and take care of you. They're the antidote to every little thing you hate about yourself. They can see past it when you can't." She shifts her whole body another inch away from him. "But eventually, you wake up and all the stuff you pushed down comes back up again. Every stupid, irritating thing about the other person becomes an argument. They get needy and demanding, they hide things from you—little things that your gut tells you are actually big things—and you start to feel paranoid and insane. You blame each other for all the ways that your lives aren't working out. For all the decisions that made sense at the time but were fucking terrible in retrospect. And suddenly there isn't any magic gluing the two of you together. You're just two idiots arguing over who gets custody of the dinnerware."

"I'm not going to take your bowl, Ari."

"She paid thirty thousand dollars in lawyers' fees to get rid of me. Do you get that?"

"That's not you and me."

She shakes her head. "But I know how this ends, too. Four years from now, I'll run into you in the Whole Foods in Park Slope. You'll be pushing your two-year-old around in one of those expensive strollers, looking for a perfect bunch of organic grapes, while your yoga instructor wife picks out kombucha. And I'll be the girl wearing some random man's Islanders jersey—"

"Islanders?"

"—double fisting bottles of cheap wine. I'll be peeking around the corner, hoping you don't see me and ask me how I've been. Because I'd have to tell you that I'm still pouring daiquiris at bar mitzvahs and writing speeches for strangers who actually have lives worth celebrating. That I still get drunk and go home with strangers I never see again. That I haven't fixed any aspect of my life. I don't want to go through that with you. I don't want . . ." Her face scrunches up suddenly. "I don't want to see you with a fucking wife and kid someday."

Her chest heaves a little bit and tears start to stream down her cheeks. Josh looks away, moving his jaw, tensing against the impulse to allow his own eyes to well up.

"I'm so tired of crying in front of you!" she shouts. "I don't do this. I'm not like this."

It feels like some third person has pressed pause on the scene and Josh sees the whole thing like it's playing out with two actors and he's just some voyeuristic creep, watching an irate asshole yell at a woman who seems to close in on herself a little bit more with each volley. He waits until her crying jag subsides and she sniffles.

"How do you know we wouldn't be buying organic grapes together in four years?" Ari's expression changes, but not in a way that helps him decipher any kind of meaning. "I will buy you whatever fucking grapes you want. The kombucha." He pauses. "The stroller. All of it."

She looks exhausted. "I don't want to get lost in someone else. I need to do something with my own life."

It feels like a half-hearted tug-of-war; the harder he pulls on the rope, the more it frays.

"What the hell do you think *my* life is like?" He stands up again, needing the higher ground, pacing in a tight circle. "I'm a complete fucking failure. My dad worked himself to death for forty years keeping his business afloat for my sister and me. And I killed it in a matter of months. Every morning I wake up and remember that I failed him in every possible way and it's too late to repair it. I have no job, no friends, and I make up a bunch of stupid bullshit to do until it's time to go to sleep and do it all over again." He stops pacing. "Do you realize the only thing I look forward to every fucking day is talking to you?"

"That's exactly why this won't work. You failed *one time* and you act like this pathetic victim of circumstance. Nothing's stopping you from trying again except your own ego. No one exiled you. And I don't *want* to be the only person you can talk to. I don't want you to take care of me. I'm an adult."

"Since when?" He should probably back the fuck off but everything's gone a step too far to walk it back. "Seems to me that you'd rather be nipple piercings and bong vapor."

Ari stares at him, eyes wide with a combination of anger and shock—like he'd just stabbed her in the stomach with a bayonet. He feels a momentary flair of regret but he can't back down.

"I'm not waiting for more time to pass. I've wasted enough of my fucking life. I'm not going backward. You're not going to insult me and pretend like we can just be friends again."

He looks into her eyes until he sees the tears well up again, and she yanks the rope back.

"I don't owe you a relationship just because we had sex."

Josh stumbles back a couple steps toward the door. He's supposed to be looking at his fucking girlfriend. He's supposed to be soaking in the new relationship energy, letting himself replay the "I love you" over and over in his head, finally allowing himself to believe it. He's supposed to have his face buried in her pussy, with her thighs pressing against his ears, so he can just barely hear her moaning.

But instead he's looking at yet another person who just wants him to fucking disappear.

Fine. FINE.

Fuck. All. Of. This.

She can have her wish.

He steps over the shirts strewn around the floor. Walking out to the kitchen, he picks his coat and his fucking overnight bag up off the floor, grabs his knife roll, and silently exits the apartment.

She can keep the pasta machine. Let it collect dust in storage.

He leaves their dinner in the oven to burn.

Two Months Later

23

ARI'S OFFICIAL TITLE IS "JUNIOR SOLUTIONS ENABLER" FOR THE FIRST two weeks of employment at WinProv LLC. Her duties include picking up her boss, Brad Hoenig (founder/CEO/head improveneur/agent of fun #1), from a variety of airports. Driving Brad around is the easiest gig she's had in years, even if she suspects she's doing it because he has a suspended license.

Brad's real name is Brian but he A/B tested first names five years ago and found that "Brad" is snappier. He's A/B tested every aspect of WinProv, including the color of the shirts his "enablers" wear for each workshop (cobalt blue—green shirts are "aggressively unfunny"). He wears a pair of wraparound sunglasses pushed up on his forehead an inch and a half above his eyes. Ari frequently finds herself staring into the reflective black abyss of the sunglass lenses as he quotes Louis C.K. bits.

He puts Ari up in a studio apartment in one of those beige corporate housing complexes with stiff, uncomfortable furniture and a tiny coffee maker. It looks like a place a newly separated dad would occupy for a few months while he sorts out his shit.

Ari hadn't brought much with her. The day before she took the train down to D.C., she packed a few odds and ends inside liquor store boxes and took a Lyft over to Radhya's.

"This is ridiculous," Radhya had said as Ari pushed the boxes into her tiny foyer with her boot. "You don't have to leave the state because of Kestenberg." It was probably the fifth time Rad had expressed this sentiment.

"This isn't about him," Ari insisted. "It's a good opportunity for me."

"I'm shocked I haven't gotten another series of unhinged texts from him." Rad leaned over to examine the remainder of Ari's stuff—an assortment of random-but-precious shit that couldn't fit in her suitcase (an aloe plant she'd managed not to kill, the blue-and-white bowl that she'd seriously considered leaving in the cabinet as some stupid show of poetic justice before chickening out). Everything else had been sold, curbed, or donated. "Since when do you have a pasta machine?"

Ari got that sensation like the teacher called on her even though she hadn't raised her hand.

"It's Josh's." Ari took care not to trip over his name, which she probably hadn't said out loud for a week.

Radhya assured her she'd return it to him. "It gives me flashbacks of rolling out endless batches of pappardelle," she'd said, shuddering.

Ari said "thanks" and decided that would be the last time she mentioned Josh Kestenberg to Radhya. Or anyone.

Instead of thinking about Josh, Ari memorizes business jargon like "hard stop," "mission critical," and "circle back to that." She watches Brad's rousing informational videos, which are all set to an unlicensed version of "Where the Streets Have No Name." She studies his A/B tested presentation script. It includes a lot of "pause for laughter." After roughly fifteen airport drop-offs and pickups and two workshops, Ari earns the title "senior solutions enabler and core faculty member." Brad reminds her that she's still in the probationary period.

Several times a week, Ari and Brad enter a Hilton or a Radisson in their bright blue button-down shirts. They do an A/V check, wire themselves up with headset mics, and pull faces in front of a sea of regional sales managers and IT specialists for three to six hours.

It's sweaty work—not like performing in front of an audience of people who voluntarily paid five or ten or sometimes zero dollars for a LaughRiot show with the goal of being entertained. The WinProv attendees need to be won over every time, whether they're happy to be away from their open-floor-plan offices or annoyed at the forced camaraderie and high probability of trust-falls.

Once or twice, Ari asks Brad if he has any reservations about servicing a client list that includes big pharma and tech companies and the sorts of places that have members of the DeVos family on their boards. He insists that "improv is for everyone. These people build the apps and services we rely on." He says, "Grocery delivery, ride sharing, text-message-based therapy. Front-end developers need to dare to fail, too."

When that line of rationalization fails, there's also Gabe's old standby in times of crisis: "Mine it for material." Ari imagines returning to New York with an incisive new sketch skewering the improv industrial complex.

But the idea of going back to the city is a non-starter now that New York and its hundreds of sidewalks and street corners and bodegas have transformed into emotional land mines. There isn't a three-block zone of Manhattan that's not tainted with a Cass memory or a Josh anecdote.

She can't even listen to music in the car. It's on the long, desolate drives around the mid-Atlantic states that her thoughts drift. Waiting at red lights. Idling in drive-thrus. Passing the billboards for Jesus next to the billboards for adult superstores. When she turns on the local FM station and a woman with a twang warbles about heartache, Ari's mind's eye draws a perfect picture of Josh's profile, better than any camera could capture.

She tries to remember the awful things they'd said, rekindling her anger just long enough to get past the heartsick feeling.

Occasionally, it feels like Ari is placing a rug over a gaping hole in the floor. But sometimes you can only address one crisis at a time.

After a few weeks of shadowing Brad, Ari leads a workshop on her own: a small session on a boat cruise around the D.C. harbor. After the workshop, while the employees of some awful lobbying firm enjoy the "premier dinner buffet," Ari stands outside on the deck, shivering in her peacoat, watching the Washington Monument pass. Incredible how humans have been shamelessly building these behemoth penises for thousands of years.

She adjusts the coat to cover the hideous blue button-down, pulls her shoulders back, and snaps a series of four selfies: two silly, one semi-silly-but-still-cute, one serious/sexy. "See," these photos say, "I'm carefree. I'm finding myself here."

She types the caption, "Enjoying the nation's #1 erect phallus," then posts all four pics, rearranging the order several times.

It's probably the first time she's taken a boat selfie since she and Cass got married. Maybe it's fitting that there's a monumental dildo sharing the frame in this one, too.

SCOURING THE BINS AT ACADEMY RECORDS IS JOSH'S PERFECT TIME-wasting activity. It feels good to put on pants with a non-elastic waistband and join the fraternity of middle-aged men who communicate by one-upping one another with their pointless knowledge of free jazz and minimal techno. For the last few minutes, he's made a conscious—some might say *valiant*—effort to tune out the insufferable manbun lecturing his normcore companion about the "auditory detritus" in Brian Eno's *Ambient 4: On Land*.

He refreshes his email app, even though he has push notifications on, and it's highly unlikely that his fucking embarrassing query to a chef in Sonoma he'd worked with briefly four years ago will get answered a mere two and a half hours after he'd composed it.

If it gets answered at all.

Still, the fact that he'd sent it is a tangible thing he can cross off his to-do list. *I'm not, in fact, spending all my time feeling a combination of bitter and heartbroken and angry and sorry for myself.*

I'm also sending emails.

Over the last three weeks, certain memories have already lodged in his brain, expanding and contracting. Walking to the train with an angry ringing in his ears from the shock of their last interaction. Waiting for her to call and apologize. Hearing *nothing*.

For a few days, he hadn't spoken to another person. Hadn't gone outside. He'd just sat on the sofa with his slowly dissipating fury, like an inflatable mattress with the tiniest leak—every fucking thing in the apartment reminding him of some stupid thing Ari had said or done.

Bill Evans's "Peace Piece" plays over the sound system, its two chords repeating like a meditation. Sometimes melancholy music has the inverse emotional impact. It's a strange form of masochism. *Can you take this plaintive piano melody? You can? Then how about this Miles Davis solo, bitch?*

> Tues, March 14, 6:03 P.M.
>
> BRIAR: Excited for tonight?
>
> Remember your POSITIVE talking points.
>
> I peeped her IG and determined that she's like five ten.
>
> A lot of people have that size kink thing where the woman is tiny and the man is a tree, but I think two people who are roughly the same height are VERY aesthetically pleasing.
>
> Btw let's talk photo filters soon.
>
> You need a better selfie strategy.

Speaking of masochism.

He taps the link to the woman's Instagram. Beach vacation pictures. Elaborate restaurant dishes. She's been a bridesmaid three times this year and it's only March.

Josh absentmindedly taps the HOME icon, refreshing his feed.

At the top of the screen is a ghost. A face he hasn't seen in months.

Thanks to this fucking algorithm that knows exactly how to toy with his brain, Ari is staring back at him, smiling.

Josh quickly shoves the phone into his pocket, as if it doesn't obey the principle of object permanence.

"The tracks on this extend past the very idea of beginnings

and endings," Manbun opines from a few feet away, his voice projecting like he's on a stage. "There's just one aural frame."

The piano melody seems to get louder over the sound system—complicated and flourishing over the constancy of those two chords.

Josh puts the record down and retrieves his phone again, holding it with both hands, reopening Ari's post. He swipes through the four photos, each one sending a completely different message. It's a post specifically devised to confuse him.

He slides the carousel of photos back and forth, looking at all of them, letting his brain memorize the slightly new angle of her face in each photo. Being careful not to accidentally tap the heart icon with the pad of his thumb.

The caption reads, "Enjoying the nation's #1 erect phallus." Does it have some meaning beyond a mere dick joke? Has she met someone? Is it code?

He's been skipping therapy. Some topics are just too big to explain in a fifty-minute session. Better to go without and wait until he gets a handle on the narrative.

He doesn't want the fucking help right now, anyway.

"Peace Piece" dissolves into discordant notes, the song almost breaking apart.

It would probably feel good to unfollow her. Or maybe he could post a selection of his own photos that suggest a productive and exciting new life. Let her be the one to check her phone too often.

But when has he ever let himself feel good?

Josh puts his phone away again. He pretends to leaf through the bins a bit more. Maybe this is a form of anchoring, too.

The melody slowly reconciles with the bass, easing into a gentle resolution.

His breathing slows.

The moment he's mentally out of the woods, his phone buzzes again in his pocket.

Tues, March 14, 6:12 P.M.

RADHYA: Hello "Chef." I have your pasta machine.

24

JOSH ISN'T HERE TO ASK ANY QUESTIONS ABOUT ARI. HE WANTS HIS GOD-
damn pasta machine, whether or not he uses it. That's why he's
finally dragged himself to Brooklyn.

He wipes his boots on the welcome mat as the door swings
open.

Radhya's wearing a pair of jeans with holes at the knees.
Her hair is down and it's longer than he would have assumed. It
must be the first time he's seen her without her kitchen armor:
no chef's whites, no hair pulled tight into a bun.

Her apartment smells like Sichuan food. From somewhere
beyond the foyer, there are sounds of low music and cans being
placed directly on a table without coasters underneath.

"Is this a bad time?" he asks, eager for any excuse to make a
quick exit.

"No. Come in." She gestures at a slightly tilting stack of
cardboard boxes at the end of the hallway flanked by a black

trash bag. His dad's pasta machine sits on top of a bulging Crown Royal box.

Josh lifts it up. His dad never actually used it for pasta—just an unsuccessful experiment with pierogi dough. Maybe it's cursed. Strange how this innocuous piece of cooking equipment has come to symbolize his misguided belief that he mattered to Ari.

There's something bright red poking out of the top of the trash bag. He bends down and grabs the wrinkled Soundgarden T-shirt.

"This is her stuff?" he can't help but ask.

Radhya nods. "I'm storing some of her things." She nudges the trash bag with her foot. "But this is going to Buffalo Exchange. I guess Cass's old gym shirt is another person's vintage 'statement piece,'" she says.

It doesn't really mean anything. Maybe she's purchased new shirts. Maybe she's sleeping naked.

He's itching to open the boxes. To examine her stuff and recapture a little bit of that feeling of knowing her.

He admonishes himself, wiping that thought away almost as quickly as it appears.

That kind of urge should have dissipated by now.

To be fair, it's fading a bit. Ari occupies less space in his brain. He's no longer agonizing over her, waiting for a call, or deciphering each social media post like it's composed of Egyptian hieroglyphics.

Or he's limiting himself to only doing that in used record stores.

"Have you talked to her?" Radhya is staring at him.

"Who?" he forces himself to ask.

"Really, Kestenberg?"

"No." *I'm giving it space, or whatever the fuck you said, so . . .*

Radhya lets out an enormous sigh. "She's—" He braces himself for her to drop a momentous piece of Ari information. *Seeing someone else. Marrying Gabe. Joining a cult in British Columbia.* "—fine. According to her."

Josh doesn't respond. It always happens this way: Just as his feelings tip over from anger into acceptance, something reshuffles the whole fucking deck. He clenches his jaw, willing his face to maintain a neutral affect.

"Did you eat dinner?" Radhya asks.

"No." Josh shakes his head once. He must really look pained. Pathetic. Friendless. "But I should get going."

"I ordered Chuan Tian Xia," she says. "Don't pretend you don't want it."

And then a way-too-familiar voice from the other room: "He can't resist Chengdu noodles."

He glances at Radhya and then follows the sound around the corner to the small living room, where his sister (*traitor!*) is sitting on the floor in front of a coffee table, every inch covered by containers, dishes, napkins, lids, and beer cans.

If Briar was capable of shame, she'd be staring up at him with wide, apologetic eyes, but instead her face is calm, even pleased. Best to maintain power position since this is an obvious trap of some sort.

"What is this?" he asks, whipping his head between them. "An intervention?"

Radhya narrows her eyes and takes a seat. She's always been good at maintaining a facial expression that simply dares people to question her further. She pushes the fortune pepper fish an inch in his direction—the Radhya equivalent of an olive branch. "This isn't about Ari."

"It's business," Briar adds. "I had an idea."

Radhya fishes a package of chopsticks out from under a stack of napkins. "She thinks we should work together on a new pop-up."

"This would be closer to a full-scale operation," Briar says, opening a beer and handing it to him. "Like a trial run for the kind of restaurant Radhya wants to open. Gujarati-inspired with a . . . well, let's call it a *nod* to traditional New York delicatessen classics."

He raises an eyebrow. There's something intriguing in the concept. His brain is already sifting through flavor combinations.

Radhya adds, "Briar assures me you can make a perfectly crispy latke to go with my cilantro chutney."

"'Moisture is the enemy of a good latke,'" Briar and Josh recite in unison.

"Do you have a location?" he asks after a beat.

The women exchange a look.

"Brodsky's," Briar says.

Josh takes a step back. "Absolutely not. We're selling the building. It's decided."

"It's *not* decided!" Briar jumps up and tugs on his coat. "It's been sitting there empty for months."

"Because it's *for sale*."

"Mom can sell any property in the city except an iconic Manhattan landmark? Do you honestly believe that?"

"It's not a landmark." *Not after I took the blue neon sign off the façade,* he silently admits. "There could be squatters in there."

"She doesn't want to let the space go. Not really. And it's a perfect solution for Radhya. And you."

"That kitchen is not a solution, it's an albatross. Or have you forgotten the last time I tried to reinvent Brodsky's?"

"Exactly! There's a built-in human interest story there," Briar says. "Former rivals working together. Josh redeeming himself on the site of his spectacular failure—"

"Hey!"

"—Radhya finally getting her chance to shine. Food writers will show up because there's a hook."

The thought of inviting more scrutiny from journalists makes his stomach turn. Time had finally started to temper all those emotions knotted up in failure. Courting publicity in the kitchen where he has so much history? Where his misadventures with The Brod will be mentioned in every article, every review? After having spent the year *not* cooking?

"I don't trust food writers," Josh says. "And having me involved could be a distraction."

"You'll be in the background," Radhya says. "I'm the captain, you're the . . . whatever Gilligan is, and Briar is the cruise director."

"With all due respect," Josh says, "Briar's claim to fame is a photo series of Taylor Swift as handbags. Not getting paying customers through the door."

His sister adjusts her posture. "Excuse me, I can get a hundred people to show up to anything."

"The beer garden pop-up was packed," Radhya adds.

"Being an influencer doesn't qualify you to run a restaurant."

"I grew up in a restaurant!" Briar shouts. She's red in the face. "And I'm tired of you underestimating me. I'm an adult. I'm good at this stuff. And I'm not going to watch while you sell Dad's legacy to the highest bidder."

Glancing at a seething Briar and then Josh, Radhya clears her throat. "It's just a pop-up to start. Give us till the end of the year to prove it's a good concept. After that, if you still want to sell, we'll . . . find a different location."

Briar huffs but she hands him a plate. "Sit down so we can discuss how this is going to work."

All his instincts urge him to flee. To let the self-righteous anger overwhelm every rational thought. To take a little bit of sick pleasure in having the last word.

He's not sure why this time is different. Why he reaches for the plate.

Maybe it's the way Briar is punctuating her thoughts with periods rather than question marks. Or that he can already taste three different traditional Jewish dishes that would work perfectly with Radhya's Indian flavors. Or because Radhya clears her throat and says, "You'll really regret it if you storm out of here without trying the wontons. They're fucking amazing."

This time he presses his boots into the floorboards. He silently names five things he can see, four things he can smell—which is easy because he's standing in front of some of the best Sichuan food in the city. He can practically feel the handle of his favorite chef's knife in his palm. His hands are definitely too sensitive to belong to a chef. Luckily he has all the time in the world to build them back up.

Five Months Later

25

WHEN ARI RECEIVES AN EMAIL FROM BRAD WITH THE SUBJECT LINE *NEVerTired!!!* she initially assumes it to be some kind of motivational tactic. Brad is prone to sending coke-fueled all-staff emails time-stamped at three A.M. featuring the "inspirational" story of how he quit his insurance sales job to "bootstrap" WinProv.

But it's a client brief. Ari will fly to Austin for NeverTired's strategic leadership retreat, featuring an "ideation and concept-ing session," followed by an afternoon improv workshop.

"They have some really big things in the works," Brad tells her over the phone. "They just hit number thirty on the App Store's business chart." He takes a huge, suspicious sniff. "They're coming for Grubhub's crown."

Still, she'd rather get paid a handsome salary to teach NeverTired executives how to play improv games than spend hours on the actual NeverTired platform for poverty wages.

Radhya calls every week. She doesn't trust Ari's emoji-filled text messages to accurately convey her friend's state of mind. It's understandable. Maybe because they lived together, they communicate with an extra layer of nuance floating just above the actual dialogue. Rad notices the little things other people miss. It compels Ari to work extra hard at expressing nothing but bland okay-ness.

"Briar's introducing me to a branding strategist," Radhya says. "We're meeting him today before my shift."

"Cool." Ari does her best to convey a supportive tone, which is really all she *can* do from five hundred miles away.

Briar has consistently commented on all of Ari's generic selfies with the broken heart emoji. It's unclear if this is intended to be a comfort or some passive-aggressive defense of her brother.

"She's really been a huge help." Suspicious pause. And then on cue: "Speaking of help, Josh came over to pick up his pasta machine."

There's a stubborn silence on each end of the line.

It's not like Ari specifically requested that Rad never bring him up. It's more of a process-of-elimination situation, like an allergy test. *Movies:* not reactive. *Briar:* mildly reactive. *Pasta machines:* highly reactive. But how does Radhya invariably find ways to steer every call down a conversational back alley toward Josh? ("Seriously, what happened?" "Have you spoken at all?" "Would it be okay if I—") Ari, just as inevitably, either changes the subject or announces that she's very sorry but she needs to hang up now.

The person who does the leaving doesn't have the right to feel anything but resignation. Ari had used up all her pity points on Cass. Better to not even scratch at the surface of the Josh thing.

There's a reason you put one of those giant cones around your dog's neck after they have surgery. If you don't, they'll go straight for the wound. They'll tear out the stitches. Even though they look adorable and confused and pathetic in that cone, they need to be protected from themselves. At least until the wound heals.

Ari has spent most of the last few months with her head inside the cone. Not talking about how empty she'd felt when Josh left her apartment without even slamming the door. Not talking about how badly she wanted to call him and say anything to make him not hate her. Not talking about the sharp pain that had yielded to a persistent, dull ache after a few days. Like terrible fucking cramps.

Still, there's something almost darkly comforting in knowing that she was right all along: Sleeping with him had truly been a mistake.

STANDING IN THE HYATT CONFERENCE ROOM IN FRONT OF A MONITOR that reads *NeverTired Annual Vision Jam* is kind of like Dorothy catching sight of Emerald City in the distance. For some mysterious reason, this company that runs on labor of under-employed actors has an "executive leadership team" of nineteen people, all of whom are undoubtedly very well-compensated and have 401(k)s.

At the continental breakfast station, Derek, head of Hustler Expansion, spoons chia seeds over his Greek yogurt and explains that the platform is "in the middle of a massive growth spurt" thanks to "exciting opportunities with contextual advertisements." Next month, instead of simply writing copy for Never-Tired clients, "Hustlers" will receive "bonus points" when they "surface" targeted products. "Your bar mitzvah speech is attached. And tap here for twenty percent off a Quip toothbrush so your smile will look its best on your big day!"

Ari wants to ask if the executive leadership team gets "bonus points" or actual dollars for coming up with the contextual advertisement idea, but she stuffs a croissant in her mouth instead. In the past few months, she's realized that this job is ten times easier if she keeps her thoughts to herself. It's kind of the opposite of being a comedic performer, which feels good in a twisted, self-pitying way.

After leading a warm-up (lots of forced smiling, energetic clapping, and A/B tested jokes courtesy of Brad's script), Ari retreats to the hotel's outdoor pool patio while the executives start their vision jam. She reclines on a lounge chair and takes out her phone. It's not the most Instagrammable setting, but it's been a while since @ari.snacks69 updated the world from a chain hotel.

Before she can open the camera, a post from Briar pops up across the screen.

> Announcing my latest collab, Ave A's hottest new pop-up:
> Shaak + Schmaltz.
> I wanted to call it Rad-sky's (guess who tried to veto) 😒 😒
> xx B

It's a photo of Radhya (in her chef's coat with impeccable posture), Briar (with a bold red lip and enviably tidy bangs), and—

The fuck? A rush of something—confusion, outrage, maybe adrenaline—courses up through her chest.

Rad picks up on the third ring, but Ari doesn't wait for her greeting. "Why didn't you tell me about this?"

"About what?" There's some strange mix of sounds in the background.

"Your new 'collab.' I didn't realize you had a new . . . partner."

"Right. Hello to you, too. Josh is helping me in the kitchen and we're using the old Brodsky's building as a temporary location. That's all."

That's all? "You don't find that a little hypocritical?"

"I've been trying to bring it up with you for weeks, Ari. You changed the subject *every time*. You shut down the conversation *every time*."

"Yes, because I thought you were about to harangue me for details. I didn't realize you were planning to hire him to peel your carrots."

"'Harangue' you? Really? Here I was, thinking I was trying to help you while you're having a nervous breakdown. It's fucking insulting that you won't talk to me about this."

Ari gets hit with a light spray from the edge of the pool where a group of kids are splashing around. "You already know what happened."

"That's not true," Radhya says. "You never told me. What kind of friendship is this where I understand Kestenberg's state of mind better than yours?"

Right. She probably already heard it all from her new bestie, Josh.

"Since when are you *his* confidante?"

"I dunno, Ari, at least I get the occasional spiraling text from him. Talking to you lately is like having a conversation with a brick wall. Do you have any idea how bad that feels? *You're* the one who left. I thought we were going to work on these pop-ups together. You left me, too."

"What do you need me for? Everyone loves your food. People respect the shit out of you. You've always been the successful one who has her life together, which is fine because one of us has to be the fuckup, right? It turns out all you were missing in this whole equation was Josh."

Ari didn't even realize this sentence was inside of her.

"Is this about jealousy?" There's a tightness to Radhya's voice, like she's barely holding something back.

"No!" But Ari's not actually sure that answer is definitive.

There's a beat of silence before Radhya says, "A best friend is the person who can call you at any hour and say, 'I have all this bullshit happening in my life and I need you to listen to me vent about it.' And the other person is supposed to unconditionally respond, 'That *is* bullshit and you're right' and then offer to fight someone. We used to have that." A toilet flushes in the background, slightly undercutting the sentiment. "I'm really proud of the pop-up." Ari stops pacing. "Josh is aggravating but he's more than pulling his weight. The location is iconic. And I feel *excited* about it. The menu, the logo, the social media Briar is doing. All of it. And I'm so fucking sad and angry that I had to tell you while I'm standing in a public bathroom."

Ari feels the blood drain from her face. "Rad—"

"I just wanted to tell my best friend that I'm excited. I wanted to tell you all the mundane details that no one else would care about. The stuff that my husband would be forced to listen to if I still had a husband. But I don't. I had *you*. And I wanted you to be excited and ask me a thousand questions and sleep over at my place and eat every test dish. I wanted you to be here for the opening. I wanted you to be part of it."

"I want to be there," Ari says, grasping for a lifeline. "I'll fly back for the weekend. We can stay up all night. You can tell me everything. I'll eat everything. Please."

At that moment, a pair of rambunctious twins in matching

swimsuits cannonball into the pool, drenching Ari in chlorinated water.

"I don't think we can, Ari. Not right now." Radhya sighs. "I should let you go."

There's just empty silence with no sense of finality when Radhya ends the call before Ari can say anything to keep her on the line. Her chest aches: the same pain as when the reality sunk in that Cass wasn't coming back. She wants THC and maybe a Xanax. Anything to keep that argument from replaying, louder and louder.

Ari wanders back to the ideation session in a daze and a damp blue shirt, standing out of the way in the rear of the banquet room that smells like stale coffee. Derek's leading the meeting at the podium and a woman is writing on a large whiteboard with neat, looping penmanship. Even at the executive team level, it's up to the woman to take notes.

As Derek describes a system in which Hustlers will have the "opportunity" to offer certain services for *free* in exchange for better placement in the NeverTired search rankings, something in Ari's brain splinters.

After a year of doing everything humanly possible to succeed on this app—keeping up with tactics on the NeverTired forums and the subreddit, sending humiliating messages begging for five-star ratings from clients, responding to every single message, even spam and harassers—it's clear as the chlorinated pool water drying on her button-down shirt.

No one is ever going to make a living at NeverTired.

"Our Hustlers are dynamic, intrinsically motivated entrepreneurs who want the flexibility of working for themselves," Derek says. "They determine the value of their own work. When the least productive Hustlers drop out of the system, the laws of supply and demand create favorable conditions for our hardest-working Hustlers."

The woman at the whiteboard checks her Apple watch, glances at Ari, and says, "Let's circle back to that. We have a hard stop for our first improv session."

Swell.

Ari walks to the front of the room, avoiding eye contact with Derek as he leaves the podium. *This young woman has something fun planned,* he must be thinking. *Maybe I'll bang her after happy hour.*

But there's a different idea forming in her head.

Because the Radhya chest pain and the Josh stomachache won't loosen their grips.

Because every khaki-wearing man in this room has profited every time Ari stayed up an extra hour to ghostwrite some blowhard's Tedx talk.

Because Ari is, in fact, VeryTired.

Whatever Brad is paying her to enable success? It isn't enough. She needs a full cleansing.

Or, at least, a little revenge.

Ari plasters a broad smile over her face and begins making shit up. "We're going to kick things off with a bang, okay? Really get ourselves out of our comfort zones with a game I call 'No, *You're* the Asshole.'" This is the closest she's come to actual improvising in a year. Feels good, feels organic. "I want half the group to form a line to my right and the other half in a line on my left." The leadership team is perfectly obedient, lining up as directed. "The two people at the front of the line are going to face off. You each have ten seconds to convince the group that the person in front of you is a huge, fucking asshole. For example, I might say, 'Derek, you're the asshole because you've been looking me in the breasts instead of the eyes all morning."

Derek's smile wavers. The eighteen other executive leaders glance around, unsure if this is a joke. Ari can feel herself teetering on the edge of losing their blind cooperation.

"I'll be honest with you all." She leans forward, speaking in a soft conspiratorial voice. "I did this activity with a team from Grubhub last week and . . . they couldn't hack it. They didn't have the balls. I have a really good feeling about this group, though. I suspect there are some *huge* assholes in this room today."

A generic white guy pumps his fist. "Fuck Grubhub, let's do this!"

BRAD HOENIG [SFW ⚠]:

It has come to my attention that you invented unapproved and inappropriate activities during a recent client engagement, in which participants were instructed to call each other "assholes" for forty-five minutes, while leveling personal insults at one another.

In addition, I've reviewed your social media accounts.

Mimicking fellatio on a United States monument during one of your contracted workshops is unacceptable and additional grounds for dissolving this professional relationship.

Good luck in your future endeavors,

Brad Hoenig

Founder/CEO/Head Improveneur/Agent of Fun #1

Three Months Later

26

ARI PACES OUTSIDE THE OLD BRODSKY'S SPACE, WHICH NOW FEATURES A hand-painted SHAAK + SCHMALTZ sign. She vapes and occasionally glances through the window, nervous. Sweaty but cold. A sad bodega flower bouquet and bag of Sour Patch Kids are safely tucked under her arm.

If the city has become a sort of ghostly memory palace, this location feels particularly haunted, even if it's barely recognizable as the place where she met with Abby nine months ago. Would Abby be proud of the scorched-earth manner of her exit from WinProv? Or disappointed?

Like Gabe. And Radhya.

For the past few weeks, she's lived like a person out on probation: subletting a windowless room from a cousin-of-a-friend-of-a-friend, cautiously cobbling together a roster of odd jobs with an "on-demand nanny service" along with two of her old catering companies. She takes circuitous routes around the city to avoid ending up on blocks such as this one—places pockmarked with awkward memories and unresolved conversations—only to pass by Brodsky's every Thursday evening around eight-thirty when Radhya's pop-up is in full swing. There's always a line of people snaking around the corner, enduring hour-long waits for tables.

Her best friend and her . . . well, whatever Josh is . . . are bustling around the open kitchen. Together. She's not going in. This is just reconnaissance. Curiosity. Ari's instinctive need to support any of Radhya's endeavors, even if it's from the other side of a thick pane of glass.

COOKING FOR ONLY FIFTY CUSTOMERS IS PLAYING A GAME ON THE EASY setting, but it feels good to fucking nail it. Briar had posted some photos of Josh's mise en place because it looked *that* good. He's still shaking off the rust—and will be for a while. But after more than a year of depriving himself of his primary source of confidence, it's some kind of triumph, even if he's the supporting actor instead of the star.

While not exactly akin to working at Eleven Madison Park, standing behind the prep tables his dad purchased secondhand back in the seventies doesn't feel as miserable as he'd anticipated. At least his dad's old equipment is no longer cluttering his apartment, thanks to his mother and her movers.

Josh plates the last of the desserts, hands tired but steady. Placing them on the pass, he glances up at the nearly empty dining room. But what catches his attention is on the other side of the front window. *That* plaid peacoat. *That* face peering nervously inside. He forces his gaze back down to the counter, knowing he'll be useless for the next few minutes, spiraling. Perhaps in his concerted effort *not* to contemplate the possibility of Ari showing up at these pop-up dinners, he'd manifested her arrival.

He has a million other things to think about: breaking down their two-person line, closing procedures, scrubbing down every surface until it's gleaming. There are twenty-three items on his highlighted task list and they're all wiped away by that nagging combination of fantasy and memory that supplies Ari imagery at inopportune moments.

In Josh's fifteen-ish years of seeing women naked, he's forgotten the specifics of most of them. They all blur together into a hazy amalgamation, the way you can't quite remember the details of a dream once you awaken.

But his mind won't let go of its tiny observations about Ari. The pointed shape of her chin. The little wispy baby hairs at the back of her neck. Her back muscles in that black dress and also out of it. Really, don't most women have those things?

It must be the recency effect. Once he completely moves on, Ari's features will be added to the compilation. He has to believe that.

Eventually, the front door swings open, jingling the bell. Ari is holding a bouquet of wilted flowers and a giant bag of candy that must have been on sale for Halloween. She raises her arms to hug Briar, causing her stomach to peek out. He thinks of tracing his finger down that exact swath of skin.

Josh quietly shuts the door of the lowboy. He ducks into the back hallway, retrieving his phone before escaping out the back exit.

RADHYA PRODUCES A BOTTLE OF CASAMIGOS BLANCO FROM UNDER THE counter as Ari approaches, holding the flowers and candy in front of her like a physical buffer.

"Twattie," Radhya says with a note of sentimentality in her

voice, reaching for the flowers. Ari keeps her coat on, unsure if she's welcome, but Radhya slides her a juice glass half-full of tequila in exchange for the Sour Patch Kids and flashes a slightly uneasy grin.

"Get over here, Briar," Radhya calls across the dining room, pouring out another glass. "We had a line out the door. You earned a shift drink."

Josh is nowhere to be seen. The whole thing feels so *okay* on the surface that Ari starts to believe that maybe it actually will be.

Briar walks past the counter, into the kitchen, returning with a plate of iced cookie pieces: broken black-and-off-white frosted circles. "I hoard the imperfect ones," she says, pushing the plate toward Ari. "They're chai-flavored. Josh's idea. I like them better than the original kind."

"Thanks." Ari looks down at the icing, applied in pin-straight lines, while Briar fills Ari in on her new minor-celebrity boyfriend.

"So many reality stars try to move right into the influencer thing, but Ryan is *so* passionate about physical fitness? He's creating this whole community. I've met so many great girls in Ryan's jogging group. We all joined to watch his ass while he runs but I've made lifelong friends?" Briar retrieves some lime wedges from the beverage station. "Can I ask you, was Gabe upset when I hard-launched Ryan on my grid?"

Ari forces herself to bite into the cookie, which is a perfect balance of spicy and sweet. "I haven't talked to him in a while, but I'm sure he's slightly jealous of Ryan . . . and probably you."

"Do you think Gabe and I could still be friends without it being weird? He encouraged me to take these storytelling classes and I think I'm really developing my craft—"

The bells above the door jingle. A tall woman with dark blond hair and a perfectly symmetrical face steps inside with all the confidence Ari hadn't felt as she paced outside like a creep.

A second later, Josh enters, letting the door shut.

Ari swallows the rest of the cookie. It suddenly tastes like sawdust.

"I just wanted to stop by and say hi," the woman says, greeting everyone with quick half-hugs, like they're old friends. Ari quickly scans for an escape route (behind the counter? Under a table?) but it's too late. "Hi!" the woman says cheerfully over the yacht rock blaring from the boom box. "I'm Harper."

"Ari," she chokes out, extending her right hand.

Harper's palm is warm, like she's just been holding hands with someone.

Which is fine.

Everything's fine.

Josh stands several feet behind the woman, perhaps deciding whether to click CONTINUE or CANCEL on the whole interaction.

Ari pastes an enormous smile on her face to indicate just how fine this is. She pours herself a tequila refill. And then another.

Of course she's a Harper. Of course she's wearing a little black dress under her coat that shows off curves that Ari doesn't quite have. Of course she has long, wavy hair and full fucking lips, and . . . well, honestly, had they met under another circumstance, Ari would be complimenting her handbag and buying her a drink.

Josh-and-Harper. A couple. Names that would pair well on a wedding website.

"I need to . . . b-be right back," Ari mumbles, dropping the cookie on the counter and sliding awkwardly off the stool. She mentally selects a color scheme for josh-and-harper-dot-com as she makes her way down a narrow side hallway.

Don't cry don't cry don't cry.

The bathroom is back here somewhere, she's sure of it, but her vision is a little clouded by the welling tears or the three rapid-fire shots of tequila. She feels along the side of a wood-paneled wall, searching for a swinging door . . .

. . . which she promptly stumbles into, landing on her knees. It's probably really painful but she can't feel anything. *Thanks, tequila.*

Still, she can't quite get up. Maybe just a minute here on the floor would be good. Ari takes some deep breaths. She pushes her tongue to the roof of her mouth. She thinks about chonky cats calmly squeezing themselves into small boxes. Anything to stop the threat of tears.

By the time the door opens, she's back on her feet and pretend-washing her hands. But it's not Josh's new girlfriend.

"Are you okay?" Radhya asks over the groan of the hinges.

Ari doesn't look up. "Will you stop asking me that?" She stares at her hands, taking heavy breaths.

"I didn't know Harper was coming tonight," Radhya says. She stands in front of the mirror, trying to repair the damage done to her liquid liner by a night in a hot, stressful restaurant kitchen. "I'm not sure he did, either. They've only been out a couple times."

"Cool. Yeah. I mean, good for him." Ari continues scrubbing her hands. They feel raw. Suddenly, Josh wants to casually date someone. He's probably going on double dates with Briar and Ryan-who's-passionate-about-physical-fitness. "It's fine." *It's all so totally fine.*

Radhya turns around. "Then why are you hiding in the bathroom?"

"Sticky hands," Ari says through gritted teeth.

Radhya stares at her, waiting to see if she'll say more. Nothing comes out. "Well, she's gone now. Thought you'd . . . wanna know." She opens the door to leave and pauses. "We're going to Doc Holliday's."

The clomp of Radhya's kitchen clogs recedes down the back hallway.

Ari shuts off the tap, closes her eyes, and sits back down on the tile floor, breathing fast, willing herself not to fall apart. She turns to stare at the wall. There's a little collection of tags and notes and phone numbers written with various pens. Humans struggling to connect with one another, trying to be remembered any way they can. She's pretty sure her number has been featured in several bathrooms throughout the city. Probably being slowly buried under dozens of other numbers.

Maybe she should dial one of them. It's not like she has anyone to talk to in real life at this point. She's managed to trigger a specific kind of loneliness that only happens when you alienate everyone who knows you—really *knows* you.

Cue the self-loathing.

Yep, there it is. Something pulling tight on her throat. All it would take is the slightest push—*one wrong thought*—to trigger the waterworks. It's a sick little game, stepping so close to the edge. The thoughts drift across her mind, almost taunting her.

Ruth Bader Ginsburg's relationship with her husband, Marty. Mel Brooks and Anne Bancroft singing "Sweet Georgia Brown" in Polish. The first ten minutes of *Up*. She can see Josh's and Harper's clasped hands with pixel-perfect clarity in her mind's eye.

It hurts, but not enough.

Ari pulls out her phone and scrolls through her text message history with Josh. What does it all amount to, really? Dumb inside jokes and too much back-and-forth over where and when to meet up. Still, the idea that there was a time when she could text him a video of James Earl Jones performing the alphabet on *Sesame Street* and he would respond within a minute seems ludicrous.

There's a giant lump in her throat but the release of tears won't come. Ari forces a couple deep breaths, rises to her feet, and opens the bathroom door.

The restaurant is quiet now, except for a blast of water from the kitchen sink. Josh's chef's coat undone, his hands busy cleaning knives. Ari's heart clenches. Actually, no—more like the cumulative effect of missing him for months punches her in the sternum. He looks up when he hears her footsteps and then looks down again quickly.

He shuts the water off. The boom box on the counter plays "What a Fool Believes."

"They went down the block for drinks," he says after a beat that seems to last minutes.

"You didn't want to?"

"Doc Holliday's smells like a swamp."

"See, I find that smell comforting," she says.

He doesn't smile. It feels like another jab to the chest. "Someone had to finish cleaning up."

"Can I help?" she ventures.

Josh doesn't respond. But it's not a "no," so she steps into the kitchen.

"I realize this isn't the right time but . . . maybe—I dunno, could we talk? There's so much, I just . . ." She pauses for a breath. "If you wanted to meet for coffee or something."

He raises his head, but doesn't look at her. "Coffee."

"I think it's great that you're cooking again and, uh, dating—"

"You think it's great that I'm dating."

No, no, no. Abort. It's already a fucking disaster. But her lips keep moving. "All I want is to talk to you again. Can't we just talk?" She shuts her mouth before it can get worse.

"That's all you ever want from me." He dries the knife and puts it down on top of a folded towel. "The two of us are not friends, Ari. We *were* friends and at some point we were something else and only one of us was able to acknowledge it."

"It's not like I'm doing great right now, you know?" Her pulse races like she just finished a 10K. "I'm—I'm feeling . . . really lonely."

Finally, he looks her in the eye. "I'm sorry it was *that* fucking difficult for you to admit you had any feelings whatsoever for me that you had to move to another state to deal with it."

A horn honks somewhere on Avenue A. The upbeat tone of the Doobie Brothers song hangs incongruously in the air between them.

"I miss—" *Shit.* Her voice is already wobbling. It's like when you scratch your hand on something and it doesn't hurt until you look down and notice you're bleeding. "I miss you. And I get that you don't want to, like, *talk,* but I need you to know that . . . you kind of m-meant the world to me." She manages to get it all out before stifling something that feels like a potential sob.

He puts his hand down on the metal prep table and it makes a booming sound. "I don't want to hear about how you used to feel." His voice sounds strained and choked. "Because you've been two hundred miles away and I'm still here and I've *been* here this whole time, waiting for you to just—"

"Josh—"

"I fucked things up, too. I know that. You told me you weren't ready for a relationship and I didn't want to hear it, so I didn't listen. I tried to center my world around you instead of actually rebuilding my life."

Except why is he finally "rebuilding" with Radhya? Why is *that* fair? How is it possible that these two people who spent the last six years resenting each other can find common ground in cutting Ari out of the picture? Sometimes the more interesting person to the left is your best friend.

There's a police siren whining in the background; he waits for it to recede into the distance before continuing. "It's taken eight fucking months and two different therapists, but I get it now," he says. "To me, that night felt like the beginning of something. You were so convinced it had to be the end. And that's not something I can control through force of will."

The lump in her throat feels like it's pressing on her windpipe. *Don't cry. Say something.*

"You're where you're supposed to be right now," he continues. "And I guess I'm where . . . I am." The tears start to make her vision blurry. Josh turns into a watery blob, but his voice is crystal clear. "I think"—he swallows—"I think there's a part of me that still loves you." There's a pause long enough to make her hope that the next word is *and.* "But I'm not going to slip back into some inane conversation with you like we're buddies. We're not going to have any late-night phone calls anymore. I'm not your coffee date. I'm not your shoulder to cry on." He inhales sharply. "I deserve more than that. Even if it's not with you."

She wants to answer. She wants to argue that he was so much more than that. But the words don't come. He *should* be with someone who doesn't make it so fucking difficult to be in love with them.

"You warned me, you know. You said we'd hurt each other. And I was so concerned with making *you* feel safe, it just didn't occur to me that . . ." He sniffles, maybe. "You were right."

Josh walks toward her, and for two ridiculous seconds, she thinks maybe it was all some big fake out. Like he might reach out his hand and just . . .

He walks right past her.

Ari watches him quietly stomp down the back hallway, leaving her in the dark kitchen.

She's still in a liminal space, where her brain hasn't quite processed the conversation. It feels like it might still be possible to rewind five minutes and try it again. Only she's not sure how it could have gone differently. They'd have to take it back so much further to make any kind of meaningful revision.

It only takes a few more seconds for her brain to turn a corner into emotional torture porn.

This is the last time we'll ever speak. This is the last time we'll ever speak.

Yeah. That feels good and painful. The sweating, the panic setting in, the churning thoughts stabbing at her brain like a needle into the skin. Like getting a really detailed tattoo over scar tissue. All her good Josh memories getting rewritten with this one.

Ari takes a wobbly step farther back into the dining room. The shock wears off and morphs into giant waves of emotion building in her chest, unstoppable and overwhelming. She covers her mouth with her hand to muffle the sobbing in case Josh can still hear. On the radio, there's a commercial for a personal injury attorney. *How fitting.*

Ari's about thirty seconds deep into the breakdown when a few familiar notes, heavy with reverb, ring out through the boom box speakers. Neil Finn launches into the first verse and it's clearly a cruel cosmic joke that the "classic feel-good hits" DJ would put on "Don't Dream It's Over" at this precise moment.

Two Months
Later

27

ARI SIPS FROM A LUKEWARM BOTTLE OF BUD LIGHT. SHE'S BOTH JEALOUS and relieved that she's not the sweating guy at the microphone with a quivering handful of index cards.

It took two trains and a bus to get here from her sublet and she'd been relieved to find that the trip wasn't for nothing: Gabe still hosts this open mic every Thursday evening. There's no better setup for an apology than showing up at one of his events.

Gabe finishes reading Brad's email and hands the phone back to her. "Did you burn that hideous blue shirt?"

"He withheld my last paycheck until I returned it."

"And now you want to rejoin our Harold team?" He checks the timer on his phone. "Is that why you're here?"

"*You* never made me perform in a button-down," Ari says.

"Well, there is no team. Tim and Kamal left for Second City. Selina went to L.A. for pilot auditions and never came back. It's been kind of hard to perform with only two people."

"Gabe." She sets the bottle down. "I'm sorry. I get that it was a sellout move, I just . . . needed a reset. And money."

"The paycheck I understand." He looks over his sign-up sheet and checks his watch. "You abandoned the group months *before* you left on your adventure in corporate America. You fed me some bullshit about being too busy. *That* was the insult. You could have just been honest."

"You're right." Ari swallows hard. "Can I cash in my spousal abandonment sympathy points for another drink?"

Gabe signals the bored bartender for another round.

"The thing is," he says, "I think you already cashed all of those in."

She peels the label from the new beer bottle. "Why do I feel like I've been running laps for the entirety of my twenties, trying to make this a viable career?"

"Ari." He looks her right in the eye, like they're in the middle of an uncomfortable acting exercise. "You feel exhausted because you're specifically not doing the thing that used to replenish your well. We came here to work shitty service-industry jobs so we could do *that*." He gestures at the makeshift stage.

"Bombing at an open mic is some kind of reward for refilling pitchers of bottomless mimosas every Sunday?"

"No, but at this point you're *only* doing the shitty service-industry part." Gabe flashes the one-minute light at the open mic performer with the glistening forehead. "At least that guy is living his dream."

"You're doing a really terrible job of cheering me up," Ari mumbles into the rim of the bottle.

"I'm not trying to cheer you up." He takes a drink. "I'm still pissed. But let me tell you a little industry secret." Gabe leans forward, gesturing for her to do the same. "It's definitely not a viable career if you never actually, you know, *do* it." He flicks his finger against her forehead. "It's not even a hobby."

"Crochet is a hobby." She nods toward the stage. "That's self-inflicted torture."

"If you really want to make it up to me, I need you to do two things." He slides off his stool. "First, LaughRiot won a grant for a series of comedy workshops for at-risk teen girls. You're teaching every session." He takes a long glance at the list of names on his open mic sign-up sheet. "Second, you're up next."

Ari plants herself more firmly on the stool. "I'm not getting up there. I don't have any material."

"You only need to fill seven minutes. I'll even give you a pseudonym." Gabe tilts his head. "You're finally at a place in your life as a comedian where you can complain about your ex-wife. That's the dream."

"Oh yes, the cliché of getting up at an open mic and treating it like a big group therapy moment."

"Exactly. You can die onstage tonight and it'll probably be the worst set you've ever done. With that out of the way, you'll feel one percent better. And then you'll get up next week and embarrass yourself again." He sets down his empty beer. "You have to start somewhere."

"No, wait." Ari grabs his forearm. "I don't have anything to say."

"You're an improviser. Ask for a suggestion from the audience."

She glances around the half-empty crowd. "They'll just say 'penis.'"

"If anyone knows how to work with a 'penis,' it's you." Gabe leads some tepid applause and jogs up to the mic. "And now, a special surprise." Ari chugs the rest of the beer and looks for an escape route or hiding place. "Please give a slightly better-than-average welcome to"—he pauses and Ari recognizes the look on his face when he's trying to generate a ridiculous character name—"Freckles McCloud."

She puts the beer bottle down and takes her time weaving through the tables up to the mic. There are maybe five people watching and ten people clearly *not* watching and Ari makes the mistake of scanning their faces. Her knees shake.

"Hi, I'm . . . Freckles." It's been years since she felt this specific brand of nervous on any kind of stage. "This is where you say 'Hi, Freckles.'" There's still some chatter, which is almost more disrespectful than absolute silence. "No addicts in here tonight? Surprising. Okay." She looks longingly at the bright red EXIT sign and the clump of smokers outside the front door. She keeps her feet planted, anyway. "Well, hi, my name is Freckles and it's been . . . approximately ten months since I sent a tasteful nude to my ex-wife."

ARI BEGRUDGINGLY ADMITS TO HERSELF THAT DOING A TERRIBLY UN-even open mic had imbued her with some sense of excitement. A little touch of the old electricity zipping up and down her limbs, swirling around her chest. The comedy holy spirit.

It gives her just enough of the necessary push to haul her ass onto the train, despite the late hour, and see the person she's been missing terribly and avoiding for months.

Ari still has the key to Radhya's but it feels wrong to knock and enter this time. She knocks and waits, staring at the nonde-script door, with its familiar scuffs and smudges. After twenty seconds that feel like long minutes, Ari hears footsteps. Radhya undoes the dead bolt and opens the door three inches.

"I'm not okay," Ari says immediately, before Rad can shut the door again. "Not fine."

There's a pause and then the door opens wider. "Grilled cheese?"

Ari follows Radhya inside and curls up on the couch under a fleece blanket. The TV is on, tuned to one of those stations for old people that only plays nineties sitcoms. They stare at an episode of *That '70s Show* while crunching into buttery grilled cheese sandwiches.

"I feel like human garbage," Ari says between bites. "Our last few conversations have been so . . ."

"Terrible?" Radhya suggests. "Fraught? Passive-aggressive dumpster fires?"

"I miss you." There's a tightness in Ari's throat. She's gotten used to the sensation over the past few months. "I'm sorry I shut you out. I'm a mess and you're the capable person with all the answers. And I was worried we had finally hit the moment where you asked yourself, 'Why am I friends with this person? Was it proximity?'"

Radhya takes a big breath in. "Are you frustrating sometimes? Yes. Have you made extremely questionable decisions? Also, yes."

"And did you judge me for those decisions?"

"Yeah," Radhya says. "I'm both imperfect *and* judgmental." She takes another bite of grilled cheese. "I don't know what the hell I'm doing." She sits forward. "Starting my own business is incredibly risky. My stomach hurts all the time. I have stress dreams where I'm surrounded by ticket printers that won't stop."

She pauses. "When Brodsky's sells, I have to figure out a new venue. And Josh might not want to keep doing the pop-ups."

Ari stops chewing. "Why not?"

"He's been talking about cooking somewhere else. California, maybe. Fresh start."

Ari tries and fails to picture Josh in any other location. He feels so rooted to the city, like he and Manhattan are in a codependent relationship.

"Do you need a sassy, charming waitress?" Ari asks, trying to push Josh out of her mind.

"No. I need a sassy, charming best friend. Preferably one who lets me give fantastic advice and then ignores it."

Ari snorts, making Radhya laugh.

"In that case . . ." Ari stares at the TV, waiting for her throat to loosen up a bit. "I need to tell you about this guy I knew."

"Okay." Radhya doesn't move a muscle, like she's afraid that the slightest flinch will send Ari fleeing into the night.

"We hated each other for a long time. And then we didn't. We became friends. And that's the hardest kind of connection for me. Obviously." She takes a breath. "He's one of those people who never has to smell items in their refrigerator before consuming them. Crumbs and misplaced apostrophes are his mortal enemies. He knows exactly how smart he is but doesn't realize he's funny. If I could get him to laugh or just, like, *hrmph* or look exasperated, it made my entire day. Which, I guess, wasn't hard because I've been miserable." It's painful to say it all in past tense. "He just *got* me. He saw me in this way that other people never do. We're really different, but I could talk to him about anything—all the stuff I tried really hard to hide from everyone else because I felt so"—she swallows—"ashamed of how much I was hurting. Even though I was at my lowest point,

he just accepted me. But then we . . . you know." Her eyes well
up again. "And I convinced myself it was this huge mistake because I couldn't deal with what it actually meant. But I—I miss
him, Rad. I r-really—"

This time she doesn't try to hold back the big, ugly sobs.

Rad wraps her arms around Ari's shoulders, getting them
both tangled in the blanket.

"Hey," Radhya says softly. "Breathe?" Ari swallows and takes
a gasping inhale, like she's finally coming up for air. "Start from
the beginning."

JOSH WALKS SOUTH ON AVENUE A, ACROSS THE WEST BOUNDARY OF
Tompkins Square Park, past a stupid new expensive kefir bar, a
Starbucks, a bodega, and whatever the Pyramid Club is now.

Everything else on the block may have changed, but despite
his cursed attempt at transforming Brodsky's into The Brod, his
mother had taken it upon herself to revert the place back to its
old form. The checkered floor has been mopped thousands of
times, but the white squares have been beige forever. As a kid,
Josh would volunteer to wipe down the tables, scour the sinks—
anything to put chaotic things in *order*.

More than that, the place has a specific scent. No matter
how many spice blends Radhya grinds in the kitchen, he'll forever detect the smell of stale cigarette smoke from the days of
smoking sections separated by nothing but a warped panel of
plexiglass. The sweet-and-sour sauce that accompanied every
serving of stuffed cabbage. Frankfurters sizzling on the flattop.
Containers of coleslaw, macaroni salad, egg salad, and some con-
coction his dad called "health salad" that only one regular ever
ordered.

Danny's food was so familiar to Josh, he couldn't properly evaluate it: the specific tang of Uncle Morrie's brown mustard, the slightly sweet glaze of brisket, the foamy head of a chocolate egg cream that clung to your upper lip. In the years of preparing absurdly complex dishes for the city's most discerning diners, Josh isn't sure he's ever made people as happy as the regulars at Brodsky's seemed to be.

In a few weeks, he could sign a pile of tabbed legal and financial documents, relinquishing custody of a hallowed institution to some "hospitality chain." Will he feel lifelong regret or will it mark the start of an exciting new chapter? Maybe working in Sonoma is the game changer he's been needing for the last year. No, two years. Fuck, possibly five or six years.

Josh sets down his knife roll and flips on the lights. It's quiet in here on Wednesdays. He's been coming in when the pop-up isn't open to try things out. Ideas for recipes. New techniques. A lot of bread. Loaves of challah. There's something satisfying about making the same thing over and over again and improving it incrementally each time.

"The Waiting" plays a tick too loud over the radio. It's fitting. Danny Kestenberg was the human embodiment of a Tom Petty song. This kitchen still feels haunted by his stubborn ghost. Sometimes Josh swears he can feel Danny looking over his shoulder, muttering as Josh pickles shallots or braises red cabbage.

Something catches his attention on the other side of the front windows: a specific cadence of heels clicking on pavement.

The bell over the door jingles as Abby walks past the tables and behind the counter, opens the beverage fridge, and pulls out a can of Dr. Brown's Diet Black Cherry. She fills a glass with ice and pours the soda just up to the rim with the practiced hand of someone who's done this a thousand times.

Without a word, she marches into the walk-in cooler and returns with a 128-ounce jar of mayonnaise and a case of eggs. Josh had hard-boiled them to prep for Radhya's egg kheema.

"What are you doing?" he asks.

Abby pulls a stack of bowls down from an overhead shelf. Her heels sink into the kitchen mat. "I told you I was bringing the offers. We need to make a decision."

"No. What are you doing with my prep bowls?" At some point in the last few months, he'd started thinking of the kitchen equipment as *his*.

"Making lunch," she says, setting up a familiar assembly line on the prep table. "Since when do we sit around a table without a nosh?"

Egg salad wasn't Josh's plan for this afternoon. But the clatter of two giant metal bowls on the stainless-steel prep table, the sound of shells gently crunching against the counter, the whip of them being tossed into the compost bin—it's all a familiar, undeniable tune. It seems to bring his dad back to life for a fleeting moment.

Danny used a dead simple recipe (hardboiled eggs, mayo, salt, pepper) with one distinction: extra yolks for a creamier consistency. "Other places use too much mayonnaise," he'd insist. Josh isn't much of an egg salad connoisseur, but he's inclined to agree. That said, he'd spent twenty years trying to convince his father to add some fucking dill.

Josh reaches for a hard-boiled egg from the carton, cracks the shell, and peels it, depositing the white in the bowl on the left and the yolk in the bowl on the right. He pushes his feet into the kitchen mat. He crumbles the "flaky-dry" texture of the yolks in his fingers. The whites are slippery and tender. Crack. Peel. Separate.

It's the closest he's come to anchoring in months.

Abby says nothing but cracks an egg against the counter in four short bursts.

"Just the Way You Are" drifts into the kitchen from the radio and rips him out of the present. It worms its way into Josh's brain with sap, easy sentimentality, and obvious allusions to Ari. Every lyric seems to have been designed by a time-traveling 1977 Billy Joel to inflict maximum damage on a defenseless 2023 Josh Kestenberg.

"Have you heard from her?" His mother is terrible at affecting a nonchalant tone.

"Harper?" he asks, just to be difficult. There's no reason things shouldn't have clicked with Harper. She works at the U.N. She's an associate-level donor to the Roundabout Theatre Company. She keeps kosher salt next to her gas stove. She has a schnauzer named Pee Wee, for fuck's sake. He'd ended it over the phone—well before the holidays, which was Briar's advice. But how do you explain to someone that you just want your conversations to spark? That you want to laugh because you can't help it, not force a chuckle out of politeness? That instead of just listening to the anecdotes you've told six other dates, you need them to hear the parts you're not saying? To know you better than anyone else?

"I think you know who I'm talking about."

"Why? Do you have another professional opportunity lined up for her?" He picks up another egg, going through the motions, cracking it too hard on the counter, letting shell pieces fly like shrapnel. "Is one of your clients launching a comedy club in Argentina or something?"

There's a brief pause in the crush of eggshell from her end of the counter.

Josh continues cracking, peeling, separating. Trying and failing to ignore the emotional grenades threatening to go off in his head: How he feels Ari's absence every single day. How she's taken root in some deep, inaccessible place that can't be edited or overwritten—just managed. Like a chronic illness.

There's an unmistakable lump in his throat now. *Anchor, dammit.*

"We danced to this at our wedding," Abby says after another quick series of *thwack*s. "I wanted Fleetwood Mac. This one was your dad's idea." Obviously. The lyrics start with his mantra: *Don't go changing.* "We even took dance lessons at a studio on Sixth Ave. He still stepped all over my feet."

With the memory of Ari in that black dress, awkwardly dancing to a song from forty years ago permeating his brain, Josh makes it as far as the song's second mention of "clever conversation" before the anchor gives way, sweeping him out past the point of no return. He spends the last forty-five seconds of the saxophone solo quietly sobbing into his sleeve, being careful not to touch his face with his yolk-covered hands.

This shirt will be forever associated with the time a maudlin Billy Joel hit grabbed him by the throat as he cried in front of his mother into a bowl of egg whites.

Thankfully, Abby doesn't turn her head to look at him. When the song ends, she hands Josh a clean bar towel off the pass. "It gets easier."

Does it? Or does it get more painful the longer your person is absent from your life? The more weeks and months you spend going over the *what-ifs*? Did those original humans become more haggard and distraught the longer they searched the world for their lost soulmates, watching everyone else reunite with their other halves?

Abby silently reaches up to a high shelf and places a bright red spice container in front of the bowls. The pop of color reflects off the stainless steel. It must be Radhya's; paprika had no place in his dad's kitchen.

Josh stares at it.

"I always thought the egg salad could use a bit of a kick," she says. "I think your dad would agree with me if he'd actually tasted it." Abby taps a finger across the counter. "He wouldn't have cared about a Michelin star, you know. But he would've been proud of what you've done here."

Josh wipes his eyes with the towel and takes a breath, looking out at the empty dining area in the same way Danny did for forty years. Standing in this kitchen isn't a capitulation or a betrayal. For the first time, it feels like the right place to anchor.

Even the little red bottle seems to belong in here. Along with the turmeric and the cardamom pods and the two kinds of coriander for the brisket rub.

Because it's Josh's kitchen now. Well, Radhya's and Josh's.

He takes a deep breath in. "Maybe we should . . . keep doing this." He removes an entire half of a shell in one piece. Josh doesn't believe in signs, but eggs never peel that easily. "And not sell. Yet."

Abby winks and nudges him with her elbow. "Should we add some dill?"

28

"THANK YOU, ZACH!" ARI SAYS INTO THE MICROPHONE AS THE HARMON-
ica notes finally fade into silence for the second time that night.
"'Piano Man' is fresh every time you hear it, right?" She points
to the sign on the easel next to the stage featuring an enormous
rainbow QR code and the title *LaughRiot: Money, Please.*

"And you can ring in the new year by subjecting this lovely
bar to whatever karaoke clichés you want for a fifteen-dollar
donation to our crowd-funding campaign. All the money goes
directly toward an entire slate of programs for queer teens. Any
of the songs on the 'Please, God, No' list require a thirty-dollar
donation. The 'Fuck You to This Entire Room' list—which
includes Journey, Adele, Queen, and more—is fifty and up. As
the host, I obviously reserve the right to heckle you and perform a very earnest rendition of 'Part of Your World' at any
point. Next up"—she consults her Notes app—"here's Cameron with *my* personal theme song, 'Return of the Mack.'"

Ari hands over the mic and awkwardly mimics nineties

dance moves, making her way through the crowd to the merch table where Gabe and Radhya are selling LaughRiot apparel at wildly inflated New Year's Eve prices.

"When it's time to go outside and wait for an Uber or walk to the train, you're gonna realize how fucking cold it is outside and desperately want one of these hoodies," Gabe tells a young man in a tank top. The guy shakes his head and walks away. "The prices are going up after midnight!" Gabe shouts after him.

"You're losing your touch, old man," Ari says, perching on Radhya's lap in lieu of a chair. "Eye contact. Compliments. Flirting. Then, 'Hey, I actually think this hoodie would look hot on you—'"

"—but it would look better on my bedroom floor," Radhya adds.

Ari grabs two plastic champagne flutes. "It's so cruel that Radhya is probably the love of my life and pretty much my only friend who isn't attracted to women."

"Don't take this the wrong way," Radhya replies, downing one serving of cheap prosecco. "But one round of living with you was enough."

"Funny, that's what my ex-wife said."

Radhya pretends to drum a *badum-tss* on the piles of sweatshirts and shorts. "Hey, I love you so much, I'm spending the number-one hookup holiday at a gay bar where I'm pretty much guaranteed to end the evening alone."

"First," Gabe says, downing his prosecco, "I'm available for all your midnight-kiss needs. And second, you're spending the number-one hookup holiday enjoying two different but equally terrible renditions of 'Piano Man.'"

In her head, Ari hears the punch line in Josh's voice: *There are* good *renditions of "Piano Man"?*

"Last year, I was working New Year's Eve," Radhya says, slurring her words a bit. "I got off at two A.M." She pauses, grinning. "Then I also got off at two thirty-five A.M."

Gabe clears his throat. "Exactly one year ago, I served hors d'oeuvres at a rooftop in Koreatown, came here to host the fundraiser"—he glances pointedly at Ari—"alone. And woke up in Alphabet City without my pants. I have no memory of how I got home, except that Ari was passed out on my futon in her evening gown, snoring and drooling." He glances at her. "I assume this year will be the same, except for the clothes. That's not an outfit that gets you laid."

Ari looks down at the LaughRiot-branded T-shirt, shorts, and sparkly rainbow tights that Gabe ordered her to wear tonight, recalling, in perfect detail, the circumstances of how she ended up on the futon last year. She's been trying not to let her mind wander to those places.

There's this mindfulness exercise she's been listening to on an app. You close your eyes and imagine yourself lying on your back, looking up at the sky, watching clouds gently float overhead. You name each cloud with an emotion you're feeling and just let it float past, and that's apparently supposed to help you sit with the discomfort instead of avoiding it.

Now, the flaw in this visualization is that you're *still feeling the shitty emotion.* That's the problem with the Josh memories. They're not puffy clouds—more like unpredictable lightning bolts that crash through her brain at inopportune times.

Maybe she hasn't quite bridged that final gap to acceptance, but this shit takes time. At some point, without Ari consciously realizing it, her hurt over Cass had morphed into something less potent. A dusting of ash rather than a burning ember.

It'll happen with Josh, too.

She has to believe that.

Radhya stares at her with what's probably intended as a look of concern, but in her squinty prosecco haze, she's giving the impression that she's confused by Ari's nose.

Suddenly the karaoke mic goes silent over the chorus of "Return of the Mack." Ari looks up. There's still over a minute until the song ends. But Cameron is pointing at someone in the crowd.

"Kyle, I just realized that it's eleven forty-five," he shouts into the microphone. "This year, I don't want to kiss my soulmate at midnight." He drops down onto one knee. Ari feels her mouth hanging open. The crowd falls silent. "I want to kiss my fiancé."

The off-brand backup vocals repeat "You *liiied* to me" as a man in a shiny suit slowly rises to his feet, nodding. The entire bar explodes in cheers as they embrace and the microphone clatters to the floor.

How many of these scenes does she have to witness? Is it some weird karmic penance for failing at marriage? Ari could probably name ten reasons for this couple's eventual demise, the first of which is proposing with a karaoke backing track to "Return of the Mack" nearly drowning out the declaration of love.

So why the stubborn ache in her chest? Why is she thinking about how she'll never get to tell Josh the story of this couple's engagement? Is it really just a matter of waiting for the hurt to subside, like a slowly atrophying muscle?

"Get up there and say something!" Gabe pushes Ari off Radhya's lap, snapping her out of the thought spiral.

"Why?"

"Sentimental crap makes people more willing to spend money. Get up there and say something fucking moving!"

Radhya holds out a plastic champagne flute in Ari's direction. "You have like two dozen wedding-related speeches on your phone, dude." When Ari doesn't take the drink, she gives a tiny shrug, pulls her hand back, and downs the prosecco herself. "Just please God, not that paragraph from *Captain Corelli's Mandolin* or the Apache Prayer."

Nodding absently, Ari makes her way around the merch table, nearly tripping on her way to the stage as the DJ fades the song out. An unsettling hush falls over the bar. She picks the microphone up off the floor, triggering a surge of feedback.

"How about that, everyone? Beautiful, right?" She takes a breath. "Gabe's been running this fundraiser for ten years and I think this is our first engagement. Congratulations to Kyle and Cameron!" There's a smattering of applause and whistles.

She swallows and scrolls her Notes app, pausing on a speech labeled "Toast from a Cynical Father of the Bride Who Doesn't Want to Mess Around with the Creep Factor of 'Giving His Little Girl Away.'" That's literally the title. It'll have to do.

"Here's the thing, Rach—er, Cameron." She clears her throat and reads off the screen. "When you fall in love with someone, you're all optimism. You have no sense of the hardships you'll face in a few years. You're thinking 'This is it!' because, uh, Kyle makes you happy. But the truth is . . ."

Ari barely remembers writing this. Maybe it happened in a fugue state. A sativa haze. A NyQuil-and-tequila fog.

"The truth is . . . happiness is really complicated. It's fickle." Radhya's face resembles the Chrissy Teigen awkward cry face meme. "People are too worried about being happy. If you want to be happy all the time, just watch cat videos. They're fucking great." There's a very light smattering of chuckles. Gabe makes a *smile* gesture with his index fingers. "No one should marry the person who makes them happy. Marry the person you want by your side at your lowest p-point. Marry the person you . . . you never get sick of. Who you always want more from. Who makes you proud to be theirs."

There's an unmistakable constriction in Ari's throat now, remembering where these words came from. Kyle and Cameron nod. She blinks rapidly, staving off the threat of tears. Because, if she's being honest with herself, the Josh-shaped hole doesn't actually feel like it's closing.

"But if you . . ?" She looks down but the phone is useless; the words are illegible now. "If you do happen to find your person, it's an act of courage to tell them that. To say, 'please love me back.' To let someone else hold your heart in their hands, knowing it could—actually, it probably *will*—end badly. Knowing that they're going to fuck up. Knowing you'll both hurt each other. But if that's *your* person, it's worth the risk. Because *your* person will see the best version of you. They'll have a whole list of reasons why they think you're irreplaceable. And they'll tell you." Ari feels hot tears slipping down her cheeks. "If you want to watch someone you love grow into the person you know they can be, that's when you get married."

A hush falls over the crowd—less a "stunned silence" than an "ummm, is she . . . done?" vibe.

She doesn't really care if they think she's crazy or drunk or incredibly moved by her own words. Somewhere on this island is the person she wants to talk to right before falling asleep. The person who knows exactly how she wants to be kissed. Who wanted to hold her hand and wake up with her and take her out for breakfast and maybe become a better person than he was eight years ago.

Gabe jogs up to the stage, gently removes the mic from her hand, gives her a little shove off the stage, and raises a champagne glass. "To the happy couple!" He signals the DJ and launches into a rendition of "Wonder of Wonders" that's bombastic even by Gabe standards.

Ari stumbles toward Radhya. There's an idea gaining momentum, moving in a straight shot through her mind.

"Are you okay?" Radhya asks, handing Ari a prosecco. "That was—"

"Where's Josh?"

Rad takes out her phone. "I think Briar's boyfriend roped him into some running thing that sounded cold and miserable. Very on-brand for Kestenberg." She opens Instagram. "Here, I think she tagged him—"

Ari snatches the phone out of her friend's hand, swiping away the low battery notification. It's a photo of smiley Briar and an extremely handsome, also-smiley man in warm jogging gear with race bibs pinned to their outer layers. To Briar's left, almost out of the frame, as if he's trying to escape the photo— very much not smiley—is a tall man dressed in all black, like a very athletic cat burglar.

"The race. Central Park." Ari drops the phone on the merch table. "I need to go."

"The streets are closed off," Radhya points out. "And this is, like, the worst night of the year for surge pricing."

Ari looks around. They're close enough to Times Square that the sidewalks are crowded, but not completely impassable. "It's only twenty blocks, I can run it."

"You can?"

Instead of answering, Ari bends down and tightens the laces on her sneakers. The crowd applauds Gabe as he hands off the microphone.

"That was good, right?" he asks, all smiles as he comes back to the merch table. "New audition song?"

"It was brilliant, Gaston," Radhya says between sips. "Total banger."

Ari grabs him by the shoulders. "We need to swap phones. He might have my number blocked."

"Who?"

"I *need* your *phone*. Radhya's battery is at three percent." Ari snatches his device out of his hand. "Is your passcode still six-nine-six-nine-six—"

"—four."

"'Four'? Wait, when did you change it?"

"The old code was too easy to guess." He looks at Radhya. "Did I miss something? She's taking my phone on New Year's Eve? On the ultimate 'you up?' holiday? When literally everyone is 'up'?"

Ari tugs at Gabe's snug LaughRiot shirt. "I think I found the other half of my black-and-white cookie and someone else might be eating it right now. I need to find him."

"We haven't even sung 'The Boy Is Mine' yet."

"It's a romantic gesture," Radhya explains. "She needs to get to Central Park."

"In twelve minutes," Ari adds. "The race starts at midnight."

"Oh my God." Gabe's eyes widen. "You're doing an airport run? Like a movie?"

Ari types in Josh's number as a new contact on Gabe's phone. "Thank you and I'm sorry."

"Where's your coat?" He turns around to search the merch boxes under the table. "I can't find it."

"Here," Radhya says, grabbing an XXL LaughRiot sweatshirt from the merch table and tossing it to Ari.

"Jesus, that entire outfit really would look better on a bedroom floor," Gabe opines. "The sparkly tights and LaughRiot booty shorts seemed like a fun idea when we were drinking at my apartment."

"Thank you. Now my confidence is at an all-time high." Ari picks up two more proseccos from the table and tosses them back. They burn going down.

"You okay, Twattie?" Radhya holds Ari's shoulders.

"No." She shakes her head. "I'm not. I haven't been okay in a long time and I've been pushing it down. But for some reason when I'm with—"

"Save it for Kes— *Josh*." Radhya nods at the door. "Now *go*."

"I love you." Ari walks backward toward the exit, knocking into at least three people.

"See?" Radhya says. "You're already saying it."

"I can't believe she's the one doing a dramatic fucking airport run," Gabe says. "I have a playlist curated for this exact situation."

29

ARI KNOCKS INTO SOMEONE'S SWEATY BACK BEFORE HER RIGHT FOOT hits the sidewalk. Technically, this part of Ninth Avenue isn't closed but it's jammed with packs of pedestrians heading south toward Times Square. Why they want to get closer to a giant teeming mass of people with no access to restrooms is a mystery.

"Excuse me! Sorry! Excuse me!" she shouts, as she makes herself small and squeezes between flush-faced revelers in their winter coats.

Ari runs north against the flow of traffic like a character in an 8-bit video game. *Right-left-left—no, right.* At some point, a trainer at her crappy gym suggested agility training. She'd laughed and wondered when the hell that skill would ever come in handy.

Apparently, Airport Run Parkour is the use case.

Her Fifty-third Street appeals of "Can I please just get around you?" evolve into Fifty-fifth Street commands to "Fuck-ing *move. MOVE!*"

Someone's cigarette singes the sleeve of the LaughRiot sweatshirt as she bobs and weaves around other people's handbags and outstretched limbs.

On Fifty-seventh, away from the bars on Ninth Avenue, the throng starts to thin out. She picks up speed, taking full strides: arms pumping, knees high, shoes only slightly slipping on the frosty sidewalk.

By the time she reaches Columbus Circle, leaping over a slush-covered open grate, Ari feels like a goddamned gazelle. A few more blocks sprinting like this and she'll reach the starting line in, like, seven minutes?

Four seconds later, she gets a stitch in her side.

Shit. Shitshitshit. She slows to a power walk down Central Park West, jamming her hand into her side.

It's fine. Walk it off. It's fourteen blocks between the location where she's currently dry heaving and the spot where Josh is probably feeling personally affronted by fireworks, silly costumes, and effusive joy.

He's probably mentally reviewing his running strategy right now.

Somehow sweating *and* freezing, she skip-walks into a jog, dodging clumps of pedestrians who are probably heading into the park to watch the fireworks.

This is fine. Keep moving. Gonna make it. Breathe in through the nose-two-three, out through the mouth-two-three. In through the nose, out through the—

Ooh . . . a pretzel stand that's not mobbed.

It turns out that it's possible to run really fast (okay, reasonably fast), while inhaling a soft pretzel and clutching a slippery bottle of blue Powerade.

She checks the time on Gabe's phone. 11:54. *Shit.*

It's like someone turned over the little hourglass timer on a board game. It's no longer just, *how fast can I get there?* It's *this is actually happening* and *my face must be the color of a cherry tomato* and *what the fuck is going to happen if I actually find him?* and *how, exactly, do you confess your love for someone?*

And, most aggravatingly: *What if he's not alone?*

There could be a Harper or a Lauren or a Maddie, and *wow,* the mind really has a knack for some perfectly timed self-sabotage. At least the pain in her tight calf muscles is a good distraction.

In the thick of the crowd at the Seventy-second Street entrance, she feels like a child sneaking into a wedding reception for grown-ups only. Everyone around her is part of a social group or a couple. They all have festive props to wave and selfies to take, and she's alone and nervous and trying to un-fuck-up a fraught situation by ambushing someone whose feelings might be bordering on hostile.

Her heart's racing—and not just because of the unprecedented amount of cardio. A series of waist-height metal barriers line the edges of the race route without an obvious entrance. Ari jogs along it, jumping up every so often to scan the crowd of runners.

It's like a bizarro, life-sized edition of *Where's Waldo?*, in which the object is to find the tree-sized emo man wearing all black running gear instead of a bug-eyed nerd in a striped sweater. "Gimme! Gimme! Gimme!" is booming through the sound system in the band shell, echoing eerily through the trees. Finding a tall, dark needle in a haystack is much more difficult when every racer is bopping around to ABBA.

Except—

There's one head that's not bopping: a man with a black knit hat, standing with his arms crossed, mouth turned slightly down, surrounded by a group of young, long-haired, heavily made-up women in matching logo shirts who are really feeling the second verse.

He couldn't look more miserable if he tried—and it's possible he did try. What kind of pretentious snob shows up to a giant fun run and puts in their earbuds before the race even starts?

My *pretentious snob*.

Hopefully.

AT FIRST, JOSH THINKS ALL THE VISUAL STIMULATION MUST BE PLAYING tricks on his mind. Because sometimes he'll be walking behind a woman with light brown hair in a messy topknot and wonder . . .

It never is.

But the girl leaning over the crowd-control barrier on the other side of the road could be Ari's twin. She's forty feet away—difficult to see details from this distance in the darkness punctured with flashing lights—but when he catches her glance, he swears her eyes grow large with recognition. At that moment, the race organizers force everyone in his starting group forward.

Fuck.

Josh takes some ineffective clearing breaths. He can't find Briar in the mob of women surrounding him—all wearing T-shirts emblazoned with the RYAN'S RACERS logo (it's just an empty pair of gray sweatpants, running—which happens to be an apt description of Ryan himself). A whole universe of art and culture and food and a half-assed jogging club organized by a former reality star is the best entertainment this fucking city has to offer? Josh can't even properly track his stats on an outdoor run where his progress will be impeded by amateur athletes.

Predictably, Briar thought this would be a good place for him to meet someone, but none of these women are here to meet a man who's the opposite of Ryan and his gray joggers. He's the only person in the vicinity not dancing around like a fool or taking selfies with practiced silly faces. It's a familiar feeling—like his whole life has been a party where everyone else is enjoying themselves while he sulks in the corner.

He cranes his neck and catches sight of the Ari doppelgänger again. She's still staring directly at him with an off-putting intensity.

She looks exhausted and flushed, but—

" . . . *thirty seconds. As soon as the ball drops, the race begins. Runners, to your starting marks please!*"

Even if he hadn't had the precise contours of her face memorized for the last eight—*nine?*—years, he would still know it was Ari because she opens her mouth and screams out—

"Josh!" It's barely audible over the growing roar of the crowd and the bouncy music, but he hears it.

His heart stops.

"Ten . . ."

"Josh!" she yells again, her voice louder but ragged.

"Okay, Ryan's Racers, you're gonna *crush this*!" Ryan holds up his hand in front of Josh and folds him into a nonconsensual bro-hug before he can avoid it.

"Nine . . ."

Josh whips back around and sees Ari reach forward and grab for the metal crowd-control barrier.

She has one leg over the top bar before a police officer

rushes over and forces her back behind it. Josh pushes a couple inches closer to the curb, as if that will somehow make a difference.

She argues with the cop. She's gesticulating. Pointing across the path. At him.

What gives her the fucking right? To show up here and shout his name like that?

"Eight . . ."

The officer walks away with a warning gesture and Ari looks back over to Josh, leaning forward against the barrier, both hands grasping the bars, with one foot resting on the lower bar of the barricade, like she's ready to push down and make another attempt.

For some reason she's wearing an extra-large logo sweatshirt over shorts and glittery tights. She must be fucking freezing. It makes his throat tight.

"Seven . . ."

Ari's mouth continues to move, like she's still yelling something important, something he absolutely has to hear, but the roar of the crowd around him is too loud to make it out.

"Six . . ."

Ari reaches into the neck of her sweatshirt and pulls out a phone from her bra. It's the least surprising thing that's happened in the last fifteen seconds.

He watches—mildly horrified—as she wipes the phone screen on her sleeve, before bowing her head slightly to type.

Two seconds later, Josh feels his back pocket buzz. He reaches for his phone, keeping his eyes on Ari. She's watching him the way contestants on *The Great British Bake Off* watch their ovens.

"Five . . ."

Sun, Dec 31, 11:59 P.M.

UNKNOWN NUMBER: There's something I need to say to you

He knows it's more bullshit. She's going to say something that seems harmless and friendly, while it actually upsets the hell out of the fragile balance of his inner turmoil.

He doesn't type a response but just looks back up at her, giving a subtle and reluctant nod of assent.

She immediately lowers her head again, stepping down off the barrier, as if this text requires serious concentration. He feels himself grinding his jaw.

"*Four . . .*"

Ari remains focused on the phone, thumbs hovering over the screen, apparently writing a thousand-word-long persuasive essay about why they should be friends again. *Webster's Dictionary defines* platonic *as . . .*

Ryan has already dipped Briar in preparation for their big midnight kiss, while one of the racers steps back to capture a video clip.

"*Three . . .*"

Ari's head is still lowered. Minutes must have passed. God-damn *minutes.*

"*Two. . . .*"

He'll have to run in a few seconds. Josh glances to either side for any kind of opening to escape from the starting line when his phone nearly vibrates out of his sweaty palm.

"*One . . . Happy New Year!*"

UNKNOWN NUMBER: I love you

That's all it says. No apology. No explanation.

Chaos, fireworks, and "Auld Lang Syne" erupt as Josh stares

at the three words he would have strangled metaphorical kittens to hear six months ago.

The man with the starter pistol raises his hand in the air.

Josh strains to look back at Ari through the crowd.

She's not typing anything else. She's just staring at him, eyebrows slightly raised, her mouth in a tight, nervous line.

The pistol fires, making him jolt.

"Let's go, racers!" Ryan shouts. The momentum of hundreds of runners presses Josh forward.

For a few seconds, he's almost glad to be literally running away from Ari.

> JOSH: You have the wrong number.
>
> UNKNOWN NUMBER: Is this not the Biggest Boy? 😳
>
> JOSH: That's it?
> This is still a joke to you?

Nothing about the two of them has ever been as straightforward as a declarative statement and a direct response.

> UNKNOWN NUMBER: There's a speech where I list out all the reasons we should be together but to be honest this is not how I envisioned this going down

"You okay?" Briar asks, nudging him as the entire pack of Ryan's Racers slowly makes their way toward East Drive. "You look like you've seen a ghost."

> JOSH: You don't just get to come back here and say that, like ntithjg happened.

For once in his life, he doesn't care about typos.

UNKNOWN NUMBER: I'm saying it because of everything that happened. Because I missed you so ducking much every moment I was away

JOSH: You cnat just show up here and ambush me and expct things to go back to what you want them to be.

Stupid fucking giant thumbs on tiny keyboards.

JOSH: I'm not doing this again. I don't want to be your friend. I don't want to be the person you crawl back to when the other thing doesn't work out.

The ellipsis reappears on the screen and Josh exhales.

UNKNOWN NUMBER: I'm not crawling.
I did an airport run to get here!!

JOSH: I don't know what that is.

UNKNOWN NUMBER: It's basic cultural literacy!!
and there is no other thing. There never was.
Just you

JOSH: Then I want the speech.
The whole thing.

UNKNOWN NUMBER: my hands are shaking

JOSH: DICTATE IT. VOICE TO TEXT.

"Hey, man," says Ryan, flanking his other side. "Can you grab some B-roll of this? My iCloud storage is full."

"No!" Josh yells, pushing him off.

"Okay. Jesus. I guess I'll just delete something." Ryan shakes his head, scrolling through his Photos app as they jog forward.

The ellipsis is still animating—*what's taking so long?*—when

Josh feels the first snowflakes. A few heads in the crowd of runners tilt upward.

ARI: Sometimes I say ridiculous things just so you'll get this
really specific look on your face where you're kind of annoyed
but mostly amused and it gives me more joy than making
other people actually laugh.

You do this thing with your mouth when you're deciding what
to say next and I find it really hot and I never told you that.

I get this Pavlovian smile response every single time I get a text
from you, even if it's just one word, because you still make me a little
nervous and excited.

I want to give you shit about the clown costume forever. It'll
never get old for me.

I want to buy the organic grapes with you.

I want to bring you chicken noodle soup when you're sick.

I want to wear your shirts.

I want you to take your shirts off me and whisper dirty things
in my ear.

I want to wake up to your voice every morning and fall asleep to it
every night.

I built my entire life around not needing anyone. But I NEED you.

I'm sorry it took me so long to let myself believe that.

I don't know if these are the right words to make you believe in it, too.

Because I'm not healed yet. My existential wound is still fucking
bleeding.

And it might be too late.

But you said there's never going to be a perfect time.

So I'm here now, saying that we deserve to be happy.

Maybe there's no such thing as soulmates, but I think you're
my person. And I'm yours.

And I don't want to wait for it anymore.

I want to wake up with you tomorrow.

ARI GRIPS THE METAL BARS OF THE BARRIER, HER HEART THUMPING IN A way that feels like a potential medical issue. Somewhere in that mass of people dressed in colorful outfits is a man wearing a dark hat and jacket, reading a sloppily dictated love declaration. It's either the beginning of a love story or a moment she'll be narrating to therapists for years to come.

Ari shuffles sideways over the slippery pavement, waiting for a face in the slow-moving crowd to look up in her direction. With each passing second, it feels a little more hopeless.

No new text message. Not even an ellipsis.

Who receives a love declaration and then just . . . disappears?

Someone like you? her brain offers.

She stumbles into a cop in front of the barrier who won't let her go farther as the runners make the left turn to go north.

"If you wanted to run the race, you should've entered," he says. Ari watches the clusters of runners slowly jog away. She wraps her hands around the barrier, hardly feeling the freezing, wet metal against her palms. "You could wait at the finish line. They'll finish the loop in an hour or so."

Oh? Just an hour of stomach-churning agony while listening to a DJ blast "Cha Cha Slide" and watching Gabe's phone light up with *Happy New Year* texts that aren't from Josh?

Ari backs away from the barrier, her mind already running

a scenario where Josh crosses the finish line and pointedly ignores her there, too. She hadn't realized how stupidly confident she'd felt until the possibility of failure became apparent.

Delicate little snowflakes float down from the cloudy sky. Ari shivers.

The cop is looking at a slight commotion up ahead on the race route—a ripple in the herd—people moving aside, as if to avoid an obstacle.

Some rogue jogger, slightly taller than almost everyone else, pushing his way through the crowd the wrong way, parting the sea of runners.

Ari allows the tiniest bit of hope to take root.

"Josh!" she yells, nearly colliding with a woman dressed up in a bathrobe and a foam Statue of Liberty crown.

A race official in a Road Runners jacket gestures wildly at Josh, trying to get him to continue north.

"Get out of the fucking way!" one of the runners shouts, knocking hard into Josh's right side.

Josh pushes past the sea of people in front of him, slowly working his way up to the barrier.

"What do you want me to say?" he shouts over the commotion. There's a weary look in his eye.

Ari breathes in.

"You could say that"—her vocal chords seem to seize up—"you're still in love with me."

She doesn't breathe out.

"All I've been doing over the last year is trying to—to just get over this."

Shit. This isn't how declarations of love begin.

"Are y-you over it?" she asks before she can stop herself.

With every second that he stares at her, his face stern and confused, her heart clenches a little tighter.

No. No no no no no.

It's impossible. Airport runs followed by dramatic speeches have a one hundred percent success rate in fiction.

Her vision is already blurry from the tears and the snow-flakes in her lashes, but she sees something immovable in his expression.

"I don't—"

Oh God.

She looks away from him, the first pangs of a familiar emotion pricking her chest before he can complete the rest of the sentence.

Oh God.

Ari takes a step back from the barrier, toward the sidewalk, backing into a smattering of people watching the fireworks. *Don't let him see this part. Walk away now. Move! Move your legs.*

Except she has no sense of which direction will lead her back to a street.

She's holding her breath. Her lungs won't accept more air.

It's just a feeling. Isn't that what the mindfulness exercises are about? *And that feeling is complete and total anguish. You can cry when you're alone again. Don't do this here. Hold it the fuck togeth—*

A hand grabs her right arm, just below her shoulder, stopping her forward movement. It feels like that one hand could lift her off the ground.

"I don't think I'll ever be over this."

There's a tug at her arm and she turns to face him, releasing the sob she'd been barely holding in for the last minute. Fresh, hot tears slip down her cheeks. There might be tears in his eyes, too, but it's impossible to tell because her entire field of vision is blurry.

Josh pulls her into his body, tucking her head into his chest and wrapping his arms around her, temporarily raising her body heat by several degrees. There's just the freezing metal of the barrier between them. They stay like that until her breathing slows to a regular rhythm.

"Tell me you mean it." He bows his head down and speaks softly into her ear. "Tell me you're not going to take it back tomorrow."

Tomorrow. The concept is too much to process.

"I can't take it back," she says into his jacket. "It's on your phone, you have the receipts."

He runs his mouth along the shell of her right ear and behind it, laying delicate kisses along her neck. Apparently, he hasn't forgotten her weak spots. She doesn't bother to dial back her reaction this time—what's the point?—letting out a little moan as he moves up her jawline until their faces are almost aligned and she can hold his gaze.

"I want you." It's freeing, telling him. Letting it spill out. Letting herself feel an untempered, raw emotion. "I. Want. You. I wish I could've said it a long time ago."

Josh nods and holds her face in his hands, tilting her chin up in a way that makes her automatically part her lips. But instead of going in for the kiss, he closes his eyes, and touches his forehead to hers.

"I really fucking missed you," he says.

"I really missed fucking you."

He sighs into her mouth.

"Brat."

"Your brat?"

He nods, stroking his thumb up and down her cheek. She moves her head against his hand, drinking in the feeling of being cared for.

She can't feel the falling snow. She can't feel the vibrating bass of the cover of "Modern Love" that's playing over the sound system. She can't feel the deep booming sound of the fireworks in her chest. The thing she feels—*the only thing*—is Josh: his lips brushing hers, his hands tangling in her damp hair, then moving down her back and under her ass, lifting her over the metal bars.

Her feet don't touch the ground on the other side. She wraps her legs around his waist, crossing her ankles, and holding tight as people continue to jostle past them and the snow continues to fall.

She breathes him in. The softness of his mouth, the way his long nose juts into her cheek, the faint trace of his nonsense cologne. She wants to capture his bottom lip in between her teeth and keep it for a few seconds. Like there's finally something that belongs to her.

"It's matzo ball soup," he says, when they come up for air. "Not chicken noodle."

"That was a test. I had to make sure you actually read it."

JOSH IS VAGUELY AWARE OF THE CONSTANT FLOW OF THE LAST OF THE joggers and race walkers streaming past, gazing at the fireworks exploding behind the trees. Nobody seems to notice a couple (a *couple*!) passionately making out against the unsteady metal barrier.

They're the only two people in a crowd of two thousand who aren't looking up.

He doesn't care that the weight of the melted snow in her clothes and hair has made her a little more challenging to carry. He doesn't care that the PopSocket on her phone, stored in her bra, is cutting into his collarbone.

She's *here*. Her ass is literally in his hands.

And she loves him.

"I want to hear you say it," he says between messy, snow-soaked kisses and heavy breaths. "Out loud."

She doesn't pretend not to know what he means this time. It's a fucking miracle.

"I love you," she says, almost shyly, into his ear, like she's still getting used to it.

He nuzzles into her neck, closing his eyes.

"What was that?"

He pulls his head back to see her face.

"I *love* you." She blinks against the snowflakes, but she's meeting his gaze. Finally.

Maybe he's pushing his luck, but . . .

"Say it again."

Her eyes narrow a bit and he feels her hand slide down into his jacket pocket and pull out his phone, turning it around for him to unlock it with facial recognition. It takes a couple tries.

"Wow. Your phone is unfamiliar with you actually smiling," she teases.

"Pointing out when someone is smiling is the fastest way to get them to stop, you know."

"Oh, I'm positive I can get you to do it again," she says, the corners of her mouth curving up into what is—objectively—the most beautiful smile in the world.

She types for a few seconds before holding it out to him, with the Notes app covering the screen.

Take me back to your place and make me scream it

Well, she's not wrong about her ability to produce smiles.

Ari kisses him again, as he allows himself to feel something like honest-to-God optimism without trying to rationalize his way out of it. For once.

Ari gives Josh one of those looks like she has another quip to add, but she bites her slightly swollen lip instead.

"So, should we go back to the apart—"

"Yes." She just looks at him with a soft little smile that he's certain he'll never get sick of seeing. "There's something I've been waiting to do with you for literal years."

30

"YOU NEED A STAND MIXER TO MAKE BREAKFAST?" THREE MINUTES INTO the cooking lesson the next morning, Ari has already splattered vanilla-infused egg custard on the STUYVESANT HIGH SCHOOL MODEL U.N. T-shirt Josh let her borrow. "What is this sorcery?"

"To whip the crème fraîche," he replies, like this is an obvious conclusion. "This is what you miss when you run away before the sun comes up."

"I have a feeling this entire relationship would have gone differently if you had fed me that first night."

"Glad I'm putting my best foot forward with matzo brei, in that case." He's breaking sheets of matzo into perfectly even pieces. "So, what did you think?"

"Of the movie?" She smiles, whisking the custard around the metal bowl. "I liked it."

"I knew you would." He scowls at a jagged piece and hands it to her.

"Well, you did say 'it's a perfect fucking movie' about twelve times," she says, munching on the matzo. "But it is a nice love story between the hot guy, Andre the Giant, and Mandy Patinkin."

"You saw *The Princess Bride* and came away with 'threesome' as the conclusion?"

"No," she says, placing the custard bowl on the counter. "My conclusion is that the secret to watching an entire movie with someone is having sex *beforehand*."

"I'm happy to test that hypothesis anytime." He slides a glass butter dish toward her. "Melt this in the skillet until it coats the bottom. Medium heat."

"So dare I ask"—she sneaks another piece of matzo—"why do you have so many individually wrapped Oral-B toothbrushes in your bathroom? Lots of overnight visitors whom you impress with your stand mixer and film criticism?"

"Yeah, dozens," he mutters. "Shockingly, I did plan on having sex again in my lifetime."

"In that case"—Ari grabs her phone—"I think I should change your contact name back to 'Biggest Boy.'"

He gives her an exasperated sigh. "Okay, then I'm updating yours, too." He reaches for his own device.

"Ooh, what am I going to be? 'Pants Hater'? 'Crumb Demon'? A simple 'Brat,' perhaps?"

Josh holds out his phone so she can see the new moniker.

GIRLFRIEND ⚭

She glances from the screen to his face, a different emotion slightly rearranging his features with every passing second of silence.

Ari looks back down at the phone in her hand and types. He braces himself—physically tenses up—when she turns it around to show him the screen.

BIGGEST BOYFRIEND 🐚🐚🐚🐚🐚🔔

Relief floods his face. His phone buzzes again.

GIRLFRIEND 🐚: Thanks for the sex!

Ari's mouth breaks into a wide smile. "Gabe might have questions when I return this—"

Josh drops the phone onto the counter. He slides his right arm around her waist and lifts her up until their faces are just about level. She's too overwhelmed to be anything but dead-weight as he kisses her hard, his nose pushing into her cheekbone.

"Can we try that again?" she asks when he slowly eases her down to the ground. "I feel like I wasn't ready for that."

"That could be the pull quote for our entire relationship." He turns his attention to the sizzling butter.

Ari hops up on his kitchen table, letting her legs dangle.

Josh turns around from the stove, his expression cycling between indignation and titillation. "There's a chair *right there* and you're sitting on the tabletop I *just* cleaned? Get off."

She feels a frisson of excitement low in her belly. "Make me . . . Chef."

"Make you what?" He takes a few steps toward the table, raising his eyebrows.

She looks him in the eye, still kicking her legs and using a measured tone. "Make me get off."

"Do I need to get the spatula?" He takes another step closer, and she's convinced he smiles for half a second, before reaching out to grab her right ankle when she swings it forward. "Or the hairbrush?"

His eyes roam down her stomach, just below her belly button.

"Still, with this underwear?"

She looks down to confirm. "Well I haven't received my two-hundred-dollar panties yet."

"These are threadbare. I can't let you walk around like that."

"So don't," she says with a hint of a smile. Ari reaches for his hands, guiding them to the worn elastic waistband around her hips. They pull it down together.

He places a hand between her breasts and pushes until she's lying back on the tabletop.

Over her heaving chest, she sees him kneel down. His nostrils flare as he grabs under her left thigh, and with a leg in each hand, pulls her forward just a bit roughly over the edge of the table. Something under her skin thrums.

"You have three minutes until your breakfast burns," he mutters, resting her legs on his shoulders.

Eight minutes later, Ari bites into matzo brei that's completely charred.

She doesn't mind one bit.

One Year
Later

31

"WE SHOULD'VE BOUGHT TICKETS IN ADVANCE." ARI BUTTONS HER COAT against the February wind as they walk up Crosby Street. "The Moth Story Slam always sells out."

"Briar invited us. I had to agree to work three closing shifts next week so that Radhya would let me off tonight." Josh turns his head to look one more time at the line snaking down the block in front of the Housing Works Bookstore. "I assumed our names would be on a list. Then again, I'm not sure we need to hear Briar's Chris Evans story. Again."

"I *love* that story." She pauses at the corner of Houston, winding the scarf around her neck. "Imagine going on a date with Chris Evans for the sole purpose of getting Jenny Slate's number so that she could call her and beg her to get back together with Chris Evans. What a hero."

"That did *not* happen."

"It totally happened. Gabe helped her workshop the monologue," she says over the dissonant sound of multiple honking horns. "Pizza?"

"Arturo's? On a Friday night?" Josh looks at her pleading face. "We can see how long the wait is."

Through the window of the enormous Crate & Barrel flagship on the corner of Broadway and Houston, he can see a couple arguing over place settings. The woman holds her phone out to scan something—probably for their registry—while the man shakes his head.

"I just got this coat back from the dry cleaners," he suddenly remembers. "I'll have to get it cleaned again."

"I'll pay for the cleaning," she says, even though dry cleaning is a luxury on an improv teacher's salary. There's a red light at the corner of Mercer. Ari stops and turns to face him in front of the Angelika while the traffic passes. "But you should know, when you smell like coal oven pizza, you're ten times more attractive to me."

"I didn't think that was possible," he says, wrapping her in his arms. He doesn't get tired of this—of holding her, or the way she looks up at him. Ari pulls at the lapels of Josh's coat and kisses him softly. He can taste her artificial cherry–flavored ChapStick on his own lips when he pulls back.

"Hey." She grins. "I like you."

"You're all right, I guess." He leans down, pulling her scarf aside, and kisses along her neck and jawline, back up to her mouth. *I will buy you an entire set of monogrammed cereal bowls,* he promises silently.

When the light turns, Ari grabs his hand and tugs him across Houston, in the other direction.

"I thought you wanted pizza."

"Always. But there's something I need to do first."

They walk south, passing the designer boutiques lining the dark street, most of which are closing up for the night.

She's uncharacteristically quiet as they cross Spring . . . and then Broome—the occasional intrusive flash of headlights cutting through the dim streetlights. She comes to an abrupt halt in front of a brick and stainless-steel storefront with one small window.

"This is the stop you wanted to make?" he asks. "Do you have a sudden need for a new vibrator? Or is that a dumb question?"

"It's our meet-cute," she replies. "One of them, at least." She tugs him by the lapels toward the CreamPot entrance. "Just imagine how the trajectory of our lives would've been different without this place."

He rolls his eyes and pulls open the door. "I'm sure the universe would have found some other way to throw us together. In another timeline, we would obviously have met at Briar and Chris Evans's wedding."

"Where I would definitely have banged you in the bathroom," Ari assures him.

"Never to be seen again. We would have gone right back to our lives."

"We should each pick something out for each other," Ari says. "Souvenirs." She glances up at something that looks like a coral-colored glass sculpture on a shelf behind his head. "Ooh, the tentacle dildo!"

"*That's* what you want?"

"It's pretty!" she insists.

"I'll pretend to look around for a few minutes while you choose some ridiculous thing for me and then we'll meet at the register."

"Have you ever used a Fleshlight?"

"No."

"Penis pump?"

"No."

"Cake-scented lube?"

"Ari."

"It's culinary!" She wanders over to the small men's section. "The possibilities are endless."

There are only a handful of people in the store—a young couple who don't appear to speak English but seem utterly delighted by the display of bondage kits and a woman in a lavender coat conspicuously turning on every vibrator display model.

It occurs to him that he hasn't been inside the store since the day Ari stole glances at him and Briar conveniently disappeared into thin air. He tries not to think about that too much—how this particular spot became the pivot point of the rest of his life.

Maybe being in love is knowing that you'd live it all over again—every part, suffering included—to get right back to the place where you're standing.

"If you had a mold made of your penis"—Ari suddenly presses up against his back, hugging her arms around him—"do you think I'd be able to identify it in a dildo lineup, using only my mouth?"

"Well now you ruined what was supposed to be your Valentine's Day present." He turns around to face her and Ari immediately puts her hands behind her back, like she's hiding something. "Are you done? Did you find something?"

"Yeah." She swallows. "Actually, I found it here two years ago, when I was lonely and horny and trying to kill time so I wouldn't have to go back to my sad apartment."

"I know. It was this." He holds up the tentacle dildo and

braces himself for her to make a little bit of a scene. It's one of the hazards of being in a relationship with someone who performs improv twice a week.

So he's not completely surprised when she slowly sinks down to her knees, letting her coat brush over the concrete floor.

She opens her right hand and holds out a large black silicone cock ring.

"I want to put a ring on it."

Josh stares at it for a moment before letting out a frustrated sigh and taking a step back.

"Very funny."

But she doesn't seem to find it funny, either, because she's not laughing.

"I want to be your wife." There's no trace of sarcasm in her voice.

He looks down, studying her expression. No grin. No smile. No joke. Her eyes are wide, like she's genuinely asking for something.

He blinks, giving his brain a chance to rapidly sift through all the evidence to the contrary. "You told me that engagements are a narrative peddled by Hallmark."

"I stand by that."

"And committed relationships are a distraction that keeps women dependent on men for validation," he points out.

"That's also true."

"You don't want to get married again."

"I don't want to go through my first marriage again." She takes a deep, audible breath. "But it means something completely different to me now."

There's a battle waging somewhere in the depths of his

brain. Voices and sentence fragments that insist that *she's joking* or *she could change her mind* or *who the fuck proposes marriage while the other person is holding an "Octopussy"?*

But somehow, he *knows*, just looking at her—making herself vulnerable in a way that's becoming more and more familiar to him—

She's serious.

Her eyes are welling up and he can't look at her for one more fucking second without kneeling down and taking her in his arms.

"I love you for doing this." He places the tentacle on the ground, brushes his hand over her hair, and cups her face. "But what's the point of being married?"

Ari's nose crinkles. "Getting up in front of an extremely small group of our friends and family and calling you my person?"

"I can't think of a single friend or family member who isn't already painfully aware of how we feel."

"I want us to belong to each other—"

"We already do, Ari."

"—legally. I want you to wake up every morning knowing that you'd have to go to great expense in order to get rid of me."

"Hey." Josh folds her into the tightest possible embrace through their thick winter coats. "I'm not getting rid of you."

Her face scrunches up a bit and she lets out a quiet sob. Josh hugs her against his chest, stroking her hair as she cries into the sweater that's peeking out of his unbuttoned coat.

"Look," he says. "I don't need you to sign a government document or wear a ring from Kay Jewelers because you think you need to prove something to me. I already know. You're always there in the morning, spooning me."

"I like being the big spoon," she says, voice wobbling. "Being the little spoon—"

"—makes you claustrophobic," he finishes. "I know."

He reaches his fingers just under her ears to the back of her neck, smoothing his thumbs over her cheeks. He takes in the contours of her face—all the little details that can't be captured by photographs. Like the scar on her forehead. Like the cute little crinkle at the top of her nose that forms when she's squinting in the sunlight. Like the little divot at the corner of her mouth that needs to be kissed to be truly appreciated.

It needs to be kissed now, actually.

The brightly lit interior of the store fades into something dark and soft and gauzy, where there's nothing but her arms around him and her hand in his hair and her artificial-cherry lips. They're the best thing he's ever tasted.

Anywhere between two and twenty minutes pass. Enough time that his knees are probably permanently damaged from the concrete floor. When they come up for air, the young bondage couple and the salesperson are all staring intently. The woman in the lavender coat turns off the vibrator she's holding.

"I'm still buying the cock ring," Ari says into his ear.

"I figured," he mutters, getting to his feet and pulling her up.

He feels her breathing slowly return to something like its normal rate and he can't tell if there's a hint of disappointment in her expression, or it's just the smudged eyeliner.

"Since you're so open-minded now"—she runs her hand along a display of restraints—"dare I ask where you currently stand on threesomes?"

"We become new people every four years." Josh bends down and grabs the glass tentacle dildo off the floor. "Anything's possible."

She raises her eyebrows. "Score."

He sets their purchases on the sleek, white counter, pausing for a beat. "As touched as I was, you know I would never agree to marry you with a fourteen-dollar silicone ring."

She zips up her gray puffy coat. "Nothing but locally raised, farm-to-table plastic for you. I can grab the one with rabbit ears, if you—"

"Actually, I was thinking of something more tasteful," he says. "Gold."

"Okay, Moneybags. A gold cock ring sounds *very* tasteful." Ari raises her eyebrows. "An investment piece?"

"More like an heirloom." He reaches into his pocket for his wallet and pulls out a small black box, placing it on the counter. "I lied before," he continues. "If we met in some other timeline, I couldn't have gone back to my life like nothing happened. You would have fucking ruined me."

The most beautiful smile in the world breaks slowly across her face.

He's been carrying the ring around for a while, waiting for a surefire *yes*. But the truth is, he doesn't need to calculate the probability that the whole thing could blow up in his face. Or the fact that most relationships fail. Or the absolute certainty of pain.

Maybe there's no such thing as soulmates. Maybe there are only people who trust each other enough to begin something without being assured of the end.

"We can't even get a proposal right on the first try," she points out.

"We don't need to do it again. Any of it." He grabs the cock ring off the counter, his eyes never leaving her face. "You were perfect for me the first time."

Acknowledgments

THIS BOOK NEVER WOULD HAVE HAPPENED IF NOT FOR AGENT EXTRAORdinaire Gaia Banks and her life-changing DM several years ago. I felt like Lana Turner being discovered at a soda fountain. I'm so grateful to you for seeing the potential through all the revisions, edits, pandemics, and time zones. There is entirely the correct amount of pepper on your paprikash.

From the very first call with my editor, Emma Caruso, I had the best vibes. You've pushed to make this book the best it can be, which makes you the greatest collaborator. You get me. I can never thank you enough. You're right, you're right, I know you're right.

The biggest thanks to Whitney Frick and the amazing team at Dial Press: Jordan Pace, Corina Diez, Maria Braeckel, Debbie Aroff, Avideh Bashirrad, Erica Gonzalez. Thank you, Donna Cheng and Cassie Gonzalez, and thanks to Debbie Glasserman for bringing a Word document to life.

I started working on this back in 2018 because Kat included

a *When Harry Met Sally* reference in one of her stories and I forced her to be my friend and help me write my first kissing scene. Hundreds of thousands of words later, she still makes me laugh every day. She's a brilliant writer, trusted confidante, and the best sounding board I could ask for. I knew the way you know about a good melon.

I was a fan of Selina before I forced her to be my friend. (Are you sensing a pattern yet?) Not only does she create gorgeous art, she's an amazing writer who devises the best and angstiest plot ideas. Your talent blows me away. We'll always have Snalps.

Kate, I'm convinced that we sat across from each other on the N train many times. You are a kindred spirit. Aisling, you are one of the funniest, most insightful people I know and you wrote the fic of my heart. Your encouragement, support, advice, and humor have been invaluable. I will always want both of your metaphorical wagon wheel coffee tables.

Ali, thank God you answered my frazzled DM years ago, explaining publishing to me. Thank you for tolerating me as a fake Italian. Forever grateful for your blurb and your absurdly hilarious prose but even more grateful for you as a human. Julie, you are my writing hero and you were with me every arduous step of the way through the publishing process. Is there anything you can't do? I will have what both of you are having.

Everyone should have a support system of fellow writers like Words Are Hard (Celia, Victoria, Sarah, Rebecca, and Jen). I literally have no idea what I would have done without you. Katie, Tam, Lucy, Claire, thank you so much for reading various drafts of this beast when it was half-formed, yet twenty thousand words too long. Thank you for the encouragement: Nat, Amy, both Kats, Julia, Elizabeth, Court, Sit, Terrestrial, Kay, castles_ and_crowns, Berit, Kayurka, Jen, and every person who left a comment on a very weird fanfic by a first-time writer. You'll never know what it meant to me. This book is an outgrowth of an amazing fandom community and our patron saint, Rian Johnson.

Josh, did I manifest you and your matzo ball soup? Tell me I'll never have to be out there again.

Thank you, Bhavi and Viv, for being the people I would love to have had brunch cocktails with at the Central Park Boathouse in 1989. (I'd bring my Rolodex.) Griffin and David of *Blank Check,* your Nora Ephron miniseries came along at exactly the right time during my revisions. Thank you for championing kissing movies. *Skytalkers,* thank you for being my soundtrack for most of 2018.

I got very lucky to have my mom and dad as parents. They are the smartest people I know and hopefully I got some of that through genetics or osmosis. My mom had lots of Harry Connick Jr. cassette tapes and I believe that's a big reason why this book exists. Someone is staring at you in Personal Growth and it's me.

Jeremy, the first time we met, I left your apartment to attend a *Twilight* release party for "anthropological research reasons." The second time we met, I cried on your couch and refused your hug. The third time we met, you ordered us a plate of bacon and kissed me before I got on the downtown 6 and we fell in love. Thank you for being the person I never get sick of. Thank you for loving me even when I'm difficult (challenging). When you realize you want to spend the rest of your life with someone . . . well, you know the rest.

You, Again

Kate Goldbeck

Reader's Guide

A Note from the Author:
I'll Have What Nora's Having

IN YOU, AGAIN, TWO PEOPLE WITH AN ACRIMONIOUS HISTORY FORM AN unlikely friendship as they help each other endure breakups. It's a romantic comedy that explores the boundaries (or lack thereof) between friendship and romance in the modern dating landscape. It's also me—a person with a background in film history and theory—trying to have a dialogue of sorts with a movie that was incredibly formative for me.

I grew up steeped in Nora Ephron's *When Harry Met Sally* because of my parents. (My mom wore out the Harry Connick Jr. soundtrack on cassette.) This idea solidified in my impressionable brain: "witty banter = grown-up romance."

Reader, this film set my expectations for banter so high, it ruined me for years of dating.

The movie depicts the evolution of a relationship over a series of conversations. There are no external conflicts. No screwball elements. The two characters barely seem to have careers. There is absolutely no explanation for why these two people can't be together except for their own hangups and neuroses.

To me, *that's* the genius of Nora Ephron. Watching two people who so clearly love each other finally move past those internal obstacles has to be one of the most satisfying resolutions in any romcom. That's why it's number one.

While writing *You, Again* (on my phone, in my dystopian open-plan office), I asked myself *What would Nora Ephron write if she were telling this story in a world without paper rolodexes?* The filmmakers posed the question: Can men and women ever truly be friends? But if we acknowledge that people of any gender most certainly *can* be friends, what questions can we ask thirty-five years later? How have our attitudes about love, romance, sex, and friendship grown more complicated? When friends-with-benefits are practically the norm, what happens when you sleep with your friend-*without*-benefits? Is it a death knell or a new chapter?

You, Again is based on some of my experiences dating in New York City. As someone who simultaneously navigates both a long-term relationship and the rollercoaster of app-based dating I regularly see the best and worst of modern romance. The characters are aspects of myself—Josh is my uptight, high-achieving anxiety brain that demands a super-secure relationship and perfect cherry tomatoes at the salad bar; Ari is the polyamorous avoidant who keeps people at arm's length and can detach sex from romance very easily. (Hi, it's also me, accompanied by my defense mechanisms!)

One of the luxuries of writing a novel as opposed to a ninety-minute film is the space to explore fully realized journeys. In *You, Again,* I wanted to add a strong element of evolution for both Ari and Josh.

"There's someone staring at you in Personal Growth" is just one of Carrie Fisher's iconic lines in *When Harry Met Sally,* and it's pretty much the essence of all romantic comedies. Romcoms aren't simply humorous stories about two people falling in love. They're all, in essence, about people who become better versions of themselves in the course of falling in love. Two people, staring at each other from across the self-help section of an independent bookstore? Now *that's* romance.

A Conversation Between
Kate Goldbeck and Kate Robb

KATE GOLDBECK IS THE AUTHOR OF *YOU, AGAIN*, AN ENEMIES-TO-friends-to-lovers debut about a commitment-phobe and a hopeless romantic who clash over the years—until friendship and unexpected chemistry bring them together. She lives in Atlanta, Georgia, where she loves bantering with her partner, falling asleep to British audiobook narrators, and scratching dogs behind their ears.

Instagram: @kategoldbeck

KATE ROBB IS THE AUTHOR OF *THIS SPELLS LOVE,* A WHIMSICAL FRIENDS-to-lovers debut about a young woman who tries to heal her heartbreak by casting a spell to erase her ex from her past—but she wakes up in an alternate reality where she's lost more than she's wished for. She lives just outside of Toronto, Canada, with her family, where she spends her free time pretending she's not a hockey mom, and she aspires to one day be able to wear four-inch heels again.

Instagram: @kate_robb_writes

KATE ROBB: So I will admit that I haven't seen *When Harry Met Sally,* which inspired your novel. I feel like it's a romance sin.

KATE GOLDBECK: Wow! I actually love when people haven't seen it.

KR: Did you always love the movie, or was this a recent thing? How did you go from the movie to writing the book?

KG: It's actually a movie that I identify more with my parents. My mom had the VHS, so it was just something I grew up with. But I would watch it with her and think: Oh, this is dating. This is what it's going to be like when I'm an adult and I live in New York City. So I wouldn't say it was a touchstone for me, but it was always something that was in my head, because it was so quotable. But it wasn't until much later in my life, when I got into Reylo fan-fiction, and decided to try writing *When Harry Met Sally* fanfic that I read the script and watched it a bunch of times. Then I started to appreciate it as a quintessential romcom and understand how brilliant Nora Ephron was, because she was able to weave specific anxieties into this timeless story that rings true thirty years later. What about you? In reading your book, it reminded me a bit of *Sliding Doors* but a completely original take on that idea and the multiverse romcom. Was *Sliding Doors* part of the original inspiration?

KR: No, actually. The idea for this novel came from the night that I met my husband. I had been planning to go to a bar with friends, but then another friend invited me to a charity ball at the last minute. I decided, why not? I'll get dressed up and go to this thing. It seemed like a very inconsequential decision at the time. I didn't even think about it, not like I had thought about other questions like: *Where am I going to go to school?* Or *What am I going to do with my life?* It was just *What are my Friday-night plans?* I was faced with two sets of plans, and I chose one over the other. But from that choice, I ended up meeting him and eventually we got married, and we have a family now. And it definitely spiraled my life in a completely different direction than if I'd chosen the other set of plans. I don't know if we would have met if those hadn't been the circumstances. Perfect time. Perfect place. I think the stars just aligned. And so that was sort of the idea that this grew from: What if you had a chance to go back and do something different with your life? If you took a slightly different path, would you end up in the same spot? Or would you just be a completely different person in a completely different place? And what are the consequences of that? When I started telling people about the book, *Sliding Doors* was an easy example from pop culture to describe the idea of "different path, different life," but the book is definitely a separate vibe than that movie.

KG: What does your husband think of the book? Has he read it yet? Is he allowed to?

KR: I will let him eventually. It's me being weird, but it's hard! You put yourself on a page and you're wondering: Is someone going to judge me? Or are they going to read into this? Will they think it's terrible and then not want to tell me? There's so much vulnerability.

KG: It's definitely weird. I remember the exact moment when I let my primary partner read my book. I was just so hyped-up and nervous. We've been together for more than ten years. We've shared everything. But there was something so raw and vulnerable about letting him read it. So I completely get that and I'm very, very careful about who I've let read it. I *just* let my parents read it because I wanted their help with the proofreading. But I was looking at their notes after, and

I thought "Oh my God, my parents have read all of this." They probably have so many questions. They're probably wondering, like, what parts of this came from my life? I was a little mortified. But I think it's almost the hardest to let the people who are closest to you read the story, not knowing what they're going to take away from it. There's so many things you can learn about a person from what they've written, far more than what they'll probably say to you in a normal conversation.

KR: Yeah, for sure. I think I'm nervous for my sister to read it, because my book has a sister relationship in it. It's very different than our relationship, but I think you take tiny little tidbits from your life, even if the characters are not based on anyone or real events or anything that's happened to you. There are always little pieces that kind of find their way in. How much of your book is based on your life?

KG: I think a lot of it is based on moments in my life with my primary partner. We had a bit of a false start ourselves. We went out on two dates, and then I kinda ghosted him. I just didn't think I could handle anything at that time in my life. So we did not see each other for more than a year. We finally reconnected when I wanted to return a DVD of his, and we had what we call our "second first date." That's when we start our anniversary from. We've always had a little bit of that second chance. A lot of the banter in the book is basically me imagining how we talk to each other. A lot of the locations are just places from my life. And a lot of the anecdotes are mine. Little moments of what it was like to be a single person and some of the bad, bad dating stories I had.

KR: I wish I wrote more in my twenties and included my terrible dating stories.

KG: Same.

KR: I used to write emails to my sister and my mom about my terrible dates, and I wish they still existed because, like, I could just write a whole short-story anthology about hilariously bad dates. But now they weave their way into my romances.

KG: Yeah, totally. It pays off later.

KR: In reading your book, it felt like you spent a lot of time in New York City, like it was a place you knew very well.

KG: Yeah, I spent most of my twenties in New York City. It's definitely where I became an adult. Not that I really feel like a total adult, but it was many years of trying to date, moving from apartment to apartment, always trying to find a better deal and never having enough money, despite working seven days a week, because I mostly worked in museums and non-profits. So much of this book is based on those memories. Speaking of which, as someone who wants to be Canadian and wishes she lived in Canada, I loved the setting in your book of Hamilton, Ontario, as well as Toronto, and the details you brought to life. As an American reader, it was all so delightful. As a Canadian author, did you ever feel pressure to set the book in America rather than Canada?

KR: I grew up in Hamilton, and it's so nostalgic for me, so I wanted to honor that. It's a place I love, and it felt like the right setting for the book. But it's funny. I hang out with a lot of Canadian romance authors. And I think, for a while, there was pressure not to set books in Canada. But lately, that's been changing. Like I have heard from some readers that it's the reason they liked the book so much. Because it was Canadian but not a stereotypical portrayal of Canada with . . . I don't know. Maple syrup.

KG: They're not running a maple syrup farm.

KR: Exactly. Hamilton is a very urban city with amazing restaurants and antiques shops and record shops and occult shops, and all the cool clothing stores. I wanted to capture all of that. And the "Canadiana" is just kind of sprinkled in.

KG: Like curling! Is curling a typical recreational activity for you or . . . ?

KR: Okay. There are hard-core curlers up here like my grandparents. I did not grow up curling regularly, but it's one of those things that, you know, you do in high school, as a unit in phys ed, like you go to the curling club, you tie a plastic bag around your shoe, and you learn how to curl for two weeks. Then you do it as a corporate team-building thing when you get your first job. It's definitely part of our Canadian culture, but we're not curling-obsessed, I would say, except for a small niche group.

KG: I kind of wanted to do it too. Honestly. Like, it seems kind of fun like bocce but on ice and like with a broom.

KR: That's exactly it. There is a ton of local beer leagues you can join to curl. A lot of people go to bonspiels on the weekends where it's just like an excuse to drink all day and get together and play a really fun sport. I have friends that do that! So I knew enough about curling. I know how to play. I had to look up a few terms, mostly so I could just make them kind of sexual puns for one scene. . . .

KG: Very important.

KR: It's my favorite scene. Now, one of the main characters in your book is an improv comedian. Did you do a lot of improv yourself?

KG: I have dated a lot of comedians, and I've always been really interested in the women who are able to hang with it. I think it's gotten better in the past few years, but it's a really hard place for a woman to thrive. When deciding what Ari's job should be, I felt like I wanted her to do something that was going to be really difficult, which requires somebody who can just totally roll with the punches, who's very spontaneous and really funny.

KR: And there is so much humor in the book, but it's also an emotional roller coaster. Both up and down. Where did you get the inspiration for the breakup in the book?

KG: I think part of that roller coaster is because this story started as fanfic. You post chapter by chapter, and you grow this built-in audience, and you have to take them up and take them down, leave them on a cliffhanger. But as I got into writing this book, I think I often felt I was arguing with myself, because I see both of the characters as aspects of myself, even though they're so different. They're arguing about things I feel that are deeply personal to me. Do you want to be in a committed relationship? How stable do you want to be versus how much freedom do you want to have? Just a lot of the internal struggles that I've had with myself over the course of my adulthood and often feeling like there are no right answers.

KR: How else do you think writing fan-fiction affected how you approach telling a story?

KG: I come from the film world. I had written some plays and tried to write a romcom screenplay. So all of my knowledge about how you build a story comes from screenwriting books and screenplays. But being in the fan-fiction community really helped me understand how to craft a longer narrative, because I had never tried to do that before. And I don't think I would have written as much as I did if I didn't feel like I had an audience. I had people who wanted to see what was going to happen next, and that was so encouraging. I don't know if I would have ever been able to write this book if I hadn't started that way. Was this your first book or had you written other books before? It doesn't really seem like a debut to me. It seems like somebody who knows what they're doing, and I'd love to know how you go about it.

KR: This was my third attempt at a book. The first book is so bad. I will save it. So one day, I can give it to people and make them laugh and show them that you can get better at things if you try. I saw a clip of Ed Sheeran on some talk show where he says how talent isn't something you're born with, it's something you need to develop. They played a clip of him playing guitar and singing earlier in his career, and he's genuinely terrible. It was the same for me. I get better with every book. My first book is like that clip: genuinely terrible. And then I loved the next book I wrote, but it wasn't the right time for it. But it was a good learning experience for me. And then with this one, I had an idea. I knew how it ended before I even sat down to write it. I had the plot in my head. And it just flew out pretty quickly.

KG: Was there any time you had to kill a particular darling? Where you had to get rid of an entire character or scene you really loved?

KR: So . . . I really hate owls. And there was this rant about owls in one scene, how they're the absolute worst, and our editor eventually had to say . . . I just don't think this rant really fits here? But other than that, no. I'm definitely an underwriter. I had to build out things a bit more, like the sister relationship, to make the story fuller. So I think I'm not one to kill darlings but add additional ones. What about you?

KG: Oh, there's literally almost nothing that hasn't been touched or transformed in this book. There are a couple of characters who were some of my favorites that had to go for different reasons. But there was a whole sequence where Ari worked as a comedian on a cruise ship . . .

KR: No!

KG: Yup. There was a whole cruise ship section, but it just seemed like a bridge too far, and so eventually I cut the whole thing, and that's probably one of the biggest changes. But maybe I'll save it for another book, because I do find cruise ships really fascinating. I did a lot of research. I've watched so many "cruiser" channels on YouTube. My YouTube recommendations are screwed forever.

KR: I love it. I actually started to write a story about yachties, because I have always wanted to be one. I thought there could be so much good scandal that would happen on a yacht. So I do understand the love of the cruise ship culture.

KG: And we also agree that, as you wrote in your book, pants are the worst.

KR: And tequila. We both have excellent taste in tequila! Each of our characters drink Casamigos.

KG: And both of our books are pretty spicy! How did you approach incorporating spice level into your book?

KR: I think steam in romance books is having its day right now. People are looking for fun stories and then some hot sex.

KG: Yeah, I feel like it can be weirdly controversial sometimes, but I do think that when you're writing romance, there's something nice about the story "paying off" in a way that you can actually describe without just emotion. It's satisfying for the reader. There's plenty of books I love that have zero steam, but I find that when people can skillfully portray sex and intimacy, it really helps to drive home the development of a relationship. And I think that was perfectly done in your book.

KR: And I think with my book, there's lots of things that wouldn't really happen in real life. Let's hope. You don't do a spell and wind up in an alternate reality. But it's fun to imagine, and then I also wanted to deliver with fun, satisfying, steamy sex as well.

KG: You know, reading your book reminded me of the 2000s era of romantic comedies, like *13 Going on 30,* or *Just like Heaven*. Where there was a sprinkling of fairy dust and somebody could live a different aspect of their life. It brought back a lot of those vibes.

KR: It's funny you say that. When I wrote this, we were smack-dab in the middle of the pandemic, and those types of movies were all I wanted. I couldn't read; my brain just wanted to watch movies where I already knew the ending. I just wanted that predictable comfort of a little bit of whimsy. That was my mind when I wrote this: I don't want to be here. I just want to escape. I want something that makes me happy the entire time I'm reading it.

KG: Absolutely. That's what made it so easy for me to just fly through it, because I was enjoying every moment. Is that what you look for when reading romance, too? For me, as a reader, there's nothing better. There's no better sign than when I can just read something straight through and don't even want to take a break to eat a sandwich. I just want to keep reading. That's the sweet spot for romance, because it just feels right to read.

KR: Yeah, I love to get my heart torn out. I love angst. Sometimes. But sometimes I just like easy, enjoyable reading. And

I think that there's a whole bunch of different types of romance books out there, and you can choose your adventure. What are you in the mood for? What's your kink? What's your trope? What are you feeling tonight? And you can find something excellent for every different situation. That's why I love romance.

Kate Goldbeck's Guide
to New York City

Restaurants

ARTURO'S COAL OVEN PIZZA (106 W HOUSTON ST., NEW YORK, NY 10012): My partner grew up nearby and he introduced me to this absolute gem. This is not a slice place. You sit down, look at the—er—eclectic paintings on the wall, order an entire pizza (I suggest bacon and mushroom), and enjoy live entertainment because there's a whole-ass piano in there. Also, several years ago, I was eating here with my partner and "It Had to Be You" came on, which I interpreted as a sign.

THE SMITH (1900 BROADWAY, NEW YORK, NY 10023): The location of Josh's date that is interrupted by Ari. The Smith is basically like a small, upscale chain that's themed like "a real New York restaurant." It's perfectly solid, and this location is right across the street from Lincoln Center.

KATZ'S DELICATESSEN (205 E HOUSTON ST., NEW YORK, NY 10002): Brodsky's is definitely a nod to this Lower East Side icon. Everyone should go here at least once, but make sure you pay attention to the ticket system. In addition to the pastrami, they have great hot dogs! Oh yeah, and I think they maybe shot a scene from some movie in here once?

THE SMILE (26 BOND ST., NEW YORK, NY 10012): The Smile, which Josh mentions is on the same block as his apartment, was a "NoHo brunch staple" for about ten years. It's now Jac's on Bond.

GRAY'S PAPAYA (2090 BROADWAY, NEW YORK, NY 10023): Iconic hot-dog stand where Ari stops on her way to the gala. No, I have never gotten the papaya drink, but I do enjoy a quality 'dog.

KING OF FALAFEL & SHAWARMA (53RD AND PARK, NEW YORK, NY 10022): When Ari suggests stopping at the halal cart for dinner after she and Josh visit The Frick, she's referring to the Manhattan outpost of the best street meat in the city. The cart is on 53rd and Park, so it would be more of a walk than Halal Guys on 6th Ave., but Freddy *is* the King. The falafel here isn't dry and everything's nice and spicy.

2ND AVE DELI (162 E 33RD ST., NEW YORK, NY 10016): It has somewhat confusingly moved from its 2nd Ave location, but this is one of my favorite classic delis and another inspiration for Brodsky's. Great corned beef.

SHOPSIN'S (ORIGINAL LOCATION) (63 BEDFORD ST., NEW YORK, NY 10014): Owner Kenny Shopsin was a fascinating and idiosyncratic character and a huge inspiration for Danny Kestenberg. I highly recommend his book *Eat Me: The Food and Philosophy of Kenny Shopsin*. The later incarnation of Shopsin's is still open at Essex Market.

MILE END DELI (CLOSED) (53 BOND ST., NEW YORK, NY 10012): This is closed now (it's still open in Brooklyn) but was ever-so-slightly one of the inspirations for "The Brod." There's something odd about opening a (pricey, hipster-aesthetic-y) Montreal-style Jewish deli in a city where local Jewish delis struggle to survive.

ODESSA (CLOSED) (119 AVENUE A, NEW YORK, NY 10009): Speaking of local establishments struggling to survive, I have to join Josh in mourning the loss of this 24/7 diner that didn't make it through the pandemic.

GRAND STREET SKEWER CART (CHRYSTIE ST., NEW YORK, NY 10002): Were you dying to know where Ari's lamb skewer came from in Chapter 2? Here you go!

THE MERMAID OYSTER BAR (96 2ND AVE., NEW YORK, NY 10003): This place really is co-owned by Zach Braff—a fact I learned while on a bad first date.

VESELKA (144 2ND AVE., NEW YORK, NY 10003): Beloved East Village Ukrainian restaurant where the food is like a warm hug.

ESS-A-BAGEL (324 1ST AVE., NEW YORK, NY 10009): There's no shortage of bagel options, but this is forever my pick. My standard order here is a scallion schmear with lox, tomato, and capers on a sesame seed bagel. Josh is correct: There's no need to toast if you're getting a fresh bagel!

ELEVEN MADISON PARK (11 MADISON AVE., NEW YORK, NY 10010): Once considered the best restaurant in the world, this is the kind of super-intense kitchen Josh references in contrast to his low-key venture with Radhya.

CHUAN TIAN XIA (5502 7TH AVE., BROOKLYN, NY 11220): One of NYC's best Sichuan restaurants. This is where Radhya strategically orders from when she invites Josh to her apartment.

LOS PORTALES (25-08 BROADWAY A, ASTORIA, NY 11105): Tacos till 3 a.m., tucked away on Broadway. This is where Ari picks up tacos (and yes, they do have the chambray onions and a man slicing roasted meat).

BOHEMIAN HALL (29-19 24TH AVE., QUEENS, NY 11105): This neighborhood institution is the inspiration for the "Bohemian Garden" where Radhya holds her pop-up. I spent so many post-work hours at picnic tables here, drinking beer and eating sausage, fried cheese, and pierogies in this gem.

Nightlife

DOC HOLLIDAY'S (141 AVENUE A, NEW YORK, NY 10009): The bar where many a bad date of mine has ended. As Josh notes, there's an extremely memorable aroma wafting out to the sidewalk, which is why he declined to join Radhya and Briar there.

THE PIT (154 W 29TH ST., NEW YORK, NY 10001): People's Improv Theater is next door to my former workplace on 29th St. It's one of the inspirations for LaughRiot.

BROADWAY COMEDY CLUB (318 W 53RD ST., NEW YORK, NY 10019): I used to pass this place on my way to and from work (I had a miraculous four-block commute at one point). It's the inspiration for the club where Ari sees Gabe's bringer show.

BURP CASTLE (41 E 7TH ST., NEW YORK, NY 10003): The gimmick of this beer bar is that it's themed as a monastery and you're supposed to keep your voice down. For some reason, men seem to think that makes it the perfect location for a first date. Ask me how I know.

PYRAMID CLUB (RIP) (101 AVENUE A, NEW YORK, NY 10009): Also on Avenue A is the former home of Pyramid, a venue with a storied history, which initially closed in the wake of the pandemic, reopened in a slightly different format (thus, Josh's line about "whatever Pyramid is now") and then closed again in late 2022. I was never cool enough to go there, but it was a favorite haunt of my partner, who used to DJ gothy 80s nights.

FILM FORUM (209 W HOUSTON ST., NEW YORK, NY 10014): Josh mentions that there's a Buster Keaton retrospective at this nonprofit theater. As a self-proclaimed "film person," I believe the cinema-going experience is incredibly transformative and powerful. If nothing else, we need movie theaters as locations for dates! (Note: movies are for fourth-date-and-higher evenings only.)

Shopping

STRAND BOOKSTORE (828 BROADWAY, NEW YORK, NY 10003): Yes, it can get really touristy at peak times and the front is mostly non-book merch but it truly is one of my top recs for a first date and I love browsing the sale carts on the street in front.

DUANE READE (WEST 4TH ST., NEW YORK, NY 10012): Duane Reade (the setting for Ari's "victorious" pervertables challenge) is an only-in-NYC drug store chain that is now owned by Walgreens, which means we can expect them all to be converted to Walgreens in a few short years.

BABELAND (94 RIVINGTON ST., NEW YORK, NY 10002): The inspiration for "CreamPot." Babeland was one of the first chains to make shopping for sex toys accessible. I was once interviewed for a trend piece in *The New York Times* where they called me a "devoted Babeland customer." I also took my mother here once and she was a great sport.

ACADEMY RECORDS (415 E 12TH ST., NEW YORK, NY 10009): My partner is a DJ, so I had to include a record store and its denizens in this story. This is where Josh listens to the Brian Eno mansplainer.

HOUSING WORKS BOOKSTORE (126 CROSBY ST., NEW YORK, NY 10012): In the final chapter, Ari and Josh are waiting in a line outside this store, for a Moth Story Slam. They host a number of events here, but it's worth stopping in just to check out the books!

Museums

NEW-YORK HISTORICAL SOCIETY (170 CENTRAL PARK WEST, NEW YORK, NY 10024): Every romcom must include an event where people are dressed up and dancing. It's the law. I had the New Year's Eve gala set here since I wrote the first version of the story in 2018. In 2022, I came here with my mom because it was an easy walk from our friend's apartment, and lo-and-behold, the actual Historical Society put on an exhibit about Jewish deli culture titled "I'll Have What She's Having." I manifested it!

THE FRICK COLLECTION (1 E 70TH ST., NEW YORK, NY 10021): One of my favorite museums, this is the former home and collection of a famous robber baron, as Ari points out. It's more intimate and easy to tackle than the Met.

BROOKLYN MUSEUM (200 EASTERN PKWY., BROOKLYN, NY 11238): Ari canvasses in front of this museum in the first scene of the book. This part of Brooklyn offers so much of what makes Manhattan exciting, but at a slightly more manageable scale. Case in point: the grandeur of the Brooklyn Museum, which sits adjacent to Prospect Park.

Points of Interest

RAMBLE STONE ARCH (CENTRAL PARK, OAK BRIDGE, NEW YORK, NY 10024): Picturesque little arch where Josh and Ari kiss on New Year's Eve. There's a trick to finding your way around Central Park (the light posts have a numerical code that corresponds to the cross streets) but the paths in the Ramble are so curvy that you *will* get lost. Enjoy.

GREYSHOT ARCH (CENTRAL PARK WEST & W 61ST ST., NEW YORK, NY 10023): This is the arch Ari and Josh pass under after witnessing the proposal at The Frick. It does smell a bit like a basement as you pass underneath.

STUYVESANT HIGH SCHOOL (345 CHAMBERS ST., NEW YORK, NY 10282): One of NYC's specialized public schools and Josh's alma mater. (He's an overachiever.) Also a tribute to my amazing, overachieving college friends who grew up as cool NYC kids.

About the Author

KATE GOLDBECK grew up in a literal village and always dreamed of living in New York, even though her parents warned her that the apartments on *Friends* were not realistic. In college, she studied film and art history—limiting her employment prospects to "film museum." This line of work did not lead to sitcom-sized living arrangements. Since earning a master's degree at an engineering school, she's designed award-winning museum exhibits and immersive experiences all over the world. She adores bantering with her partner, falling asleep to British audiobook narrators, and scratching dogs behind the ears.

kategoldbeck.com
Instagram: @kategoldbeck
Twitter: @kategoldbeck
TikTok: @kategoldbeck